ALEXANDER WILSON was a writer, spy and secret service officer. He served in the First World War before moving to India to teach as a Professor of English Literature and eventually became Principal of Islamia College at the University of Punjab in Lahore. He began writing spy novels whilst in India and he enjoyed great success in the 1930s with reviews in the *Telegraph*, *Observer* and the *Times Literary Supplement* amongst others. Wilson also worked as an intelligence agent and his characters are based on his own fascinating and largely unknown career in the Secret Intelligence Service. He passed away in 1963.

By Alexander Wilson

The Mystery of Tunnel 51
The Devil's Cocktail
Wallace of the Secret Service
Get Wallace!
His Excellency, Governor Wallace
Microbes of Power
Wallace at Bay
Wallace Intervenes
Chronicles of the Secret Service

a&b

Get Wallace!

ALEXANDER WILSON

Allison & Busby Limited
12 Fitzroy Mews
London W1T 6DW
allisonandbusby.com

First published in 1934.
This paperback edition published by Allison & Busby in 2015.

A CIP catalogue record for this book is available from
the British Library.

10 9 8 7 6 5 4 3 2 1

Paperback ISBN 978-0-7490-1820-7

Typeset in 10.5/15.5 pt Adobe Garamond Pro by
Allison & Busby Ltd.

The paper used for this Allison & Busby publication
has been produced from trees that have been legally sourced
from well-managed and credibly certified forests.

Printed and bound by
CPI Group (UK) Ltd, Croydon, CR0 4YY

CONTENTS

CHAPTER ONE

Cousins Goes Shopping

The Christmas rush was at its height. An almost solid mass of humanity crowded both sides of Oxford Street; taxis, omnibuses, private cars, commercial vehicles panted their way forward by painfully slow degrees, every now and then coming to a protesting stop as the traffic signals barred their progress with scarlet warning. The shops were packed with jolly, clamouring people bent on purchasing gifts for friends and relations, all of them imbued with the spirit which only Yuletide can bring.

In one of the great stores, of which London has such a large number, a little man, slim, barely five feet in height, made his way from department to department with surprising ease. Unlike so many of the men and women round him, he showed no signs of confusion or agitation. Utterly unperturbed, he progressed by a series of rapid, eel-like wriggles, while others, pushing and jostling, almost remained at a despairing standstill. He managed also to get served without appreciable delay, one or other of the hardworked, but always courteous assistants seeming ready to place herself at his disposal when called upon. It may have been that they were attracted by his deep brown eyes, the brightness of which almost fascinated, or perhaps the mouth, full of humorous curves, proved irresistible. Altogether he was a remarkable individual, compelling attention wherever he went. His extraordinarily wrinkled face was utterly incongruous, when one noticed the slim, boyish figure neatly attired in a dark grey overcoat, grey suit, grey Stetson hat. Whenever he smiled, which he frequently did when conversing with the girls who served him, the wrinkles turned into a mass of little creases, each one of which appeared to be having a little joke on its own. He proved a rare tonic to quite a number of assistants who, previous to his advent, had felt as though they were about to collapse from sheer fatigue.

By the time he reached the wireless department, he was loaded with parcels. He spent some time inspecting valves and loud speakers; then turned his attention to the display of cabinets. Customers desirous of purchasing radio sets were being shown the latest models by polite young men; in various parts of the room were listening-in to scraps of the programmes broadcast from London Regional, National, Radio Normandie and other stations. Suddenly above the medley of music and song came the rapid, insistent tap of a Morse message. A young salesman standing close to the little man with the wrinkled face gave vent to an expression of annoyance.

'That blessed row keeps butting in and spoiling our demonstrations,' he remarked, as though looking for a sympathiser. 'You'd hardly believe it, sir, but there are some people who know so little of wireless that they imagine the dot-dash-dot business to be caused by a flaw in the set.'

'You surprise me,' returned the little man. 'I suppose it is actually a ship sending a message.'

'I can't make out what it is. To tell you the truth I feel rather puzzled about it. It is butting into all the stations, and is so loud and persistent—'

'What you might describe as remorseless,' murmured the other, his bright eyes twinkling mischievously.

The demonstrator eyed him more in sorrow than in anger; was about to turn away when, sharp above the strains of a melody played by a symphony orchestra, came the staccato note of the wireless message once more.

'There it is again, blow it,' grunted the salesman. 'Odd that it should keep coming through like that, isn't it?'

But the little man was not paying any attention to him. He was listening to the rapid series of dots and dashes coming over the air with such force. The first time he had heard the interruption he had been too much engaged to take any notice of it. Now he was spelling out the message to himself with surprising results.

X. S. B. Seven, it ran, *wanted at Headquarters immediately. Most urgent.*

As the sound of the last dot died away, leaving the music triumphant, the man with the wrinkled face turned to the demonstrator.

'Where is the nearest telephone?' he demanded.

On receipt of the information, he rapidly wriggled his way through the crowds to the telephone department. The number he murmured to the operator acted like a charm. Without the slightest delay she indicated a box, eyeing him with great curiosity as she did so. Carefully shutting the door behind him, he placed the receiver to his ear.

'Cousins speaking, sir,' was all he said.

'Good,' came a quiet voice from the other end of the wire. 'We've been trying to get hold of you for the last hour. Where are you and what are you doing?'

'In Selfridges – shopping,' replied Cousins.

A soft chuckle seemed to indicate that the other man was amused.

'Sorry to interrupt your laudable endeavour to help trade, Cousins,' he observed. 'But I want you here – at once.'

'Very well, sir. I'll be with you in ten minutes.'

Having given instructions for his numerous parcels to be sent to his flat in Lancaster Gate, the little man, whose name was Cousins, and who was down as *X. S. B. Seven* in the records of a certain important government department, quickly went from the congestion and noise of Selfridges into the rattle, roar, and crush of Oxford Street. Hailing a taxicab he directed the driver to take him to Whitehall, giving explicit instructions about the route to be followed. Few people know London as Cousins does. He gave a lesson to the taxi driver that afternoon, concerning the way to get from Selfridges to Whitehall by the shortest and least congested route, that was an eye-opener to a man who had previously considered his knowledge of the metropolis unique.

Seven minutes after concluding his telephone conversation, Cousins alighted near the Foreign Office. Paying off the taxi he walked across to the building which is the headquarters of the British Intelligence Service. Less than two minutes later he entered the office of Major Brien, one-time officer of cavalry, now head of the office staff and second in command to Sir Leonard Wallace, Chief of Great Britain's Secret Service. The tall, upright man, whose fair hair was rapidly thinning, and whose good-looking face was beginning to show signs of the strain of years in the most exacting profession in the world, greeted Cousins from behind a desk literally buried under a mass of documents of all shapes, colours, and sizes. His blue eyes twinkled merrily, as he surveyed the dapper little man, who ranked very high in the list of those devoting their lives to their country's service, as members of that very silent but very efficient corps of patriots.

'I'm beastly sorry to interrupt your Christmas shopping, Cousins,' he observed, 'and as our French friends would say, utterly desolated at calling you back in the midst of the first leave you've had for about three years. But *que voulez-vous*? It is the service calling. Take a pew, and help yourself to a cigarette, if you can find one.'

He pushed aside a heap of reports, uncovering a large silver cigarette box. Cousins, preferring his pipe, filled and lit it before sinking into a comfortable leather armchair close to the desk.

'I hate leave,' he pronounced with a smile; 'always feel lost. To quote Ruskin—'

'Don't quote anybody,' interrupted Brien hastily. He helped himself to a cigarette, lit it, and sent a spiral of grey-blue smoke rising towards the ceiling. 'We telephoned to all sorts of places in an attempt to find you,' he resumed presently, 'before getting the Admiralty to send out a wireless message in the rather vain hope that you might pick it up somewhere. If the matter had not been extremely urgent I shouldn't have bothered you. But I am very short-handed at the moment. Most of the experts are spread over Europe engaged on other jobs. Maddison is here, but he's as puzzled as I am. There is nobody else I dare rely upon in an affair of such gravity as this. I shall be heartily glad when Sir Leonard gets back from the United States.'

'What's the trouble, sir?' queried Cousins.

Major Brien sat reflectively stroking his small military moustache for a few seconds; then leant forward.

'Two of our most cherished military secrets,' he observed, 'have, during the last few days, been offered for sale to the governments of France, Germany, and Russia. One consists of the plans of the Wentworth gun, the other the Masterson monoplane. I received information to the effect that negotiations had been opened in Moscow and Berlin, from Reval and Gottfried respectively, early this morning. This afternoon Lalére informed me from Paris that the Quai d'Orsay had been invited by some mysterious agency to make an offer for the plans.'

Cousins took his pipe from his mouth, and whistled.

'This looks serious,' he murmured. 'Is there any clue to show how the leakage occurred?'

'Not the slightest. Neither the War Office nor the Air Ministry have had any reason to suspect leakages. Both were astounded at my information. Lindsay, from the Special Branch, and Maddison have both been investigating without result. The only people who had access to the plans are beyond suspicion; nobody else could have touched them.'

'Still somebody has,' remarked Cousins, 'unless—'

'Unless what?'

'The whole thing may be a hoax. Some enterprising crook may have hit upon a new idea for making money. The plans may be dummies.'

Major Brien shook his head.

'Not a chance,' he commented. 'Governments don't buy other nations' secrets until they are pretty certain they are getting the pukka goods for their money. Which brings me to the second part of my yarn: the Foreign Office has received a cryptic sort of communication stating that the writer has full information regarding the secret plans of France for certain offensive and defensive alliances in the near future; he also states that he can sell intelligence regarding certain German secrets of the utmost importance. On the assumption that the FO is prepared to negotiate, a carefully worded announcement is asked for in the personal column of *The Times* stating as much, and assuring him of safe conduct and freedom from any sort of espionage.'

Again Cousins whistled.

'Well, that beats the band,' he declared. 'It almost looks as though somebody has hit upon a new kind of profession. Making a corner in national secrets, and selling them to foreign powers should be a profitable kind of business, if it is genuine.'

'I don't see how such a thing can be possible,' objected Brien. 'Of course, we know that very carefully guarded information does leak out occasionally, but it would be impossible for any man or organisation to collect national secrets indiscriminately, and sell them to the highest bidder.'

'It does seem a tall order,' agreed Cousins; 'still, one never knows. Unless the whole thing is a big bluff, however, it looks mighty serious. If the plans of the Wentworth gun and Masterson monoplane have, by some means, been copied, and are in the possession of unauthorised people, we've got to make an attempt to get them back before they are secrets no longer, or, as the lines in La Mascatte have it, *"Entre nous, c'est qu'on appelle Le secret de polichinelle."*'

Brien grinned at this example of the little man's passion for quotations, but immediately became grave again.

'It's all very well to say we must get the copies of the plans,' he complained, 'but how is it to be done? Instructions were immediately sent to Reval, Gottfried, and Lalére to leave no stone unturned to prevent their being sold, and you can bet they will do all that is humanly possible. The trouble is, however, that they have no clue to the identity of the organisation that is offering to sell the plans. Read these!'

He passed across a sheaf of papers to Cousins, who read what was written on them carefully, before handing them back.

'H'm!' he grunted. 'They certainly don't know much. Each has obtained his information from a private source in the foreign offices of the three countries. If only they had been able to find out from where the communication to each power had been dispatched, we'd have something to work on. I suppose there is nothing to help us in this way at all?'

'Nothing. We have ascertained that, as you have seen.' He tapped the bundle of papers lying before him. 'There have been no other wires. It looks as though both the secrets of the monoplane and the gun will be fairly common property before we can do anything.'

'There's one hope,' pointed out Cousins. 'Paris, Berlin, and Moscow are places at considerable distances apart. Obviously the fellow who is bent on selling the plans cannot be in three spots at once, and, as he is offering them to three governments, the negotiations must take place by letter or wire. That means a certain amount of delay, which will be further increased by the haggling that will necessarily take place before he disposes of them to the highest bidder.'

'Very comforting,' murmured Brien, with a slight note of sarcasm in his voice, 'but I can find numerous objections to all that. If it is an organisation, and not an individual, or even if it is an individual, behind it all, negotiations may be conducted by agents with full power to accept a certain figure. If that is the case the whole business could be concluded in a few hours.'

'Then the plans would have to be taken or sent to whatever government paid the sum demanded.'

'Why shouldn't each agent have a copy? If one can be made, so can three.'

Cousins shook his head.

'The fellow behind the deal would never risk entrusting such precious documents in the hands of others. Besides, he wouldn't sell them to three nations at once.'

'Why not?'

'They'd lose their value. He could make more from one than three. Each would be told that they are on offer elsewhere, and invited to bid. The highest bidder will obtain the spoils, but naturally he would make a condition that they were not to be sold elsewhere as well.'

'How would he know?'

The little man smiled.

'Britain is not the only country with a secret service,' he reminded the ex-cavalry man. 'We know that the plans are being offered for sale in Moscow, Berlin, and Paris. You can be pretty sure that each of those capitals is aware that they are being offered elsewhere as well. No; our enterprising seller of secrets will act as auctioneer, and it will be some time before he decides that he has obtained a price worth accepting.'

Brien sat gently tapping the desk with his fingers for some moments.

'You may be right,' he remarked at length, 'but that doesn't bring us any nearer solving the riddle of the identity of the person or persons in whose possession are the copies of the plans.'

The little man with the wrinkled face sat very still for some time considering the position. Before he spoke again, a small, keen-eyed, grey-haired individual carrying a file entered the room.

'You're just the man we want, Maddison,' commented Major Brien. 'Is there anything you can tell Cousins about your visits to the War Office and Air Ministry which is likely to give any clue, no matter how insignificant it may be, regarding the manner in which the leakage of the plans occurred?'

The newcomer shook his head slowly.

'Not a thing,' he confessed. 'Both sets of plans are locked up in burglar-proof safes to which only the Air-Marshal and Vice-Marshal have access in one case and General Warrington and the permanent Under-Secretary in the other. The plans themselves were quite intact, and showed no signs of having been tampered with. With the exception of the models no attempt has yet been made at construction, and the only people, apart from the inventors, who have so far seen the plans, are the two bodies of experts who tested and adjudicated.'

'All of course beyond suspicion,' put in Brien. 'I was at both demonstrations, and can vouch that no unauthorised person was present.'

Cousins looked sharply at him.

'How do you know that all were beyond suspicion?' he demanded. 'I grant you that it seems ridiculous to suspect men of their position and record, but somehow those plans have been copied, and, until we find out who did it, everybody concerned is under suspicion.'

'Even the Air-Marshal and General Warrington?' queried Brien with a twinkle in his eyes.

Cousins nodded.

'I said everybody,' he insisted.

'You're a suspicious beggar, Cousins,' smiled Maddison.

'Aren't we all, in this service? If we're not, we jolly well should be.'

'Well,' demanded the deputy-chief, 'what do you suggest?'

'I'm going round to the Air Ministry and War Office myself,' was the reply. 'I don't suppose I'll discover anything, as Maddison hasn't, but there's just a chance. After, all,' he glanced slyly at the grey-haired man, his face creasing into one of his inimitable smiles, 'he was once a policeman, and that's bound to have cramped his style somewhat.'

'I always thought you were a bit jealous of my Scotland Yard experience,' retorted Maddison.

'Nothing like that about me,' Cousins assured him. '"O! beware, my lord, of jealousy!"' he quoted. '"It is the green-eye'd monster which doth mock The meat it feeds on!" That's Othello, in case you don't know.'

'For heaven's sake don't start him off, Maddison,' pleaded Brien. 'We'll never get anywhere, if we allow him to break out with those infernal quotations of his.'

Cousins sighed deeply.

'It's appalling to reflect upon the lack of appreciation noticeable in my fellow men,' he murmured. 'As Bunyan has it—'

'Let him keep it,' interrupted Maddison, grinning broadly.

He turned to Major Brien. 'I came in to tell you, sir, that I have decoded two wires received a few minutes ago, one from Gottfried in Berlin, and the other from Reval in Moscow. Here they are.'

He opened his file, laying it on the desk before the deputy-chief. The latter read the messages eagerly; looked up at Cousins with shining eyes.

'This certainly helps,' he announced. 'The offers received by Berlin and Moscow were both dispatched by registered post from Sheerness. Replies, indicating willingness or otherwise to negotiate, are to appear in the London *Times*.'

'Ah!' came Cousins' soft exclamation. 'How interested in *The Times* we shall be for the next few days! A nice little job for one of your promising young men, Maddison.'

'I think I'll undertake it myself,' replied the grey-haired man.

'It looks pretty evident that the same organisation that made the offers to Paris, Moscow, and Berlin is behind the communication to the Foreign Office, offering to sell those French and German secret plans. Will you ring through to the Foreign Office, sir,' he asked, 'and find out where the letter they received came from?'

Major Brien turned to one of the telephones on his desk, took up the receiver, and asked for the Under-Secretary of the Foreign Office. As that particular wire communicated direct with the department he required, there was no delay. Almost immediately he received the necessary information, and imparted it to his companions. The document in question had been sent by registered post *from Sheerness*.

'That settles it,' declared Cousins. 'Somebody has obviously opened business as a dealer in national secrets, and his headquarters *pro. tem.* seems to be in Sheerness or its vicinity. The Isle of Sheppey is not at all a bad place in which to stage a conspiracy. I'll go down, and have a look round after I've been to the War Office and the Air Ministry.'

'How in the name of all that's wonderful,' ejaculated Brien, 'can this fellow have come into possession of secrets affecting so many different nations? It's astounding. If all this is genuine, he must be amazingly ingenious and resourceful.'

Maddison nodded.

'There's no doubt about that, sir,' he agreed, 'which makes me wonder why he has fallen into such a stupid blunder.'

'What blunder?'

'Why, to dispatch all his communications from the same place, and to request that replies from each country interested should appear in *The Times*.'

'H'm! That certainly doesn't seem very clever.'

'There may be method in the seeming madness,' put in Cousins. 'At all events I'll go down to Sheppey and have a look round.'

'Would you like to take anybody with you?' asked Brien.

'No, thank you. One is less conspicuous than two, and it is quite likely that a watch is being kept.'

'It is also quite likely,' put in Maddison drily, 'that you will be on a wild goose chase. I very much doubt whether the sender of these communications actually lives in or near Sheerness. They are probably only posted from there as a blind.'

'Maybe,' returned Cousins, 'but wild goose chases or not, I'm going down. That is, of course,' he added rather belatedly to Major Brien, 'if you agree, sir.'

'Oh, rather – of course,' nodded the latter. 'It is possible you may stumble on something. But be wary, and don't run any unnecessary risks. There's probably a great deal more behind this business than meets the eye.'

Cousins smiled.

'*Mens tuus ego*,' he murmured. 'I'll take the excellent advice of Haliburton: "'Mind your eye, and take care you don't put your foot in it.'"

CHAPTER TWO

How the Plans were Copied

Cousins spent the rest of the afternoon, and a good deal of the evening, interviewing various officers, clerks, and commissionaires at the Air Ministry and War Office without result. He saw neither General Warrington nor the Air-Marshal, but that made no difference, as the permanent Under-Secretary of the War Office and the Vice-Marshal both accorded him interviews, did their utmost in fact to help him in every way they could. He even took a trip to a street in Pimlico, where he had a chat with the head night watchman of the War Office, who, like the others, was unable to supply him with any information that appeared of importance. It is true that the man informed him that General Warrington had rather surprisingly appeared at the War Office with a staff officer late at night about ten days previously, and had remained in his room for well over an hour. It was so unusual an event that it had caused a certain amount of comment among the members of the night staff, but Cousins decided it had little significance. It was absurd to suspect the Chief of Staff himself of having ulterior motives, the officer with him was quite well known, apart from which his honesty of purpose was proved by the fact that he had accompanied the General. 'Still,' reflected the little man, as he entered a taxi and told the driver to take him to Lancaster Gate, 'I'd like to know why they spent over an hour in the War Office at that time of night. Not my business of course – couldn't possibly have anything to do with the plans. If, by some abominable freak, the General is a wrong 'un, he could make copies of the things at practically any time of the day. There would be no need to go to his office at dead of night; neither would he take a staff officer with him. Don't start getting imaginative in your old age, Jerry.'

But that astute mind of his, which, during his long service as a member of the Intelligence Department had become accustomed to weighing up, sifting, and examining every item of information that reached him in his work, continued to dwell on that belated visit of the Chief of Staff to the War Office at dead of night, when neither war, rumours of war, nor manoeuvres required his presence there. An idea suddenly occurred to him. He directed the taxi driver to take him to the Air Ministry where he knew he would find the night staff already on duty. He had had a conversation with the head watchman, who had rooms in the basement, during the afternoon, but he wished to ask a question which had not occurred to him before. He found the man after some difficulty.

'How often does the Air-Marshal work in his room here at night?' he demanded.

The watchman looked at him in surprise.

'Never, sir,' he returned; 'leastways very rarely. In fact I don't think I've known him come back o' nights more than two or three times since he's been Marshal. The one before him used to be a terror for night work.'

'How long ago is it since he was last here at night? Now think carefully before you answer, as I am most anxious to know.'

The man was obviously intrigued by the questions, but made no comment. He had been instructed to give whatever information his interrogator might demand, and he did his best to oblige. For some time he stood thoughtfully scratching his chin.

'It was a little over a week ago,' he declared at length. 'I remember quite plain, for I'd had kippers for supper, and they weren't agreeing none too well – must have been a bit high.'

Cousins' sharp eyes held his.

'Why should you know it was just over a week ago because you had kippers for supper?' he asked.

'Well, you see, sir, the missus never gives me fish except on Friday. It wasn't last Friday I know, so it must have been Friday week.'

'Sure it was not longer back than that?'

'Certain, sir.'

'Today is Monday,' mused Cousins, 'that makes it ten days ago.' His eyes gleamed. 'Was he alone?'

'No, sir. He had one of his staff with him – a group-captain, who goes about with him a lot.'

'What time did he arrive, and how long did he stop?'

'It must have been after midnight, sir. He stopped until near two. I remember looking at my watch as he went.'

A very puzzled Cousins left the Air Ministry, and he re-entered his taxi.

'It begins to look,' he chuckled to himself, 'as though the Air-Marshal and General Warrington are the villains of the piece. They must have gone to their offices on the same night or, at least, on adjacent nights. I'll probably get rapped on the knuckles, but I'm going to find out why. *Fortiter in re, suaviter in modo.*'

He was driven to the General's residence in Knightsbridge, and sent in his card, on which he had pencilled some figures and a letter of the alphabet. The General was dressing for dinner, but did not keep him waiting, ordering the butler to bring him to his dressing room. A valet, obviously an ex-soldier, who was brushing his master's dinner jacket, was told to leave the room, and the two were alone. The General, tall, straight as a ramrod, with grizzled hair, and a moustache rather larger and bushier than is generally worn in Army circles nowadays, gazed curiously at his diminutive visitor.

'You're from Intelligence I take it,' he observed. 'What can I do for you?'

'Are we likely to be overheard?' asked Cousins. On being assured that they were not, he went on: 'I won't take up much of your time, sir. I merely came to ask a question.'

'Ask it!' General Warrington was obviously a man of few words.

He put on the waistcoat which he had been holding in his hand, and began to button it, still eyeing Cousins intently.

'I am making investigations concerning the offer of copies of the plans of the Wentworth gun to Russia, Germany, and France.'

'I gathered that.'

'About ten days ago I understand, sir, you and an officer of your staff spent over an hour late at night in your room at the War Office. May I ask if you were there on business concerning those plans?'

The General's mouth opened wide in most unmilitary fashion. He stared at the wrinkled countenance of the man before him harder than ever.

'What the devil are you talking about?' he demanded. 'The latest I have been at the War Office for three or four months is seven in the evening. I was certainly not there late at night ten days ago.'

'Ah!' A little sigh escaped from Cousins. 'You are quite certain of that?'

'Of course I'm certain. Who told you I went there late at night ten days ago?'

'The head watchman, sir.'

'He's a fool – must have been drunk.'

'He seemed very certain. In fact he told me that your going there was such an unusual event that it caused a certain amount of comment.'

'What is behind all this?' The General frowned portentously. 'The night staff must be mad, if they think they saw me there after seven. What time did this very – er – unusual event take place?'

Cousins smiled slightly at the sarcastic intonation.

'As far as I could gather,' he replied, 'you were seen to arrive just after ten, and left about quarter past eleven. All that time you were shut up in your room with the officer who accompanied you.'

'Rubbish!' The Chief of Staff turned away, but almost immediately swung round to face Cousins again. 'What is this leading up to?' he snapped. 'Am I to understand that I am suspected of copying and selling those plans?'

'Hardly.' This time the little Secret Service man smiled so broadly, and the wrinkles on his face became such a mass of cheery-looking creases, that in spite of his evident annoyance the General smiled also. 'It would be almost a crime to suspect you of such an offence, sir.'

'You're wasting your time listening to such cock-and-bull stories. I—'

'I don't think I've wasted my time at all. In fact,' went on the little man, 'I believe I have discovered how the copies were obtained.'

'How?' he queried eagerly.

'I'll tell you when I have had a chat with the Air-Marshal,' returned Cousins. 'May I use your phone? It will save my going all the way to Teddington where he lives.'

'You needn't bother,' was the reply. 'He is due to dine here tonight. If you like to wait, you'll be able to speak to him personally.'

'That,' declared Cousins, 'is what I might describe as a bit of luck. As Virgil has it: "*Audentes fortuna juvat.*" I'll wait.'

Attempts to draw him failed, rather to the General's chagrin, He was presently conducted to the morning room, and supplied with refreshment, while his host completed his dressing. It was not very long before the Air-Marshal arrived. The General drew him apart from the other guests, and explained who was waiting to see him. Together they entered the morning room. The Air-Marshal, who, as a slim, alert flying wonder, had performed great deeds during the war, had grown, under the weight of authority, somewhat pompous and fussy, as well as stout. Cousins noted that he was about the same height as the General, though he appeared shorter, owing to a slight stoop.

'I understand you want to see me,' he observed, after introductions had been effected. 'In connection with the alleged offer of copies of the plans of the Masterson monoplane to foreign countries, I presume?'

Cousins nodded.

'That is so, sir,' he responded. 'May I ask, though, why you speak of the *alleged* offer? Don't you think it is genuine?'

'No; I don't,' returned the Air-Marshal bluntly. 'The plans in question are in a particularly strong safe to which only the Air Vice-Marshal and myself have access. It is utterly impossible for anyone else to obtain them, and make copies of them, without our knowledge.'

'About ten days ago,' declared the little man quietly, 'you and a group-captain of your staff arrived at the Air Ministry about midnight, and spent nearly two hours closeted in your room. Would you mind telling me why you were there?'

General Warrington appeared startled. He had been asked a similar sort of question, and it struck him as significant. He frowned in deep perplexity, as he glanced from the wrinkled face of the Secret Service agent to the astonished countenance of the Chief of the Royal Air Force.

'What are you talking about?' demanded the latter after a short pause. 'I seldom go to the Ministry at night, and I most certainly did not spend two hours there ten nights ago.'

'Yet the night watchman and certain members of his staff are convinced that they saw you; just as the night staff of the War Office are convinced that General Warrington spent some time in his room on the same night or a night contiguous.'

The Air-Marshal turned to the soldier.

'What does it all mean, Warrington?' he asked irritably. 'Either this man is demented, or my night watchmen are. I have not been at the Air Ministry as late as that since my appointment.'

The General shrugged his shoulders in rather a helpless manner.

'I also,' he asserted, 'have had no occasion to go to my office late at night for some considerable time; yet, according to Mr Cousins here, the night staff of the War Office definitely state that I was there on or about the same night as you are supposed to have gone to the Air Ministry. It is very puzzling.'

'It is ridiculous,' snapped the other. 'What do you expect to discover by manufacturing cock-and-bull stories of this nature?' he demanded, glowering at Cousins.

The latter was not discomposed by his manner. In fact he seemed to be quite amused.

'"How now, thou core of envy! Thou crusty batch of nature,"' he murmured softly.

'What's that? What's that?'

'Merely a quotation, sir. I assure you,' he went on, 'that I am not manufacturing cock-and-bull stories. I have merely repeated what I have been told, and I am convinced that neither the head watchman of the War Office, nor his contemporary of the Air Ministry were suffering from hallucinations on the night or nights in question.'

'Are you giving me the lie, sir?' stormed the Air-Marshal.

General Warrington drew himself up, frowning ominously.

'I do not disbelieve either of you gentlemen,' Cousins assured them.

'But, damn it all, man,' remonstrated the General sharply, 'you have just said—'

'Just a minute, sir,' interrupted Cousins patiently, 'I know what I have said, and I have no reason whatever for doubting the information given me, either by you or by the watchmen—'

'But you can't believe both sides of the story. They're contradictory.'

'Yet I do. You see, General, there is no doubt whatever in my mind now that, on the night or nights in question, you and the Air-Marshal were impersonated.'

'What!' cried the airman.

'Good Gad!' exclaimed the soldier.

'That is how the copies of the plans were obtained. On each occasion the man who impersonated you both was accompanied by a fellow disguised as a staff officer. Naturally no suspicion was aroused, and the two quietly went to your rooms, removed the plans from your safes, and copied or photographed them.'

'Rubbish, utter rubbish!' sneered the Air-Marshal. 'You have let your imagination run riot. I have all along contended that the offer of copies of the plans to foreign powers was a scare or a hoax, nothing more. Even if some enterprising criminal and a companion had made themselves up to resemble me and one of the members of my staff, they could not have taken the plans from the safe in which they are stored. The combination is altered frequently, and the safe is burglar-proof.'

Cousins' smile suggested the tolerant indulgence of a grown-up person dealing with an argumentative child.

'I have seen both your safe and the safe in General Warrington's room at the War Office, sir, and I beg leave to differ from you. Neither of them are really burglar-proof. An expert would open them without a great deal of difficulty. The supposed staff officer in each case was, I am convinced, a cracksman thoroughly experienced in his job, and he opened the safes. Whoever the men are, they are undoubtedly past masters in the art of impersonation. It is going to be a difficult job to run them to earth, but we have what might turn out to be a clue to their whereabouts. Now that I have discovered that you two gentlemen were impersonated, and the manner in which the copies of the plans were made, I must beg you to excuse me.'

The Air-Marshal was still sceptical, but General Warrington was undoubtedly convinced. Both strove to detain Cousins, desiring to ask innumerable questions. However, firmly, but politely, he insisted on leaving; was driven to the Foreign Office, where he obtained permission to inspect the letter received from the mysterious individual who had offered to sell French and German secrets to Britain. He made a careful examination of the type-script, the texture of the paper, and the watermark. Eventually satisfied, he returned to his flat in Lancaster Gate.

He had a bath and a hasty meal, after which he spent some time ransacking a wardrobe, at length bringing to flight the uniform of a naval gunner. This he donned as though enjoying the experience. It was obviously not the first time he had worn the garb. Only after considering the matter deeply had he decided to adopt a disguise. People who had proved themselves so complete and clever in the impersonations of an air-marshal and a general were likely to be no mean opponents, and it behoved him to be careful. He wished to be as inconspicuous as possible, and nothing, in his opinion, would attract less attention in a naval port than a naval uniform.

His preparations completed, he took a taxi to Victoria, arriving there in time to catch a fast train to Sittingbourne, where he had to change for Sheerness. With several naval ratings he was crossing the platform towards the waiting local when his attention became riveted on a tall, broad-shouldered man standing under a lamp. Involuntarily he pulled up, whistling softly to himself. There was no mistaking the clear-cut features, determined chin, and powerful form of Captain Hugh Shannon, the strong man of the Secret Service. What surprised Cousins was to find him in Sittingbourne railway station when he was supposed to be in Italy. The little man wondered if by any chance he were on the same errand as himself. It was quite possible that Shannon had returned from Italy that afternoon, reported at headquarters, and been sent down to make independent investigations in the neighbourhood. On the other hand he may have been deputed on some totally different mission. In any case it was a moot point whether he desired to be recognised, though the very fact that he was on the platform at Sittingbourne suggested that he was waiting for someone, perhaps Cousins himself. The latter decided to walk by him once or twice, thus showing himself. If Shannon did not desire to be recognised, he would make no sign, and Cousins would go on to his destination without further delay.

Having come to this decision the little man sauntered along the platform, passing close to Shannon; stood for a moment looking up at a notice board so that the halo of light thrown from a lamp would illuminate his features; then walked back. This time, as he approached his colleague, he looked directly at him to find the other's eyes fixed intently on him. He gave an almost imperceptible wink which was immediately answered. The broad-shouldered man stepped cautiously towards him, glanced up and down the platform, and bent down ostensibly to fasten a shoe lace.

'What did Major Brien say?' he asked softly.

Cousins felt a trifle puzzled.

'About what?' he murmured.

'It's obvious,' returned the other, still engaged with his bootlace, 'that you haven't seen him since I returned from Italy. Well, listen! I'm down here on the same job as you, and I've a lot to tell you. We can't speak here, and it isn't wise to be seen together too much. I've a car outside the station. Give me a couple of minutes; then join me, and I'll drive you to the spot you're looking for.'

'You seem to know a lot,' muttered Cousins.

'Quite a lot. I bet I'll astonish you.'

Without another word he straightened himself; strode away towards the exit. Cousins watching him go, admired, as he had so often done before, the swing of those powerful athletic shoulders.

"'Tis the sunset of life gives me mystical lore,'" he quoted, "'And coming events cast their shadows before.'"

He waited for a few minutes; then handed over his ticket to the collector, and left the station. There were two or three cars standing outside and, in the gloom, it was difficult to see much, but presently he became aware of a dim form in the driving seat of one, and caught sight of a beckoning finger. He walked across the station yard.

'That you, Hugh?' he asked.

'It is,' came the well-known voice of Shannon. 'Come and sit next to me, unless you prefer to ride in solitary state inside. It'll be warmer there.'

'I'll sit by you.'

Cousins stepped into the car and took his place by Shannon's side.

CHAPTER THREE

Adrian Saves His Father's Life

The White Star liner *Majestic* was being slowly warped to her berth. Among the passengers on her decks, eagerly looking for friends awaiting their arrival, stood Sir Leonard Wallace with his beautiful wife. The years had dealt very lightly with Molly, for, though well on in the thirties, she hardly looked a day older than twenty-five. Her complexion was as flawless as it had ever been, her perfectly shaped lips as deliciously scarlet without any aid from a lipstick, her deep blue eyes as clear, her lovely chestnut hair as naturally wavy. She and Sir Leonard had, after many postponements, accepted the invitation of friends in the United States to visit them; had had a short, though gloriously happy holiday. It was a vacation that Molly would always treasure, for it was the first time she and her husband had had a real holiday together for years without the constant fear being present in her heart that he would be called away on one of those dangerous missions, which always caused her the most acute anxiety lest he should never return.

As head of the British Secret Service, Sir Leonard was, she knew, in almost constant peril. Often, she felt, he undertook enterprises which a man with less strength of character would have left to others, but she never made any attempt to dissuade him from them, never tried to keep him at home in the comparative security of his office. Like other women she had experienced the agony of suspense during the war years, but whereas they had reaped a reward of peaceful and contented happiness, and freedom from dread anticipation on the signing of the Armistice, she had perforce been compelled to suffer on, knowing that almost every moment he spent away from her, on ventures necessitated by plot and unrest, international intrigue and conspiracy, might be his last. In her way Molly had given herself to her country's service with as much devotion, loyalty and courage as her husband. Hers was the agonising duty of patience, of waiting, of smiling, when her soul was sick with dread, of realisation without murmuring against it, that the man she adored was constantly carrying his life in his hands. Often when alone she visualised, despite frantic attempts to suppress her imaginings, the long, empty, ugly years of utter and desolate loneliness which would be hers if she lost him, but still she held high her head, smiling bravely, showing no sign of inward pain or trepidation, praying only in her heart for the day of his retirement to come with the blissful peace so ardently desired by her.

As she stood on the deck of the mighty *Majestic*, gazing down at the eager faces of the people waiting on the quay, she suddenly felt a great lump come into her throat, tears rose in her eyes. Instinctively she realised that her joyful little holiday was over. Despite the fact that she was warmly wrapped in furs, that the sun was making the December day almost balmy, she shivered. Her hand, resting on her husband's arm, involuntarily tightened. Sir Leonard looked quickly at her; as quickly turned away. He knew what she was thinking, almost as though she had told him herself; the greatest grief of his life lay in the fact that he understood her sufferings without in any way being able to mitigate or lessen them. Their little son, Adrian, now a sturdy youngster of twelve, who had accompanied them to the States, came running up; clutched his mother's arm.

'I can see Auntie Phyllis,' he announced, 'and Uncle Bill is there, too, but I don't think they've brought Peter or John or Vera or Joan with them.'

Sir Leonard laughed.

'You don't think that Uncle Bill can afford to take all the family with him wherever he goes, do you?' he asked. 'It would be like moving an army corps. You thank your lucky stars you're the only child in this family, my lad. Think what you'd miss, if you had a lot of brothers and sisters, and had to stay at home.'

'Oh, Daddy, you've lots of money,' returned the little chap, 'I know you have. And even if you didn't have,' he added rather wistfully, 'I'd like to have a brother or sister, like other children.'

Sir Leonard pinched his ear.

'Perhaps you will some day,' he observed. 'Who knows! Now run away and collect your goods and chattels. We'll be landing presently.'

They watched with shining eyes as he wriggled his way through the crowd of passengers. Both were as devoted to the little fellow as they were to each other.

'Bless him!' murmured Molly. 'What on earth would we do without him, Leonard?'

'I'm hanged if I know. But we don't have to do without him,

so why imagine such a thing. By Jove! Bill looks doleful. I wonder what's the matter with the fellow.'

'He does look rather worried. I – I hope there is nothing wrong.'

Sir Leonard patted her hand.

'Of course there's nothing wrong,' he assured her, though he was far from feeling sanguine himself. It was so unusual to see the cheery countenance of his great friend and chief assistant clouded by gloom. 'He is probably trying to appear that he has been overworked during my absence.'

He filled and lit his pipe carefully but quickly. An observer realising that his left arm was artificial would have been astonished by the celerity of his movements. But only those who knew him, or sat with him at table, were aware of his handicap, the latter simply because of the glove he always wore. He had trained himself to use one hand where others would have to use two, and so natural were his movements that there never appeared anything odd about them. Occasionally the artificial hand was brought into action, but without ostentation. Even his intimates were apt to forget that Sir Leonard Wallace was a one-armed man until some amazing feat of strength reminded them. Although slightly built and of medium height, he is astonishingly muscular. His right arm is a great deal stronger than an average man's two, a fact that has more than once disagreeably dawned on people who imagined that in him they had an easy victim. His general air of indolence, too, is calculated to deceive those who do not know him. Sir Leonard Wallace possesses an utterly calm and cool disposition which is reflected in his attractive good-humoured face, his almost lazy manner. But behind his unruffled exterior, his unexcitable temperament, is the brilliant brain which has carried him so often to success against the men that international conspiracy has caused to be pitted in opposition to him. It is only when able to look deep into those steel-grey eyes of his that one realises the dynamic force hidden somewhere within that frame of slim nonchalance.

Sir Leonard, his wife, and son were among the first to step ashore when the *Majestic* was tied up. At once they were greeted by Phyllis Brien and her husband, who had motored from London to meet them. Like Molly, Phyllis showed few signs of the ravages of time, even though she was the mother of four strapping children. Her sweet face and manner retained all the vivaciousness of the days when she had first met and fallen in love with Major – then Captain – Brien. Her fair hair had lost none of its gloss, her eyes none of their sparkle. The two beautiful women made a lovely picture as they stood greeting each other with all the deep affection of their long and intimate friendship. The meeting of Wallace and Brien was typical. Their hands shot out and gripped hard, a few desultory sentences fell from their lips while in the presence of their women-folk, not a word concerning their work. But how their wives understood them! With significant glances at each other they wandered away, taking Adrian with them, and leaving Sir Leonard's manservant Batty to attend to the baggage. Wallace watched them go with a slight smile; then took Brien by the arm; drew him into a deserted corner of the customs' shed.

'Well, Bill,' he demanded, 'what's the trouble?'

'How do you know there's any trouble?' queried the other.

'I saw it in your face long before the ship docked. Is it anything serious?'

'There's a hell of a mess,' came bluntly and feelingly from the other. 'If I hadn't had your cable to say you were sailing by the *Majestic*, I should have begged you to come. I know my limitations, Leonard, none better. I bow to nobody where staff and routine work is concerned, but when it comes to matching my brains against the subtlety of—'

'Never mind all that. Get on with the story.'

At once Brien plunged into an account of the offers made to Germany, Russia and France, the counter offer to Great Britain, and the discovery of the fact that all the communications had been dispatched from Sheerness.

'I recalled Cousins from leave, because I was short-handed, on the day before you sailed from New York,' he concluded. 'He went down to Sheerness the same night. Since then there has not been a word from him. He has completely disappeared.'

'Cousins disappeared!' repeated Sir Leonard. 'That sounds bad. Have you no idea where he is at all?'

'Very little. Cartright and Hill have been making exhaustive enquiries for the last two days, and they have ascertained that a naval gunner descended from the 9.45 train at Sittingbourne, was about to cross to the local for Sheerness, but apparently changed his mind and, according to a ticket collector, left the station. Further information, elicited from an old taxi driver, who was waiting in the hope of picking up a fare at the time, makes it seem apparent that Cousins entered a Morris-Cowley car, and was driven away by a big, burly man. We have been unable to find out the number, but Hill was able to trace the car for some distance on the road to Sheerness, but from that point on all trace of it was lost. We succeeded in getting a repair gang at work on the bridge across to Sheppey in order that traffic would be delayed, and forced to crawl. Cartright is with the labourers working a "Go" and "Stop" sign, which enables him to scrutinise every car that passes, but so far without result.'

'Good work,' approved Wallace. 'I'm afraid, though, that

blocking up the road won't help much. For one thing you have only a vague idea whom you are looking for. There are hundreds of big, burly men about, and it would be impossible to suspect everyone who motors across the bridge between Sheppey and the mainland in a Morris-Cowley car.'

'Still, there is a chance. I was hoping that, if Cousins had been taken across to the island, his captors might presently remove him to some other place, in which case our men would spot him.'

Sir Leonard smiled.

'If Cousins has been kidnapped, as you seem to think,' he remarked, 'and his captors wanted to move him from the island, there are several ways of accomplishing it, without using the road. There is only a narrow channel separating it from the mainland, which a rowing boat could cross in a few strokes; then there are aeroplanes. Besides, Cousins may never have been taken to the island at all. I think we can take it as obvious that he has been kidnapped, otherwise he would not have left you without word of some sort for five days. What puzzles me is that he apparently entered the car of his own accord. What happened about the plans? Have any answers appeared in *The Times* in reply to the letters?'

'Yes. France has apparently ignored the one sent to her, but two very well-guarded notices, which we were able to find out emanated from Moscow and Berlin, were printed in the personal column yesterday. The Foreign Office also inserted the requested reply, but so far has heard nothing further.'

'And probably won't, now that this mysterious organisation is aware that efforts are being made to unmask their activities. I'd like to know how copies were made of the plans.'

'I can tell you. From conversations I have had with General

Warrington and the Air-Marshal since the disappearance of Cousins, it seems that—'

'Daddy, look out!' a frightened childish treble interrupted.

A little form threw itself against Sir Leonard Wallace, causing him to stagger a yard or so. At the same moment something hummed by his ear like an angry wasp, almost coincident with the report of a revolver. Cries of alarm rose from every side; two or three women screamed; men came running towards them. Brien, however, who had swung round at the first startled cry from Adrian, was already tearing towards the dockside.

'This way,' he roared.

Immediately a general pursuit of the would-be assassin took place. Sir Leonard, however, had neither eyes nor ears for anybody but Adrian, who had fallen to the ground after the impact with his father. Tenderly the latter raised the little chap.

'Are you hurt, old man?' he asked, and there was an unwonted huskiness in his voice.

'No, Daddy; I only fell after I tried to push you out of the way.'

'You're sure?'

'Quite sure. Daddy, that – that man didn't hit you, did he?'

There were tears in the little fellow's eyes now, but he made strenuous efforts to hide them. There was a suspicious moisture in Sir Leonard's eyes also as he looked proudly at his son, afterwards transferring his gaze to a tell-tale mark in a packing-case close by.

'No, sonny,' he murmured; 'no, he didn't hit me.'

Adrian took his father's hand and held it tight.

'I hope he is caught,' he said tremulously. 'Why do you think he wanted to shoot you, Dad?'

Sir Leonard smiled down at him.

'I don't suppose he wanted to shoot me,' he replied. 'Probably he was examining the revolver, and it went off.'

But Adrian was not to be put off in that manner. He shook his head.

'He did want to shoot you,' he insisted. 'I was coming across the shed, when I saw him raise the pistol. I looked to see what he was aiming at, and it was you. You were talking to Uncle Billy, and had your back turned to him. He was trying to kill you, Daddy. Why should he do such a terrible thing?'

Sir Leonard suddenly became aware, possibly for the first time, that his son was no longer a baby. He was growing up, and already there were indications of the man in him. It is quite likely that his experience that morning had swept away quite a lot of the illusions of childhood. Wallace realised that it would be futile to attempt further to deceive him.

'I don't know who he was, or why he should try to shoot me,' he remarked quietly, 'but I do know that you have saved my life, Adrian, and that I am very, very proud of you.'

Instinctively the little chap squared his shoulders. His eyes gleamed with pleasure, but were quickly clouded by a look of fear.

'Oh, Daddy,' he cried, 'do you think he will try again, when – when—'

'When you are not near to save me?' smiled Sir Leonard. 'No; you needn't worry about that. He'll probably be caught and, even if he isn't, he'll have to go into hiding, because the police will be on the look-out for him. Where's Mother?'

'She is waiting in the car with Auntie Phyllis. She sent me to tell you they were ready.'

'She knows nothing about this?'

Adrian shook his head.

'Then we won't tell her, will we? This must be our secret, old chap. We don't want to alarm her.'

'I won't say anything, Daddy, but perhaps Uncle Bill will.'

'I'll ask him not to. Run along to the car now, and say we'll be coming in a minute. And mind! Don't let Mother see any signs of distress on your face, or she'll guess something has happened. She's very clever, you know.'

'You're sure you'll be all right?'

'Quite.'

After hesitating a moment, the little fellow ran off, making his way through the crowd, mostly composed of women and customs officials, who had not joined in the chase, and had been watching father and son with curious, and, in some cases, fearful eyes. Sir Leonard walked rapidly towards the dock, where he met the disappointed pursuers returning. Brien was in earnest conversation with a man who proved to be a police inspector in plain clothes. He had apparently been told who the intended victim was, for he showed marked deference on being presented to Sir Leonard.

'He got away in a speedboat, which was apparently in waiting, sir,' he explained. 'But I have dispatched a man to send out calls to all police in the vicinity of the river. He was making down the Solent when last seen, and is being pursued by some colleagues of mine in another boat, while several other speedboats are taking up the chase. I think we'll get him,' he added confidently.

'Recognise him?' asked Sir Leonard of Brien.

The latter shook his head.

'I've never seen him before. He's a greasy-looking specimen; looks like a Maltese.'

'A Maltese!' mused Wallace. 'I did not know I had offended any of that race. He was probably hired by someone else to do the job. You'll find the bullet embedded in that packing-case over there, Inspector. You'd better collect it as evidence. I'm not usually vindictive, but this time I am. I'll be very disappointed if you don't lay the fellow by the heels.'

'We'll do our best, sir.'

'Let me know when you have him. I'll come down. I rather fancy a little conversation with him myself.'

Nodding to the police officer, he strode through the curious crowd accompanied by Brien.

'You owe your life to Adrian,' observed the latter softly. 'The little chap showed courage and resource which many men would have lacked.'

Sir Leonard turned, and looked at him. Brien's eyebrows rose slightly as he noted the expression on his companion's face.

'Do you realise, Bill,' muttered Wallace, 'that if that bullet had been aimed at my heart instead of at my head, it would, in all probability, have got Adrian? That's the reason I'm so anxious for the police to capture the fellow.'

Brien nodded understandingly.

'I wonder if he has anything to do with the people who seem to have kidnapped Cousins,' he mused. 'They may have heard that you were due home, and sent down a man to put you out of action before you could butt in on their game.'

'Possibly you've hit it. I only hope so for, whether the police catch him or not, I shall then have a chance of settling my account with him, or with those who sent him. There's the car. Not a word to the ladies about this business.'

'Of course not, but what about Adrian?'

'He won't speak. I told him not to. By Jove! look at him playing round the car as though nothing had happened.' He smiled proudly, and added: 'Bless the boy, he has the right stuff in him.'

'A chip off the old block,' murmured Brien. A somewhat fatuous remark, perhaps, but nevertheless sincere.

'What a time you men have been,' commented Molly as they strode up. 'Can't you gossip in the car? You seem to forget that today is the twentieth of December, not midsummer's day, and that even Billy's luxurious new car is not a hot-house.'

'Sorry, dear,' returned Wallace lightly, climbing in beside his friend, and sending the protesting Adrian into the tonneau with his mother and Phyllis. 'Billy's taken to road-mending while I've been away, and finds it suits him so well that he is thinking of handing in his resignation.'

'It's the first I've heard of it,' laughed Phyllis.

'Beg pardon, sir,' came a voice.

A short, stout man with a round, red face to which twinkling blue eyes and a snub nose imparted a delightfully cheery expression, stood respectfully by the car. He wore a very neat serge suit, neat bowler, and neat patent leather shoes; in fact, everything about him was neat. This was Sir Leonard's confidential servant, an ex-naval seaman, who had been with him ever since taking his discharge, a man who had made himself so necessary for the welfare of the Wallace family that he had become an institution and was regarded more as a friend than a servant.

'What do you want, Batty?' asked his employer.

The ex-sailor jerked a thumb over his shoulder. His eyes glittered angrily.

'I've just 'eard—' he began.

'You mustn't believe everything you hear,' interrupted Sir Leonard sharply, accompanying his words with a frown of warning. 'Is all the luggage on the train?'

'Yes, sir. Saw it all packed aboard meself.'

'Then you'd better take your seat lest the train goes without you.'

'Aye, aye, sir, but I'd like to say as 'ow—'

'We'll take it as said, Batty. Are you ready, Bill? Then right away.'

'You're very abrupt with the poor man all of a sudden,' remarked Molly, as the car sped towards the dock gates.

'Not really,' returned Wallace, 'but we can't hang about all day, while he makes observations. We're in a hurry.'

'You did not seem to be in a hurry a short time ago,' was her sarcastic comment.

Adrian suddenly laughed a trifle hysterically.

'What's the matter, darling?' his mother asked.

'I – I was only thinking of something – funny, Mother,' he replied.

'He's a little overwrought,' muttered Brien.

Sir Leonard nodded.

'Will you stop at Smith's in Above Bar,' he requested. 'I'll get him a book or a boy's journal to keep his mind occupied.'

CHAPTER FOUR

Sir Leonard Takes a Hand

On the way to London, Brien told Sir Leonard what he had learnt from General Warrington and the Air-Marshal concerning the conversation Cousins had had with them.

'There seems no doubt that he was right,' was Wallace's comment, when he had heard all his assistant had to tell him.

He fell silent for some time, appearing to be occupied in studying the scenery. Despite the fact that it was shorn of the beauty which delights in spreading its cloak over the county of Hampshire during other seasons of the year, the countryside was still attractive. Mighty trees, most of them leafless, proudly raised their heads as though calling witness to their hardiness; others still retained a certain amount of foliage coloured with the warm tints of late autumn, a few evergreens combined with the rolling meadows to add that verdant touch which is so typical of the English country. Here and there they passed old-fashioned thatched cottages, nestling among the trees, made more fascinating and attractive by contrast with the ugly, modern buildings which, erected on the virgin breast of nature, almost suggested sacrilege. They had passed through Basingstoke before Sir Leonard spoke again.

'The impersonation must have been amazingly good to have taken in Cousins,' he observed, 'especially after he had discovered how the copies of the plans had been obtained.'

'What impersonation?' queried Brien in tones of surprise.

'I have been wondering why Cousins suddenly changed his plans at Sittingbourne and, instead of catching the connection for Sheerness, walked out of the station, and entered a car which was waiting there. You made certain, I suppose, that he had a ticket for Sheerness?'

'Yes.'

'Then he must either have met somebody in the train, or on the platform at Sittingbourne, who influenced him to alter his arrangements.'

'According to the collector, who seems to have been an observant sort of fellow, he actually went towards the local; then changed his mind, eventually handing over his ticket, and leaving the station. As far as we have been able to ascertain, he spoke to nobody on the platform at all.'

'Yet to judge from the taxi driver's story he entered a car of his own free will and apparently without hesitation. That shows that he knew it was there, and waiting for him. Of course he may have arranged for it to be there. In that case why did he take a ticket for Sheerness? It's a bit of a puzzle, Billy.'

'Bit of a puzzle! It seems a crazy enigma to me. Do you think that the man who impersonated the Air-Marshal and Warrington also impersonated someone Cousins knew, and deceived him so effectively that he accepted a lift?'

'It looks like it.'

'But how on earth could he have known that Cousins was going to Sheerness, where did he meet him, and how did he know him?'

'Those are questions I am unable to answer at present.'

'Another thing you must remember,' went on Brien, 'is the fact that Cousins was wearing a naval uniform which would render him inconspicuous in a train crowded with naval ratings, and in a place where sailors are as frequently seen as civilians.'

'That's true. But it is possible that Cousins made himself known to the man who kidnapped him.'

'What!' The car swerved violently, as Brien forgot the wheel in his surprise. 'Why on earth should he do that?'

'Because he recognised, or thought he recognised, a friend who would be of use to him in his investigations. The only man he would be likely to accost when engaged on a job of that sort would be one of us. Therefore, I am playing with the notion that one of us was impersonated. Cousins fell into the trap, and was kidnapped.'

'But, man alive,' protested Brien, 'you are bestowing almost supernatural, or rather I should say satanic, powers on these people. We don't move about under a halo of publicity with pictures in the papers, and all that sort of thing. How on earth can outsiders know us or anything about us?'

'We're up against a pretty big thing if I'm any judge,' observed Wallace. 'Men who have among their number fellows who can impersonate people like the Air-Marshal and the War Office Chief of Staff, walk boldly into their offices, and make copies of plans supposedly secreted in burglar-proof safes, are not ordinary. They must have a pretty complete organisation behind them. Meddling with affairs which they must know are bound to bring the Secret Service on their track, it is pretty certain that they first found out a good deal about the Secret Service, and set a watch. Apart from that, have you forgotten how the triumph of Miles, Cousins, and Shannon in India, which ended incidentally with a popular double wedding, brought the three into an almost worldwide glow of publicity? Isn't that the reason why we generally give Cousins and Shannon jobs where it doesn't matter whether they are recognised or not?'

Brien nodded.

'I forgot that for the moment,' he confessed. 'I remember your remark at the time that their usefulness as Secret Service agents was badly impaired.'

'Of course that was three years ago, but people of the type we are generally up against always remember anything that is likely to turn out useful later. Cousins is probably a marked man, and – by Jove!'

The sudden exclamation with which he interrupted himself, caused Brien to glance at him sharply. In consequence the car swerved again, bringing a duet of protest from within. Billy glanced round with a grin.

'Sorry,' he apologised. 'Leonard becomes so dashed interesting at times that I forget I'm driving.'

'Shall I do it for you?' enquired Phyllis sweetly; 'then you two can come inside and gossip to your hearts' content.'

'No, thanks, dear. I'll be careful in future.'

'Mind you are,' begged Molly; 'we'll soon be getting among the traffic, and I've no ambition to return from America only to be killed or maimed for life in a car smash.'

'Why did you give that sudden exclamation?' demanded Billy of his companion in aggrieved tones.

'The significance of my own remark struck me rather forcibly, that's all. I was saying that Cousins is probably a marked man, was going to add that it is very likely Shannon is too.' He waited as though expecting Brien to make some comment. When the other remained silent, he went on: 'Apparently the same idea does not occur to you. Taking into consideration the fact that Cousins and Shannon are publicly the two best known men in the Secret Service, isn't it probable that they have been watched and studied? Then, as soon as this organisation or gang, or whatever you wish to call it, thought its activities were likely to bring the Secret Service on its track, precautions were taken. Cousins goes to Sheerness, or rather gets as far as Sittingbourne. There he walks into a trap already set for any Secret Service man who might go nosing round. He sees Shannon on the station and accosts him. He is invited into the car, goes innocently, and there you are.'

'Good Lord! You mean to say—'

'I mean to say that the man who impersonated the Chief of Staff and the Air-Marshal quite possibly impersonated Shannon also. You said the fellow in the car was big and burly; well, so is Shannon.'

'But this man was not seen on the platform.'

'You mean nobody has volunteered the information that such an individual was seen. Well, we'll make certain of that. I'll go down to Sheerness or rather Sittingbourne myself, and conduct enquiries along those lines.' He chuckled. 'I may even meet the sham Captain Shannon myself, though that's not very probable. I don't think the head of an organisation showing such skill and resource would blunder like that.'

'He's blundered pretty badly in one respect anyhow,' observed Brien.

'How?'

'Why, in dispatching all his communications from Sheerness,

especially as we seem to have proved that he is actually somewhere in that neighbourhood.'

'That's true. It certainly seems a slip, but it can't be. There must be something behind it. The brain that has conceived all that we know, or guess at, wouldn't make an error of such rank idiocy.'

'Very often,' declared Brien somewhat sententiously, 'it's the little things that trip people up. But seriously; do you really believe that business about Shannon being impersonated? It seems so utterly fantastic to me.'

'Perhaps so, but it is the best of several notions that have occurred to me. It all fits in so admirably. Shannon is in Rome on embassy duty; has been for some time. These people possibly know that. They also possibly know that he is likely to be there for some time longer. There is no particular secrecy about his present job.'

'But how could they have known that Cousins would travel down by that particular train? How; in fact, could they have known that he was searching for them?'

'Perhaps he was watched; they may even have picked up your wireless message; guessed what it meant; and set a watch at once. But what is far more likely; they knew nothing about Cousins' activities at all, and the station at Sittingbourne was kept under observation merely as a precautionary measure.'

'What about the road? We might have sent somebody down by car.'

'You may be sure the road is under surveillance as well, and, if their headquarters is on the Isle of Sheppey, the watch is being kept on the bridge.'

'Then you think we are up against something big?'

'Billy, I think we're up against the biggest thing we've struck for a long time, bigger perhaps than we realise yet.'

Major Brien gave a deep sigh.

'Well, I'm jolly glad you're home. If I'd had to tackle it alone I should have made an awful mess of it. As it is,' he added rather despondently, 'I've lost one of our best men. Cousins has probably been murdered by now.'

'You aren't responsible. Dash it all! If he has walked into a trap, it's not your fault, and we all have to take our chances of life and death in the big game. I hope he hasn't gone though. In many ways it would be almost impossible to replace him, and he's such a darned good fellow. Oh, well, it's no use getting despondent. You may be sure that, if Jerry can possibly hold on to life, he'll do it.'

They spoke of other subjects for a while. Going through Camberley, memories of days gone by crowded through their minds, when, as cadets, they had worked and played together, eventually to pass out of the Royal Military College at the same time, as subalterns in the same regiment.

'Happy days, Bill,' sighed Sir Leonard.

'Happy days,' echoed his second in command.

They had reached the Brentford by-pass before Brien reverted to the subject which was uppermost in both their minds.

'I'm beginning to feel convinced,' he remarked, 'that the attempt on your life at Southampton was instigated by the people who are behind this organised theft of national secrets. You have made me realise what a big thing it is, and if, as you suggest, they know so much about Shannon and Cousins, they're bound to know you, and fear the consequences, if you take a hand in the game. You'll have to keep your eyes skinned, old chap. They won't throw in the sponge just because they've failed once.'

Sir Leonard shrugged his shoulders.

'The Southampton affair was probably engineered by somebody

who has a grudge against me. I'm afraid there are quite a few of that type about.'

'Carter is due back tomorrow from Turkey. Keep him with you as a bodyguard in case of any further danger. He's a quick-witted fellow, and a splendid man in an emergency.'

Wallace laughed.

'What do you take me for?' he scoffed. 'You'll be asking me to wear a bullet proof waistcoat next.'

'Not a bad notion,' commented the other.

'A damn silly idea,' grunted Sir Leonard. 'A bullet proof waistcoat would be wonderful protection against a bullet aimed at the skull, like the one that missed me this morning, wouldn't it? What's the matter with you, Bill? Are you getting premonitions or something?'

'I've an uneasy feeling knocking round inside that I don't like. Sounds absurd I know, but there it is.'

Sir Leonard eyed him with a smile, but he spoke seriously enough.

'Look here, old man,' he observed. 'You and I have been in the game for fourteen or fifteen years now and, during that time, we've both been on the brink of eternity pretty often. In fact we've had some devilish narrow squeaks. You don't think I'm going to start hedging myself round with a host of safety gadgets and precautions now, do you? I've quite a lot of faith in my lucky star. It's seen me through up-to-date, and I'll continue to trust in it. At any rate I've always been a fatalist, so have you – one has to be in this service. Look out!'

His sudden cry of warning was hardly necessary. Brien had already sensed the menace. They were passing the Chiswick Empire at the time, when a large car, driven at an absurdly reckless speed in such traffic, overtook them; suddenly swerved towards them. Only Brien's coolness and skill prevented a disaster. He swung the wheel over, at the same time jamming on the brakes. The car skidded on to the pavement scattering people in all directions, but doing no damage.

'Keep going, Bill!' came the level voice of Sir Leonard. 'There may be someone waiting with a gun.'

Almost in the same movement as it had mounted the pavement, the car was in the road again, narrowly missing a young tree, had shot between a tram and a lorry, was going on its way as though nothing had happened. Behind could be heard the shouts and cries of frightened and angry people, a police whistle. Sir Leonard turned to soothe the startled women and Adrian in the tonneau, found them all indignant at the criminally reckless behaviour of the vehicle that had almost wrecked them, and was now lost in the distance.

'People like that should be forbidden to own cars,' cried the angry Phyllis.

'They ought to be sent to penal servitude,' declared Molly. 'But why did you continue, Billy? It wasn't your fault, and a policeman is blowing a whistle behind us as though he intends to burst his lungs.'

'Didn't want to be surrounded by a crowd of people all talking and telling lies together,' he replied with a wink at his companion. 'We'll be held up soon enough.'

He was right. A policeman stopped them just as they were approaching Hammersmith. Wallace promptly handed him a card, which he scrutinised, whereupon, saluting smartly, he stepped back, and waved them on.

'Narrow escape that, Leonard,' muttered Brien, when they had crossed the Broadway, and were heading towards Olympia. 'There's not much doubt that these people, whoever they are, are bent on stopping you from taking a hand in the affair.'

'And they gamble with the lives of two women and a child! God! I'll make them regret it, if I ever come into contact with them.'

The cold fury in the speaker's voice caused a grim smile to play round the lips of Major Brien. He knew that from that moment Sir Leonard's efforts to run down and smash the gang that was beginning to prove itself such a menace would be implacable, deadly. Nobody was more chivalrous to an opponent, whose efforts in opposition to him or his cause were governed by the canons of fair play, than Sir Leonard Wallace, but, if his adversaries overstepped those bounds, resorted to foul means to encompass their ends, or endangered innocent lives, he could be utterly ruthless.

No further attempt was made to molest them before they reached Sir Leonard's house in Piccadilly. They all lunched together, after which Lady Wallace and Mrs Brien went out shopping while their husbands drove together to Whitehall. Batty had already arrived with the luggage, and had been warned to say nothing to anybody about the affair in Southampton Docks. Always exceedingly solicitous about his wife's happiness, Wallace saw no reason why she should be made anxious by an event which, after all, had terminated without hurt to him, when already she suffered so much anxiety on his account.

A glowing fire, burning cheerfully in the large fireplace of his office, seemed to extend a hearty welcome to him. For a moment he stood at the door, his gaze wandering round the comfortable room, taking in the shelves packed tight with reference books and reports which took up the whole of one side, the maps on the other walls, the massive mantelpiece with its beautifully carved clock and relics of the War, the three deep leather armchairs. Finally his eyes came to rest on the great oak desk, and he sighed. Brien, who was still with him, was unable to decide whether the sigh was one of relief or regret.

'A comfortable office is a good place in which to spend one's working hours, Bill,' observed Sir Leonard, as he divested himself of his overcoat, hanging it with his hat on a peg in the small lavatory adjoining. 'The trouble is that so many of my working hours are spent elsewhere.'

Brien looked at him with a certain amount of surprise. It was unusual to hear his companion give tongue to such sentiments.

'Are you getting tired of – of the other life?' he asked curiously.

Wallace shook his head.

'I was thinking of Molly,' he explained.

He walked to the desk, and, seating himself in his swing chair, began to study a pile of reports placed ready for his perusal. Brien watched him for a few minutes; then took out his cigarette case, helped himself to a Virginian.

'Are you beginning to get premonitions now?' he demanded.

Wallace looked up at him with a smile.

'Nothing like that about me,' he assured the other. 'I want to think – do you mind?'

Brien took the hint, and left the room. Twenty minutes later Sir Leonard pressed one of the numerous buttons under the ledge of his desk. Almost at once Maddison appeared. He was unable to add anything to what Sir Leonard had already learnt from Brien concerning the disappearance of Cousins and the activities of the gang, which presumably had kidnapped the little man. However,

Wallace insisted on going through the affair step by step with him in the hope that some point would arise, which would be of help in the investigations he intended to make. Afterwards he paid a visit to the War Office and Air Ministry, had interviews with the Chief of Staff and the Air-Marshal, inspected the safes, carefully examined the plans. He questioned the night watchman very thoroughly, only to be convinced that the men who had carried out the impersonations must have been perfect in every detail. No item of interest likely to aid him in his search emerged from the enquiry. Nothing could be added to the information Cousins had apparently already acquired.

On his return to his office Wallace was told that the Foreign Secretary had been asking for him on the telephone. He immediately rang through on the line connecting directly with the statesman's room in the Foreign Office.

'That you, Wallace? . . . Good,' came eagerly from the other end. 'Can you come over? There is a gentleman here who is very keen to speak to you. I'd send him across only he is not exactly the type of individual you would care to have wandering round your premises.'

'Who is he?' asked Sir Leonard with interest.

'Monsieur Damien.'

'Not *the* Damien?'

'Yes.'

Wallace whistled softly to himself. What could the head of the French Secret Service want with him!

'I am coming at once,' he assured the Foreign Secretary.

CHAPTER FIVE

The Anxiety of Monsieur Damien

The tall, good-looking man who controlled Great Britain's foreign affairs greeted Sir Leonard warmly, expressing his pleasure at seeing him back in London.

'It is a good thing your short holiday ended when it did,' he declared, 'otherwise, I am afraid it would have been interrupted. Events have been happening lately which badly require your intervention.'

For a while they spoke of the daring manner in which copies of the plans of the Masterson monoplane and Wentworth gun had been obtained, of the offer made to the government concerning the sale of certain French and German secrets. Sir Leonard was shown the letter received by the Foreign Secretary, and studied it with great care. It consisted of a sheet of ordinary writing paper obtainable in almost any stationer's shop, on which the words had been typed by a machine which obviously had no peculiarities. There was neither signature nor address, not even a date.

'Not very helpful,' commented Wallace, after he had examined the envelope which, with the exception that it bore the postmark 'Sheerness', was of no more assistance than the letter.

'Still, I'll keep them, if I may?' The statesman nodded. 'I understand that nothing further has transpired since you put the requested notice in *The Times*?'

'Nothing at all. Really, Wallace, I am inclined to think the whole thing is a hoax.'

'I might agree with you were it not for the fact that Cousins has obviously been abducted and probably murdered. Also, two attempts have been made on my life today, which I am rather persuaded to believe were engineered by the same people.'

'Attempts on your life!'

Wallace told of the narrow escapes he had had in Southampton and Chiswick. The Foreign Secretary was horrified, particularly at the wanton manner in which the lives of Lady Wallace, Mrs Brien, and Adrian had been jeopardised by the unknown assailants.

'Who can these people be?' he cried, 'and what is behind all this?'

'I don't know,' returned the other grimly, 'but I'm going to find out – soon! Now how about Damien. What does he want?'

'I do not know. He wouldn't tell me. But he is very much perturbed about something. He is waiting in the office of one of the secretaries. Shall we have him here?'

'Please.'

The Frenchman was ushered in, and presented to Wallace. He bowed profoundly; gracefully accepted the seat offered to him.

'We have met before, monsieur,' he said in excellent English. 'At times the duty we owe each to our countries has – what shall I say? – prevented us from seeing eye to eye on certain matters; is it not so?' Sir Leonard nodded. 'Always,' went on Monsieur Damien, 'pardon, I should say, nearly always, our interests have clashed – we have even been antagonists; nevertheless, I think you will agree with me that we have had much respect for each other. Am I not right, monsieur?'

'You are quite right,' agreed Wallace, wondering what all this was leading up to. 'At least,' he added, 'I can certainly say that I have always respected you.'

'And I you,' declared the other earnestly. 'Today, I come to you in the presence of your eminent Secretary of Foreign Affairs' – he bowed to the statesman – 'to ask your assistance.'

'I am flattered,' smiled Sir Leonard, reflecting none of the surprise which the Foreign Secretary showed in his face. 'In what manner can I be of assistance to you?'

Monsieur Damien leant forward. He was a thin, sharp-featured man with a pair of keen brown eyes, but little else of an impressive nature about him.

'It is my intention, messieurs,' he proclaimed, 'to lay all my cards on the table, if I may use one of your excellent idioms. May I proceed?'

The Foreign Secretary looked enquiringly at Wallace, who nodded.

'Please do,' urged the former.

'Very well, messieurs. Some days ago a mysterious communication reached the Quai d'Orsay. The writer claimed to possess copies of certain secret plans regarding British inventions of military importance, and stated that he was prepared to accept the highest offer for them. It would be idle and hypocritical of me to pretend that France was not interested, gentlemen. You know and I know that all nations are eager to learn each other's secrets.

France and Great Britain, though very friendly disposed towards each other, are not above buying the secrets of each other, if it is felt that those secrets are of value. You see, messieurs, I am frank. But naturally, negotiations would not be entered into without the Quai d'Orsay being satisfied that the offer was genuine. In the case of which I speak the writer asked for a reply in the London *Times*, stating that France was prepared to negotiate.'

Wallace smiled slightly.

'Why do you smile, monsieur?' asked the Frenchman.

'I will tell you presently,' replied the Englishman. 'Please go on.'

'*Bien*. Before replying as requested, it was necessary to make investigations, but I confess that everything was so wrapped in mystery that nothing could be discovered. The letter was typed on ordinary paper in French of the most faultless; there was no indication to suggest address or name or, in fact, anything about the writer. All we knew was that the document had been posted in England at a place called—'

'Sheerness,' put in Wallace.

The Frenchman's eyebrows rose slightly.

'No, monsieur, it was Southend. Why do you say Sheerness? Have you reason to—'

'Pardon my interruption, Monsieur Damien. I was merely guessing. Certain communications which presumably emanated from the same source, were posted in Sheerness. I find the fact that the letter, of which you speak, was dispatched from Southend quite interesting.'

'Then you know of the communication to the French Government?'

'I do. I also know that similar communications were sent to

Berlin and Moscow. They, I may as well tell you at once, were posted in Sheerness.'

The Frenchman smiled. He was not in the least surprised by the revelations.

'It is amusing, this game of international espionage,' he commented. 'If we knew how – but I am not here to talk of matters so delicate. As I have said, I am here to beg your assistance. As you know so much, my task is made a little the easier. Having this knowledge, you will guess I am aware that an offer was made to your government of certain French plans for alliances of an offensive and defensive nature. Circumstances all seem to point to the likelihood that these offers are inspired by the same individual.'

'I quite agree with you there,' nodded Sir Leonard. 'It appears that an organisation has arisen which intends to make money by stealing the secrets of one nation, and selling them to the highest bidder among the others.'

'Exactly, monsieur. But unless the whole thing is bluff, how can this organisation have obtained so many secrets? One or even two, yes, but more it seems impossible. Yet to France has been offered two of Great Britain's cherished secrets and one of Germany's; Britain has been offered a secret of France, perhaps also others; to Germany has been offered the same secret, and I very much fear another. Tell me, monsieur, do you think it is all fraud, this?'

Wallace emphatically shook his head.

'Since you have been so frank with me and, as you say, are placing your cards on the table, I will be equally frank with you. There is no bluff about this thing. There is an organisation which has certainly obtained the secrets it claims to possess, and intends to enrich itself at the expense of the nations concerned. I say this, fully convinced of the truth of it.'

Monsieur Damien's eyes gleamed.

'Then I have not come for your help in vain, I hope,' he remarked. 'These people, it seems, are in England. You will do your best to exterminate them, and quickly?'

Wallace eyed him thoughtfully for some moments. The Foreign Secretary looked from one to the other, appearing to be rather puzzled. Presently Wallace spoke:

'You told us, Monsieur Damien,' he observed, 'that you intended to lay all your cards on the table.'

'But certainly.'

'At present there are one or two missing, and I believe they are more important than the others. It appears to me that, measuring what Britain is likely to lose against what France is likely to lose by the sale of the national secrets under discussion, Britain stands to suffer the bigger blow. Why, then, are you so eager for this organisation to be smashed? Why do you come in this apparently frank manner? There is something else influencing you and those who sent you, monsieur. What is it?'

Monsieur Damien nodded slowly. His manner became impressive.

'You are right,' he declared. 'The sale of our plans for offensive and defensive alliances to either Britain or Germany is a serious matter, but not of paramount gravity. Sooner or later the world will be aware of those arrangements, though naturally the nation that knows them now could act very much to our disadvantage. I confess, however, that, if those plans of France were placed by her in the balance against the purchase of copies of Britain's two military inventions, she would risk the loss of them to obtain the others. As you guess, monsieur, that is not the real reason I have come to you. The organisation apparently exists in this country;

you have the best chance of ferreting it out, and destroying it. And it must be destroyed, monsieur. It is becoming a terrible menace to the peace of Europe. The French Government is greatly perturbed.'

'Why?' asked the Foreign Secretary.

'Blackmail is now the trump card,' replied the Frenchman quietly, but with grim deliberation. 'Think of it, gentlemen; the blackmailing of a nation. Last night another letter was received at the Quai d'Orsay, posted this time in London. You, of course, have heard that the whole frontier of France has been strengthened until it is considered now to be almost impregnable? Well, the writer of the letter claims to have complete copies of maps and details, even to the smallest item, regarding the fortifications. These he promises will be handed over intact to France on payment of two hundred million francs. If that sum is not paid by January the fifteenth the plans will be sent to Germany.' He paused, noting the effect of his pronouncement on his hearers. The Foreign Secretary looked decidedly startled; Sir Leonard Wallace appeared almost uninterested. 'You see now,' continued Damien, eyeing the latter with some disappointment, 'that there is grave reason for my presence here today. It seems impossible that the plans of the fortifications can have been copied, they have been guarded with care of the greatest. Yet what sense could there be in making such a – what you would call – gigantic bluff?'

'I don't think it's bluff,' remarked Wallace. 'In fact, knowing how copies of the plans of the British military secrets were obtained, I am convinced it is not.'

'You will do your utmost to destroy the gang?' asked the Frenchman earnestly.

'You may rely on that, monsieur, and for more reasons than one. For our own sakes it is urgent that their activities must be ended once and for all. It is now evident also that the peace of Europe will be broken, if they are not suppressed very soon, which gives me more reason than ever for getting on their track at the earliest possible moment.'

'Good Lord!' exclaimed the Foreign Secretary. 'Fancy daring to hold a revolver to the head of a whole nation in that barefaced manner. Who, in Heaven's name, Wallace, can these people be? They must comprise a pretty powerful organisation, and be *au fait* with everything that goes on in government and diplomatic circles.'

Sir Leonard Wallace nodded.

'Yes,' he agreed, 'there is no doubt about it now. I think we will be startled to find who is behind it all, if we are fortunate enough to bring the gang to book.'

'Why,' queried the Frenchman, 'are you so certain that everything is not bluff? You say you know how copies of the British military secrets were made. Would it be injudicious on my part to ask how it was done? You see, monsieur, the French plans may have been copied in the same way.'

'Very likely they were; in fact it is pretty certain, I think. There is no reason why you should not know, Monsieur Damien. This organisation, of which we speak, appears to possess men who are past masters in the art of mimicry and make-up. The high officials in whose possession were the plans in question were impersonated, and so perfect was the impersonation that not the slightest suspicion was roused. Either on the same night or on adjacent nights these officials were apparently seen to arrive at the buildings in which the plans were secreted. They were in each case accompanied by a staff officer. Enquiry proved that in reality neither of the gentlemen has visited his office at night for some considerable time, thus it is obvious that men made up to represent them were seen, not they. Both officials are of similar height, and were probably impersonated by the same individual. It is also significant that the staff officers impersonated are of like build. It is my opinion that the man masquerading in each case as a staff officer was an expert safe-breaker. If that was done in London, it could equally well be done in Paris.'

'*Mon Dieu*!' The startled look on Monsieur Damien's face was almost ludicrous. 'What effrontery! What impudence! No longer can I hope that the letters to my government were the work of a fraud or an imbecile. Messieurs, it is a very grave situation. Undoubtedly the villains are domiciled within the shores of England, therefore I am helpless to assist, but my wishes, and the wishes of all good Frenchmen, will be with you in your efforts to destroy the organisation. You have my word on behalf of the French Government,' he added somewhat naively, 'that the advances of these people will be treated with contempt. France will, under no circumstances, purchase the copies of the plans of the military secrets which have been stolen from Great Britain.'

Sir Leonard smiled at the Foreign Secretary. Almost it seemed as though his left eyelid fluttered in a wink.

'It is gratifying to be assured of that, monsieur,' he observed drily. 'In return, I am in a position to be able to inform you that His Majesty's Government is not likely to bid for information concerning the secret treaties which were offered for sale. You asked me a little while ago why I smiled. I will tell you: all nations that have been approached by this organisation have been invited to insert a notice of their willingness to negotiate in the personal column of *The Times*, just as you were. It is good to know that

France does not intend to make a bid. Unfortunately, however, that decision helps Great Britain very little. Germany and Russia were approached in the same manner, and both have inserted the required acceptances in *The Times*.'

'I see,' murmured Damien. 'I regret very much that the decision of my country is of so little help to Great Britain. It appears now that we are asking for much, but in return giving nothing. I am sorry.'

'You forget, monsieur,' returned Wallace, 'that in endeavouring to save France from a great blow, we shall also be serving ourselves. It is necessary for us to obtain possession of the copies of the plans that have been stolen from us, and—'

'Ah, yes, monsieur, that is true,' interposed the Frenchman earnestly, 'but what comparison can there be between certain secret details in the construction of a gun and an aeroplane being made public, and Germany being put in complete possession of all details concerning our frontier fortifications? The latter would probably mean tragedy and disaster for France, the former merely inconvenience to Britain. Even if France agrees to the demands of these blackmailers, and preserves her frontier secrets, she will be compelled to pay two hundred million francs. Think of it, gentlemen!'

'In any case,' observed the Foreign Secretary, 'it is essential that this band should be broken up. With Europe in its present unsettled state, this general auctioning of national secrets must eventually mean serious trouble. It is bound to increase distrust and cause bitterness between the powers.'

'Tell me, Monsieur Damien,' solicited Wallace; 'in what manner is your government expected to reply to this latest demand?'

'If the money is not paid by January the fifteenth—'

'Yes: I know that, but to whom is the reply to go? Another notification in *The Times*?'

Monsieur Damien nodded slowly.

'That is so,' he affirmed. 'It is to appear no later than the twelfth, and must be worded thus: "France desires to preserve the peace of Europe." Instructions – that is the word used, mind you; the *canaille*! – instructions will then be sent regarding the time and place for the exchange to be made.'

'January the twelfth,' commented the Foreign Secretary. 'We have twenty-one days then.'

'Twenty-one days to save two hundred million francs for France,' put in Wallace, 'but nothing like that to prevent our own stolen secrets from being sold to Russia or Germany. Negotiations may even now be proceeding.' He rose from his chair. 'For our own sake and for yours, Monsieur Damien,' he declared, 'you may rest assured that every effort will be made to break up this organisation, and obtain possession of all copies of French and English plans now apparently held by it.'

The Chief of the French Secret Service rose also, and bowed.

'You will find France very grateful I assure you, monsieur,' he proclaimed. For a moment he stood as though irresolute. 'There is one thing more I have to beg of you,' he added presently.

'And that is?'

'In the event of your proving successful, and documents of secret and vital importance to France falling into your hands, may I ask for your assurance that you will not divulge anything you read in them?'

'I expected you to ask that,' smiled Sir Leonard. 'Will you, on your part, give me your word that there is nothing contained in them of a nature inimical or damaging to Great Britain, her dominions or colonies, or to any country or person receiving the protection of Great Britain?'

'Most assuredly, monsieur,' returned the Frenchman at once. 'Of our frontier fortifications you will gather that the plans and details cannot contain anything inimical to your country or its dependencies. With regard to the plans for offensive and defensive alliances, there is nothing in them which Britain can object to. Their publication at this time would be of great inconvenience, that is all. It may be necessary for you or your assistants to look through the documents to ascertain that they are the correct ones – you will thus be able to see for yourself that they are in no way damaging to your country. You have my word of honour, monsieur.'

'Thank you,' acknowledged Wallace. 'I can promise with a clear conscience, therefore, that nothing seen by me, or anybody representing me, in the documents belonging to France will ever be divulged.'

He held out his hand which Monsieur Damien grasped warmly.

'I go from here with joyful heart,' he declared. 'I feel already that France is saved.'

'Don't be too sanguine, monsieur,' warned Sir Leonard. 'I may fail.'

Damien smiled.

'It has been said, and with great envy, by colleagues in my department,' he confided, 'that Sir Leonard Wallace never fails. Whenever you are in France, or passing through, it is a matter of the greatest concern, and I may add the gravest concern. You see, monsieur, I continue to be frank with you?'

'That is why I am invariably shadowed I presume,' commented Sir Leonard drily.

For a moment the Frenchman was nonplussed; then he smiled again.

'Since you know, why should I deny it?' he observed with a shrug of his shoulders; adding slyly: 'In a way I suppose such vigilance is useless. If Sir Leonard Wallace did not want France to know he was on her shores, I am very much afraid France would not know.'

Shortly afterwards he took his leave, after thanking the Foreign Secretary for his courtesy in receiving him, and reiterating his gratitude to Sir Leonard Wallace. Although he was not aware of it, Monsieur Damien was shadowed all the way to Paris, a surveillance that did not relax until he actually entered the office of the French Minister for Foreign Affairs to make his report. Wallace was taking no chances. Although he had met him before, and was fairly certain that Monsieur Damien was in truth *the* Monsieur Damien, he had already had sufficient proof of the ability of certain individuals to impersonate others to cause him to take every precaution against a repetition of that sort of thing. He could not see what object a man could have in masquerading as the head of the French Secret Service, and obtaining an interview with him and the Foreign Secretary still, as he put it to himself, one never knew.

He remained for some time talking to the Foreign Secretary, during which the latter made a few well-meant but rather futile suggestions anent the manner in which it might be possible to checkmate the activities of the organisation that was playing ducks and drakes with the closely guarded secrets of France and Great Britain; not to mention Germany, and possibly other countries as well. The Foreign Secretary was too much of an aesthete and idealist to fit satisfactorily into his high office. He believed as much in the League of Nations as Charles I had believed in the divine right of kings, and spent a considerable amount of his time in Lausanne and various capitals of Europe in consultations with foreign statesmen, which never came to anything. He was utterly unable to deal with the kind of situation that had now arisen, and was perfectly honest in his oft-repeated statement that he was relieved and glad that Sir Leonard Wallace was back in harness.

It was getting late when the latter left the Foreign Office, but he returned to his own department, where he shut himself up in his room, and remained for a considerable time in deep thought. He felt almost certain now that the organisation he was so anxious to destroy had its headquarters in reality in the neighbourhood of Sheerness. He had come to the conclusion that the posting of three of the letters from the naval port had been an oversight or a blunder. Of the two others, received by France, one had been dispatched from Southend, easily reached from the Isle of Sheppey by a boat – a fast motor launch for example – the other from London which was not a great distance away. At any rate it was at Sittingbourne, close to Sheerness, where Cousins had disappeared, and, whether there had been a mistake made in the posting of the letters or not, everything pointed to Sheppey as the spot where his investigations should commence. Having definitely made his plans, he sent for Maddison, and gave him certain explicit instructions. That keen-eyed individual listened attentively, made a few notes, and departed.

Big Ben was striking seven as Wallace left his office to find his car – for which he had telephoned ten minutes previously – drawn up to the kerb. The chauffeur – an ex-corporal of his own regiment whom he had engaged soon after the War, and who had been in his employ ever since – saluted him respectfully.

'Have you enough petrol for a journey to Sittingbourne, Johnson?' he asked.

'No, sir,' replied the man.

'Drive me home; then fill up the tank. I shall want you to take me there after dinner. I'll be ready about eight.'

'Very well, sir.'

While he dined, alone with his wife, Sir Leonard told her that he would probably be away for the greater part of the night. She paled a little, but made no comment. The sigh which rose to her lips was stifled before it found expression. Promptly at eight Wallace, wrapped in a warm overcoat, a muffler round his neck, a soft hat pulled well over his eyes, entered his car, which, as soon as he had given the driver instructions to stop a hundred yards or so from Sittingbourne station, started on its journey. He lay back in the well-upholstered seat, lit his pipe, and gave himself up to reflection. The latter did not last very long, however. For some minutes Sir Leonard's eyes had been fixed, at first casually, afterwards alertly, on his chauffeur's back. The well-tuned car was running smoothly through Herne Hill when he chuckled softly to himself.

'Really,' he murmured, 'these people depend a lot upon impersonation. But I wonder what they have done with Johnson!'

CHAPTER SIX

Cousins is Trapped

Cousins, sitting by the side of the man he had imagined to be Captain Hugh Shannon, had had no suspicion for some considerable time that he had fallen into a trap. The car was driven rapidly along the road leading to the bridge crossing over to the Isle of Sheppey, and the driver scarcely uttered a word. Cousins' numerous questions either went unheeded or were replied to with grunts or in monosyllables. At length the little man had grown exasperated.

'Look here, Hugh,' he exclaimed, 'this is ridiculous. We are alone in a car; there doesn't appear to be a soul within miles of us; surely now is the time to spill the beans. Why all the mystery?'

'You'll know before long,' grunted the other.

Something in the tone of voice caused Cousins to start. With a gasp he quickly turned his eyes on his companion, striving to pierce the darkness, examine the other's features. But all he could see was the dim outline of a face that certainly looked like that of Shannon. Yet he began to have doubts. The clever impersonation of the Air-Marshal and General Warrington recurred to his mind. Perhaps he had also been taken in. He had not had a perfect view of the man. Even when he had been standing under the lamp in the station, the latter's face had been in shadow; nevertheless Cousins had seen it clearly enough not to be deceived; besides the figure, the voice, even the walk had been so typical, and he had known Shannon for years, had worked with him, been in daily, hourly contact with him. But the doubt persisted. He hardly knew what had caused it. And, like most doubts, it momentarily grew stronger.

It certainly was curious that Shannon should suddenly appear on the scene. Of course he may have been recalled, but, if so, surely Major Brien would have said something about it. Shannon may have returned of his own accord, bringing home information that could not be trusted to the usual channels, and incidentally have arrived in time to hear news which had reached Major Brien after Cousins had left him. News which it was important he, Cousins, should know. Shannon had been sent down by car to inform him; the man by his side had hinted as much. That seemed reasonable enough. Knowing that Cousins was not travelling down by train till late, but unaware of the actual time, the other had decided to meet the London trains. There another doubt assailed the little man. Surely, if this man was Shannon, he would have looked along the row of coaches, searching for his colleague, instead of standing aloof apparently taking no interest in the arrival of the train.

It was at this point in his reflections that the Secret Service man became certain that he had been trapped, that the man by his side was an impostor. The other had hinted that it was unwise to be seen, yet had been standing under a lamp, showing himself off to anybody who cared to look in his direction. And the reason he had been standing in such an ostentatious position suddenly became obvious. Suspecting that a member of the Secret Service might appear in the neighbourhood to investigate, a man made-up like one of them – apparently the people he was in search of were well acquainted with certain of his companions – had been stationed on the platform of Sittingbourne station in the hope that the investigator would recognise him, thereby giving himself away. And Cousins had obliged.

'Fool!' he muttered to himself. 'You'll never be able to lift up your head again after this – if there is an after,' he added grimly.

'What did you say?' came the voice of Shannon from the man by his side.

'Oh, I was just quoting,' replied Cousins.

Again he began to wonder. That voice! It was so perfectly Shannon's that it seemed impossible that his companion could be an impostor. If he were, then Shannon must have, at some time or other, been studied by a master in the art of mimicry and make-up; perhaps for this very purpose. Cousins strove to persuade himself that he was merely letting his imagination run away with him. But the demon of suspicion had obtained strong hold upon him now; various little matters came uppermost in his mind. The reluctance of the man driving the car to speak. Was that not proof that he feared to give himself away? Surely Shannon would have been only too eager to confide in the other once they were upon that lonely stretch of road, absolutely safe from eavesdroppers! At that point in his reflections the car swung giddily round a bend. Cousins, unprepared, was flung against his companion. Then, despite himself, he chuckled. He knew only too well what would have happened had he collided with Shannon's massive shoulders. His whole body would have been jarred by the shock. Nothing like that occurred in this case. He hit something that was soft and gave to the impact – padding!

'Why are you laughing?' asked the bogus Shannon.

'Only because I overbalanced, and was flung against you,' replied Cousins.

'You laugh easily.'

'Haven't you ever noticed that about me before?' was the cool retort. He broke into a long quotation from Shakespeare. 'Very apt, isn't it?' he concluded.

'Very.'

Again Cousins chuckled, this time very softly to himself. The real Shannon professed to loathe quotations, always nipped Cousins' efforts in that direction in the bud, sometimes with more force than politeness.

'What I like about you, Shannon,' went on the little man, 'is your readiness to listen to me when I quote poetry. As you know, the others generally do their utmost to shut me up. But there, you're by way of being a poet yourself. What became of that ode you sent to the *Windsor*? Was it published?'

'Er – not yet,' came the hesitating reply.

'It ought to be. I loved the bit about the moon shimmering on the water like a mantle of rapturous delight. How does it go again?'

'Do you think I can break out into poetry now?' snapped the other hastily. 'I've other things to think about at the moment.'

'Once a poet always a poet,' retorted Cousins.

In the darkness his extraordinarily mobile face creased into a broad smile. Having assured himself that the man by his side was an impostor, his mind now began to work furiously in an effort to decide what was best to be done. The simplest thing was to produce the automatic he carried in his pocket, hold it against his companion's head, command him to stop, and get out of the car, or order the fellow to drive him back to Sittingbourne. In that case nothing would be gained, and probably a great deal lost, for his quarry would, in all likelihood, take fright and make his headquarters elsewhere. If he refrained from holding up the driver until they reached their destination, his chances of escaping with information concerning the present hiding place of the organisation were practically nil. Even if he succeeded in getting away, it was certain that there would be nobody to arrest when he got back with help. 'On the whole,' he decided, 'it's just as well I was fool enough to walk into a trap. It's the simplest way of getting into the headquarters of these people. Once in I shall be able to study ways and means of getting information to Brien, if they don't kill me right away.'

In order to have at hand a means of defending himself in the event of his adversaries deciding on such an unpleasant course, Cousins spent some minutes considering where he could hide his automatic so that it would be overlooked when he was searched, as he was bound to be. It was a small Webley, but even so was too bulgy to pass unnoticed in his clothing. Eventually he slipped it cautiously from his pocket.

'Have you a collection of mosquitoes in this bus?' he asked the man by his side.

'What do you mean?' demanded the latter.

'Something's irritating my leg.'

'Scratch it!' tersely advised the impostor.

'Just what I am about to do,' Cousins informed him. 'At the same time I object to the necessity of having to do such a thing.'

He lifted up his left leg; subjected it to a vigorous rubbing. During the process he managed to push the weapon into his sock. It did not make for comfort, but there was no danger of its falling out, as the sock was securely held up by a suspender. He muttered a prayer that it would not be discovered.

'Obviously some prowling insect has bitten me,' he observed.

There was no answer. The car was approaching the bridge over the channel that separated the island from the mainland, and began to slow down until it was merely crawling along. The driver gave three quick blasts on the electric horn. Cousins, wondering why, was at once on the alert. Suddenly two men appeared in the glare of the headlights, waving their arms.

'I wonder what is wrong,' muttered the pseudo Shannon.

He put on the brakes, bringing the motor to a standstill.

'There's trouble ahead,' warned one of the strangers.

'There's always trouble,' replied the driver.

'Spoken as per arrangement,' muttered Cousins to himself.

He became aware that the other man was standing at his side of the car; could just discern the revolver held close to his head.

'Get out, and jump in the back,' ordered the fellow. 'Hurry up!'

'Hullo! What's all this?' protested Cousins. 'Are you holding us up?'

'Do what you're told, and be sharp about it.'

'Do we submit or fight, Shannon?' asked the little man. He was actually enjoying himself.

For answer the masquerader turned on him, and gave him a push.

'Out you get,' he commanded roughly, and the voice was no longer the voice of Shannon.

'Good Lord!' ejaculated Cousins. 'Surely I haven't made a bloomer. You're Shannon, aren't you?'

'Shannon be hanged! Get a move on. Something might come along at any moment, and—'

'Then I'll wait here until something does come along.'

'If you don't hop into the back at once,' came the grating tones of the man with a revolver, 'I'll fill you so full of lead that you'll rattle.'

'Oh, well, if you put it like that,' sighed Cousins, 'I have no option.'

He descended to the road; was immediately hustled into the back seat. The two newcomers stepped in, and sat on either side of him. The car proceeded rapidly on its way.

'What is the meaning of all this, and who are you?' demanded the little man. 'I could swear that Captain Shannon—'

'Shut up, and remain shut up!' snapped one of the men. 'Tie a handkerchief round his eyes, Swede. It'll be just as well in case of accidents; though, if he does see where he's going, he won't live long enough to be able to talk about it.'

'That doesn't sound very cheerful,' commented Cousins.

They both laughed roughly. The Secret Service man's eyes were bound tightly, after which his hands were tied together behind his back.

'I think we better gag him,' suggested one.

'Not necessary,' returned the other. 'If he makes a noise, I'll dot him on the head. Do you hear?' He shook the captive.

'Oh, yes,' replied Cousins. 'I'm not suffering from deafness, merely from a kind of offended curiosity.'

'You're for it, and that's all there is to it. Better take things philosophically.'

'"Philosophy will clip an Angel's wings,"' quoted Cousins, '"Conquer all mysteries by rule and line, Empty the haunted air, and gnomed mine—"'

'Will you shut up!'

'Don't you like poetry?' asked the little man in aggrieved tones.

All the reply he received was a sound expressive of disgust. He fell silent, striving to sense in which direction they were taking him. But, owing to the frequent turns he became baffled. One thing was obvious; Sheerness would be avoided. They were not likely to take a man whose eyes were covered by a handkerchief, and whose hands were bound behind his back, through the lighted streets of a town. Presently he caught a whiff of the sea. That suggested that the car was close to the coast, heading probably for somewhere near Minster, perhaps between Minster and Eastchurch. He was very interested; felt that he might be able to guess fairly accurately after all in what part of the island the headquarters of the organisation was located. He knew Sheppey rather well. At last the car stopped, the engine was shut off, and he immediately became aware of the dull boom of the sea. It sounded very close by, and his curiosity was aroused. Was it possible that he was to be taken in a boat to some place abroad! Immediately he put the idea aside. It was hardly likely that people who had their headquarters in a foreign country would take the trouble to post letters in Sheerness, and keep a watch on Sittingbourne station. His cogitations were rudely interrupted.

'Get out!' bade a curt voice.

He rose; was pushed over the step, and fell headlong. Owing to his hands being tied behind his back, he was unable to do anything to diminish the force of the fall. He crashed to the ground, hitting his head with such violence that he lay half stunned. In a daze he heard a callous laugh.

'That will upset his poetical tendencies,' remarked a voice.

He was jerked to his feet; someone took him by the arm, led him forward up a hill. It seemed to him in his benumbed state that he was climbing for a long time, actually it was a matter of a few minutes. Eventually his feet were guided up three or four steps, he heard a door open, was pushed along what sounded to his keen ears like a stone passage.

'Who the hell have you got there?' asked a voice.

'Don't know,' replied one of his captors. 'The guvnor'll know him I daresay.'

'Bring him upstairs.'

Cousins counted the steps he was forced to climb. There were twelve; then apparently a landing, followed by four more. He was propelled six or seven feet, and pushed into a chair. Hands went carefully over his person, searching his clothing thoroughly, removing everything from his pockets. Every moment he dreaded lest the automatic in his sock be found, but it remained undiscovered. He breathed an inward sigh of relief as the searcher desisted in his efforts.

'Nothing more,' he heard the fellow say. 'The most dangerous weapon on him appears to be the pipe.'

'Might as well let him have that and the baccy pouch,' remarked the voice of the newcomer. 'He'll probably like a smoke or two before he gets his.'

His hands were untied, the handkerchief removed from his eyes. The sudden transition from darkness to a brilliant light caused him to blink owlishly. Before he had become accustomed to the glare, and was able to take stock of the two men, they had gone, closing a door on him. He heard it being locked on the other side, footsteps receding in the distance.

The first thing Cousins did, when he had ascertained that he was alone, was to make sure that the automatic was still where he had placed it. He had become so used to the feel of it that it no longer inconvenienced him, and, at first, experiencing no discomfort, he feared that, when he had fallen, it had slipped out of its hiding place. However, it was still there. Having relieved his mind on that important point, he took stock of his prison. It was a small room without windows, not much larger than a good-sized cupboard in fact. It had probably been intended originally as a box room. The cane chair on which he was sitting, a very small, cheap-looking washstand, an iron bedstead with no mattress, and two or three dirty blankets was all the furniture it contained. Cousins grimaced; allowed himself a moment's regretful recollection of his own cosy, well-furnished bedchamber in the flat in London.

Expecting every minute to be summoned to an interview with the ruling spirit of the gang that had captured him, he sat for a long time waiting. However, he was not disturbed, and, deciding eventually that he was to be left alone till the morning, removed his overcoat, jacket, collar and shoes, wrapped himself in the blankets, and went to bed. With the facility of a man who had, on innumerable occasions, been compelled to seek slumber when and where he could, sometimes under the most uncomfortable circumstances, and in unwholesome surroundings, he was quickly asleep.

He awoke with a bad headache, due to the lack of air in the room, looked at his watch, which had been left on his wrist, found the time was five minutes to seven. The brilliant light, so out of keeping with the size of his prison, still burnt fiercely.

He had forgotten to switch it off. He did so now, and lay in the darkness with his eyes closed, hoping thereby to ease his aching head. He was shivering with the cold, the three blankets being quite inadequate to keep him warm. Eventually he reached up to his overcoat, which was hanging over the bedrail, pulled it over him, and felt a little warmer, or perhaps it would be more correct to say, less cold. At length he dozed off to sleep again, awaking nearly two hours later to find the light on once more, and a man, with the battered face of a pugilist, standing by the bed, holding a tray in his hand.

'Hullo!' murmured Cousins drowsily.

'Hullo to you,' returned the man in almost friendly tones. 'You believe in having your whack of sleep, don't you?'

'If you shut me up in a room without much air, you must expect me to be drowsy,' retorted Cousins. 'I feel as though I've been drugged.'

'Shouldn't worry about your quarters if I was you. They're a sight better than you're like to have after the guv'nor's come back and seen you.'

'Oh, and where do you think he'll confine me? In a dungeon?'

The fellow grinned.

'Call it a dungeon if you like,' he remarked. 'I've generally heard it called a grave.'

Cousins sat up.

'You give me the shivers,' he confessed. 'Why on earth should I be buried, what have I done, why have I been abducted, and who are you?'

'Here, steady on! I'm not here to answer questions. You'll know all you want to soon enough, and a great deal you don't want to know as well. Take this, it's your breakfast.'

He handed the tray to Cousins. It contained a cup of tea, and a plate of bread and butter.

'I prefer coffee in the morning,' observed the little man, 'and toast.'

'Oh, you do, do you? Lord! You're a cool customer. Here are you on the brink of – of—'

'Eternity,' supplied Cousins.

'That's it. And anybody would think you were spending a holiday at a friend's house. You've certainly got guts.'

'Vulgar, but you mean well,' commented Cousins. 'Tell me: when do you expect the gentleman you call the guv'nor to be back?'

'Don't know for certain. Probably tonight or early tomorrow.'

'Dear me! Am I to wait all that time for the pleasure of seeing him?'

'Pleasure!' laughed the pugilistic one. 'You won't call it a pleasure when you've had a little time with him.'

'It all depends upon how one looks at it. Aristotle helps us considerably in deciding what is pleasure, and what isn't. Have you read Aristotle?'

'No, I haven't. Is it a book or a magazine?'

'Tut! tut! The ignorance of the man.' The multitude of wrinkles on the little man's face seemed to express positive pain. 'Aristotle was a great philosopher. He founded the Peripatetic school.'

'Did he? Well, I hope it was a success. It sounds awful. Look here, you and I have talked enough. Get on with your breakfast; it'll help to keep you quiet.'

He crossed to the door.

'Just a minute,' called Cousins. 'You don't seem a bad sort. Suppose you forget to lock that door, and—'

'None of that!' The fellow's manner changed. His apparent

friendliness vanished. He looked positively evil, as he stood glaring at the little man in the bed. 'If you want to get a taste of what hell's like,' he snarled, 'you'll get it quick, if you try bribing me.'

'Why?' queried Cousins coolly. 'Are you so well acquainted with it as all that? All I know about it is: "Five hateful rivers round Inferno run. Grief comes the first, and then the Flood of tears, Next loathesome Styx, then liquid Flame appears, Lethé comes last, or blank oblivion."'

The jailer stamped out of the room, the door slammed behind him. Then came the sound of the key turning in the lock. Cousins shrugged his shoulders.

'Another whose soul has not risen above mundane things,' he murmured. 'It seems that I am never to find a kindred spirit in my wanderings.'

He turned his attention to the tea, and bread and butter.

The day passed slowly, almost agonisingly. Shut up in that tiny chamber with the minimum of air to breathe, always in artificial light, for not the slightest glimmer of daylight penetrated into the room except when the door was open, Cousins suffered acutely. The same man brought him a kind of stew, very unappetising, at one, and a large plateful of bread and cheese at six, with a cup of discoloured water which he guessed was supposed to be coffee. The fellow had become very surly, refused to answer questions, hardly spoke at all. It was with a very bad grace that he brought soap, a towel, and water – there was none in the jug on the washstand – and procured a razor. The blade of the latter was not too sharp, but Cousins had shaved with worse. At eight, after dipping his aching head in the icy cold water, the Secret Service man went to bed.

He slept badly, found it impossible to get warm, while the

lower his head lay the more it ached. Eventually he dozed off in a half-sitting, half-reclining position in which attitude his jailer found him when he brought in his meagre breakfast. Cousins drank the tea, but refused the bread and butter, the very sight of food nauseating him.

'How long do you intend to keep me confined in this black hole?' he asked.

'It isn't my doing,' replied the man showing more disposition to talk than he had done since the previous morning. 'I wouldn't shut up a dog in a room like this. There's no need to make you suffer before the guv'nor decides what he'll do with you.'

'Those sentiments do you credit,' remarked Cousins. 'I agree with you entirely. By the way, hasn't the guv'nor, whoever he may be, arrived yet?'

'Expected at ten,' answered the other. 'I daresay he'll want to see you at once, so it won't be long before you get a change of air.'

'Well, that will be very welcome, even if it does mean interviewing your guv'nor. I'll let him talk while I do breathing exercises.'

'Take my advice, and don't rile him,' warned the jailer. 'He's got the temper of the devil himself when he's roused. If you're nice to him, he'll probably only order you to be shot, but, if you get his rag out, as like as not, he'll have you cut to pieces.'

'He must be a charming individual,' murmured Cousins. 'I am getting quite thrilled at the prospect of meeting him.'

The fellow eyed him with grudging admiration. 'You're only half a man to look at,' he observed, 'but damn it, you've got pluck.'

He departed, leaving Cousins alone once more. The latter rose wearily from his uncomfortable couch, poured what remained of the water into the basin, and thoroughly rinsed his face and head. Afterwards, feeling a little refreshed, he sat in the rickety chair, filled his pipe and lit it but the stuffy atmosphere was not conducive to the enjoyment of tobacco, and reluctantly he put away the briar. Ten o'clock came, and eleven, but still he was not summoned to the presence of the 'guv'nor'.

'Dash it all!' he muttered. 'I hope he doesn't neglect me. I'm aching for that fresh air.'

The thought that perhaps the man might visit him, instead of sending for him, made him groan. Just then Cousins was not at all concerned about the fate likely to be meted out to him. His mind was fixed on the necessity to escape, if only for a short time, from the fetid atmosphere of that box room. It was twenty minutes to twelve when the fellow with the battered face of an old-time pugilist opened the door, and entered. He jerked his head backwards.

'He's waiting for you, below,' he announced. 'Come along!'

Cousins did not wait for a second invitation. He shot out of the room with such rapidity that the other grabbed hold of him, fearing that he was attempting to escape.

'Here!' he growled, 'not so fast. What's the hurry?'

'Fresh air,' gasped Cousins.

'I'll leave the door open so's some air can get in, in case you're sent back.'

'You may be a crook and a scoundrel,' commented the little man, 'but you're not devoid of humanity. There's probably a seat for you somewhere in paradise in spite of your sins. Lead on, Macduff!'

He filled his lungs with good, wholesome air as they descended the stairs, feeling a great sense of relief and an almost immediate decrease of the pain in his head. He was shown into a room on the ground floor, which offered a striking contrast to the apartment he had just left. It was furnished lavishly and with taste. Not a speck of dust appeared anywhere; not an article was out of place. But Cousins was not interested in the furniture. He found himself confronting a most impressive-looking individual.

'I presume you're the guv'nor,' he remarked coolly. 'How do you do?'

CHAPTER SEVEN

An Interview with the 'Guv'nor'

Seated in a deep chair behind a large mahogany desk was a man whose great head and extraordinary breadth of shoulder looked almost grotesque. The physical strength denoted by his bull-like neck and massive torso was equalled by the mental power suggested in his face. Short iron-grey hair grew above a high, broad forehead; thick shaggy eyebrows overhung cold slate-blue eyes. The nose was broad and straight; the mouth large but well-shaped; a small moustache, iron-grey like the hair, adorned the upper lip. But the strength displayed by his other features faded almost into insignificance when compared with the huge, square, altogether brutal jaw. A magnificent specimen of manhood, thought Cousins.

This apparent colossus surveyed the captive for some moments in silence; then rose to his feet, walked round the desk, and continued his inspection. Cousins received a shock. Expecting a man of such development to be tall in proportion to his breadth, he was astonished to discover that he was not more than five feet seven in height. His legs were remarkably short; so short, in fact, that, standing up, he appeared deformed, an impression that was confirmed by the length of his arms. 'The Gorilla-man,' Cousins mentally dubbed him.

'So you are the prisoner, eh?' he asked, speaking at last in a heavy, deep voice with the slightest suggestion of a foreign accent. 'A Secret Service man posing as a Naval Officer. Like a fly you walk into the web of the spider.'

'Pardon me,' remarked Cousins, 'a fly doesn't, as a rule, walk into a web. It flies.'

He rather expected to incur the other's wrath, on account of his levity, but was agreeably surprised when the big man broke into a low, rumbling laugh.

'Whether it walks or flies is no matter. It is certain that you have played the part of fly.'

'"Methinks I hear in accents low the sportive kind reply: Poor moralist! and what art thou? A solitary fly."'

'Ha! you quote poetry. Those are lines from your poet Gray: am I not right?'

'You are quite correct,' beamed Cousins, 'and, if I may say so, it is a pleasure to meet one who knows the poets so well that he can recognise a quotation when he hears it.'

'Poetry is my passion,' the 'guv'nor' told him. 'It is interesting to find that you combine your particularly hazardous calling with a study of the muse. Sit down, Mr Cousins.'

'So you know my name,' murmured the little man.

'Of course I know your name.' The gorilla-man walked round the desk, and resumed his seat. Cousins sank into a comfortable armchair. 'I have made it my business,' went on the former, 'to study, as far as possible, members of your profession. I thought it might be useful to know the men who would try to get on my track when I commenced my activities.'

'I see,' commented Cousins.

'I must admit that I am astonished. It is at present a mystery to me how you knew in which direction to start your search. Perhaps you will inform me presently. I was saying that I and others endeavoured to learn who were British Secret Service men in order to know them when we see them. Alas! Your men are so secretive that it was a task of great difficulty. With you and Captain Shannon it was easy, also, of course, with Sir Leonard Wallace and Major Brien—'

'Why was it easy to get to know Shannon and me?' queried Cousins curiously.

The other laughed.

'Your memory is short,' he replied, 'but mine is not. Two or three years ago you two and an American obtained much publicity through an affair in India. Ah I see memory reasserts itself.' Cousins had impatiently clicked his tongue. 'Thus we knew of you, and have done our best to study you. In my organisation is a man who was once an actor and a mimic. If he had not unfortunately killed another man, he would, no doubt, be a star of the greatest magnitude in the theatrical world today, because his impersonations and his ability in the art of make-up are perfect. You have been able to judge that for yourself, is it not so?'

'You are referring to the man who posed as Shannon?'

'Exactly so. He deceived you, who have been a colleague of Captain Shannon for many years. What greater tribute could there be than that?'

'He also impersonated the Chief of Staff at the War Office, and the Air-Marshal at the Air Ministry, I presume,' remarked Cousins.

'Ah! You know that?'

'Of course I do. What of the man who posed as a staff officer? Is he also a mimic?'

'He was drilled in the parts by the other, who also arranged his make-up, my dear Mr Cousins. He is a very wonderful man with safes.'

'I thought as much. What I would like to know, since you are being so informative, is: how was it that the bogus Shannon was waiting on the station at Sittingbourne when I arrived there? Was he expecting me?'

'Yes; but we had one difficulty to contend with. He did not know you. He was, therefore, instructed to stand in a prominent position so that when you left the train, you would mistake him for Captain Shannon, and accost him yourself. After that, we expected that it would be easy to deal with you, and it was. We knew Shannon was in Rome, we also knew you had been on leave, and might not be acquainted with his movements. It was very simple, after all, to take you in, much more simple than I anticipated. Of course our man had spent much time where he could be near enough to hear the real Shannon's voice, learn tricks of movement, and any other peculiarities. You see, Mr Cousins, we anticipated that impersonating Captain Shannon would be a trump card in defending ourselves against the activities of the Secret Service.'

Cousins leant forward.

'Why are you telling me all this?' he demanded.

The other shrugged his huge shoulders.

'What harm is there?' he asked. 'You will never be able to repeat what I say to you. Dead men have never been known to tell tales yet.'

'You intend to kill me?'

The gorilla-man appeared surprised.

'Why, of course,' he replied. 'It is regrettable but necessary. Surely you can recognise that yourself.' He spoke as though he were merely discussing a business proposition. Unconcerned though he appeared, a shiver ran down Cousins' spine. 'From the time that you reappeared at your headquarters,' continued the deep voice in conversational tones, 'that was the day before yesterday, I have been forced to face the fact that you must be killed. It would in the ordinary way have happened by accident somewhere. Since you have walked into our hands, we will just shoot you or knife you. You were followed everywhere you went on Friday. Anticipating that he might be required, a wire was sent to John Hepburn – ah! I see you remember the case – telling him to make himself up as Captain Shannon, and drive to London. In the meantime you had been followed from your flat to Victoria, a man was standing by your side when you took your ticket, and thus knew where you were going. Hepburn arrived directly after your train had left, and was immediately sent post-haste to await you at Sittingbourne station. His motor car beat your train by seven minutes exactly.'

'I congratulate you on your espionage system,' said Cousins. 'It seems fairly efficient.'

'As efficient as the British Secret Service, eh?'

'Not quite,' came the quiet response. 'You haven't come up against Sir Leonard Wallace yet.'

A frown appeared on the broad brow of the colossus.

'Not yet,' he admitted, 'but we soon will. We have information that he sailed yesterday for England in the *Majestic*. Soon after he lands in this country he will be a dead man.'

Cousins started, his face paled.

'Why?' he demanded. 'What has he done to you that you should seek his death?'

'Nothing – yet,' was the reply, 'but Sir Leonard Wallace is the only man we really fear. We know too much of his achievements not to fear what he may accomplish in the future, if he is allowed to live.'

'You rotten murderer!' shot out Cousins. 'You callous brute!'

'Quietly, my dear Mr Cousins, quietly. I do not like to hear things like that.' The big man's eyes glinted.

'Good! Then I'm glad I'm the one to say them. And beware, Mr Seller of Secrets: Sir Leonard Wallace's life has been threatened before, but he has always escaped to turn the tables on his intended murderer. You would be wise if you abandoned your scheme of stealing and auctioning national secrets.'

'Impossible, my friend. We have great world-shattering plans ahead. If you were to live, you would be astounded by the mighty schemes my partner and I have in view.'

'Oh, you have a partner, have you?'

'But yes. He is a man with a wonderful brain. He has the ideas, I develop and execute them. His name is a household word – you know, admire him! Ah! That makes you wonder. But, even though you are to die, I must forgo the pleasure of viewing your amazement, for I shall not divulge his name to you. Nobody knows he is connected with me but myself.'

'Is he an Englishman?' asked Cousins.

'No, he is a Greek like me.'

'I wasn't far out. I took you for an Armenian.'

'Armenian, me! Bah! Do I look like one of that breed? I, Stanislaus Ictinos, am of ancient Greek blood.' He smacked himself on the chest, stuck out his formidable chin, and glared at Cousins. 'Do you mean to say,' he demanded, 'that you think there is a resemblance between the Greeks and Armenians?'

'Quite a lot,' returned Cousins coolly.

It looked for a moment as though the big man was about to break out into a towering rage. His lips came together in one long line, his nostrils dilated, his eyes glared murderously. Then suddenly his anger passed. He gave one of his deep rumbling laughs.

'You do not know of what you speak,' he grunted. 'I was foolish to allow a man of no account like you to anger me. But do not do it again, my friend, it is not safe.'

Cousins laughed.

'If you have made up your mind that I am to die,' he observed, 'it doesn't seem to matter much to me whether it is safe or not.'

'Ah! But there are many ways of dying. You would prefer to die like a gentleman?'

'I suppose I would.'

'And you shall, if you do not aggravate me or insult me. But remember! The men I command know well how to prolong the agony of death, if I order it.'

'You seem to have trained your scum well,' was Cousins' contemptuous retort.

Again the Greek laughed.

'It would not be pleasant for you, Mr Cousins, if they knew you had called them scum. Some of them, as you have perhaps noticed, are countrymen of your own. Do you also designate them as scum?'

'More so than the others. Men who would sell or help to sell their own country are the lowest of the low. There are not words descriptive enough for such perfidy.'

Stanislaus Ictinos studied him for some moments with a thinly veiled sneer on his lips.

'All that is what you English call moonshine,' he said. 'Most of the men in my organisation have been outlawed by their countries. Why should they not sell them, if they find the opportunity? John Hepburn is wanted for murder, so are many of the others. The man who brought you here is required by the police for many crimes. Is it not reasonable that they feel a hatred for their country, and are eager to exact vengeance?'

'No,' replied Cousins firmly; 'the worst possible injury can be no excuse for turning traitor. And, by your own showing, these men have not been injured. It is they who have injured themselves by becoming criminals. I suppose,' he added, 'it is because they are criminals that they serve you. You bind them to you by threat.'

'That is so. And, believe me, it is the safest way to bind a man to you. Fear is the greatest assurance of faithful service in the world.'

'But those who fear sometimes turn on those they fear.'

'Bah! That would never happen in this case. They are well-treated, if they do their work well, and make no mistakes. They are also well-paid, and are satisfied. I am their chief, and they respect me. Besides, each of them knows that I could break him in two like a little stick, if I were so minded.'

The swagger of the man was amusing, but Cousins did not laugh. He was not taking much notice of what Ictinos was saying, but was meditating on the possibility of drawing his automatic, holding up the other, and compelling him under pain of instant death to accompany him to the nearest police station. But further reflection showed him how futile such a course would be. Even if it succeeded, and he had no means of knowing how many desperate men he would have to run the gauntlet of, little would be gained. The copies of the plans would still be in the hands of the organisation, and there was a partner who, even this braggart admitted, was the brains of the concern, and who probably held the all-important documents. On the whole, Cousins decided that it would be better to wait in the hope that chance, or the talkative Ictinos, would give him a clue to the whereabouts of the copies, and only attempt to fight his way to freedom, if his life were threatened. Nevertheless, he felt sorely tempted to make a desperate bid, if only in the hope of being able to warn Sir Leonard Wallace of the attempt that was to be made to kill him. The wrinkles on his face suddenly creased into a smile, as he reflected that, if he made such a dash for liberty with the odds about a hundred to one against his getting away alive, and succeeded, Sir Leonard would not thank him for it. His reward would be a sharp rebuke for not stopping where he was until he had obtained important information, or until he was compelled to try and fight his way out to save his own life. Having weighed up all the pros and cons, Cousins again turned his attention to the loquacious Greek.

'The organisation is thus well-nigh perfect, as you must admit, my friend,' the latter was saying. 'Before long the nations of the world will be in terror of it. We shall control priceless secrets, be able to command fabulous sums, dictate to the world. It is a great prospect.'

He rubbed his hands together with an air of immense satisfaction. Cousins brought him down to earth.

'You certainly have accomplished a lot, and quite cleverly,' he admitted, 'but in one respect you have committed a blunder which only a thoughtless fool would make.'

Ictinos frowned.

'How?' he asked. 'I demand to know.'

'I have no objection to telling you. You seem to have forgotten that I had come down to this district to look for you. I was about to go on from Sittingbourne to Sheerness, when I saw the man whom I took to be Captain Shannon.'

'Sheerness!' repeated the Greek, adding involuntarily: 'So near?'

'Yes, so near,' smiled Cousins.

Ictinos bit his lip, angry at his own carelessness.

'I was going to ask you what made you go to Sittingbourne,' he declared. 'Tell me: there must have been something to make you decide to visit Sheerness – what was it?'

'The simplest thing in the world,' replied Cousins sarcastically, 'the postmark on the envelopes containing communications sent to various governments. Your well-nigh perfect organisation slipped up badly on that point. Really, Ictinos, if you don't want it to be known where you are, you shouldn't have posted letters near your hiding place. That's the most childish blunder I've ever heard of.'

The gorilla-man was staring at him as though he had not heard aright. His hands were clasping and unclasping while over his face was gradually stealing a look such as Cousins never expected to see in a human countenance. It became distorted with terrible fury until every feature spoke of brutal savagery.

'What is that you say?' he hissed.

For a moment Cousins hesitated. He wondered why the man was looking so fiendishly murderous.

'Letters you sent to the British Foreign Office, to Moscow, and to Berlin,' he repeated, 'were postmarked Sheerness. There may have been others, but I—'

Suddenly Ictinos was on his feet. He strode to the door, flung it open.

'Danson, Farrell, Moropos, Ibsen,' he shouted, 'all of you, come here!'

There was the sound of approaching feet, and he returned to his desk. Cousins, who had risen, stood partially in his way; was swept aside with one movement of the man's great arm as though he were a piece of paper blown by the wind. He lost his balance, fell, but Ictinos took no further notice of him. Into the room crowded four men, all eyeing their chief with curiosity, which turned to consternation when they saw the expression on his face.

He stood glowering at them for some seconds, his face still distorted with passion. Cousins rose to his feet; dusted his clothes carefully, though there was not likely to be any dirt on them from contact with the well-brushed carpet of that spotless room. Thereafter he stood looking from the 'guv'nor' to his men and back again, sensing the tension in the air, the dread on one side, the rage on the other. Suddenly Ictinos spoke, and the burning fury in his tones caused even the Secret Service man to stiffen apprehensively.

'I have called you here,' he roared, 'so that you can all witness the punishment I measure out to those who do not obey my orders, or are careless and lazy.' He shot out a finger in the direction of a stout, greasy-looking specimen of humanity, whose swarthy face, dark eyes, sleek, oily black hair proclaimed him as a son of one of the Balkan races.

'You, Moropos,' he thundered, 'have been entrusted with the dispatch of certain letters of great importance. What did you do with them?'

Moropos, whose face had gone a sickly yellow, cowered back against the wall.

'I-I posted them,' he stammered in a husky whisper.

'Where?'

'In London – in Southend—'

'You lie. I instructed you to post them in London or in Southend, but three, at least, were sent from Sheerness.' The fellow made no answer to that, and Ictinos went on, this time in a smooth, silky voice which sounded even more menacing than his previous outbreak. 'Answer me, my Moropos, it is so, is it not? You thought it was too far to go to London or Southend every time, but Sheerness it was only a little way – who would know, what difference would it make! And there would thus be much time for you to sit in a drinking house, and fill your belly with wine.'

'I-I was ill at the time I put the letters in the box at-at Sheerness,' gulped the man. 'I-I thought it would not matter.'

'So! In spite of my very particular orders, you did that!' Suddenly his voice changed to a roar again. 'You dolt, you imbecile, you fool! You have perhaps ruined all our plans, brought to naught schemes that would shake the world, make us all men rich beyond dreams. Look at him, you others; to you and to me, and to the one whose knowledge and brains are behind our work, he is a traitor, a cursed betrayer, for by his imprudence he has given a clue to our enemies of our whereabouts, possibly may bring disaster upon us. Look at him I say, and remember that it is not only your hope of obtaining much money that is threatened with disappointment by his carelessness, but your liberty and your lives as well. You know what will happen to you, if you fall into the hands of the police.'

There was an ugly murmur from the three men standing with Moropos. Threatening eyes were turned on him, fists clenched. The wretched culprit threw himself on his knees, his hands raised in supplication.

'Mercy, mercy!' he whined. 'I did not understand. I did not know. I will never offend again.'

'No; you will never offend again,' hissed Ictinos; 'you will not have the chance.'

Moropos seemed to know what penalty would be his, either from instinct or from previous knowledge of the methods of his leader. He was white to the lips; his terrified eyes stared unblinkingly at the other.

'Spare me! Spare me!' he croaked. 'I will atone, master.'

Ictinos watched him for some moments, his lips curled in a cynical smile. His attitude was that of a cat playing with a mouse, about to make the final spring.

'And how will you atone, my Moropos?' he purred. 'How will you repair the damage you have already done?' His manner changed again. 'It is safest that you are obliterated,' he snarled. 'You can then do no further harm. There is no room for men who are careless or who make mistakes.'

With lightning-like swiftness he picked up a long, thin-bladed knife from the desk and, almost in the same movement, sent it glittering across the room with unerring aim. Cousins made a desperate attempt to stay his hand, but his actions had been too rapid. A scream rose to the lips of the doomed man, was killed at birth as the weapon buried itself deep in his throat. With a horrible gurgle, Moropos toppled over on to his face, his body shuddered convulsively once or twice; then lay still. For some seconds there was not a sound in the room. Cousins stood gazing down at the dead man with horrified, pitying eyes; Ictinos gently rubbed his hands together, once or twice shrugged his shoulders; the other men remained where they were as though transfixed. Suddenly their leader's heavy voice shattered the silence.

'What are you standing there for?' he demanded harshly. 'Can't you see his blood is soaking into my beautiful carpet? Remove him at once, and you, Farrell, bring something to mop it up.'

Farrell, the man with the battered face, who had acted as

Cousins' jailer, left the room, the others lifted the still form of Moropos in their arms, and presently followed him.

'That sort of thing is distasteful to me,' observed the Greek, when he and his prisoner were again alone, 'but you will realise that, at times, it is necessary in an organisation of this kind to preserve discipline.'

'I realise nothing,' returned Cousins through clenched teeth, 'except that you are a foul and cold-blooded murderer.'

'Those are hard words, my friend,' remarked Ictinos softly. 'I do not kill for the lust of killing. That man disobeyed my orders – he has paid the penalty. It is finished.'

'It is not finished. It will be finished, when a noose is placed round your neck, a trap released, and a crowd of curious loungers reads on the notice board, outside one of His Majesty's prisons, that the sentence of the law on Stanislaus Ictinos has been duly carried out.'

The big man frowned, his face paled a little as Cousins spoke. He stared unseeingly at Farrell who had returned with a pail of water and a cloth, and was endeavouring to remove the blood from the carpet. Indubitably Ictinos was momentarily agitated, but he pulled himself together. He made a sound expressive of impatience.

'Ah, bah!' he snapped. 'All you English are squeamish fools.'

'It seems that my father has been losing his temper again,' came in silvery tones from the doorway.

Both men swung round in the direction from whence the voice came. Cousins blinked. Standing there, one hand holding a long cigarette tube to her lips, the other idly swinging the stiletto that had ended the life of Moropos, was a tall, slim girl of little more than twenty-one. Clad in a close-fitting gown that showed to perfection every curve of her sylph-like form, with a beauty that caused the little Secret Service man to gasp, she seemed utterly out of place in a room where murder had been so recently done.

Her face, flawless in its texture as satin, was absolutely devoid of colour, made more noticeable by the deep scarlet of her perfectly shaped lips. Her nose was rather long, but finely moulded; her eyes, slate-blue in colour like those of the man she called father, were almost too large; long curling eyelashes with daintily pencilled eyebrows provided them with a setting which would have enraptured an artist. Her sleek black hair was drawn lightly back allowing the full depth of her forehead to be seen, exposing without stint the shell-like beauty of her little ears, from each of which hung a perfect pearl. Yet there was something about her that spoke of a lawless nature, of cruelty, of a lack of the finer susceptibilities of femininity. But she was glamorous, fascinating, magnetic.

'What are you doing here?' demanded Ictinos. 'Did I not tell you that I did not wish to be disturbed?'

She shrugged her shoulders; advanced into the room, every movement suggesting feline grace. Throwing the stiletto on to the desk, she sank into one of the armchairs, and turned her wonderful eyes on Cousins.

'What a quaint little man!' she remarked. 'Are you forgetting your manners, Father? Please present him to me.'

The Greek regarded her with a frown for a moment; then retired behind his desk, and sat down.

'I wish to be alone, Thalia,' he reminded her. 'Please leave us.'

'You have already been alone far too long it seems,' she returned calmly. 'If I had been with you when you became angry, poor Moropos would not now be dead. I would not have allowed you to kill him. What had he done?'

'He posted some of the letters in Sheerness. It was unforgivable. This man is of the Secret Service – he came to investigate. He is in our power, but there will be others. Moropos perhaps has ruined our schemes – he deserved to die.'

She nodded her head slowly.

'So!' she murmured. 'I did not know. I agree with you that it might be very serious. Moropos was a fool.'

'I think it will be necessary for us to change our headquarters.'

'That will not be difficult.'

'It will not be easy,' he snapped. 'It will mean a complete change of plans, and everything was working well. Damn Moropos!'

Farrell finished his unpleasant work and retired. The girl removed the cigarette end from the holder, placed it in an ash tray; turned her eyes back to Cousins.

'So you are an agent of the Secret Service,' she observed. 'I find that very interesting. As my father has not introduced us properly we must do the best we can. My name is Thalia Ictinos. May I know yours?'

'Cousins,' returned the little man, 'Gerald Cousins. If I may say so, Miss Ictinos, I sympathise with you in the possession of such a father. I was a witness of the cold-blooded murder he recently committed, and he knows my opinion of him.'

'He is not so bad. Of course he does kill people sometimes, but they generally deserve it, and he has such a bad temper, you know.'

Cousins regarded her with amazement, wondering how such beauty could conceal a heart which was apparently as utterly callous as that of her father.

'Enough of this,' interposed Ictinos roughly. 'Leave us, Thalia. I have some questions to ask this man before—'

'Before he dies, I suppose,' she interrupted. 'Why not let him live – at least for a while? I like him – all those wrinkles on his face are unique; they amuse me.'

'It is impossible – you know it is.'

'But why? You have told me of his activities, and how he was captured. Well, now he is our prisoner, he is no longer dangerous.'

'We have quite enough to do without looking after a captive; besides, think what would happen, if he escaped.'

'He will not escape,' she asserted confidently. 'I will guarantee that. I will also take on the post of jailer. When I grow tired of him, you may kill him.'

Cousins felt more amused than dismayed at the discussion, despite the fact that it was his life that hung upon the result. He found it singularly revolting, nevertheless, that a young girl like Thalia Ictinos should be so lost to all sense of humanity that she looked upon murder with such utter indifference. Human life appeared to mean no more to these two than the life of an insect. Ictinos, frowning deeply, rubbed his massive chin.

'This is absurd,' he protested. 'How can you guarantee that he will not escape?'

'Leave that to me, Father,' she returned. Leaning forward, she added: 'Did you not say that Sir Leonard Wallace might soon be searching for us?' He nodded. 'Well, don't you think it would be as well if we kept Mr Cousins alive as a hostage in case—'

Ictinos was impressed. He considered the suggestion.

'There is perhaps something in what you say,' he agreed. 'Well, he shall live for the present, but you will be responsible for him.' He turned to Cousins with a gesture as though conferring a great favour. 'I present you with the gift of life for a few days longer. You may thank my daughter for it.'

'*Timeo Danaos et dona ferentes*,' murmured Cousins.

'It is good to know you do fear the Greeks, little man,' retorted Thalia; 'it may help to prevent you from attempting anything rash. Come along! I have not had a pet since my dog died some time ago. Perhaps you will make a good substitute.'

The indignity of being regarded as a possible substitute for a pet dog did not anger Cousins. He followed her obediently to the door.

'You mustn't forget the licence,' he remarked.

She threw him a glance over her shoulder.

'We will dispense with that,' she returned, 'but perhaps it would be as well to buy a chain and a collar for you.'

'Be careful, Thalia,' called Ictinos after them. 'You had better summon Farrell to help you with him in case he is foolish enough to attempt to escape.'

She laughed scornfully.

'He will be very sorry if he does,' she declared.

CHAPTER EIGHT

Through the Tempestuous Night

The car bearing Sir Leonard Wallace tore on through the bitter cold of a wild December night. After an extremely mild, sunny day, the weather had changed suddenly. A strong east wind was blowing, carrying with it the threat of snow. Inside the car Sir Leonard sat feeling warm enough, but hardly noticing the violence of the wind or the sleet which pattered against the windows. The discovery that in some way his chauffeur, Johnson, had been abducted, and his place taken by the man impersonating him at the wheel necessitated certain alterations in his plans. It was a little thing that had first aroused Sir Leonard's suspicions that all was not as it should be: merely the fact that the driver was not sitting at the wheel in the manner to which Wallace had become accustomed. Johnson, perhaps because of his military training, always sat bolt upright; the man now driving was reclining in an indolent manner which would have roused the ex-soldier's scorn. Once he had observed one thing, Sir Leonard noticed others. The wheel was being held differently, the gears were not changed with the same smooth precision. The impersonator of Johnson, although made-up very cleverly as the soldier–chauffeur, had overlooked the little details that count for so much in a scheme of that sort, especially when the man in the tonneau of the car possessed the well-trained and keen powers of observation for which Sir Leonard Wallace was noted.

Although anxious concerning the fate that had overtaken his driver, Wallace was rather pleased than otherwise at the turn affairs had taken. He was debating within himself the best use he could make of the knowledge that the man driving him was obviously a member of the organisation he was determined to break up, and that he was unaware that the deception had been detected. At length, his mind made up, Sir Leonard took up the speaking-tube.

'Stop at the first decent-looking public house you come to, Johnson,' he instructed. 'A hot whisky will help to keep the cold out.'

'Very well, sir,' came back the answer.

Listening carefully, Wallace was able to detect the very slight difference between the real voice of Johnson and the imitation. The man was decidedly clever; might have made his fortune on the stage as a mimic. Sir Leonard was wondering if the impostor would obey orders, when the car drew up before an inn on the outskirts of Chatham. He descended into the road, told the chauffeur to go into the bar, and order whatever he required; then strolled into a cosy lounge where, sitting in a secluded nook close to a roaring fire, he dallied over his hot drink. He had not been there above three minutes when the door opened, and the keen eyes of Maddison glanced into the room. Wallace beckoned to him.

'Whom have you brought with you?' he asked.

'Reynolds and Cunliffe, sir.'

'Where are they?'

'Outside in the car.'

'Well, listen,' Wallace spoke rapidly. 'Johnson has been knocked on the head or doped, and his place taken by a man masquerading as him. I don't know whether this fellow happens to know you and the others by sight, it's very doubtful, but if they enter the bar they will in all likelihood think he is Johnson and speak to him. Go and warn them!'

'I've told them to keep well out of sight, sir, and not to enter into conversation with anybody. When we reached this place, and I noticed your car standing outside, I concluded that you wanted to speak to me. I thought they had better stay where they are in case there was any risk.'

'Good man. How long had you been waiting in Piccadilly before I left?'

'About five minutes, sir.'

'You noticed no suspicious movement near the car?'

'No; it was standing outside your house with the man we took for Johnson at the wheel. Of course our view was obscured by the traffic on several occasions, for we were a good distance from it.'

'They must have lured him away on some pretext or other, and hit him on the head while the other man took his place. They're pretty clever, Maddison. Now the question is, where is the show-down, as the Americans would call it, going to take place? Was I followed?'

Maddison nodded.

'Three men in a Buick,' he informed his chief. 'They did not keep very close behind you, or I would have been here sooner.'

'Where are they now?'

'Went on ahead, sir. I daresay they're lurking somewhere along the road.'

'Well, look here, I'm going to contrive, if possible, to get captured. That seems the only way to find their headquarters without a long search that will possibly take weeks, and thus mean our losing the game. They've obviously abducted Johnson in order to get me into their power. Well, we'll let 'em, but don't lose sight of my car, if you can help it. As soon as you've discovered where they've taken me, you must raid the place.'

Maddison nodded somewhat sombrely.

'Perhaps they have no intention of capturing you, sir,' he reminded his chief. 'It is far more likely that they intend to shoot you offhand, isn't it? They have already tried twice today to kill you, you know.'

'You may be sure that I am not going to let myself be assassinated, if I can help it, Maddison. If things begin to look too ugly, I think I can contrive to escape them. They are not likely to be acquainted with the peculiarities of my car.'

Maddison smiled.

'Why not let Reynolds or Cunliffe hide in the luggage compartment, sir?' he suggested.

Wallace shook his head.

'There's only room for one there, and it's possible I may want to use it myself. Don't worry about me. Everything will be all right so long as you don't let my car out of your sight. My driver is probably waiting by now. Go and ascertain if he is suspicious of your car or not.'

Maddison left the lounge to return presently with the information that the fellow masquerading as Johnson was standing by the limousine waiting for his passenger to continue the journey. He had taken no interest in the other car beyond a casual glance or two. Sir Leonard expressed his satisfaction, finished his drink, and went out. The driver opened the door for him.

'Now no more stops till we reach Sittingbourne railway station,' remarked the Chief of the Secret Service. 'Beastly night, isn't it?'

The fellow mumbled something. Apparently he was not too sure of himself, possibly because he had had no opportunity of ascertaining the manner in which Johnson spoke to his employer. He was not to know that they were on rather unusual terms for master and servant. Wallace had a habit of treating those in his employ more as friends than inferiors. He switched off the interior lights, and made himself comfortable on the well-padded seat.

The car splashed its way through the muddy streets of Chatham without incident. There were few people about, the wildness of the night keeping at home all but those whom business or necessity compelled to be out of doors. The Sittingbourne road was practically deserted, an omnibus being the only vehicle to be met with over a stretch of two or three miles. The rain was now falling heavily, the wind lashing it furiously against the car as though overcome with rage that its pitiless force should be defied by man. The glaring headlights appeared to lose a considerable amount of their power in that storm; the electric screen-wiper, working rapidly, was unable to keep the glass clear. The man, sitting huddled up over the wheel, his eyes aching with the strain of attempting to keep the road ahead in view, was finding his job well-nigh beyond him. Inside sat Sir Leonard Wallace in comparative comfort, ever on the alert, allowing an occasional smile to appear on his lips at the realisation of his driver's distress.

Suddenly, about a mile from Sittingbourne, they came upon a man standing in the road frantically waving his arms. They were scarcely a dozen yards away when the driver first saw him, and applied his brakes so hastily that the car skidded, coming to a dead stop barely more than a foot from a deep ditch that ran along the left-hand side of the road. Full in the glare of its lights could be seen another car lying on its side, its bonnet half buried in the mud. Sir Leonard at once recognised it as a Buick, and it immediately flashed into his mind that the accident had been staged, and with such realism that his suspicions would not be aroused.

'No need to allow myself to be captured after all,' he reflected. 'They'll have to use this car – it would take hours to move the other.'

His mind was made up at once. The limousine had hardly stopped, when his finger sought for and found a knob cunningly concealed under the arm of his seat. He watched the spurious Johnson descend from the car, and join the men in the road – there were now three of them. With much waving of arms, they appeared to be explaining how the accident had happened. Feeling quite assured that his movements could not possibly be seen, Wallace pressed hard on the button, at the same time rising from the seat, which ascended rapidly until it was quite two feet from the floor. Through the aperture thus formed Sir Leonard promptly crawled into the large luggage compartment. Once there, he pushed down a small lever which, to the eyes of the uninitiated, would have merely appeared to be part of the hinge that enabled the door of the baggage chamber to be opened. The sliding panel and the seat descended into place with a click. Wallace had had the bodywork of the car constructed with an eye to just such a contingency as this. The luggage compartment, a good deal larger than is usual, was part of and not additional to the body. Inside there was ample room for a man to sit comfortably, while air was admitted by two small and cunningly hidden ventilators. A simple micro-phonic device enabled a person concealed therein to hear practically every sound in the tonneau. There were other secrets in that limousine known only to Sir Leonard, Johnson, and one or two others, while its powerful engine was the pride of its builders, the famous Rolls-Royce Company.

Sir Leonard settled himself as comfortably as he could on a rug, and waited for eventualities. Two or three minutes went by; then he distinctly heard a door open.

'These gentlemen,' commenced a voice in admirable imitation of Johnson's tones, 'have had an accident, as you will have observed, sir. They ask me to—'

The speaker broke off with an exclamation not in the ex-soldier's voice. Wallace heard a click as the lights in the interior of the car were switched on.

'He's not here!' cried the man in incredulous tones.

Various exclamations of a distinctly forcible nature came from his companions, after which there was a significant silence for some seconds. Wallace, picturing four amazed faces staring into the empty car, smiled to himself.

'He's smelt a rat, and hopped it,' presently observed one of the others. 'What are we going to do now?'

'How the devil could he have got out?' came in exasperated accents, obviously from the fellow who had impersonated Johnson. 'We should have been bound to have seen him.'

'I don't mean here. He must have jumped out while you were coming along.'

'Rot! We travelled too fast for that – he'd have been killed or badly injured, if he'd tried it.'

'How about when you were coming through Chatham?' asked another voice. 'You must have slowed down then.'

'Not enough to enable him to land safely.'

'Perhaps,' persisted the other, 'after you had stopped at that road house, he got out again when you thought you had shut him in.'

'Why should he do that?'

'How do I know? He's gone anyway, and there'll be the devil to pay when the guv'nor knows.'

'I tink Mr Hepburn are for it,' put in a fresh voice in distinctly foreign tones.

'Shut up, Ibsen. I don't see how I am to blame. I've done my job, and it's been the trickiest piece of work I've ever tackled.'

'Well, it seems to have come unstuck,' was the dry remark of one of the others. 'Obviously you didn't take him in. We'd better get on – I don't relish hanging round here in this storm, I'm soaked to the skin now.'

'I've come to the conclusion that you're right, Danson,' came slowly from the driver. 'He must have got out again at that pub. Another car arrived while we were there. I didn't take much notice of it at the time, but I wouldn't mind betting now that it was one of his. He probably had it following us. You were spotted, and that's why he did the disappearing act.'

'Perhaps he still follow,' remarked the foreigner.

There was silence. They were apparently engaged in straining their eyes in an effort to see back along the road through the darkness and rain, for, after some time, one observed that there was not a thing in sight.

'Fool,' snapped Hepburn, 'if we're being tracked, you can be damn well certain that they're lying in wait somewhere along there with their lights out. We can't see them, but they can see us.'

'Why don't they come along, and try to arrest us then?' asked one of the others.

'Because they're after bigger game than us. Bundle in, all of you, we'll have to leave the bus where it is – blasted nuisance now that you upset it – I suppose there is nothing about it to give a clue of any sort?'

'Not a thing,' was the reply. 'It was carefully searched before we started and, as it was a stolen car, it can't be traced to us.'

'Mr Ictinos can't get sore about tat, anyvay,' remarked the man called Ibsen. 'He it vas ordered us to ditch eet.'

'That's a consolation,' grunted Hepburn. 'You come in the front with me, Swede. Danson, you and Farrell sit in the back, and keep your eyes skinned. If they're after us, they'll have to show a light or crash to kingdom come. We'll lead 'em a dance, and soon shake 'em off. This beauty'll walk away from anything short of Campbell's Bluebird.'

'Damn risky, I call it, running round in a car like this,' muttered one of the others. 'It may be known to all the police in the country.'

'Well, if they know the car, they'll know the driver, won't they?' snapped Hepburn, 'and I'm he. Jump in!'

The limousine glided away from the derelict lying in the ditch, was soon tearing through the storm-racked night, the needle on the speedometer rising from forty to fifty, to sixty, eventually to reach seventy. In that weather the driver was taking a tremendous risk, and he knew it, but it was a risk well worth it for his own sake, for the 'guv'nor's', and for the sake of his companions. White-faced sat the latter, the Swede with eyes shut that he dare not open, Danson and Farrell looking through the window at the back of the car at the headlights of the motor they now knew for certain was pursuing them. In the luggage compartment crouched Sir Leonard Wallace, aching in every limb, but smiling grimly to himself at this utterly futile effort to shake off the men of the Secret Service, for whether or not Maddison lost track of the Rolls-Royce, it was certain that he himself, unless some unforeseen occurrence took place, would be there at the end of the chase.

Maddison, sitting by the side of Cunliffe, who was driving the other car, had his eyes glued on the tail light of the speedy vehicle he was following. He realised that his presence had been discovered, that the men ahead were endeavouring to shake him off, but his orders were to keep Sir Leonard Wallace's car in sight, and that he intended to do until it was no longer possible. Cunliffe sat at the wheel like a graven image. The speedometer indicated a rapid advance from fifty to sixty; was still rising. The needle trembled over the figure seventy, began to fall back a little; then went forward to seventy-two. They had turned aside from Sittingbourne which was soon left far behind, were now on the Dover road.

'She can't stand the pace,' shouted Cunliffe, endeavouring to make his voice heard above the combined roar of the elements and the engine. 'They're drawing away from us.'

Maddison nodded. It was only too evident. They followed for a few miles farther, tearing through rain-drenched hamlets, avenues of naked trees bent almost double by the screaming wind, up desolate hills, down into valleys rendered gloomy and sinister-looking by the wildness of the night. The red light ahead grew ever smaller, vanished for a time, showed again dimly for a fleeting minute and at last disappeared altogether. Maddison gave orders to the young man by his side, and the car gradually slowed down, presently coming to a stop.

'There are few cars in England could catch Sir Leonard's when it is all out,' he remarked, apparently not greatly concerned by his failure to keep the Rolls-Royce in sight. 'We're not beaten yet, though. If I'm not mistaken they've been leading us away from their destination to put us off the scent. There is still a chance that we'll be able to pick them up again.'

At his orders the car turned, was presently speeding back towards Sittingbourne. In the meantime, Hepburn was continuing to risk the lives of his companions and himself, not to mention that of the passenger they did not know was with them, in reckless fashion. His skilful driving, combined with a great deal of luck, saved them from disaster on several occasions. The storm had rendered the roads comparatively free from traffic, but once he shaved a motor coach by a quarter of an inch; missed a steam roller, laid up at the side of the road for the night, by a similar narrow margin; avoided a skid at the bottom of a hill, which would have spelt certain death, by sheer good fortune. Luck was certainly with him. His companions had become almost paralysed with fear, but none of them attempted to get him to slow down. They knew only too well the fate in store for them, if they fell into the hands of the dreaded men of the British Secret Service.

The car was travelling at over eighty miles an hour when, at last, Danson's quivering voice through the speaking tube informed Hepburn of the fact that their pursuers had been shaken off. Even then the latter continued driving at the same headlong pace for some minutes longer, and it was not until another five miles had been covered that he began to slow down. The relief to Sir Leonard Wallace, cooped up in the narrow confines of the baggage compartment, was immense. Every nerve and muscle in his body was aching, his head throbbing fiercely, his breath coming in laboured gasps. It had been one of the most painful experiences of his life; one which he certainly hoped would never be repeated. The speed of the car dropped to a mere crawl.

'Are you certain we've done them?' asked Hepburn, his voice sounding thin and tremulous from the strain he had undergone.

'Absolutely,' Danson assured him; 'we lost them several miles back. It was just hell, Hepburn. I thought every second would be our last.'

'So did I,' came the grim response. 'It was all very well for you fellows, but what about me? I'm all in. I never expected that blasted car to be able to hang on like that.'

He put on the brakes, and stopped; sat for some time lolling over the wheel, his head resting on his arms. The Swede produced a brandy flask from his pocket, removed the stopper, and forced it into the other's hand.

'Drink,' he advised. 'Eet vill do you goot.'

Hepburn accepted the invitation gratefully, handed back the flask half-empty.

'That's better,' he coughed. 'Pretty strong stuff that, Ibsen.'

'Eet's goot,' agreed the Swede, taking a long drink himself. 'Now vat ve going to do?'

'Double back, of course. The guv'nor'll be wondering what's happened to us. I wish I could trust one of you fellows to drive;

I'm absolutely cooked. If it wasn't for the brandy, I wouldn't be able to do it.' He put his lips to the speaking tube. 'Better continue to keep a look-out, Danson. We don't want to risk being picked up again, and not realise it.'

He seemed to know the country well, for he drove back another way. This time he was content to keep the speed down to the neighbourhood of thirty miles an hour, much to the satisfaction of Sir Leonard. By the time Sittingbourne was reached the rain had ceased, but the wind was still blowing a gale. The town was apparently asleep, but at the window of a house on the road to Sheppey, stood a man, who watched the car go by; then hurried to a small compact wireless apparatus on which he deftly tapped out a message in Morse. Maddison, sitting in his car, hidden behind a group of trees in close proximity to the Sheppey bridge, with earphones over his head, spelt out the message and smiled his relief.

'They're coming,' he told Cunliffe. 'Get ready to follow. It's a good thing we were able to get in touch with Cartright.'

He tapped out an assurance that he had received the communication; then, removing the earphones, fitted them into their place on the miniature wireless set before him. At a touch the whole slid into position flush with the instrument board, leaving no indication whatever that the car possessed any equipment of that nature.

Before long the neighbourhood was illumined by the headlights of an approaching car. Trees, looking stark and naked, some bending almost double before the force of the howling gale, were thrown into sharp relief; the countryside appeared grim and ghostly; a tumbledown thatched cottage close to the bridge stood clear-cut in its depressing loneliness; the bridge itself showed up spidery and sinister-looking. Maddison shivered slightly, whether because he was cold, or on account of a vague foreboding which suddenly possessed him, he would have found it difficult to decide.

Sir Leonard's car swept by. Immediately the other drew out from its hiding place, and followed. Cunliffe, obeying orders, did not switch on his lights. Maddison had directed him to steer as far as possible by the glow spread by the lamps of the Rolls-Royce, and only to use his own headlights when it became absolutely necessary – a difficult task on any moon-shrouded night, but trebly difficult in that wintry and tempestuous darkness.

It was a nerve-racking ordeal. The young Secret Service man sat at the wheel, his eyes strained ahead, his attention entirely taken up with this will o' the wisp pursuit. Neither he, nor Maddison, nor Reynolds sitting in the back of the car, noticed the baleful eyes glaring at them from the shelter of the dilapidated cottage. None of them saw the revolver steadily raised at their approach. None of them could have heard the shot above the din and clamour of the gale. But Cunliffe suddenly sagged sideways, his nerveless hands slid from the wheel; the car swerved violently, made headlong for the parapet guarding the drop to rocks and water below. Before Maddison could raise a finger to save them, the machine collided violently with the weather-worn masonry, crumbling it to a heap of stone and rubble. For one sickening second it appeared to hang there; then toppled over, crashing to its doom.

A shadowy gorilla-like figure emerged from the shelter of the cottage, walked to the spot where the disaster had occurred, and looked down, taking care not to lean on any of the broken stonework. A powerful torch threw an inquisitive ray of light on to the wreckage twenty feet below. Apparently satisfied with what he saw, the grotesque, powerful-looking creature returned to the hut, came out presently wheeling a motorcycle. This he pushed across the bridge. The road was undergoing repairs at one point, indicated by a red lantern. A watchman sat crouched inside a shelter behind a glowing brazier. Too intent on keeping warm, and unable to see more than a yard or two beyond the fire, he failed to notice the man and motorcycle passing silently by.

Stanislaus Ictinos walked for some distance beyond the bridge; then, starting the engine, mounted his machine, and rode after Sir Leonard Wallace's car.

CHAPTER NINE

Stanislaus Ictinos is Exultant

Unaware of the tragedy that had taken place at the bridge, John Hepburn, murderer, traitor, and masquerader, drove on towards his destination. From time to time Danson and Farrell, seated in the back of the car, had assured him that there were no further signs of pursuit. None of them had observed Maddison's machine hidden behind the clump of trees, neither had they any reason to suspect the presence of the 'guv'nor' in the ramshackle cottage they had barely glanced at in passing. As the Rolls-Royce drew nearer to its goal, the wind, blowing in unhampered from the open sea, became stronger until it appeared to be savagely doing its utmost to retard the progress of the powerful limousine. Hepburn sat crouched at the wheel, his bloodshot eyes fixed on the muddy surface of the rough, badly kept road ahead. They skirted Minster, turned on to what was little more than a track, now churned up into a mixture of water and slush by the heavy rain, and headed for a house standing solitary within high walls at the top of a cliff exposed to the full force of the elements.

The gate was wide open, which fact caused Hepburn to raise his eyebrows in surprise, but he drove through, bringing the car to a standstill before the front door. Shutting off the engine, he stepped stiffly to the ground. His companions soon followed him, and the four grouped themselves together in the porch, apparently reluctant to enter the house, and face the man whose anger they so greatly feared. Eventually, however, one of them rang the bell, the door was quickly opened, and they disappeared into the interior. A few minutes went by; then cautiously the head of Sir Leonard Wallace looked out from the luggage compartment. It was impossible to see much in that almost Stygian blackness, while the velocity of the wind rendered any attempt at listening for voices or footsteps a sheer farce. Nevertheless, he presently became aware of the beat of a motorcycle engine. He listened intently, his head being withdrawn at the identical moment that the machine panted laboriously through the gate.

Stanislaus Ictinos came to a stop close to the Rolls-Royce, and sat for a moment surveying it, a smile of satisfaction on his powerful face. Presently he dismounted, pulled his motorcycle back on its stand, and strolled round the car. He opened a door and, switching on his torch, surveyed the interior, giving vent to a deep exclamation of admiration. Stepping inside, he sat on the seat, allowing himself to sink back into the comfortable depths of the upholstery with a murmur of almost childlike delight. The man in the baggage compartment smiled to himself, his hand strayed towards a lever pedestal; then fell back to his side. Sir Leonard felt convinced that he was within a few inches of the chief of the organisation whom he was so keen to meet, but the time had not yet come, although the fellow at the moment was utterly in his power.

Ictinos sat for some minutes enjoying his luxurious surroundings, after which he stepped from the car, and walked to the front door of the house. In answer to his ring he was admitted by a small, deformed creature, whose beady eyes, squat nose, and large, big-lipped mouth made him utterly repulsive. The Greek patted the fellow on the head much in the same way that he might have fondled a dog, gave orders for the gates to be locked and the motorcycle to be put away; then strolled up the stairs, turning into a room which might have been a Mayfair boudoir, so elegantly was it furnished. Clad in a long, clinging dress of some soft, shimmering material, Thalia Ictinos lay languorously on a divan, her graceful arms behind her head. Opposite her sat Cousins reading aloud. Round his waist was a steel belt from which a chain ran to a staple in the wall to which it was padlocked. Thalia showed little pleasure at the sight of her father.

'What is it you want?' she asked ungraciously in English.

'Is my coming then of so little account?' he returned, frowning a little. 'A dutiful daughter would be happy to see her father.'

'Please let us be sensible,' she pleaded. 'I am not interested at the moment in rules and regulations for daughters. Why have you entered my room?'

'Your manner is strange, Thalia,' he protested. 'I do not understand. Is this man influencing you against me?'

His slate-blue eyes became coldly menacing as he turned them, for a moment, on Cousins. Thalia laughed scornfully.

'My little pet dog-man influence me!' she echoed. 'Oh, that is indeed funny. I like him; he amuses me. Some day I will grow tired of him, and then he will be finished – dead, is it not so?'

'That day is now. His usefulness as a hostage has passed.'

'How?' cried the girl sitting up. 'What do you mean?'

Cousins also looked enquiringly at the Greek, waiting for enlightenment. During the five days of his imprisonment he had paled considerably, appeared to have gone even thinner than usual. But his eyes were as bright as ever, his manner as light-hearted, despite the ordeal of nights spent in the stuffy atmosphere of the box-room, the humiliation of being chained to a wall during the greater part of the day, and treated like a captive animal.

'I mean,' proclaimed Ictinos in triumphant tones, 'that the so-great Sir Leonard Wallace is no longer in a position to do me harm. He is in my power. It was to inform you of this news, my dear, that I came to you.'

Thalia rose gracefully to her feet.

'It is indeed excellent news,' she declared. 'Take me to see him. My eyes are eager to look upon such a paragon. Perhaps you will let me have him as a pet instead of this little man. It would be amusing to see Monsieur Wallace chained to a wall.'

The idea seemed to appeal to her father also. One of his deep, rumbling laughs echoed through the room.

'Come, Thalia,' he invited her; 'you will help me interview this idol whose feet are after all, it appears, of clay. It is time Mr Cousins was back in his most pleasant bedroom. Afterwards we will discuss in what manner it will be best to dispose of him.'

He left the room. The girl stood for a moment contemplating the man upon whom she had heaped humiliation after humiliation.

'It will be a pity to lose you, my friend,' she observed, 'but it is good to have change. Sir Leonard Wallace, in your place, would entertain me greatly.'

'May I remind you,' remarked Cousins quietly, 'of the comment made by the slave to Ancaeus.'

'And what was that, my learned little man?'

'"There's many a slip 'twixt the cup and the lip."'

She shrugged her shoulders.

'My father seldom makes slips,' she pronounced.

Cousins was left to his own reflections, and the mask disappeared from his face, leaving it bleak and dismal. For once in a way he was feeling thoroughly perturbed and apprehensive. If Sir Leonard were actually in the hands of Ictinos, his chances of life were small indeed. Cousins knew very well how intensely the Greek feared and hated the Chief of the Secret Service, realised that the latter would receive very short shrift from his captors. He thoughtfully felt the automatic which he still managed to retain hidden in his sock. There was only one thing for it, he decided, that was to knock out the man who came to release him and escort him to his room, directly he was free, and dash down to the rescue of Sir Leonard. The latter was almost certain to be with Ictinos in the room the Greek used as an office.

Cousins looked round for a weapon, but saw nothing powerful enough to render unconscious a fully grown man, especially the type of the bullet-headed Farrell. Suddenly his eye caught sight of the chain which connected his steel belt with the wall, and he smiled. A quick snatch at it, directly the padlock was removed, and a hefty swing at the man's head, should prove adequate. He sat waiting impatiently for the coming of his jailer. But time passed slowly by, and still he was left to himself. It began to look as though he had been completely forgotten, and gradually his spirits, which had risen at the thought that he might be able to rescue Sir Leonard, sank until he felt utterly depressed.

Arrived in his room or the ground floor, Ictinos sank into the chair behind the great mahogany desk, and rang a small bell. Immediately the deformed man, who had opened the door to him, hurried in and stood looking at him questioningly.

'Tell the others I await them, Paul,' ordered the Greek genially in his own language. 'They can bring their prisoner with them.'

'Prisoner, excellency!' exclaimed the other.

'Yes, prisoner. What else do you expect me to call him – a guest?' He laughed as though at a good joke.

'But there is no prisoner, excellency. You must have been misinformed.'

For a moment Ictinos glared at the misshapen creature standing before him. Gradually the geniality left his face to be replaced by a look of mad fury. The dwarf began to cringe in fear.

'Tell Hepburn, Ibsen, and the others I want them,' suddenly roared the big man. 'Do not stand there like a fool. Begone!'

The fellow called Paul needed no second bidding. He shot out of the room like a bullet from a gun, almost colliding with Thalia, who was just entering.

'What has happened now, Father?' asked the girl. 'You are not going to tell me that the excellent Wallace has been allowed to escape?'

'I don't know what has happened,' he snapped, adding with a sneer: 'It seems that my trusted assistants have failed in some manner again. I do not understand. Outside undoubtedly is the car of Sir Leonard Wallace, but Paul tells me there is no prisoner.'

'Oh,' she pouted, 'am I then to be disappointed? I was hoping so much to see this man in your power.'

He gave vent to a forcible oath. With a slight shrug of her shoulders she sank into an armchair. Presently Hepburn, still disguised as Johnson, Farrell, Danson and Ibsen crowded sheepishly into the room. Ictinos glared from one to the others.

'Fools, dolts, idiots,' he snarled in English, 'am I to understand that again failure is to be reported to me? Villinoff blundered at Southampton this morning, you failed to crash the car in which Wallace rode at Chiswick, and now, when everything was planned to perfection tonight, after my brain had conceived that he would make a journey to Sittingbourne, you spoil everything by your stupidity. What has happened? Where is this man? In preference to seeking another retreat I stayed here, even when I knew so much about us had been discovered, hoping to exterminate Wallace and others who sought us, and you fail me, when I think failure is impossible. Where is he, I say?'

'It isn't our fault, guv'nor,' sullenly muttered the stocky, overfed-looking man known as Danson. 'He's a devil, is Wallace, if ever there was one. Hepburn'll tell you that he was in the car as far as Chatham, but when we stopped it as arranged, he had disappeared. I don't see how you can blame any of us for that.'

'Oh, don't you?' shouted Ictinos. 'Who am I to blame, if not you, you fools?'

'Anyway, we shook off the blokes that were trailing us,' put in Farrell; 'took them right away from this direction altogether.'

The Greek's manner changed. His tones became soft and silky, but, if possible, his eyes looked more savage and dangerous than before.

'So you think that, do you?' he purred. 'Well, in that case, you will be surprised to hear that they were waiting behind some trees near the bridge when you passed, and at once started to follow you.'

Four pairs of startled eyes bored into his, to drop one by one from that malevolent glare. For some seconds there was a deep silence then Hepburn spoke.

'They must have turned back when they found they could no

longer keep up with us,' he remarked. He swung round on Danson fiercely. 'I thought you said there was no sign of anything following either before or after we crossed the bridge?'

'The other car showed no lights,' interposed the silky voice of Ictinos, 'and they were not permitted to follow you long.'

'Why?' demanded Hepburn, the relief showing in his face. 'What prevented them?'

'I did,' returned the Greek in tones of great satisfaction. 'When you were so long in coming, I rode on my motorbicycle to the bridge, thinking that perhaps I might be of use. I had just crossed when I saw the car come and hide behind the trees. I concealed myself in an old cottage and waited. At last the limousine I knew belonged to Sir Leonard Wallace went by, and I thought all was well. The other motor began to follow and, as it drew near the wall, which is in need of repairs, I shot the driver. The car, as I anticipated, plunged through the broken wall, and fell on to the rocks. All in it are surely killed.'

There was dead silence for a moment or two after he had concluded his recital. Thalia appeared to be the only one unaffected by the announcement. She showed neither elation nor regret. Suddenly Hepburn gave a cry of delight.

'You have nothing further to fear from Wallace,' he declared triumphantly.

Ictinos eyed him questioningly.

'What is it you mean?' he demanded.

'He was in that car!'

The slate-blue eyes of the Greek gleamed.

'How can you know that?'

Hepburn proceeded to relate how he had been commanded by Sir Leonard Wallace to stop at the wayside inn, the arrival of the other car of which he had taken little notice at the time, but subsequently felt assured could be no other than that containing the Secret Service men who had trailed them.

'It was impossible for Wallace to jump out of the car between the time we left the public house and Danson stopping us on the Sittingbourne road,' he concluded. 'He would either have been killed or badly injured. It looks pretty obvious that when he re-entered the Rolls-Royce, and I shut him in, he stepped out of the other door, and joined the men in the second car.'

The anger slowly left the Greek's face. The genial expression began to return. He rose, and walked thoughtfully to and fro, his great right hand caressing the large, forbidding jaw. At last he came to a stop in front of Hepburn.

'My friend,' he observed, 'it is possible you are right. I am inclined to think you are. Circumstances certainly seem to indicate that your conjectures are correct. If so, as you say, we have no longer anything to fear from the great Wallace. I am sorry I did not suspect that he might be one of those hurled to their deaths, otherwise I should have gone down to make certain. From the top I was able to see three forms lying among the ruins of the car, but that is all.'

'Three, did you say?' demanded Hepburn excitedly.

'Three, most certainly.'

'Then Wallace was one of them. There were only two in the car when I saw it outside the inn.'

'You are sure?'

'Positive.'

'Excellent. I feel that a load has been lifted from my back.'

'The name of Wallace seems to have filled you with dread,' jeered Thalia. 'Why is it that you feared him so?'

'*Ma chérie*, you have not heard of the things he has done, as I have. Since I became interested in international espionage, I have found that Wallace was the most feared and hated of any Secret Service man.' He turned again to his four assistants, standing in a group. 'You can go,' he told them. 'I forgive you for your failures, but I still think you are fools, all of you. Remember that it was I – I, Stanislaus Ictinos – who succeeded where you blundered, who put an end to the activities of the British Secret Service.'

They filed out without comment.

'Perhaps those activities are not at an end even now,' put in Thalia drily when they had gone. 'The death of three men, even if one of them is Sir Leonard Wallace, is hardly likely to prevent others taking up the quest.'

Ictinos shrugged his huge shoulders.

'It matters little,' he returned. 'At least a shattering blow has been struck at them. Before they can recover, our headquarters will have changed, and the damage done by the lazy Moropos repaired. Tomorrow I meet the representative of Russia in London, the day after comes my interview with the German ambassador. After that we will disappear from here, leaving no trace.'

'Has it not occurred to you, my father,' she said, reverting to the Greek language, 'that the finding of three bodies near the bridge, one of them that of Sir Leonard Wallace, another with a bullet in it, will lead to this island of Sheppey being searched from end to end? If that is done, how can you expect to avoid discovery?'

'A search like that would take many days,' he replied with a complacent smile, 'and I am always ready. The motorboat is prepared to depart at a moment's notice. Now leave me, my child. I must start preparing for our move.'

'And what of the good Cousins?' she asked. 'I think that, as

I cannot have Monsieur Wallace now, I should like to retain the small man as a pet a little longer.'

He frowned.

'It is absurd,' he commented. 'However, he shall be permitted to live until we go from here.' She rose, and walked towards the door. 'Before you retire, Thalia,' he called to her, 'please instruct Hepburn to make certain that the car of Sir Leonard Wallace is locked up securely, and not to allow the key of the garage out of his possession. We cannot risk prying eyes catching a glimpse of it. Tomorrow we must endeavour to alter it beyond recognition; if that is impossible it must be broken up and destroyed.'

She turned and looked at him.

'Of what prying eyes were you thinking?' she asked softly.

He shrugged his shoulders.

'None in particular,' he assured her, 'but one must take precautions.'

'Your mind was not dwelling on the Englishman Wallace?' she persisted.

'Of course not. He is dead, or at least severely injured.'

'Are you so sure? It has occurred to me that, if he is the clever man he is supposed to be, it is very unlikely that he is dead, or even injured. Perhaps he may even now be close to us preparing to strike . . . Goodnight, my father.'

She walked away humming a tune. He stood glowering at the door for some seconds after she had gone then, once again shrugging his shoulders, returned to the desk and, for well over an hour, was busy with certain documents he took from cunningly contrived receptacles, putting them back after he had examined and apparently placed them in order.

Thalia conveyed her father's instructions to Hepburn, after

which she walked slowly upstairs, still humming. Whatever doubt she may have felt regarding the surmise that Sir Leonard Wallace had been involved in the tragedy on the Sheppey bridge, she appeared to be in no way perturbed. Inheriting her father's callousness and a good deal of his cruelty, she yet possessed a cooler, more calculating mind than his. When she had first been introduced into the organisation which her father and his mysterious partner controlled, the men who comprised the gang had, to use an Americanism, immediately fallen for her. Her beauty and grace had been more than they could resist. Very soon, however, they had learnt to recognise the savage in her, not before one or two of them had suffered with a violence they would remember to their dying days. Before long they realised that it was safer by far not to be on friendly terms with her, and she was generally left severely alone. Although not outwardly acknowledging her as an associate in his enterprises, her father relied to a rather surprising degree on her, considering the brutal forcefulness of his own character, often taking her advice, and deferring to her opinion. It was a cruel whim of hers that had resulted in a steel belt with chain attached being procured for Cousins. It delighted her to see him chained to the wall like a savage dog, while giving assurance to all of his utter inability to escape. In both the room where he was confined at night and in her boudoir by day he was always fettered. He never once gave a sign to show the humiliation and indignity he was suffering, but she knew how he felt, and delighted in his torment.

She looked into the boudoir now as she was passing on her way to her bedroom, was surprised to find her captive still sitting where she had left him. He looked eagerly at her, and she noticed the anxiety in his eyes.

'Hallo, my little man,' she said. 'I thought you had long gone to bed. The bad Farrell, it seems, has forgotten to take you to your kennel. I will call him.'

'Tell me,' pleaded Cousins, 'what have they done to Sir Leonard Wallace?'

'Ah! You think then more of his safety than of your own. Are you not worried because my father has said that the day of your usefulness as a hostage has passed?'

'Not a bit,' replied the little man coolly. 'I certainly did not expect a murderer like your father to allow me to remain alive once he had me in his power.'

'You are hard on my father, and I do not like the word murderer, my little pet man.'

She bent down, caught his ears in either hand, and twisted them unmercifully. He made no effort to resist, merely rubbing them somewhat ruefully when she desisted.

'Now that you have had your little bit of fun,' he ventured, 'perhaps you will answer my question.'

She looked thoughtfully at him, her beautiful brows meeting together in a little frown.

'I wonder if it is that you have no feeling, or are a very brave man,' she debated. 'It does not please me when I hurt you, and you show no sign of pain. It gives me much pleasure to see people suffer.'

Cousins eyed her almost in wonderment. Although he had been constantly in her company for five days he still found it difficult to believe that a girl with her charm, beauty, and grace could possess a character the very antithesis of her gentle outward appearance.

'You wish to know about Sir Leonard Wallace,' she went on. 'Very well, I will tell you. He did not arrive after all. His car came, and my father concluded rather prematurely that Sir Leonard must have come in it, but alas! He did not.'

Cousins made no attempt to keep the elation he felt from showing in his face. She noticed it, and a pitiless smile, for an instant, curved her scarlet lips. She walked to the door; looked back at him over her shoulder.

'Monsieur Wallace,' she asserted, 'was in another car that unfortunately was travelling without lights. It was very unwise on a dark, stormy night like this. The car collided with the frail wall at the beginning of the Sheppey bridge, and fell over. Sir Leonard Wallace and his companions are dead.' She turned back to watch the effect of her words; smiled again. 'I will tell Farrell to take you to your room. Goodnight, little man.'

Cousins sat as though crushed. He did not doubt her story, except in the conviction that the accident was no accident at all, but a tragedy contrived by a monster in the person of Stanislaus Ictinos. He felt there could be no mistake; the Greek would surely make certain that the man he feared was in reality dead. In his anguish the Secret Service man lost sight of the fact that Thalia would be only too ready to exaggerate, if by so doing she could cause him distress. He hardly noticed Farrell, when the latter arrived to unlock the padlock, and conduct him to his unventilated cell. He walked along the corridor in the wake of his jailer apathetically; watched the chain being fastened to the iron bedstead with listless eyes. Farrell made one or two remarks, which passed almost unnoticed; looked curiously at his prisoner, and was about to leave the room, when Cousins spoke for the first time.

'Is it true that Sir Leonard Wallace has been killed?' he asked.

The fellow nodded.

'There was a bit of a smash-up,' he stated, 'and he along with two others lost their lives. His car's here – just been locked in the garage.'

He hesitated as though about to say something else, changed his mind, and went out. Cousins stretched himself wearily on the bed. For a long time he lay staring almost unblinkingly at the brilliant light above him; then turned on his side, and shut his eyes. Two or three hours passed slowly, agonisingly by, but sleep did not come to the little man whose heart was aching, only memories of the chief, to whom he, like all other members of his Service, had been devoted. Cousins, who would gladly have given his life for Sir Leonard, was facing the fact that he lived while his chief had died. No thought of his own desperate situation intruded on his thoughts. The wrinkled face was creased ludicrously, but not now with laughter. Pain distorted it, and the effort to restrain the threatening tears.

Suddenly his ears caught a tiny scraping sound. At first he thought it had been made by a mouse, but, as it persisted, he listened, presently deciding that it came from the direction of the door. He sat up, wondering what it could be, and saw the handle turning slowly, as though the individual manipulating it was exercising the most extreme care. Then inch by inch the door opened, until there was just room enough for a moderate-sized man to enter. A figure slid quietly into the room, finger to lips, and Cousins almost cried out in the sudden revulsion of feeling, as an immense relief and great joy annihilated every other emotion.

It was Sir Leonard Wallace.

CHAPTER TEN

Legitimate Burglary

The Chief of the Secret Service had remained for some considerable time in the luggage compartment of his car after Ictinos had entered the house; then only by slow and very cautious stages had he opened the small door, and ventured out. After that, however, having assured himself that there was nobody nearby, he set about examining his surroundings without delay, as far as such a task was possible in the darkness. The house he found was a rambling affair of two storeys standing in the centre of a neglected garden overgrown with shrubs and untrimmed plants. Several out-buildings, one of which was obviously used as a garage, stood in a cluster at the back. A high wall, a somewhat anomalous adjunct to what was, after all, an ordinary residence, encircled the property. Close examination showed it to be of recent erection, thus suggesting that the present occupiers were bent on keeping out possible intruders. A pair of powerful gates, now open, were the only means of egress.

Sir Leonard slowly crept round the house endeavouring to obtain a glimpse of the interior, but not a glimmer of light showed from any of the windows either on the ground floor or above, indicating fairly conclusively that they were all carefully and heavily curtained. Having assured himself of this fact, he made his way to the gates, went through, and walked round the wall on the outside. He discovered that the place was built on a high cliff, exposed to the full fury of the wind. It was as much as he could do at times to move forward in the teeth of the gale. From below came the thunder of the angry waves as they clashed themselves violently on the rocks. Except for a dim light some distance away, and slightly inland, there appeared no habitation anywhere near. Altogether a more desolate spot, at least for at that time of the year, it would be difficult to imagine.

He had barely re-entered the grounds, when the front door of the house opened, and a diminutive figure, looking more like an animal than a human being, appeared. He was quickly swallowed up by the darkness, but his footsteps could be heard as he approached the gates, which he closed with a clash as though in a hurry to return to the warmth of the house. He had left the front door open, and Sir Leonard, from his vantage point behind a hedge, could see into a comfortably furnished hall. There seemed to be nobody about, and he wondered if he could possibly get inside without being observed by the fellow at the gate. He began to creep towards the house, but had not gone very far, when the other man passed quite close to him. However, the latter had another job to perform before going in. He lifted the motorcycle from its stand, and wheeled it round the side of the building. That was Wallace's opportunity, and he promptly took it. As silently as a shadow he glided into the hail. Doors on either side of him drew his eyes speculatively to them, but the sound of a voice apparently raised in anger attracted him on. He came to a sudden turning and, glancing cautiously round the corner, found that he was looking into a brilliantly lighted room. Three or four men stood bunched together, their backs to him, while another, who could not be seen, was talking loudly and wrathfully. '. . . you fail me, when I think failure is impossible,' he was complaining. 'Where is he I say?'

Sir Leonard looked hurriedly round. It was impossible to stay where he was. At any moment the little man, who had gone to put the motorcycle away, might re-enter the house, and discover him. But he intended, if possible, to hear all the speaker had to say. A curtain a few yards farther on to his left close to a staircase, offered possibilities. Without hesitation he crossed to it, risking the chance that one of the men in the room would turn and catch sight of him. Luck was on his side, no alarm was raised, and he found himself in an alcove containing a curious assortment of articles of which three very modern rifles were the most significant. To his great satisfaction he discovered that he was still able to hear distinctly every word spoken in the room across the passage and, as he listened, the expression on his face became gradually sterner. He heard the front door close, and footsteps come rapidly along the hall. Glancing cautiously round a fold of the curtain, he caught a glimpse of a deformed, repulsive little creature, who hurried along towards the back of the house. Thereafter nothing occurred to divert his attention from the conversation taking place within a few yards of him.

He smiled grimly as he listened to the discussion concerning his own supposed demise, but his heart was heavy with the knowledge of the fate that had befallen Maddison and his companions. For some time he had been wondering why they had not arrived;

had taken it for granted that the pursuit had been shaken off, now he knew the real reason, and his thoughts boded ill for the scoundrels who spoke so callously of a foul crime. The girl's voice intrigued him. He wondered who she was. He was not particularly shocked at the discovery that a woman was connected with the organisation. It was not the first time that Sir Leonard had found a female among his antagonists, and he was perfectly well aware that a woman could sometimes be more dangerous than a man.

The conference ended on a more pleasant note than it had apparently started, due obviously to the conviction that Wallace had been killed or seriously incapacitated, and the leader's evident complacence in his own imagined infallibility. Four men filed from the room, and Sir Leonard succeeded in obtaining an excellent view of each. Even he, a man who seldom showed surprise, raised his eyebrows in grudging admiration at the excellence of Hepburn's disguise. He was the chauffeur Johnson to the life. Previously he had only viewed the man in shadow or in a very poor light; there, with the strong illumination of the hall throwing up every line, he was unable to detect a flaw.

The conspirators walked away to the rear of the premises, but their leader continued speaking to the woman. Unfortunately they lapsed into the Greek language, one of the few European tongues of which Wallace had little knowledge, but not before he had heard, and mentally noted, that interviews had been arranged with representatives of the German and Russian governments presumably to discuss the purchase of the plans of the two British inventions. He was able to understand certain references, caught his own and Cousins' names mentioned; then the girl left the room. She walked along the passage softly humming to herself, came back a few minutes later, and ascended the stairs. He was just able to catch a glimpse of her face, the beauty of which gave him rather a pang. It seemed very terrible that a woman so handsome and so young could be associated with such men, that the grace and charm, which she almost seemed to irradiate, could possibly cloak a heart that must be entirely without feeling, brutal in its callousness. While he was thinking of her, the man who had impersonated Johnson, and was still wearing the disguise, passed along the hall; went out by the front door. Five minutes later he returned, and disappeared in the direction from whence he had come.

Wallace waited behind the curtain, expecting the leader, who had unconsciously but fortuitously announced his name to the listener, to emerge from the apartment opposite, but, when some minutes had gone by, and Sir Leonard could hear the rustle of paper, he decided to attempt, if possible, to find out what Ictinos was doing. By slow degrees he emerged from his hiding place, and surveyed his surroundings. Glancing to his left along the passage he found that there was a baize door at the end, obviously leading to the domestic quarters of the house. Another door halfway along, under the staircase, stood slightly ajar, and from within came the murmur of voices. He concluded that the apartment there must be a kind of general room for the rank and file of the gang.

For some seconds he stood listening; then tiptoed quietly across the passage to the room in which Ictinos sat. Suddenly, however, came the sound of quick footsteps overhead, and he had barely time to dart back to the shelter of the alcove before the girl came running lightly down the stairs. She called someone by the name of Farrell, and was presently joined by one of the men Wallace had previously seen.

'You have forgotten my little man, Farrell,' she observed. 'You know it is your duty to take him to his room, and lock him up every night. I shall have to complain to my father, unless you are more careful. You do not think he is to be allowed to enjoy the comfort of my boudoir all night, do you?'

'Sorry, miss,' came in surly tones from the man. 'I hadn't forgotten, but last night you told me I had come too soon.'

'Do not be impertinent. Take Mr Cousins to the box room at once.'

She returned up the stairs, followed by the man she called Farrell. Sir Leonard breathed a sigh of great relief. Cousins was still alive! He made up his mind to discover where the little Secret Service man was incarcerated, even though the risk to him seemed stupendous. Expecting every moment that someone would appear and discover him, he crept up the stairs. But luck was on his side again. He came to a landing in which was a curtained alcove similar to the one he had just left. From there he was able to see a considerable part of the corridor above, reached from the landing by a further four steps. He had not been there long before Farrell emerged from a room at the front of the house followed by Cousins. Sir Leonard's lips came together in a thin straight line when he observed that his assistant was being led by a chain attached to a steel belt round his waist. They entered a room close to the top of the stairs. Four or five minutes passed by; then Farrell reappeared, shutting, and locking the door behind him. That done he descended, passing so close to the hidden watcher that his arm actually touched the curtain, drawing it a little to one side. Sir Leonard almost anticipated discovery, but the fellow went on without a pause, utterly unconscious of the fact that in the alcove crouched the man whom he and his companions appeared to dread so greatly.

Wallace was half inclined to attempt the rescue of Cousins without delay, but decided that the chances of success, while the household was awake, were too slender. He cautiously went down the stairs, therefore, halting awhile at the bottom, and listening intently, before once again stepping across the passage to the room which Ictinos had apparently not left, for an occasional cough and the rustle of papers denoted that he was inside. The door was still wide open, a fact that helped considerably. Sir Leonard wanted to find out what the man was doing if possible, without being detected himself. As he stood on the threshold, he knew that, if anybody came along, he was bound to be discovered, but that did not worry him. By slow degrees he insinuated his head into the room until he was able to see the man who sat behind a great mahogany desk examining a document which he held in front of him.

Wallace noted the powerful face, the great breadth of shoulder, but his most urgent attention was occupied in searching for a place within the room where he could conceal himself. It was impossible to remain where he was; it looked equally impossible to enter the apartment without the man at the desk seeing him. The latter sat facing the door. Behind him thick heavy curtains were drawn closely together, doubtless covering windows; a great fire burnt cheerfully in a large open grate, but apart from the glow which it threw into the room, the only illumination now was supplied by a desk lamp, the shade of which projected most of the light on to the papers in the Greek's hands. If he could only reach the curtains, Wallace knew that he would be able to watch in comparative safety, but the chances were all against his getting across the room undetected, even though the man at the desk was undoubtedly deeply engrossed in his occupation. He resolved to make the attempt. He had become convinced that, if he were to succeed in finding out what Ictinos had done with the copies of the plans, it was absolutely necessary to watch the fellow closely. The remark, which Wallace had overheard concerning the appointments with the Russian and German representatives rather suggested that Ictinos was even then preparing for the interviews. Possibly the papers, at that moment in his hands, were the very ones of which Sir Leonard was so anxious to obtain possession.

He went down full length on the floor, and, without hesitation, began to worm his way into the room. It was not an easy task for a man handicapped by the fact that he possessed only one arm; his heavy overcoat also proved a hindrance, but he advanced slowly, the thick carpet deadening any sound he might otherwise have made. Every moment he expected a cry of alarm to break from the lips of the Greek, but it did not come, and he reached the comparative safety of the desk. He rested there a second before attempting the greater hazard of passing close to the man in his endeavour to reach the curtains. A soft chuckle came from the other side of the desk; a muttered remark. For an instant Sir Leonard feared that he had been observed, that Ictinos knew he was there, and was playing with him as a cat plays with a mouse, but the rustling of the papers went on. The Greek had been amused apparently by something he was examining.

Wallace reached the end of the desk; began to wriggle his way along within three or four feet of the man sitting there. It seemed out of the question to expect to get by, when the slightest movement of his head in Sir Leonard's direction, or even a glance out of the corner of his eye, would have been bound to disclose to Ictinos the presence of the man on the floor. But he was so utterly absorbed that the crawling figure was able to pass without his knowledge. The curtains opened slightly, closed again, shook a little, and were still. Sir Leonard had reached his objective. He made a little opening between the folds in order that he could watch everything that went on. The remarkably broad back of the Greek obscured the papers over which he was poring, but occasionally he raised them in a manner that enabled the watcher to catch a fleeting glimpse. Once part of a diagram came into view with certain technical terms well known to gunnery experts written in the corner, and Wallace smiled to himself. He felt reasonably certain now that actually on that desk were the papers he was so anxious to possess.

For a moment he was inclined to take them at the point of his revolver; force Ictinos to go upstairs with him and release Cousins then accompany them back to headquarters, but the absurdity of such an attempt became immediately apparent. Ictinos might have a secret means of communicating the alarm to his followers, Wallace had no certainty that all the papers he desired were on the desk while, in any case, there was always the possibility that one of the others might appear and turn the tables on him. Apart from this the Greek might refuse to be overawed by the sight of a revolver, in which event, being averse to shooting a man in cold blood, a rough and tumble would take place. Wallace could hardly expect to get the better of it with one arm against a man whose physique would have earned the admiration of Hackenschmidt. He was in no hurry. He decided to wait and watch until the Greek went to bed; then secure the papers. Once he knew where they were hidden, he had no doubt of his ability to open the receptacle in which they had been placed, and take possession of them.

An hour passed by, and still Ictinos sat at the desk. Sir Leonard was feeling very weary, but, except to change his weight from one leg to the other, he was careful to make no movement for fear that he might be heard. At last the Greek yawned loudly; stretched his great arms above his head. He gathered his papers together in four heaps; then, bending down, took hold of the handle of the bottom right-hand drawer. Instead of pulling it out he turned the knob half a dozen times to the right, after which he pressed inwards. Immediately a portion of the bottom part of the desk, about three feet long, two wide, and four inches deep, slid outwards. It appeared to be constructed of steel, and contained four compartments all of which were unlocked by separate keys. Wallace watched intently as Ictinos lifted the various lids, and deposited his papers within the receptacles. He saw the Greek close and carefully lock each division, put the keys away in an inner pocket of his jacket then manipulate the knob on the drawer, causing the steel tray to slide back into place. A few minutes later, after glancing casually round the room, Ictinos rose to his feet, switched off the lamp, and went out.

Sir Leonard remained where he was for some time in case the man came back. It was well he did, for the dwarf, through whose carelessness he had been able to get into the house, suddenly entered the room without the slightest sound, giving no warning whatever of his approach. He busied himself raking out the fire, a duty he performed as though in a hurry to withdraw; then departed, closing the door behind him. The clock on the mantelpiece slowly ticked away ten minutes before Wallace emerged from the shelter of the curtains. Walking across the room, he opened the door gently, and looked out. Not a sound reached his ears and, as the hall light had been extinguished, he came to the conclusion that everybody had gone to bed. Satisfied, he closed the door, and returned to the desk.

A tiny torch not much bigger than a fountain pen shot a powerful beam of light at the right hand bottom drawer. Clasping it somehow in his artificial hand by means known only to himself, he took hold of the knob in the other, and manipulated it exactly as he had seen Ictinos do. The steel tray duly slid out, and the ray of light hovered inquisitively over each keyhole in turn. From an inner pocket, Wallace drew out a flat leather case, which he opened, disclosing to view a set of small, beautifully made steel instruments of graduated sizes. He selected one, and set to work immediately on the locks. So complicated were they that it took him some time, and he required the help of two other of the little tools, before he succeeded in getting the lids of the four compartments open. At last his task was accomplished; he gave vent to a sigh of relief. Quickly he removed the documents from their receptacles, placing them in four piles upon the desk; then, extinguishing the torch, he crossed once more to the door, where he stood for some minutes listening intently. Convinced that nobody was about, he returned to the desk, switched on the lamp, and sat down to examine the papers before him.

It was not long before he came across copies of the plans of the Masterson monoplane and Wentworth gun, with voluminous notes concerning each. A little exclamation of satisfaction escaped from him as he stuffed the papers into the inside pocket of his overcoat. Thereafter he found a good deal to interest him among the remaining documents, including a memorandum of the times and places decided upon for the Greek's interviews with the representatives of the Russian and German governments. He made a careful note of these in his pocket-hook. Copies of Russian and German official secrets, two or three letters, and details of the

French schemes for defensive and offensive alliances were there, and were also pushed into his pockets, but there was no sign or indication anywhere that Ictinos possessed copies of the plans of the French frontier fortifications or any details concerning them. Sir Leonard searched carefully without success. Returning the papers, which he did not wish to take away with him, to their compartments, he locked the lids, and manipulated the steel tray back into its place. He then set to work to search every drawer in the desk. Some were locked, others were not, but he opened them all. Nothing of interest was discovered except a list of the men serving Ictinos. Against each name were notes concerning crimes they had committed, with dates and details of police investigation. Wallace found the list interesting, and decided to keep it. Scotland Yard, he felt, would be gratified.

He examined every inch of the desk in an endeavour to ascertain if it contained any other hidden partitions, but, as nothing further came to light, he turned his attention to the rest of the room. The bookcases, fireplace, pictures, even the walls and floor came under careful inspection, but he found no sign that anywhere, but in the desk, was there a secret cavity. Satisfied at length that if Ictinos possessed copies of the French fortification plans they were concealed elsewhere, he gave up the search. He felt that it was time he released Cousins, and got in touch with his own headquarters.

Extinguishing the light, he walked to the door, opened it, and stood in a listening attitude for several minutes. Then treading with the greatest care, for fear of causing the stairs to creak, he ascended slowly to the upper regions. At the top he again stood listening, before approaching the door of the room in which he knew Cousins was imprisoned. A gleam of light showing underneath caused him to frown a little, but, without hesitation, he inserted into the lock one of the small steel instruments, which he had retained in his hand when putting the case away. Slowly, but with hardly a sound, he worked. He felt the lock turn, and devoted his attention to the door handle. A second or two passed, and he stepped into the room, his finger to his lips, taking care to close the door behind him.

CHAPTER ELEVEN

The Flight of Ictinos

The pallid face of Cousins lit up, his eyes showed plainly the joy he felt, his lips whispered 'Thank God!' He sat up in bed so suddenly that the chain attached to the steel belt round his waist jangled noisily. Again Sir Leonard's finger went to his lips. He stepped up to the bed.

'I didn't expect to find you alive, Cousins,' he murmured. 'From what I have discovered about these people, it seems that murder is a pastime they indulge in without the slightest hesitation.'

'I suppose I have to thank the girl for being permitted to remain alive as long as this,' returned Cousins. 'She used to have a pet dog, and it tickled her sense of humour to appoint me its successor for the time being. Hence the chain.'

Wallace eyed it with a frown, his teeth clenched tightly together.

'Have they given you a very bad time?' he asked sympathetically.

'It could have been worse,' replied the other. 'Being shut up here at night, with practically no air to breathe, has been the most unpleasant part, if one excepts the humiliation of the chain. But I was told you had been killed, sir. I can't say what a relief it is to find you are alive after all.'

'There was never much danger of my being killed,' Wallace told him simply, adding with deep feeling, 'but I'm afraid Maddison, Cunliffe, and Reynolds are gone.'

Their eyes met and, in each pair, an indomitable resolve showed, proclaiming their intention to avenge their companions, if and when opportunity offered.

'We can't waste time talking,' declared Sir Leonard. 'I must free you from this beastly contrivance.'

He bent down, and examined the belt. It was fastened round Cousins' waist by a padlock similar to the one locking the other end of the chain to the bedstead. Presently he straightened himself and, from his case of instruments, took a strangely shaped implement which, after a little manipulation, fitted into the keyhole. A couple of turns, and the padlock opened; the belt was removed, and Cousins freed. One of his inimitable smiles showed for a fleeting second on his wrinkled countenance.

'Love laughs at locksmiths, sir,' he commented, 'and so do you. It's a lucky thing for me that you brought that little case with you.'

'It was fortunate in more ways than one,' muttered Wallace. 'Come along, and tread quietly. The slightest sound may bring the whole gang on us. I'm sorry I haven't another revolver to give you.'

For answer Cousins bent down, and removed the automatic from its hiding place in his sock.

'I managed to hide it there,' he explained, 'when I discovered I had been duped. They never found it. It was my intention to wait until I had ascertained where the plans were hidden; then make a break for it. That was before the girl adopted me as a pet,' he added ruefully, 'and had me chained up.'

Wallace nodded understandingly, and led the way to the door, which he opened with extreme care. All seemed well, not a sound disturbing the silence into which the house was plunged. They descended the stairs, an occasional ray of light from Sir Leonard's powerful little torch helping them. Before long they were in the room used by Ictinos as a study, the door closed on them. Wallace rapidly told his companion how he had come to the place, and what he had heard concerning the disaster that had overtaken Maddison and his assistants.

'The first thing we must do,' he added, 'is to get in touch with headquarters by means of the wireless installation in my car. I've a pretty good idea where we are, and the sooner we get down a force strong enough to raid this building, and capture everyone in it, the better I shall be pleased. Wait a minute, though.' An idea had suddenly occurred to him. 'Hill and Cartright are at Sittingbourne. Major Brien had planted a repair gang on the Sheppey bridge with Cartright working a "go and stop" sign until today, in order that every car that passed could be scrutinised. Both men are now in a house on the Sheppey road. From their room they can see everything that passes, and are provided with a wireless outfit. I'll get in touch with them, and tell them to bring along a strong force of police. We'll save a great deal of time that way. I badly want the Greek under restraint, Cousins, and the police will be glad to take the rest into custody. They seem to be a particularly choice collection of criminals.'

'Have you found out who Ictinos' partner is, sir?' asked Cousins.

'Partner! I didn't know he had one.'

'He has: told me so himself. According to the Greek, he is a man with a wonderful brain, who has all the ideas.'

'An admission like that from Ictinos,' commented Sir Leonard drily, 'is worth recording. I should imagine, from the little I know of him, that there is only one man worth describing as wonderful in this world, and that is Ictinos. Who is this partner? Have you any idea?'

'No. Ictinos was pretty frank. I think it pleased him to tell me things, being certain in his own mind that I could never repeat them, as he intended me to die; but he admitted that the partner's name was a household word, and that he was a Greek like himself.'

'H'm!' Sir Leonard rubbed his chin reflectively. 'It's a pity he's not in this house. I'd like to capture the whole gang, and put an end to its activities once and for all. We shall have to find out who he is. I have the copies made of the plans of the Masterson monoplane and Wentworth gun, and various other interesting documents, but there are other things I want as well.'

Cousins' eyes glistened in the dark.

'By Jove!' he exclaimed, 'that's good work, sir. How did you find them, and what—?'

'There's no time to tell you now. We must get out to the car, and send the message to Cartright. I think we'd better go by way of the window.'

He walked across the room, and pulled aside the curtain. Switching on his torch, he and Cousins looked carefully for burglar alarms, feeling certain that in a house of that nature precautions would have been taken to guard against possible intruders. Cousins' heart was light. After his days of captivity and humiliation, with the shadow of death ever hovering over him, he felt it good to be alive and free.

"'How good is man's life, the mere living! how fit to employ,'" he quoted softly, "'All the heart and the soul and the senses for ever in joy!'"

Wallace smiled to himself, but made no comment. They discovered various cunningly hidden wires, which were cut one by one. Whatever he may have said about his mysterious partner, Ictinos himself was undoubtedly a man of ideas. The electric plant attached to the house was obviously used for more purposes than to supply light. Satisfied that at last all alarms connected with the windows of that room had been put out of action, the two men raised the lower sash of one preparatory to climbing out. At that moment a light flared up and, with a hiss, something sped past Sir Leonard's head through the open window. With one accord he and Cousins swung round. Standing by the door was Thalia Ictinos, a revolver held steadily in her hand; by her side was Paul the dwarf, his repulsive features distorted in a malevolent grin.

'So my little dog-man would escape, eh?' observed the girl mockingly. 'I think it is very ungrateful of him. You, sir,' she added to Wallace, 'came I presume to release him. If Paul had not thrown the knife so badly you would now be dead, but perhaps it is as well you remain alive. You can explain to my father how you come to be here. No; do not move! I shoot very straight.' She turned to the dwarf; spoke rapidly to him in Greek. Cousins, who understood the language, knew she was directing him to call her father and the other men. Paul disappeared. 'It is fortunate,' went on Thalia in English, 'that I had a headache, and came down to get some tablets that my father—'

With extraordinary rapidity Sir Leonard drew his revolver from under his artificial arm, where he had placed it for convenience, and all in one movement, fired at the single glowing electric bulb, hanging in a cluster with two others from the ceiling. It was a wonderful shot, and the room was immediately plunged into darkness. Thalia Ictinos also fired, but she was just a trifle too late, Wallace having gone to the floor.

'Quick! Through the window,' he cried, at the same time dragging down Cousins behind the desk. 'Crawl round to the side near the fireplace,' he breathed urgently in the little man's ear.

Thalia, screaming for help, took three or four seconds to find the other switch. By the time the lights were on, Wallace and his companion were kneeling close together behind the far side of the desk, not exactly a hiding place, if any of the crooks glanced round the room, but Sir Leonard calculated on their making for the window. By now the place was in an uproar. Men came tearing down the stairs calling out to know what was wrong. Ictinos was the first on the scene, the others crowding behind him. Thalia met them at the door.

'Cousins and the other man have escaped – through the window,' she cried.

The Greek proved himself a man of action. He did not stop then to ask who the other man was.

'They may have guns, and shoot to keep us in,' he snapped, promptly switching off the lights again. 'Danson and Farrell, through the window after them. Hepburn and Ibsen, go out the front way. Search the grounds thoroughly; they must not escape. Paul, fetch torches. Quick, all of you!'

His orders were obeyed immediately, and he and his daughter were left alone.

'Who was this other man?' demanded Ictinos, still speaking in English.

'I do not know,' she replied 'it is the first time I have seen him.

He was a man of middle height, with a strong thin face and, I think, grey eyes. I have never seen anyone so quick with a gun before. He wore a big overcoat.'

'I do not care what he wore,' he snarled, adding in a quieter voice, which was almost a whisper. 'It sounds like that devil Wallace, but it cannot be; it cannot be. Thalia, you stay here. I must help in the search.'

'I will get a coat and come too,' she declared.

Sir Leonard and Cousins rose cautiously to their feet.

'Nice of him to switch off the lights,' commented the former quietly. 'It will enable us to get across the room without being spotted from outside.'

They waited a few minutes; then, at a signal from Wallace, the little man followed his chief to the door. They stood there a short while, after which, hearing no sound in the house, they crossed the hall, and ran quietly up the stairs, entering one of the front bedrooms. The light had been left on, but the windows were closely covered by thick curtains, and there was no fear of their being seen from outside.

'We're safer up here than down below,' observed Sir Leonard. 'It's a pity that girl came along when she did. Our chances of getting in touch with Cartright now are not very bright. Still, I can't always expect to have the luck on my side.'

Cousins cast an appreciative eye round the apartment. Obviously that of a woman, it was furnished most tastefully. Gold and enamelled toilet articles adorned the dressing table, delicately worked cushions lay everywhere, while silken curtains hung round the bed.

'Must be her bedroom,' remarked the little man. 'She certainly believes in comfort, even in this out-of-the-way spot.' He chuckled softly. 'Those fellows will find it a bit draughty out there in that piercing wind. I daresay most of them are in pyjamas. "Except wind stands as never it stood, It is an ill-wind turns none to good."'

He was bubbling over with good spirits, probably due to the fact that he was no longer a prisoner. Neither he nor Sir Leonard were in any way perturbed by the fact that they were apparently in a hopeless position. Their chances of escaping from the house were certainly very slender. While the six men were outside searching the grounds, it was impossible for them to get away, especially when it meant attempting to open a barred and locked gate or scaling a high wall, and it was certain that, failing to discover his quarry outside, Ictinos would order every corner of the house to be examined. Wallace sank into an armchair, and considered the problem.

'Go and have a look into the other rooms up here,' he at length directed Cousins. 'If any of them offer a fairly safe hiding place in the event of a search, come back and let me know at once. Be careful! If you hear anybody approaching, return to this room immediately.'

Cousins departed on his errand. He was away for over ten minutes; then came back shaking his head.

'There are cupboards and various other hiding places, of course,' he informed his companion, 'but not a place that is likely to be overlooked in a search.'

'Then there's nothing for it,' decided Wallace, 'but to stay here, and act as circumstances direct.'

Half an hour went by before they heard the sound of voices. Sir Leonard and Cousins quickly withdrew behind the curtains at the farther side of the bed, both holding their weapons ready for action. They heard nothing further for several minutes; then, almost without warning, two people entered the room. One was

Ictinos, the other his daughter. The former appeared very agitated to judge from the excitable manner in which he was speaking to her. She was much calmer and did her best to soothe his apparently ruffled feelings.

'It is of no use behaving in this way,' she protested. 'It is a matter in which you can blame nobody. Whoever the man is who got in, he must have had a perfect knowledge of the house, and probably had been studying it for some days.'

'If you are right, it cannot have been Wallace. He only reached England this morning, or rather yesterday morning.'

'Does it matter whether it was Monsieur Wallace or somebody else? The fact remains that a man did get in and rescue Cousins.'

'Yes; and they are probably far away by now. But how did he get in?'

'How do I know? I only reached your study in time to see them about to get out. I wish I had shot them both at once. If Paul had not missed with his knife all would have been well. Afterwards, when I had them covered with my gun, I thought there would be no attempt to escape. I was not to know that the stranger was so clever. Never have I seen such rapidity of movement as when the light was shot out.'

'That sounds as though he *was* Wallace,' growled Ictinos. 'He is known to be marvellously quick with a pistol. But it seems they have got away. We must go, too. It will be ruin to stop a moment longer than necessary now. Pack only what you require, my child, and hurry. The motorboat is fortunately always ready.'

'Will you put to sea on a night like this?'

'We must, there is no choice.'

'But search the house first. They may have got in somehow when everyone was outside.'

'That is absurd – they could not have done it. The doors and windows were watched. This man must have had a rope over the wall, and they escaped by that means. However, Hepburn and the others can search while I collect my papers.'

'Perhaps they have been taken.'

Ictinos laughed gruffly.

'Impossible. Only I know where they are, and that is a place that could be tampered with by nobody. Be quick, Thalia, we must be away in half an hour. Most of us are ready to go. Are you?'

'It will not take me long. How will you communicate with the caretakers? Some day we must recover possession of the furniture and other articles here. It would be very sad to lose them.'

'We have more important things to think of than caretakers just now,' he responded sharply. 'There will be time tomorrow to send a telegram to them.'

He left the room. The men hidden behind the curtain heard the girl moving about for some minutes, once she actually approached close to them, and Wallace made ready to spring out on her, but she walked away again directly afterwards, leaving the bedroom probably to get something from her boudoir. While she was away, Cousins rapidly, and in a whisper, gave his companion the gist of the conversation they had overheard. Sir Leonard had been able to gather what some of it was about, but his lack of knowledge of the Greek language made it impossible for him to understand much.

He chuckled softly.

'So his papers are hidden in a place that nobody could find, are they?' he commented. 'If I'm not mistaken, there'll be more fireworks presently.'

He had hardly finished speaking when a commotion broke out below. The deep voice of Ictinos could be heard raised in apparent anger, other voices forming a sort of chorus to it. Wallace and Cousins smiled at each other. Thalia re-entered the bedroom, dropped something on the floor that sounded like a suitcase, and ran out again, calling down to her father to know what was wrong. He shouted back something, and she descended rapidly to join him.

'How about making an attempt to get away now, sir?' suggested Cousins. 'While their attention is occupied down below, we might be able to lower ourselves from the window, and escape.'

Sir Leonard shook his head.

'If possible,' he returned, 'I mean to find out their destination. I haven't finished with Ictinos yet. There is something else I want from him, which it seems is hidden elsewhere.'

Cousins eyed him curiously, but made no comment. The hubbub downstairs continued for some time; then could be heard the movement of several people on the upper floor. It was evidently a search party. A man actually came as far as the bedroom, but a voice from somewhere farther away told him it was no use searching Miss Ictinos' room.

'She's only just come out,' he added, 'and if there had been anyone there, she would have spotted him.'

'It's a waste of time, anyhow,' returned the fellow at the door. 'You can bet they're well away by now. I'm going to put some clothes on. I don't fancy a trip in that perishing motorboat in this get-up. I'm almost frozen stiff now.'

He moved away, and the two men in the room breathed again.

'Luck doesn't seem to have deserted us after all,' muttered Wallace.

Thalia Ictinos came running up the stairs. She was apparently accompanied by the dwarf.

'These two, Paul,' she said, as she entered the room. There was a grunt, and the sound of unsteady retreating feet, suggesting that a heavy burden was being carried. Wallace, taking a chance, looked cautiously round the curtain. He saw her, dressed in a fur coat, pulling a waterproof over her shoulders. A sou'-wester covered her glorious hair, while her legs were encased in gum-boots. She turned in his direction, and he drew back out of sight. A minute later the light went out; they heard the door close, and all was quiet. Quickly Wallace was across the room, looking through the keyhole. He saw her descending the stairs. She was presently followed by two men who appeared from the other end of the passage; then Ictinos emerged from a room close by, a suitcase in either hand. He paused at the top of the stairs, and called out to someone. A voice answered from below and, apparently satisfied, he switched out the corridor light, and went down. Whispering to Cousins to follow carefully, Sir Leonard quietly opened the door. The two of them, treading cautiously, descended in the wake of the crooks, who were apparently gathered together some distance along the hall towards the back of the house. Ictinos, still in a great rage, was talking to them.

'I do not care what you declare or swear,' he was saying. 'I am convinced that it was Sir Leonard Wallace and no other who was in this house tonight. He was never in the second car, and our belief that he was killed is nonsense. Somehow he tracked you here and got inside. He must have watched me at work in my study and, when I went to bed, stole the papers I have lost. After that he rescued the man Cousins, whom I should have killed, when he first came here. You are bunglers, all of you. Three times in one day Wallace has been allowed to escape death or capture. By whom am I served – men or suckling babes?'

'You can't blame us for tonight's episode,' retorted the voice of Hepburn harshly. 'Miss Ictinos should have shot both of them when she caught them in the study. And none of us asked you to keep that little rat Cousins alive, did we? If we have bungled, so have you, and a great deal more. You've even lost plans worth hundreds of thousands which Danson and I got for you. What have you got to say to that? Nothing; except to blame us. I'd like to know where you'd be without me, anyhow.'

'How dare you talk to me like you – you murderer,' roared Ictinos.

'Murderer!' laughed the other sarcastically. 'A case of the pot calling the kettle black, isn't it? Why, almost lily-white compared with you.'

'Perhaps you would like to stay behind, and face the music,' came in tones that had altered to a soft, silky utterance. 'You can if you like, my friend Hepburn. Now that it is known about your ability to impersonate people, you are not of much further use to me.'

Hepburn again laughed.

'I can see you agreeing that I should stop,' he sneered. 'I know too much for that.'

'Ah! So you threaten me, eh?'

'Not a bit of it. I'm willing to stay with you and be loyal to you, so long as you don't push the blame for everything that goes wrong off your own shoulders on to mine or these fellows here.'

'I put the blame where the blame should be, and I will not be dictated to by—'

'You men are absurd,' interrupted Thalia impatiently. 'You stand here quarrelling when, at any moment, the house may be raided. What is past is past. Let us go!'

'She is right, except for one thing,' came from Ictinos, after a short pause, during which he had calmed down.

'We will forget the blunders made, and have no further recriminations. I have perhaps been a little hasty. But what is past is not past where Wallace is concerned. Unless we kill him, I am convinced our endeavours will fail or suffer badly. He stands in the way. From now on we must resolve to spare no efforts to remove him. Remember always, when the opportunity arrives: get Wallace! Now no more talking. We will proceed.'

'Are we really going to try to reach the yacht?' asked Danson.

'Not only try, but succeed, my friend.'

'But it is still blowing hard, and I doubt if the motorboat will live in that sea.'

'She would live in a hurricane. It will be wet, but not too dangerous. Our friend Hepburn is the best of pilots.' The light in the hall was extinguished.

'I thought I was not of much further use,' retorted Hepburn, who was apparently still nursing his grievance.

Ictinos made some reply as they were moving away, which the listeners did not catch. The latter's curiosity was aroused by the fact that the gang did not make for the front door, but went on towards the back of the house. Followed closely by Cousins, Wallace quickly ran down the remainder of the stairs. At the bottom he craned his neck over the banister, but could not see where they had gone, the green baize door having closed behind them. Softly he tiptoed along the passage, pushed open the door a few inches, and looked through the gap. He found that the corridor continued, a lighted apartment at the end throwing out sufficient illumination to enable him to see that two or three more rooms, probably kitchens and a pantry, opened into it. But he was not interested in these. From the sound of voices he gathered that

Ictinos and his followers were in the rear, probably about to go through the back door. Bidding Cousins stay and keep watch in case all were not there, and holding his revolver ready, he crept along the passage; found himself peeping into a large scullery. A trapdoor in the centre of the room had been raised, and, through it, the conspirators were descending one by one. Ictinos was the last to go, and Wallace succeeded in obtaining a good view of him, marvelling once again at his extraordinary breadth of shoulder, and noticing, for the first time, how short he was in comparison to his width. The watcher dodged back as the Greek gave a glance round the scullery before switching off the light, and following the others through the trap. Then Wallace hurried back to Cousins; told him where they had gone.

'There is probably a cave underneath this house where the motorboat is kept,' he added. 'I'm going after them. If possible I want to find out the name of the yacht they spoke about, otherwise it's going to be a devil of a job to find them again. I'll leave the trapdoor open, and you keep watch. If you hear a shot, come down to my assistance, but don't show a light; the reflection might be seen.'

He went back to the scullery, found the handle of the trapdoor without much difficulty, and lifted it. Pushing the revolver within easy reach in his breast pocket, he felt round, discovered the steps, and began to descend gingerly. There were far more than he expected, and he seemed to be going down an interminable time. As far as he could ascertain he was in a narrow shaft dropping almost perpendicularly, and the steps were rungs of an iron ladder or ladders riveted to the rock. He was wondering how much farther he would have to descend, when something struck his head and shoulders with tremendous force, tearing his hand from its grip, and hurling him downwards. Fortunately he had been near the bottom, but even so the impact with the rock shook most of the breath from his body. In a daze at first, he felt something on top of him, clawing at his throat, and uttering low snarling cries like a savage animal. He began struggling desperately to tear away the hold but, with one hand, was at a disadvantage, while the creature mauling him seemed to be possessed of considerable strength. The clutch on his windpipe increasing, he had a difficulty in breathing, flames began to dance before his eyes. Abruptly he changed his tactics; his hand dropped away from the claws of the creature on him; he lay inert. His assailant relaxed its grip, probably thinking it had rendered its victim unconscious, the pressure on his chest was relieved, and Wallace was able to slide his hand to his breast pocket. Taking hold of his revolver by the muzzle, he suddenly threw himself on one side. Caught unaware, the creature was for the moment at his mercy. He felt for, found its head; then, just as the clawing fingers reached him again, brought down his weapon with sickening force. There was a grunt, the body fell back, and lay still.

Sir Leonard rose somewhat shakily to his feet. There was not a glimmer of light anywhere; an impenetrable blackness seemed to cloak him on all sides. He felt, therefore, that he could risk a light for a moment. Presently a ray of brilliant illumination stabbed the darkness and was focused on the body lying at his feet then was switched off again.

'The dwarf!' he mused. 'That's a nuisance. Somebody will probably come back to look for him. I wonder where he came from.'

He ventured another look at the recumbent man, decided that he would probably remain unconscious for some time then, having found in which direction to go, proceeded cautiously on his way.

Before long he collided with the rock, discovered that the passage took a turning to the right; went carefully on. He could hear the howling of the wind now, and the lapping of water. Presently the opaque blackness seemed to diminish. He turned another corner; stopped abruptly. Electric torches lit up the scene, giving him a perfect view of what was ahead of him. Twenty or thirty yards farther on lay a large motorboat in an inlet from the sea. Although sheltered to a great extent from the storm that still raged without, she was rocking violently, her fenders every now and again coming into sharp contact with the ledge of rock to which she was moored. The latter made an excellent landing stage. Two men stood there looking somewhat anxiously in the direction of the cave. As Wallace watched, Ictinos appeared from the cabin amidships, frowning portentously. He said something to one of the men, who reluctantly began to walk in Sir Leonard's direction. The fellow had almost reached the turning, when the Greek's voice came booming along the gallery.

'Hurry!' it cried. 'It will be daylight before we are aboard the *Electra*.'

Sir Leonard smiled to himself.

'Thank you,' he murmured softly, 'that's all I wanted to know,' and stepped back into the darkness.

CHAPTER TWELVE

The Organisation is Reduced by Two

He retreated for some distance; then stood still awaiting the coming of the man he could not see, but whose footsteps were plainly discernible. It had occurred to him that, as he had been more or less forced by circumstances to have one prisoner on his hands, he might as well have two. The little fountain-pen-like torch was in his hand now, nestling by the side of the revolver. The approaching man also carried a flash lamp, but, as he kept its ray focused on the ground, he was not aware of the presence of Sir Leonard until the latter switched on his own light; then, for a moment, did not know who stood before him.

'Where the devil have you been, Paul?' he growled. 'You're keeping us all waiting. The guv'nor—'

'Don't make a movement, or you're a dead man,' came Sir Leonard's stern command. 'I am covering you with a revolver.'

A startled gasp broke from the alarmed man. His jaw dropped ludicrously; his eyes, wide open with fear, strove owlishly to pierce the brilliant light full on him, in an effort to discover who was behind it in the gloom.

'Who – who are you?' he stammered.

'That doesn't matter. You can drop that torch. I've enough illumination here for two.' The flashlight fell to the ground obediently. 'In case you feel like playing any tricks,' went on Sir Leonard, 'this will perhaps warn you to refrain.'

He fired rapidly twice, the bullets humming close by the right ear of the now thoroughly frightened man. He ducked apprehensively. From the mouth of the cave could faintly be heard cries of consternation; directly afterwards came the staccato beat of a motor engine, at first in a hesitant manner; then more continuously, as it warmed to its work. Wallace smiled. He had counted on Ictinos taking alarm, and fleeing.

'Your friends, it appears, have decided to leave without you,' he observed. 'Come along; this way, and remember that a revolver as well as a torch will be pointed full at the middle of your back.'

With a sound that was something between a curse and a groan, the man obeyed orders. Sir Leonard crushed himself against the wall of the cave to allow him to pass, following closely behind as he stumbled his way along. Suddenly another torch flashed out ahead.

'Put your hands up,' cried the voice of Cousins.

'It's all right,' Wallace reassured him. 'This chap is with me, and well covered. There's another at the foot of the ladder having a little rest.'

'Yes; I noticed him,' chuckled Cousins; 'in fact I stepped on him. I heard the shots, found a torch, and came down, expecting to find you in difficulties, sir.'

'The only time I was in any difficulty,' returned Sir Leonard, 'was when that dwarf hurled himself down the ladder on me. Where did he come from? Didn't you see him?'

'No. Do you mean to say he followed you down?'

'He did. Probably he was in the pantry, or hidden in the scullery, and saw me pass.' They reached the foot of the iron ladder. Paul was still lying there unconscious. 'Pick him up,' ordered Sir Leonard, prodding his prisoner in the back. 'You'll have to carry him to the top. You go first, Jerry, and keep your gun handy.'

His orders were obeyed. Cousins hastened up, and stood by the trapdoor, his torch lighting up the shaft, and his automatic covering the man, who laboriously followed with the dwarf slung over his shoulder. Wallace stood at the bottom until all were up then, pushing his torch and the revolver into his pocket, ascended in his turn. In the scullery he examined Paul, who now lay on the floor breathing stertorously, after which he quietly inspected the man he had captured. The latter, whose battered face and large, ill-shapen ears denoted that he had once been a pugilist, stood sheepishly with downcast head, while Cousins, quickly and expertly searched him. He possessed no weapons.

'Who are you?' demanded Sir Leonard.

Cousins answered for the fellow.

'His name's Farrell, sir; the only one of the bunch who possesses any feelings of humanity. He did his best to give me a certain amount of fresh air in the box room by leaving the door wide open when I was not inside, and he actually found courage enough to protest when the steel belt was fastened on me and orders given for me to be kept chained. For that indiscretion Ictinos knocked him down, and kicked him.'

'H'm!' commented Sir Leonard. 'You are apparently a little less poisonous than the rest of your crowd.' He took from his pocket the list of those serving Ictinos, and consulted it. 'William Farrell,' he read, 'wanted by the Bristol police for robbery with violence, by the Metropolitan police for being concerned in three smash and grab raids, and by the police of Leeds for blackmail. A pretty hefty record, my man, which will probably get you anything from fifteen years upwards. Still, as you don't appear to be wanted for murder like the rest of your companions, we might make things a little easier for you – if you are willing to give us all the information you can about the activities of Stanislaus Ictinos.'

'Who are you?' asked Farrell hoarsely.

'Does that matter? However, if it will interest you at all to know, my name is Wallace.'

The battered face turned pale.

'Hell!' ejaculated the fellow. 'Then you weren't killed after all! The guv'nor was right.'

'Yes; the guv'nor, as you call him, was right. Well, what is it to be? Are you coming clean, or refusing to talk? I might as well tell you that, apart from your criminal operations, I have the most utter contempt for you. A man who will take part in betraying his own country for gain or otherwise is, to my mind, the most despicable of worms. I can find no excuse for traitors whatever. Nevertheless, if you show willingness to assist us by telling us everything you know about Ictinos, I will use my influence with the police on your behalf.'

Farrell hesitated for some moments. At length he appeared to make up his mind.

'What do you want to know?' he asked sullenly.

'I'll tell you when we get to London,' returned Wallace curtly. 'Throw some water on the dwarf's face. It's time we brought him to.'

'Take my advice,' grunted Farrell, 'and tie him up before he comes to his senses. When he finds he's a prisoner he'll be like a wild cat. I know him.'

Sir Leonard's eyebrows lifted slightly.

'Thanks,' he said. 'Cousins, look round and see if you can find some rope.'

'There's some in that cupboard over there,' indicated the ex-pugilist.

It certainly looked as though he had made up his mind to be of assistance. The rope was procured, and Cousins deftly trussed up the dwarf. Then Farrell emptied a basin of water on his face. Such drastic treatment on that icy cold morning proved quickly efficacious. Paul stirred; presently his eyes opened. He gazed in wonderment round him, a puzzled frown crossed his face when he became aware that he was bound; then, as memory reasserted itself, and he realised he was the prisoner of the man he had attacked in the shaft, he broke out into a high-pitched torrent of blasphemy in a mixture of Greek, French, and English, struggling madly the while to release himself. Sir Leonard watched him for a few minutes.

'You were right,' he observed to Farrell. 'There is quite a lot of the wild cat about him. Tell me,' he went on; 'why did you warn us, when it was possible that, being ignorant of his character, we might have been taken by surprise, thus enabling you to make a bid for liberty?'

'Oh, I guess I'm not so sorry it's all over,' replied Farrell in a somewhat shamefaced manner. 'I'm pretty tough, but I couldn't stomach some of the things the guv'nor did, and I'd had about enough. Besides it's hell to be always wanted by the police; it gets on your nerves after a while. You can take it from me, sir, that I wouldn't have got mixed up with Ictinos' racket, if it hadn't offered a fair amount of security. I was only with the gang six months, and that was just about five months and a half too long. Anyhow, it's quite a relief to be shot of them, and I can take my medicine without whining.'

'How did the Greek get in touch with you?'

'Came to the place where I was hiding up, and got me to join him. How he found out where I was, I don't know, but I reckon he's pretty well in with people who give shelter to fellows like me. He recruited his gang from those who have a price on their heads – it gives him a hold on them – but you seem to know all about that.'

'Yes; I know all about that,' agreed Sir Leonard. He turned to Cousins, and drew him aside. 'Go out and see if the car is locked away,' he whispered. 'If so, let me know, and I'll come and get the door open. If you can get to it, wireless headquarters – you know where the installation is, don't you?' Cousins nodded. 'Tell them to send down two or three men to join Cartright and Hill, and also phone through to Lady Wallace that I'm all right. Then get in touch with Cartright, inform him about the disaster on the bridge, and tell him to get an ambulance out there. Notify him also that we'll be along in about three quarters of an hour.'

Cousins hurried off, and Sir Leonard turned back to his prisoners. Farrell stood dejectedly with his hands in his pockets; the dwarf still continued to scream maledictions, but Wallace took no notice of him. He let down the trapdoor, and fastened it, after which, ordering Farrell to accompany him, and holding his revolver handy, he made a tour of the house, switching on all the lights and cursorily inspecting every room. He hardly expected that anything of importance would have been left in the building, and he had no time to make a meticulous examination, but the men he would send down would go through every apartment as though with a small-tooth comb. Cousins returned while he was still on the upper storey.

'The garage was unlocked,' reported the little man. 'They had searched it and your car pretty thoroughly, I should imagine, though how they could have expected us to get in, and lock the door on ourselves, I can't think.'

'Perhaps it never had been locked,' remarked Wallace.

'Oh, yes, it had, sir. You told me so, didn't you?' he asked, turning to Farrell.

'That's so,' nodded the latter.

'Well, it doesn't matter,' observed Sir Leonard. 'Is everything all right?'

Cousins drew him out of earshot of the crook and, keeping his automatic turned on the man, told Wallace in a low voice that he had carried out his orders to the letter. He had one item of news, however, which relieved Sir Leonard's mind a great deal. Maddison and Reynolds had not been killed in the smash, though both were badly injured, particularly the former. The wireless apparatus in the car had been shattered, but Reynolds, although suffering from a broken arm, two fractured ribs, and a badly cut face, had made his way to the house where Cartright and Hill were staying, and had informed them of the disaster. An ambulance had been immediately sent to the scene, and the police notified, Cartright telling the latter that Secret Service headquarters would get in touch with them concerning the affair. Maddison, with a fractured skull, and several other injuries, and Reynolds were now in hospital, but both were expected to recover. Poor Cunliffe was dead – had been shot through the head. Sir Leonard listened without comment, except to express his sorrow at the death of the young man, and his relief that the others were alive.

A few minutes later they left the house, Farrell carrying the dwarf who had now discontinued his ravings, but whose eyes glared hatred at the men into whose power he had fallen. Wallace locked the front door, and retained the key. The big gates were unbarred and opened and, with Cousins at the wheel, and Sir Leonard inside keeping a watchful eye on Farrell and the dwarf, who had been deposited on the floor, the car was driven rapidly towards the bridge connecting Sheppey with the mainland.

Glancing at his watch as they drew near the scene of the tragedy, Sir Leonard found that it was close on five. The wind had decreased considerably, and the sky had cleared a good deal, but it was still bitterly cold. A breakdown gang from Sittingbourne was already working to haul Maddison's smashed car back to the road as they passed, and several members of the local police force stood by, but they did not stop, and no effort was made to detain them, though curious glances were turned in their direction. The fact that they were abroad at such an early hour no doubt caused a certain amount of surprise to men who did not know who they were.

The house in which Cartright and Hill had taken up their quarters was found without much difficulty. The former was awaiting them. Sir Leonard handed over the key of the house near Minster to him, giving him instructions to proceed there as soon as he was joined by the men from London. Enquiries elicited the news that Maddison had not regained consciousness, but that both he and Reynolds were doing as well as could be expected. A few further injunctions, and the car proceeded on its way. On arrival in London, Farrell and Paul were taken to Scotland Yard, and handed over to the inspector of the special branch then on duty, to be locked up and kept there until Wallace sent for them. Farrell walked to his cell quietly, without uttering a word, but the dwarf, as soon as he was released from his bonds, fought and screamed like a wild animal. It eventually took three stalwart constables to carry him to a cell, where he was deposited none too gently, as a little punishment for his obstreperous behaviour, and the door locked on him.

Wallace found a very relieved Major Brien awaiting his coming at headquarters. The latter greeted Cousins first almost as he might have done an acquaintance risen from the grave; then turned eagerly to his friend.

'By Jove! I've been anxious,' he confessed. 'I stopped here all night, expecting to hear from you, but, as hour after hour went by, and no news came through, I almost went dippy. Molly kept ringing up, too, but I did my best to reassure her.'

'You've told her that everything's all right, I hope.'

'I have, my son. Rang her up as soon as Cousins' message came through.'

Sir Leonard sank wearily into a chair, and yawned.

'You'll never be an ideal member of this service, Billy,' he observed. 'You are too prone to allow individual affections to cause you anxiety, and thus interfere with duty.'

'Well, I like that,' protested the indignant Brien. 'No matter how I may feel, I have never—'

'Another of your shortcomings,' went on Sir Leonard, 'is that you never know when your leg is being pulled.' He drew out the documents which had filled his pockets, and threw them on the desk. 'Lock these away carefully,' he directed; 'among them are the copies of the plans of the Wentworth gun and Masterson monoplane.'

Brien gave vent to a cry of delight.

'Then you have succeeded,' he exclaimed; 'the job is done, and this is the end of the business.'

Sir Leonard sighed.

'On the contrary,' he returned, 'it is just the beginning.'

Major Brien questioned him eagerly, demanding to know what he meant. Sir Leonard related the conversation he had had with Monsieur Damien, and the promise he had made.

'Until we have recovered the plans of the French frontier fortifications or France has been forced to pay up,' he concluded, 'we cannot consider the business finished. Apart from that, I shall never rest until I have smashed this gang and put *finis* to the activities of Ictinos. Of course, he may get me first; I believe he is very keen on doing so. In that case,' he added grimly, 'I shall certainly rest. He has murdered Cunliffe, and very nearly Maddison and Reynolds as well. In addition, he set his jackals on to us yesterday when your wife and mine and Adrian were in the car. That was unforgivable, and he'll answer to me for that, if for nothing else.'

It was exceptional for Wallace to show vehemence, but on this occasion he permitted his companions to see a little of the force underlying his usually genial, easy-going manner. They knew, of course, of its existence. Nobody who had worked with him could fail to do so. But it was so rarely that he allowed it to come to the surface that they were a little awed. On his face was an expression of inflexible resolve, of almost ruthless determination. He noticed the way in which they were regarding him, and laughed – a little harshly.

'Tell us what happened to you, Cousins,' he suggested, turning to the little man. 'How did you get trapped?'

Cousins related everything, from the time he left Victoria

arrayed as a naval gunner until rescued by Wallace. The story took some time in the telling, though neither of his listeners interrupted, except when he spoke of the impersonation of Shannon; then Brien, glancing at the chief with admiration showing in his eyes, said: 'That is exactly what you conjectured might have happened.' Wallace nodded slightly; bade Cousins continue. The former paid most attention to the latter's interview with Ictinos, but it added little to what he already knew.

'Was that the only time you had a talk with the Greek?' he asked at the end of the recital.

'The only time he said anything of interest about the organisation, sir. He frequently entered the boudoir when I was chained up there, jeered at me, and reminded me that he intended to have you killed as soon as you set foot in England.'

'Did the girl ever say anything which might give us a clue to their intentions after being compelled to leave Sheppey?'

'Never. She generally avoided all topics that might afford me any information. When I was in her boudoir, she usually made me read to her, or discuss poetry with her – she could be very charming when she tried – the rest of the time she did her utmost to make me squirm by humiliating me or inventing some new physical torture.'

'Charming girl!' commented Brien. 'The Ictinos family seems to be utterly callous and brutal. Fancy murdering that poor beggar – Moropos, was it you said? – simply because he posted some of the letters in Sheerness!'

'I can imagine how Ictinos felt,' grunted Sir Leonard. 'It was a terrible dereliction of duty from his point of view. That one blunder put us on his track, remember.' He rubbed his chin, and frowned. 'I wonder who this mysterious partner of his is? That's got to be ascertained somehow. Perhaps he's on the yacht. Listen, Bill: I want you to get busy on several matters right away, while I go home, and have a bath and a shave. First of all find out whom the yacht *Electra* belongs to, where she is – in fact all you can about her. Secondly, recall Shannon from Rome – order him to fly back. It is possible I may find a use for him in this business. Then ask Scotland Yard to send the two prisoners round here under a close guard at ten. I think that will do for the present. By the way, have you found out what happened to Johnson, by any chance?'

'Yes; he was found bound and gagged in a corner of your garage by a policeman, who noticed the door slightly open at three this morning. He'd been chloroformed.'

'He's all right, I hope?'

'I believe so.'

Wallace rose from his chair, and stretched.

'I'm not so young as I was,' he remarked. 'I get tired too easily nowadays.'

'Dash it all!' remonstrated Brien. 'You've had a pretty stiff time, and not a wink of sleep, since you left the *Majestic* yesterday morning. What can you expect?'

'One can't afford to be subject to the usual human failings in this job,' retorted the other. He turned to Cousins. 'You'd better continue your leave, Jerry,' he suggested. 'You'll be able to have a Christmas holiday after all.'

Cousins looked pained. His face creased ludicrously as he eyed Sir Leonard in dismay.

'Anaxagoras is to blame for a lot,' he complained. 'It was he made this holiday business popular, but, if you don't mind, sir, I'd rather forgo mine; at least until this affair is settled.'

Wallace stifled a yawn.

'Just as you like,' he smiled. 'I'd rather have you on duty, of course.'

Every wrinkle on the little man's face appeared to develop a grin of its own.

'Thank you, sir,' he said with real gratitude, as though a great favour had been conferred upon him. 'I wonder if the ghost of Shelley would object, if I adapted a verse of one of his poems to my feelings about leave: "Out of the day and night a joy has taken flight; Fresh spring, and summer, and winter hoar, Move my faint heart with grief, but with delight No more – oh, never more!"'

'Thalia Ictinos doesn't seem to have curbed your instincts,' commented Wallace. 'I'll be back just before ten, Bill. Find out every item of information you can about the *Electra*. It's possible I'll want to board her before the day is out.'

'Aren't you going to tell me how you found out where this fellow, Ictinos was living, and how you obtained possession of the plans?' asked Brien in disappointed tones.

'Not now, my lad. Have a heart! I'll tell you sometime during the course of the day. At the moment I feel I shall not regain the full use of my faculties until I've revelled in a bath.'

He walked out. The sight of his car brought a momentary frown of reflection to his brow. Despite his handicap, Sir Leonard still managed to drive, though he seldom did so, but it was not on account of that reluctance that he was hesitating now. Although he felt fairly certain that he was safe for the time being from the machinations of the gang controlled by Ictinos, he intended to take no risks. The car had been left unattended. There was just a chance that in the meantime emissaries of the indefatigable Greek had arrived, and had laid a trap for him. He walked for some distance up Whitehall, and took a taxi. Eight o'clock boomed out from

Big Ben as he directed the driver. A thin sleet was falling, making more depressing the new daylight of a typical December day. He was quickly home, to be greeted happily by a wife who, though she would never divulge the fact to him, had spent the long hours of the night overcome by a gnawing anxiety that was only partially relieved by the message received from Major Brien that all was well. She did not question him concerning the business that had kept him away for so long, but he, feeling that some sort of explanation was due to her, gave her the information that he had gone to the Isle of Sheppey to recover certain plans that had been stolen; spoke of the house at Minster as though it had been deserted when he arrived there; scorned the idea that he had been in danger at any time. She listened to him, and understood, filling in the blanks as her own imagination and knowledge of him directed. And thus the great game, engendered by their love, was played, as it would always be played by those two, while he was Chief of the British Secret Service.

CHAPTER THIRTEEN

Farrell is Offered a Chance

There was no intention of taking a short rest in Sir Leonard Wallace's mind to make up a little for the strenuous night he had spent. As soon as he had bathed, shaved, and partaken of breakfast, he had a talk with Johnson. The chauffeur, looking rather pale, but otherwise little the worse for his ordeal, was unable to give any information about the attack made on him, except that he had been about to drive the car from the garage, when a pad, soaked in chloroform, had suddenly been pressed over his nose and mouth, and held there, despite his struggles, until he had lost consciousness. Sir Leonard warned him to be on the *qui vive* during the course of the following days.

'We're up against a gang that will stick at nothing,' he remarked. 'One of their amiable intentions, between you and me, Johnson, is to put an end to my career, and it is quite likely that a lot will depend upon your watchfulness and care. Do you feel fit enough to go and fetch the car back from Whitehall?'

Declaring that he was quite all right, Johnson departed on his errand, his face reflecting some of the grim resolution of his employer's.

At ten minutes to ten, Wallace walked into his office looking as fresh as though he had recently risen from bed after eight or ten hours' untroubled slumber. He found Major Brien awaiting him, standing with his back to a roaring fire, hands in pockets, a pipe in the corner of his mouth.

'Good Lord!' groaned that worthy, 'how on earth do you manage to look so indecently fit? I did get a snooze in between times during the night; even so I feel a rag.'

'It's your riotous living, my son,' returned Wallace.

'Riotous living be damned! I'm the hardest-worked man in Europe, chained to a buzzing hive of industry by the whim of a martinet.'

'Don't stint yourself, Bill. Make it the hardest worked man in the five continents.'

'Shouldn't be far wrong.' He knocked out the ashes of his pipe on the fender. 'Shannon left Rome ten minutes ago,' he informed the other.

'Good work,' applauded Sir Leonard. 'What news of the *Electra*?'

Brien nodded to the desk.

'Full information on that sheet of paper there,' he observed.

Wallace strode across, took up the slip, and perused it eagerly.

'*Electra* – steam sea-going yacht of 1,200 tons,' he read, 'at one time the property of Sir Peter Nikoleff, sold two years ago to Michael Senostris, the Greek millionaire and philanthropist. Now lying in the Medway off Rochester. Has accommodation for twelve guests, and usually carries a crew of twenty officers and men. Can attain a speed of twenty-two knots.'

He allowed a look of triumph to show fleetingly in his face.

'Billy,' he proclaimed, 'you have surpassed yourself. It looks as though Mr Michael Senostris is the mysterious partner of Ictinos.'

'It certainly fits in with the description,' agreed Brien. 'Man with brains, household name, Greek and all that sort of thing. But why should a millionaire want to mix himself in a game of this sort? He has all the money he can possibly want, and a lot over. Besides, he seemed quite a decent Johnny when I met him, not at all the sort of bloke to be hand in glove with a bloodthirsty ruffian like Ictinos.'

A clerk entered the room.

'Inspector Graham from Scotland Yard to see you, sir,' he informed Wallace. 'He has two men with him in the custody of several constables.'

Sir Leonard nodded. He was about to order the visitors to be shown in, but changed his mind; turned instead to Major Brien.

'Is Cousins still here?' he asked. Brien nodded. 'Well, look here, Billy, I want you to examine these fellows, and see what you can get out of them. Cousins can help you. Farrell will talk readily enough, but I don't suppose he can tell us much. You'll probably find the other – a dwarf – a hard nut to crack. I'll interview them at Scotland Yard later in the day.'

'What are you going to do?'

'Have a word with Sir Peter Nikoleff, if he is in London. He'll probably be able to give me some useful information about Senostris.' He looked at the clerk. 'Show Inspector Graham and the men with him into Major Brien's room, Stevenson, and ask Mr Cousins to go there.'

'Very well, sir.'

Wallace waited until he and Brien were alone again; then:

'Before you start the pumping process, Bill, get in touch with the powers that be in Rochester, give your authority, and ask them to detain the *Electra* if she shows any signs of sailing. Also get hold of Cartright if you can, and tell him to send one of his men to keep an eye on the yacht until he hears from me. If you can't get hold of him, you'll have to send down the best man you have available here.'

'We're almost an empty house,' remarked Brien, 'but I'll see what I can do. You're keeping me busy, aren't you?'

'You may be a good deal busier yet. It is possible I shall want you to accompany me on a visit to the *Electra* later on.'

'That will be a change. By the way does the dwarf, under Graham's tender care, bite or do anything nasty like that?'

'He probably would, if he got half a chance,' smiled Sir Leonard. 'But I think you'll find him safely handcuffed. He's a repulsive-looking beggar and a thorough savage.'

'What a little pet!' commented Brien, 'it seems as though I am in for an interesting time.'

Sir Leonard drove to Grosvenor Square, where dwelt Sir Peter Nikoleff the financier, diplomat, art connoisseur, and man of a host of other interests made possible by his enormous fortune. Although of Greek extraction, Sir Peter was a naturalised Englishman, and had accomplished great work for his adopted country. But his reputation was international, not merely national. He had financed revolutions, supported causes of all kinds, even propped up tottering kingdoms. Nothing that was great enough was too great for Sir Peter to champion. Time and again his operations had caused tremendous fluctuations in the money markets of the world. He was perhaps the most significant figure in finance and politics that had lived for a century.

Wallace was fortunate to find him at home. He was shown into a study furnished with antiques and *objets d'art* that must have cost a fortune. A secretary informed him that Sir Peter would see him in five minutes, and in exactly five minutes he came, a short, rather stumpy figure, whose bright eyes, ruddy complexion, bushy white hair and white, somewhat unkempt beard, gave him an air of genial benevolence. He shook hands warmly with his visitor.

'I am intrigued,' he declared with a smile. 'What can the mystery man of the Foreign Office want with me at this early hour of the morning?'

'Not much of the mystery man about me,' returned Wallace.

'In some countries you are not only regarded as a mysterious, sinister figure,' insisted the old man, 'but to you are attributed almost satanic powers as well. In fact I once overheard an official say that he was perfectly convinced you were in league with the powers of darkness.'

Sir Leonard smiled ruefully.

'Simply because I was endeavouring to do my duty to my country I suppose,' he observed. 'It is a pity one is misunderstood so easily in this world.' He accepted a cigarette. 'I have come to you, Sir Peter,' he went on, 'to ask you one or two questions. I shall not take up much of your time.'

'I shall be glad to answer them if I can.'

'Thank you. Two years ago, I believe, you sold a yacht called the *Electra* to a Greek gentleman of the name of Senostris. Is that correct?'

Sir Peter nodded.

'Quite correct,' he replied. 'What of it?'

'Of course most people have heard of Michael Senostris. I

myself have met him once or twice. But do you know him well – that is to say intimately?'

'Quite; in fact he is a very old friend of mine. We have often been partners in various enterprises in the past.'

Wallace gave a little exclamation of satisfaction.

'I am going to be perfectly frank with you,' he declared. 'We have reason to suspect that Senostris is engaged with another man in procuring and selling to the highest bidders various national secrets. Do you think he is the kind of man to associate himself with such a business? It is a delicate question to put to his friend, I know, but I am asking you as a man who has proved his loyalty to his adopted country, and Great Britain is very much concerned.'

Sir Peter stared at his visitor for a moment then lay back in his chair and laughed heartily. When he had recovered from his amusement:

'You say you have met him. Did he strike you as a man who would engage himself in international intrigue of that nature?'

'No; he certainly did not.'

'Well, you can take it from me, Sir Leonard, that he is not. Every enterprise with which he has ever been connected has been strictly honourable. He would not stoop to anything of a shady nature. You can take my word for it.'

Wallace rubbed his chin reflectively.

'And yet,' he remarked, after a pause, 'it is a fact that he owns the *Electra*, and to the *Electra* has gone the man, and certain members of his organisation, whom we know obtained copies of military and air force secrets, and offered them to three European powers.'

Sir Peter opened his eyes wide with surprise.

'Are you sure of this?' he demanded.

'Absolutely certain.'

'It is strange – very strange.' He sat thoughtfully tapping his knees with his hands. 'Very strange,' he added again. 'But,' he went on, 'that hardly proves, does it, that Michael Senostris is a partner in this affair?'

'No; it does not prove it, but the facts are very significant. The man, of whom I am speaking, himself a Greek, has declared, within the hearing of one of my most reliable assistants, that he has a partner of the same nationality, whose name is a household word, and whose brains supply the ideas. As this fellow, when in danger, fled with his gang to the *Electra*, you will agree that everything points to Senostris as the partner.'

The genial look departed from the financier's face, leaving it hard and stern.

'If I thought for a moment,' he began; then shook his head. 'It cannot be,' he insisted. 'I have known Senostris since we were boys together. It is utterly out of the question that he could be engaged in work of such a nature. Is there any reason why I should not know the name of this other man?'

'None at all,' returned Wallace promptly, 'though you are hardly likely to be acquainted with him. He is one of the most callous, bloodthirsty scoundrels I have had the misfortune to be arrayed against. During the last few days he has committed two brutal murders.'

'Decidedly he must be a fiend. And you think that my friend, Michael Senostris, is likely to be associated with a ruffian like that? You certainly do not know Senostris, Sir Leonard. Who is this man?'

'His name is Ictinos – Stanislaus Ictinos!'

At once Nikoleff was on his feet staring down at his visitor, his eyes and mouth wide open with amazement, Wallace eyed him curiously.

'Then you do know him?' he observed.

'Know him! Of course I know him. He also is a friend of mine. In fact only recently has he come from Greece with his daughter to spend Christmas with me. They are in this house now.'

In his turn Sir Leonard was on his feet.

'In this house!' he repeated.

'Certainly. They are my guests. I will present them to you, if you care to meet them, but I fear you must be labouring under some great misapprehension.' He took up a house telephone, and dialled a number. 'Is that you, my dear Stanislaus?' he asked presently. 'I hope you have slept well. Has your daughter, Thalia, risen yet? Good. There is a friend with me who is anxious to meet you both. May I bring him to your drawing room and present him? Thank you.' He put down the receiver and turned to Wallace. 'Will you come with me, Sir Leonard?'

They left the study, and ascended the great wide staircase to the first floor. Sir Peter knocked on a door, a voice bade them enter, and a moment later they stood in a beautifully furnished drawing room, confronting a dark-visaged man of about forty and a pretty girl in her early teens. Sir Leonard had never seen either before.

'Allow me to introduce you,' came in Sir Peter's quiet tones. 'Mr and Miss Ictinos – Sir Leonard Wallace.' Sir Leonard shook hands with the man, bowed to the girl who dropped him a graceful curtsy. 'Sir Leonard was of the impression that one of his assistants had met you,' went on Sir Peter, 'but I hardly see how that could be possible.'

'I also have seen the people of whom I spoke,' remarked Wallace. 'Did I not convey that to your mind?'

Sir Peter raised his eyebrows.

'No,' he replied; 'I understood from what you said that only your assistant had met them. This lady and gentleman are not they?'

Wallace smiled, and shook his head.

'Not at all,' he demurred. 'My – er – friends were certainly of the same name, but there the resemblance ends.'

The man laughed, displaying a row of white, even teeth.

'In Greece,' he remarked, speaking the English language with difficulty, 'the name Ictinos are not rare, but your friends would not the first names have the same. My first name Stanislaus, my daughter her first name Thalia.'

'The people of whom I am speaking,' returned Wallace quietly, 'had both their initial names and surname identical with yours.'

'How extraordinary!' exclaimed Sir Peter.

'It is most strange,' agreed the second Stanislaus Ictinos.

Wallace and his host remained there talking for a few minutes, and they all partook of coffee together, after which the former declared that he must depart. Sir Peter accompanied him down the stairs, and took leave of him at the front door.

'It is obvious that the people you told me about knew of my friends, and took their names for some reason of their own,' remarked the financier, 'or else you have been misinformed.'

'I have not been misinformed,' Wallace told him. 'Although I have not actually spoken to them, I have been in close proximity to them, and know they are passing under those names.'

'And you are certain they were going to the *Electra*?'

'Positive.'

'The whole business is very strange,' commented Sir Peter, 'but I cannot think that Senostris can be mixed up with them. It is beyond credence. I thought that Michael was sailing the Mediterranean with a party of friends, but your information rather suggests that the *Electra* is in England. If that is so, why don't you pay a visit to her?'

'That is exactly what I intend to do,' Wallace assured him. 'Goodbye, Sir Peter. I hope I haven't caused you any inconvenience by a visit at this hour?'

'Not at all,' was the courteous reply. 'I wish I could have been of some real assistance to you. By the way,' he added, as Wallace was about to leave, 'if you know that this scoundrel, who calls himself Stanislaus Ictinos, has committed a murder, why don't you have him arrested?'

'There is something I want from him, or from his partner, first,' was the reply, spoken in a resolute voice.

'I see,' nodded Sir Peter. 'You have my best wishes for your success.'

As his car threaded its way through the traffic on the way back to Whitehall, Wallace sat back in his seat, and pondered the fresh problem that confronted him. He felt sure it was not merely a coincidence that the names of Sir Peter's friends and those of the man and woman he had so recently seen in the house on the Isle of Sheppey were identical. The fellow whom Cousins called the gorilla-man, and his daughter, must have adopted the names for some reason of their own. Various conjectures occurred to him, but were not suggestive of a very satisfactory solution. He was still thinking deeply, when the car drew up outside headquarters, and Johnson had been standing holding open the door for some seconds before he rose from his seat, and alighted.

He found that the examination of Farrell and the dwarf was still proceeding. Entering Major Brien's room, he stood listening for some minutes, while his deputy and Cousins strove by every means in their power to get the dwarf to talk. But where before he had screamed with rage and hurled maledictions at his captors, he now stood sullen and silent, hanging his head, and looking the picture of dejection. He answered not a word to the patient questions put to him, whether they were in English or Greek; it was as though he did not hear. Brien cast a despairing eye in the direction of Sir Leonard, and the latter thereupon took a hand in the proceedings, but it was fruitless.

'Take him away,' directed Wallace at last. 'Farrell can stay. I'll send him along to you,' he added to Inspector Graham, 'when I have finished with him, or at any rate let you know what I've done with him.'

'The CID are anxious to have him, sir,' the police officer informed him.

'Well, they'll have to wait,' retorted Wallace. 'He's my prisoner, and they can't prefer any charges against him until I've finished with him. Give them my compliments, and tell them that.'

Inspector Graham smiled.

'Very well, sir. I'll leave a couple of men outside in the corridor for him.'

'You needn't do that. I'll see that he reaches you all right.'

The inspector saluted, and retired, taking with him his men and Paul the dwarf. Wallace studied the sheet of paper on which Brien had jotted down the answers Farrell had given to his and Cousins' questions. There was little there that was not already known to him, certainly nothing of great interest.

'Have you kept anything back?' asked Sir Leonard, eyeing the crook sternly.

'Nothing, sir,' replied the latter earnestly. 'I've told everything I know.'

'You have never been on the *Electra* or met the partner Ictinos speaks about?'

'Never, sir.'

'Haven't you even heard his name?'

'No, sir. The guv'nor always kept that a dead secret from all of us. Even Hepburn didn't know it, and he knows a great deal.'

'H'm!' Sir Leonard took the list of men serving the Greek from his pocket, and held it before the other's eyes. 'These apparently,' he said, 'are the names of men in the organisation. It's in English, so you can read it. There are eighteen names there, but apart from yours and those of Hepburn, Danson, Moropos and Ibsen, I have not heard of them. Where are they?'

Farrell took the list, and studied it carefully. A scowl crossed his face as he noticed the details concerning the crimes, which were written after most of the names. A muttered oath escaped him.

'These two,' he pointed out, 'are in Rome—'

'Just a minute. Make a note of it, will you, Cousins?' The little man drew up a sheet of paper, and commenced to write. 'Go on, Farrell. Those are in Rome—'

'These three are in Paris, these in Berlin, this one in Moscow, these two in Washington, I don't know where this one is. Zinescu, the name without any crimes against it, is the dwarf, Paul. He was a sort of servant to the guv'nor. The other is in England.'

'Where?'

'He was at Southampton yesterday. He is the fellow who had orders to shoot you when you came off the boat.'

'Ah!' exclaimed Sir Leonard softly, 'so his name was Villinoff, was it? I shall remember that. It sounds more like the name of a Russian than a Maltese, Bill,' he added.

'He certainly looked like a Maltese,' grunted Brien.

'He's a Bulgarian, sir,' Farrell told them.

'So we're both wrong,' commented Wallace. He looked through the list Cousins had made. 'Quite an espionage system apparently,' he remarked. 'Italians in Italy, Frenchmen in France, Germans in Berlin, etcetera – England alone has a cosmopolitan crowd, probably because the headquarters of Ictinos are, or were, here.'

'Whenever the guv'nor wanted a job done,' volunteered Farrell, 'Hepburn used to be sent to the country where it was to take place. The blokes on the spot would give him the low-down on routine, details of the safe to be cracked, and that sort of thing. Then Hepburn would spend a long time studying the fellow he was going to impersonate, learning all about his habits, his walk, and getting near him to hear him speak. When he was sure he had studied all that was necessary, Danson would join him. Hepburn would make him up like some other official, and the job would be done.'

'Very interesting,' murmured Wallace. 'I gathered Damson was the safe-breaker from the details of his crimes. He seems to be wanted for a lot, including the murder of a policeman who tried to arrest him. Hepburn must be a linguist to be able to carry out impersonations in so many countries.'

'He speaks a hell of a lot of languages,' was Farrell's emphatic reply. 'The guv'nor couldn't do without him, and Hepburn knows it. That bloke seems to be able to do anything. Can't think what he wanted to go and ruin his life for by croaking the husband of a girl he was sweet on.'

A slight smile appeared on Wallace's face. He studied the ex-pugilist carefully for some minutes; then, apparently making up his mind, he leant forward.

'Would you like to earn the King's pardon, Farrell?' he asked.

The man's eyes opened wide, a look of hope began to dawn on his face.

'Would I!' he repeated. 'Just give me the chance and see. I'd go straight for the rest of my life, and—'

'Not so fast, my man; I'm not asking you for any promises regarding your future life. If you were pardoned, with the list of crimes against your name you have collected, and went wrong again, you'd be the biggest fool in Christendom, but that would be your pidgin, not mine. I'll guarantee to obtain a pardon for you under certain conditions, and they won't be easy. You'll have to work jolly hard for it, and carry your life in your hands. What do you say?'

'I'd do anything that gave me a chance to get clear,' was the reply.

'Well, tonight I want you to join your late companions on the *Electra*. I don't care how you reach her; swim if you like. I'll see that you are taken down to Rochester. Once on board, you can tell some tale about being captured with Paul and breaking away. Say you hid up all day today, and dare not get out to her until after dark. Of course you'll be thoroughly pumped about Cousins and me, but I'll put you wise about what you're to say before you go. Once back with them, you will do your utmost to find out all their plans, discover where certain documents I badly want are, and keep me posted about all other developments. Do you agree?'

Farrell's face had paled as Sir Leonard spoke.

'You mean you want me to turn stool pigeon?' he said slowly.

'Exactly; but I don't see what there is to hesitate about, if you're honest in your statement that you want to wipe out the past. You've been a traitor to your country, apart from your other crimes, and it's the only way you can eradicate that stain. And it isn't as though you are betraying your former comrades. We know who they are and enough about them already without wanting to make a collection of further charges to lay against them.'

Farrell looked him in the eyes.

'I'll do it, sir,' he declared.

'Good. But remember; you'll be taking a tremendous risk. You know as well as I that if Ictinos catches you spying, or suspects you in any way, your number will be up.'

The ex-pugilist nodded.

'Don't I know it,' he remarked grimly, 'but I'll chance that. You can be sure that I'll be careful. And about that pardon, sir; you will get it for me, if I satisfy you?'

'You can rely upon me,' Wallace assured him. 'I'll see you again this evening, and give you all your instructions. Until then you'll stay in this building; it will be safer than risking the possibility of being seen by somebody antagonistic to us. There is a room where we keep visitors like you, Farrell, but you'll be given your meals, have papers to read, and generally be well looked after. You'll find it much better than a cell at Scotland Yard. Take him down below, Cousins, will you?'

When the two had departed, Major Brien looked rather dubiously at his friend.

'You're taking a big risk, aren't you?' he queried.

Wallace shook his head.

'No,' he replied; 'what harm will it do us if he does tell Ictinos that I've sent him. The fellow already knows we're on his track, and Farrell cannot give him any information about us or our plans of any value.'

'But between them they may set a trap.'

'Then we'll fall into it gracefully, Bill. Have you forgotten that you and I were not born yesterday? As a matter of fact, I believe Farrell is genuine in his desire to reform. The only thing I'm anxious about is that Ictinos may ferret out that he's working for us, and have him murdered.'

Stevenson, Wallace's confidential clerk, knocked and entered the room.

'A message for you, sir, from Rochester,' he informed Sir Leonard. 'The *Electra* sailed early this morning – destination unknown.'

Brien looked dismayed, but Wallace did not show any particular concern.

'That's a nuisance,' was his only comment.

'There's also a report from Mr Cartright, sir,' added the clerk. 'He and his assistants have searched the house on the Island of Sheppey thoroughly, including the grounds and the underground passage, and have found nothing whatever of importance.'

'I thought they wouldn't. Recall them to London, Stevenson; the police will be taking possession today.'

The clerk departed noiselessly.

'What are you going to do now?' asked Brien.

'You, my lad, will set to work to find out where the *Electra* is. That shouldn't cause your locks to get any scantier. I am going to keep an appointment for Ictinos, which it is probable he will break.'

'Keep an appointment for Ictinos! What the devil are you talking about?'

'He was meeting the representative of the Russian government to discuss the purchase of the stolen plans today at three o'clock. As he no longer has those plans, and must realise that I have discovered the arrangement, the chances are he will not turn up.

On the other hand, he may alter the meeting for some other place, for he still has something left to offer. Whether he does or not, I will visit the Russian emissary. And in order that I may not miss them, I will make arrangements for the gentleman to be closely shadowed from now on. His name is Moskevin, and he is staying at the Savoy.'

'What about Farrell? He won't be able to get on the *Electra* now.'

'He might; you never can tell.'

He left the room, and walked along the corridor to his own office.

'I begin to see daylight,' he murmured to himself. 'It is quite possible, after all, that Ictinos will keep his appointment, though not in the same locality as was first arranged.'

CHAPTER FOURTEEN

Ictinos Meets Wallace Face-to-Face

Back in his own room, Sir Leonard was engaged very busily for a considerable period. Most of the little buttons under the ledge of his desk were pressed at one time or another during the course of the next hour, bringing to him men from various departments to whom he gave careful instructions. He spoke several times on private telephone lines, once at great length. Two or three reference books, taken from the large number packed on the shelves, were carried to his desk, where he opened them and studied certain pages. He became so engrossed that, when calls from the Air Ministry and War Office were put through, and he discovered that they were merely from high but enthusiastic officials, who desired to congratulate and thank him for his success in preserving the secrets of the Masterson monoplane and Wentworth gun, he was abrupt, almost sharp, in his replies. Even when the Foreign Secretary himself spoke on the private line running direct between his room and Sir Leonard's office, he listened impatiently, and rang off at the earliest possible moment. He had no desire to listen to a laudatory speech delivered by a statesman, who was noted for his command of the English language and little else. Ictinos and his organisation had been checkmated in the attempt to sell British military secrets and, as far as Wallace was concerned, that was the end of that part of the affair. But he had pledged his word to Monsieur Damien to do his utmost to save France from the outrageous threat of blackmail overshadowing her. He was also determined to break up the organisation which was proving a menace to so many countries, and had promised himself a private settlement with Ictinos. He had no time or desire, therefore, to spend the morning receiving compliments.

It was nearing one o'clock when he sent for the papers he had brought away from the house on the Isle of Sheppey. The copies of the plans of the Masterson monoplane and the Wentworth gun were placed in sealed packets, and sent by special messenger to be delivered into the hands respectively of the Air Marshal and Chief of Staff. From the remaining documents Wallace took several sheets of foolscap pinned neatly together, the remainder he sent back to be locked up. Rapidly he made copious notes from the pages before him in a small leather-bound book with a lock attached, putting it away in his own private safe when he had finished. The sheets of foolscap he folded, and placed in the inside pocket of his jacket. Brien entered the room as he was preparing to go.

'I say, Leonard,' he proclaimed, 'there's a deuced queer sequel to the sailing of the *Electra*.'

'Oh, what's that?'

'She left Rochester without giving any destination, as you know. At nine she anchored off Gravesend, remaining there until eleven, when she sailed. Since then not a sign of her has been seen. She's just disappeared.'

Sir Leonard had been washing his hand. He came now from the little anteroom drying them, and whistling softly to himself.

'That gives support to my suspicion,' he observed.

'What suspicion?'

'Never mind now. It's only very hazy at the moment.'

'What can have become of the *Electra*? She can't have sunk – report says that the storm has quite abated. And even if Ictinos and company had decided to scuttle her, something or somebody would have spotted her. You can't sink ships in a busy place like the Thames without causing comment.'

Wallace laughed.

'Why should they want to scuttle her?' he asked. 'It's not reasonable to destroy something that is providing one with shelter.'

'You don't seem very perturbed about her disappearance.'

'I'm not. It is fairly obvious that for some reason or other her identity has been altered.'

'You mean that she has been disguised?'

'Exactly.'

'But could that be done without the transformation being observed?'

'Yes; especially if there were already means on board for alterations to be made. She would probably slink into some quiet inlet, and in less than no time might have another funnel, an extra mast, different shaped stern or bows and, of course, a new name. They might even paint her another colour, but that would be a lengthy business, and there are few inlets along that coast where it could be done without someone observing the process sooner or later.'

Brien thoughtfully regarded his companion.

'There is only one reason that occurs to me why she should be disguised,' he decided, 'and that is that, somehow or other, Ictinos suspects that we know all about the *Electra*.'

'You're very probably right,' smiled Sir Leonard. 'Help me on with my overcoat, please.'

Brien obliged.

'It's going to be a devil of a job to find her, if you're right,' he grunted. 'Why, she might be disguised as anything – a tramp or—'

'Or an Atlantic liner,' Wallace finished for him.

'Don't be an ass! But you see what I mean?'

'Yes, Billy, I see what you mean. You're quite right; it will be a difficult job, if we have to organise a search for a boat when we have no idea what she looks like. But I trust that won't be necessary. I am hoping that we shall be taken down to her without trouble.'

'What's the notion?'

'I'm not sure yet, but I'll tell you when I am. At any rate, I have a feeling that the final settlement between us and Ictinos and co. will take place on or near the *Electra*.'

He did not return to his office after lunch, but sat in his study at home writing letters, occasionally glancing at the clock on the desk before him. It was getting on towards three when the telephone bell rang. Taking off the receiver, he gave his name, listening with a slight smile to the information transmitted to him over the wire.

'Splendid!' he remarked at length. 'A pastry cook's shop close to the Camden Town station, you said? Right; I'll soon be there.'

Two or three minutes later his car, with Johnson at the wheel, and Batty, his personal servant, sitting by the driver's side, was on its way along Shaftesbury Avenue. It turned up Tottenham Court Road, was able to increase its speed along the Hampstead Road and

Mornington Crescent, eventually coming to a stop near Camden Town underground station. Sir Leonard quickly stepped out.

'If I'm not back in a quarter of an hour,' he said to Batty and Johnson, 'come and find me.'

'Aye, aye, sir,' replied the ex-sailor, taking out an enormous watch, and fixing his eyes on it.

'There's a clock on the dashboard,' Johnson reminded him.

'I prefer me own,' retorted Batty. 'I've carried it aboard, man and boy, for thirty years, and it's never gone adrift once.'

Sir Leonard had walked on towards a tiny confectioner's establishment. He was a few yards from it, when a neatly dressed man, with a small, well-trimmed moustache, passed slowly by.

'He's in the room behind the shop, sir,' he whispered.

Wallace nodded almost imperceptibly. Turning into the shop, he walked straight towards the door of the inner room.

'Hi!' cried a man, standing behind the counter. 'Vere are you going?'

Sir Leonard ignored him, opened the door, stepped through, and closed it quickly behind him. Exclamations of astonishment greeted him from two men sitting opposite each other at a rickety table covered by a dirty cloth. They both looked out of place in that small dingy apartment. One, a sallow, thin-faced man, wearing pince-nez, was dressed in correct morning garb, his silk hat resting on the table by his side; the other, a bearded individual with tortoiseshell glasses, was clothed in a neat grey lounge suit, but there was no mistaking the great head and shoulders, the cold, slate-blue eyes and broad forehead. It was Stanislaus Ictinos. He sprang to his feet, his right hand going ominously to his coat pocket.

'What is this?' he demanded in a deep, threatening voice. 'Who are you?'

Sir Leonard noted with a certain feeling of pleasure that his face had paled.

'I have reason to believe that you know me by sight, Stanislaus Ictinos,' he observed quietly. 'Take your hand away from that pocket, and sit down. Before you could draw a revolver or a knife, or whatever it happens to be, your wrist would be shattered. I'm a fairly useful shot, as perhaps your daughter observed quite recently.'

Slowly the Greek sank back into his chair. Sir Leonard heard the door opening behind him; drew to one side in order that he could see the newcomer as well as keeping an eye on the men at the table. It was the shopkeeper.

'He came in too quick for me to stop him,' he told Ictinos in trembling tones. 'Vill I throw him out?'

Sir Leonard smiled at the idea of the fellow attempting to throw him out. He was an undersized, rat-like individual who looked a thorough weakling.

'Get out yourself, and stay out,' commanded the Chief of the Secret Service; 'and I warn you, if you try any tricks you'll find yourself in difficulties. There are several men outside awaiting my return.' The fellow slunk out and, still facing the others, Wallace locked the door behind him. 'We do not want to be interrupted,' he observed, walking across to another door on the opposite side of the room, and fastening that. 'Now we can talk in peace.'

He sat down at the end of the table. The thin-faced man had not uttered a word since his initial cry of surprise at Wallace's entrance. Now he leant on the table, and fixed his eyes on the intruder.

'What is the meaning of this?' he asked in excellent English. 'Who are you, sir?'

'I am the head of the British Intelligence Service,' Sir Leonard told him, 'and I am here to warn you, Monsieur Moskevin, that you are running a grave risk in coming to England, and negotiating with this man for the purchase of certain confidential documents.'

At the announcement of Sir Leonard's status, Moskevin gave a startled exclamation, his sallow face paled. He made one or two attempts to speak; then turned apprehensive eyes to Ictinos, as though leaving the responsibility to him. The latter sat clenching and unclenching his hands, a look of concentrated fury and hatred in his face. He said nothing, however, and the Russian was forced to speak.

'How did you know my name and hear of this meeting?' he asked weakly.

'I am not here to answer questions,' returned Wallace sharply, 'but I have no objection to telling you that certain letters and other documents came into my possession. I discovered that you were meeting this man today at three in your suite at the Savoy Hotel. As he knew that I had found out about that meeting, it was obvious the place, and perhaps the time, would be altered. It was not a difficult matter to ascertain the new arrangement. You would not be altogether ignorant of methods adopted in such a case, since you were a little while ago Commissary of Police in Petrograd.'

'You are well informed, sir.'

'Very,' replied Sir Leonard drily.

The Russian seemed to have recovered his composure to a great extent.

'So you are the Sir Leonard Wallace I have heard so much about,' he observed. 'Your name is not popular in my country, sir.'

'It is not popular anywhere,' suddenly burst forth Ictinos. 'This man is a devil.'

'Perhaps he is,' returned the Russian sharply, 'but you, my

friend, have done badly to land me in a position of this nature. You should have taken precautions to guard against such a contretemps. What is your intention?' he added, turning to Wallace,

'First of all to show this fellow up,' was the reply. 'As he has dared to meet you, despite certain events that took place last night, let me inform you that he has nothing to sell to you. He is here to get money from you by false pretences if possible. The copies of the confidential plans which were offered to the highest bidder among certain governments, of which yours was one, were recovered by me last night. If he has told you he has them, he lies. Furthermore, Monsieur Moskevin, I have here full details of the proposed disposition of the Russian air force and armies corps in the event of mobilisation. They were offered by this man's organisation to my government, but I obtained them from their hiding place with the others.'

'So it *was* you,' snarled Ictinos.

'Have you only just gathered that? I remarked just now that your daughter recently had a demonstration of my skill with a revolver.' He turned back to the Russian emissary, who was glowering at the Greek opposite him. 'You see, monsieur – I suppose I really ought to call you Comrade – Moskevin, there is, or has been, a widespread conspiracy to steal confidential information from various nations and auction it – a pretty way of making money, you will agree, in which millions would be involved, and not only that, but powers rendered suspicious of and bitter towards each other. Behind it all is a mysterious figure, whom this man Ictinos calls his partner, a mysterious figure who is aiming, I think, to become dictator of Europe. In order that you may recognise Ictinos, if by some chance he escapes my net and goes to Russia, cast your eyes on him, and look well!'

Suddenly he leant forward, and tore off the Greek's false beard, displacing the glasses in the same movement. A great cry of rage broke from the big man. He sprang to his feet, but was checked by the revolver which had appeared with lightning-like swiftness in Sir Leonard's hand.

'Sit down, Ictinos,' snapped the latter.

It looked for a moment as though the Greek would defy him but, before the steel-grey eyes of the Englishman, his own slate-blue ones fell, and presently, with an oath, he resumed his seat.

'You see now,' went on Wallace to the Russian, 'Stanislaus Ictinos, conspirator and murderer, as he really is. Under the Official Secrets Act of this country, Monsieur Moskevin, I could have you arrested and tried with him, but I am not particularly anxious to see you sent to prison, while the time for my reckoning with him has not yet come, though it is approaching rapidly. You can go, therefore, and take this with you.' He removed from his pocket the folded sheets of foolscap, and threw them on the table. 'It will interest you, and probably not please you, to know that I have copied everything of importance.'

Moskevin picked up the package, opened it, and glanced through it. His face grew dark as thunder, and there was that in his eyes, as he shot a look at Ictinos, that boded ill for the Greek, if the latter ever fell into his power. Without a word he rose, and put on his overcoat. He walked to the door; then spoke.

'I have your permission to unlock the door?'

Sir Leonard nodded.

'If I were you,' he advised, 'I should return straight to the Savoy, pack my belongings, and leave England at the earliest possible moment.'

Moskevin bowed coldly, and went out. Wallace turned his eyes on the Greek.

'So we are alone – face-to-face, Stanislaus Ictinos,' he remarked softly. 'You heard me say that the time of my reckoning with you is not yet. Nothing would give me greater pleasure than to settle with you now, but I must wait. I'll tell you this, however, that I am going to get what I want, and then smash you and your gang without mercy.'

The Greek shrank back before the deadly menace in Sir Leonard's tone. Despite his great physique, like all bullies, he was a coward at heart. He had learnt to fear the name of Wallace without having previously come face-to-face with him; now personal contact made him fear this man the more. And the greater his fear, the greater his determination to destroy the Englishman, who was threatening to bring down all his cherished plans like a house built of cards. As he sat there, inwardly he was seething like a volcano, but retained control of himself, knowing full well that he was at a disadvantage with this quick-thinking, quick-moving man. He wondered why Wallace did not have him arrested then and there – not that he would have succeeded, for Ictinos would die rather than that should happen; besides, there was a method of getting away from that house without appearing in the road, which should render his escape certain. As he remembered that fact his courage revived. He resolved to try the pose of a much-abused and misunderstood person.

'Why is it you speak to me like this?' he asked in unctuous tones. 'It sounds as though you hate me. Why is that?'

Sir Leonard regarded him, very much as he might have eyed a particularly loathsome reptile.

'During my career,' he announced, 'I have had the misfortune to meet some pretty vile specimens of humanity, but few as thoroughly foul as you, and I warn you now that I intend having no mercy on you. Since I arrived in Southampton yesterday morning I have received proof after proof of your utter brutality. You're not a man but a fiend. I am not holding anything particularly against you because you attempted to have me murdered, but your callousness in endangering the lives of two women and a child in your efforts to get me, the cold-blooded manner in which you shot one of my assistants and caused a motor smash near Sheppey bridge, and one or two other acts of yours, have made me resolve not to rest until either I see your body lying dead at my feet or know you are safe in the hands of the hangman. You have tried your utmost to finish me, Ictinos, but you have failed, and you will continue to fail, but I won't. I may let you go today, but before long – it may be tomorrow, the next day, a week hence – sooner or later you'll pay your price to the very last farthing.'

By the time he had finished, the Greek's face had turned a dirty yellow colour, fear showed from his eyes. He made a feeble attempt to continue his bluff.

'You are mistaken,' he bleated in unusually high tones for him. 'Why should I want to have you killed? There has been no attempt on my part to—'

'Be quiet!' snapped the Englishman. 'Lies won't help you. Have you already forgotten what Mr Cousins saw; what you told him? In your astounding self-conceit you have said enough to convict yourself a dozen times over. I myself heard you describe how you had caused the disaster on the bridge; heard you browbeating the bunch of ruffians you employ, because they had been unable to carry out your orders regarding me.'

Ictinos managed to pull himself together.

'What I told the estimable Mr Cousins, and what you say you heard,' he had the audacity to declare, 'was just foolishness. It meant nothing. If I was all you say about me, why is it I have not taken the opportunity you give me of killing you here now?'

Wallace smiled cynically.

'Are you trying to be humorous?' he demanded. 'One of the reasons why you dare not molest me is that you know I have men outside; the other is here.' He indicated the revolver in his hand. 'You are a brave man, Ictinos, only when your prospective victim is unarmed or unsuspecting, and your cut-throats are within call.'

There came the sound of voices from the direction of the shop, the connecting door flew open, and Johnson and Batty walked in, followed by the volubly protesting confectioner. The ex-sailor regarded him with an impatient frown.

'Look 'ere, Alphonso,' he observed, 'we're 'ere under orders, so sheer off, an' find another anchorage.'

The fellow continued his protests, but showed no signs of going. Batty, therefore, screwed him round by his hair, administered a well-placed kick, which sent him back into the shop rather abruptly, and closed the door.

'Come aboard, sir,' announced the valet, 'a quarter of an hour 'aving passed since you entered this 'ere building.'

'It's all right, Batty; I was just about to rejoin you.' He was turning away, when an idea occurred to him. 'Go through this man's pockets, both of you. We may find something interesting in them.'

His face now black with anger, the Greek sprang to his feet.

'You will not touch me,' he roared. 'Stand back!'

But Sir Leonard's revolver quickly cowed him into submission. Johnson and Batty seemed to enjoy their job, performing it with thoroughness and celerity. There was not a great deal in his pockets – a case full of banknotes, some loose change, a few innocuous letters and papers, a Browning automatic, a stiletto in a sheath, and a long envelope containing diagrams and memoranda. Wallace studied the latter, and whistled softly to himself. Presently he looked across at Ictinos.

'Having lost the real thing,' he commented, 'you thought you'd fake plans from what you remembered of the others, and sell those to Moskevin. There's no limit to your roguery apparently. But you've made at least one glaring mistake in each of these, which the Russian would have been bound to spot. It would have been interesting to know what he would have said – nothing polite I should imagine. Perhaps it would have ended in your adding his name to your list of victims.' The Greek made no reply, and Wallace went on. 'Tomorrow you have an appointment with the German ambassador. I intend visiting him after leaving here. In the circumstances it might be safer for you, if you refrained from keeping your engagement; that is, if you are then in a position to keep it.'

Ictinos growled something unintelligible.

Batty was examining the stiletto with an air of great interest.

'What shall I do with this 'ere toothpick, sir?' he asked.

'Take charge of it, and the automatic as well. Give him back the pocketbook and the letters.'

Sir Leonard returned the diagrams and memoranda to their envelope, which he put in his own pocket.

'You have not the right to take from me my weapons,' protested Ictinos. 'They are my property.'

'In this country it is illegal to carry weapons without a permit. I am possibly saving you from arrest and prosecution.'

'That would be a great grief to you,' sneered the Greek.

'Very great indeed at the moment,' replied Sir Leonard calmly.

'I prefer to wait until I have placed you in the dock myself with the certainty that you will be condemned to death for murder.' He walked to the door, waited until Johnson and Batty had gone through; then turned back to the man whose baleful blue eyes were watching him with an intensity of hatred in them. 'You heard what I had to say to you, Ictinos. Remember it! In a short while you and I will meet again, and you will not be allowed to get away then. It will be your finish.'

He strode out, leaving the cursing Greek to call angrily and hastily to the shopkeeper. Outside Sir Leonard met the neatly dressed man who had told him where Ictinos and the Russian emissary were to be found.

'He'll be out presently,' he said, putting away his revolver. 'You've made all the preparations I suggested to have him followed?'

'Yes, sir.'

'He'll know he's being watched, and will be up to all kinds of dodges to give you and your men the slip. But he must not be lost sight of for a moment. It may be disastrous, if he succeeds in getting away.'

'He won't, sir,' the man from the Special Branch of New Scotland Yard assured him. 'We'll let him think he's shaken us off, as you directed, but some of us will hang on.'

Wallace nodded. The car came gliding up; he entered, and was driven away, just as a small crowd of Camden Townites – sensing with the amazing instinct of Londoners that something out of the usual was happening – began to collect. Ten minutes went by; then from a house in Park Street, a hundred yards from the pastry cook's establishment in which he had spent such an unpleasant quarter of an hour, emerged Stanislaus Ictinos. He had not troubled to replace the beard and glasses so rudely torn from his face by

Wallace, but the collar of his overcoat was turned up, and the brim of his soft hat pulled well down. Looking cautiously round, he set off walking briskly towards Albany Street. Two or three taxis passed by, but he ignored them, eventually signalling to one coming from the opposite direction. Sitting well back in its interior, he allowed a slow smile of satisfaction to cross his face. That devil Wallace would have difficulty in finding him now. He had not known that there was a very convenient secret exit from the pastry cook's establishment, by which it was possible to cross several back yards, and make one's way through a house into Park Street. Wallace's agents, hanging about in the vicinity of the confectioner's – from the windows of an upper room, Ictinos had noticed two or three loungers who were quite possibly Secret Service men waiting to trail him – would have a long and bitterly cold vigil. A deep chuckle broke from the gorilla-like Greek. He lit a cigar, began to smoke appreciatively. Gradually the expression of venomous hatred returned to his face, as he thought of the Englishman who, in one day, had so disagreeably upset his plans; and through his mind passed schemes of vengeance. At Oxford Circus he dismissed his taxi, and took another; at Cannon Street Station he repeated the performance. He felt perfectly assured that he had got away from Park Street unobserved, but he was not running any risks. All the time his thoughts were fixed firmly, malevolently on Wallace.

'Not my finish, my friend, but yours,' he muttered once, through clenched teeth. 'Whatever happens you must be destroyed – and without delay.'

CHAPTER FIFTEEN

Major Brien is Promised an Outing

Sir Leonard drove to the German Embassy after leaving Ictinos. He was fortunate in finding the Ambassador at home, and had ten minutes interview with that gentleman, which opened the latter's eyes considerably. It left him also feeling a trifle resentful that his country should entrust a task to him which brought an unwelcome visit from a stern, grey-eyed Englishman who, though exceedingly polite, spoke caustically and to the point.

On returning to his office, Sir Leonard found Brien waiting for him, eager to know how he had fared. He related the events of the afternoon to his deputy, afterwards, at the latter's request, giving him an account of his adventures of the previous night on the Isle of Sheppey. Brien listened entranced, occasionally giving vent to an exclamation of amazement or horror, but not otherwise interrupting.

'Good Gad!' he cried at the end, 'what a fiend this bloke Ictinos appears to be. Seems to me, Leonard my boy, he's somewhat the same *jat* as our old friends Levinsky and Dorin.'

Wallace smiled reminiscently.

'You've just about hit it,' he agreed. 'He's the same cold-blooded, callous kind. In addition, from the look of him, I should say he has enormous physical strength, although I don't think he has much courage. But brutes of his rotten type seldom have.'

'Are you quite sure he won't get away from the men you've got watching him?'

'As sure as I can be of anything.' He leant back in his chair, puffing contentedly at his pipe. 'I think we ought to be able to clean up this business in a couple of days, and have a peaceful Christmas after all. At one time I feared that there would be another wash-out this year. Do you realise that it's four years since we have had one of our old-time Christmases in Hampshire; that is with you and Phyllis, Cecil and Dorothy, and all the children complete? Last year I was in Syria, the year before in Egypt, the year before that Cecil was stationed in Palestine and I was in China. I think I'm due for a Yuletide at home and,' he added a trifle wistfully, 'I hope I get it.'

'It seems to me a pity you didn't collect Ictinos today,' ventured Brien. 'After all you've done the main job and, if he'd been handed over to the police for trial, there'd really be nothing to worry about, and Christmas would have been safe. With the information we could have given to Scotland Yard, they wouldn't have had much difficulty in laying the rest of the gang by the heels. Besides, while that man's at liberty, your life's in hourly danger.'

Wallace shrugged his shoulders.

'I pledged my word to Damien,' he reminded the other, 'and I'm going to keep it. If I had had Ictinos arrested, the partner – the fellow who, I am convinced, really is at the head of the organisation – would lie low for a time; then commence operations from a totally different direction, probably somewhere where it would be impossible to get at him. In his hands, I believe, are the documents which are so vital to France, and it is only through Ictinos that I can reach him; that is, get a grip on him to enable me to unmask him and obtain the plans.'

'Ah, well! You know best, but, for Heaven's sake, be careful. It would be a fat lot of good spending Christmas at home as a corpse, wouldn't it?'

'Billy, you're crude. I have no intention of spending Christmas at home or anywhere else as a corpse. Have you heard from Shannon?'

'Yes,' nodded Brien; 'he'll be in Croydon at eight.'

'Splendid. That's jolly good going.'

'Carter arrived at two, full of beans as usual. It's topping to have the old hands around when there's an emergency like this on.'

'How's Maddison?'

'The operation was successful, and he's regained consciousness. It'll be a long time before he's in harness again of course, but Reynolds will be about in a few weeks. Cunliffe's body has been taken to his home in Twickenham.'

'Poor Cunliffe.'

The two of them became quiet, almost unconsciously paying that silent tribute to the dead which the thoughtful sympathy of His Majesty the King had originated. Suddenly a telephone bell rang, and Sir Leonard took up the receiver of one of the instruments on his desk.

'Yes, put him through,' he directed.

Thereafter he listened attentively for some time, eventually expressing his satisfaction, and asking for further information to be phoned to him as soon as possible. He replaced the receiver, and regarded his companion with a smile.

'From Seymour of the SB,' he announced. 'He is in charge of the men I had out this afternoon to track Ictinos. It appears that there was a secret way out of the confectioner's shop where I met him – I thought there might be. He emerged in Park Street about a hundred yards away and, after ignoring several taxis he might have taken, engaged one going in the opposite direction, and drove to Oxford Circus. There he changed into another, and went to Cannon Street, where he repeated the process. He is now at Finsbury Park having tea in a small restaurant.'

'He seems to be touring London,' commented Brien. 'How was he picked up, if he used a secret exit? Did Seymour know of its existence?'

'No,' smiled Wallace, 'but I arranged with him to have twenty taxis at his command, driven by men from the Yard of course. When he found where Moskevin went – he followed him from the Savoy – he had the twenty taxis patrolling the streets in the neighbourhood, and the police had orders to divert all others. Ictinos naturally took one, probably thinking he had bamboozled our fellows; several of the others followed at discreet intervals, one of them having picked up Seymour. When the Greek changed at Oxford Circus and Cannon Street, things were manoeuvred in such a manner that he merely left one of our cars to enter another. Now he is in a teashop at Finsbury Park almost opposite a taxi rank, and the first three cabs on the rank are in charge of Seymour's men. If he is lost trace of after this, I shall almost be inclined to eat my hat.'

Brien chuckled his approval.

'Poor old Ictinos,' he commented. 'It almost seems a shame,

when he has taken such trouble to put us off the scent, to keep hanging on to him like that.'

'I only hope he leads us to the *Electra* or wherever his new headquarters is. We'll raid tonight if possible; there is nothing like striking while the iron is hot, so to speak. Will you give instructions for Cousins, Carter, Hill and Cartright to stand by, and leave a message for Shannon to the same effect?'

Brien nodded.

'What are you going to do with Farrell?' he asked.

'Take him with us. He might come in useful; anyway I want to give him the chance I promised him, if I can.' He pressed one of the buttons under the ledge of his desk. His clerk entered almost immediately. 'I am going home, Stevenson,' he informed the man; 'see that all telephone calls for me personally are switched on to my house, and get in touch with me immediately, if anything important turns up.'

'Very well, sir.'

The clerk was turning away, when Brien gave him the orders to be conveyed to Cousins, Cartright, Carter and Hill, and also Shannon when the latter arrived.

'And now, Bill,' suggested Wallace, 'come home with me, and have a spot of tea. You can also help me convey the news to Molly that I shall probably be out all night.'

'Coward!' jeered his friend. 'I say,' he added anxiously, 'you're taking me with you, aren't you? You said—'

'I know what I said, my lad, and if you're good you shall come. It'll be a little outing for our fair-haired boy. But, for the love of Mike, don't stop a bullet – what on earth would the office staff do, if you deserted them in that cavalier fashion?'

'It's a consolation to know that I would be missed, if an

unpleasant accident of that nature happened,' murmured Brien drily. 'I have my uses then.'

'Yes, Bill, you have your uses. Come along.'

'Those kind words almost overwhelm me,' observed the tall, fair-haired man as he accompanied his friend to the lift. 'Sometimes I have been inclined to believe that I am but an amorphous soul.'

Sir Leonard chuckled.

'What you want, Billy,' he declared, 'is a delicately toasted muffin nicely buttered, and a cup of China tea.'

'But look here, Leonard,' demanded Major Brien, as they stepped out of the lift on the ground floor, 'when on earth are you going to get any sleep? You were up all last night, and look as though you're going to be up all this. You can't carry on like that for long.'

'When there are no more muffins to eat, and you've been cleared off the premises,' replied Wallace, 'I'll have an hour or so – perhaps.'

'M'm,' muttered Brien *sotto voce*, 'perhaps!'

On arrival at his house in Piccadilly, Sir Leonard was told that his wife was out shopping. He and Major Brien, therefore, had tea together, after which the latter departed for his own home. Wallace went to his bedroom and, without troubling to remove much clothing, lay down. He suddenly discovered that he was feeling very tired, and, before long, fell fast asleep. Returning from her shopping expedition nearly two hours later, Lady Wallace peeped into the room, but took care not to disturb him. However, she had hardly tiptoed quietly away before the telephone – he had had it connected through to the instrument in his bedroom – rang. At once he was awake, all his faculties about him, and lifted the receiver to his ear. It was Seymour of the Special Branch.

'I am speaking to you from Shifton, sir,' he announced.

'Where is that?' queried Sir Leonard. 'I don't think I have ever heard the name before.'

'It is a tiny village about three miles beyond Tilbury, the only place in this neighbourhood which seems to possess a telephone.'

Sir Leonard whistled softly to himself.

'How did you get there?' he replied.

'The Greek brought us down here, sir, or rather,' he added with a little chuckle, 'we brought him, on his instructions, of course. When he left the teashop at Finsbury Park, he again took one of our taxis, and drove to Bethnal Green. There he changed once more, walking some distance before he entered another car, but we took care that it was one of ours. He asked the driver to take him to Tilbury. There was not a great deal of traffic on the Tilbury road, but hadn't much fear that he would discover that his taxi was being followed. We didn't show headlights and, whenever it was possible, switched off the others also; besides we kept well in the background. At Tilbury he discharged the cab and, after looking round him ten minutes or thereabouts, as though he were waiting for somebody, strolled down to the docks. I shadowed him myself, Willingdon tracking me. He went to a deserted wharf, and signalled with a flash lamp. He was answered from the river, and soon afterwards a large motorboat ran alongside, and took him aboard.

'I thought we were going to be done, but luck was on our side – luck and Willingdon, I ought to say. Somehow in pushing off, the boat's propeller fouled a rope hanging over the side of the wharf. How such a thing happened, I can't say, but an idea occurred to Willingdon. He is a little slim fellow able to hide himself in places where a bigger man couldn't. He crept up to the boat and, while the crew were astern trying to find out what had happened, he slipped aboard, concealing himself in the bows. It took quite ten minutes before she was clear of the rope; then she headed down river.

'I went into the office of the dock superintendent, knowing that if Willingdon wasn't caught he'd phone me there. Sure enough, after I'd been waiting about an hour, he rang through from here. The motorboat, he told me, had gone to what seemed to be a little tramp steamer, lying in a secluded spot behind a small island at the mouth of a creek. When the launch was tied up, and her crew and the Greek had gone aboard, Willingdon shipped over the side, and swam ashore. It took him some time to find this village, but he eventually did. Directly I knew where he was, I joined him with another man, MacAlpine, who is now down on the shore of the creek keeping watch. Luckily it's a clear night, and the moon's nearly at the full, so he can see fairly well.'

'Smart work, Seymour,' approved Sir Leonard, when the inspector had concluded his report. 'Very smart work indeed. I shall have a word to say to Willingdon when I see him. By the way, I hope he is taking precautions after that swim of his. It must have been bitterly cold.'

Seymour was heard to laugh.

'He's one of those cranks who go swimming in the winter, sir, but his clothes have been dried in the inn here, and he's had some hot grog.'

'Good. Well, look here; I'll be down with half a dozen men about eleven, and we'll raid the steamer. It's possibly the yacht I want, disguised. Are there any boats handy that we can use to get aboard? If not we'll have to get the assistance of a police launch from Tilbury.'

'There are several boats hereabouts, sir. I ascertained that – one or two flat-bottomed affairs, and quite a number of dinghies.'

'That's splendid. Well, describe the place to me, and how one gets there.'

He listened attentively while Inspector Seymour carefully gave the necessary directions; then reiterating his intention of joining the other at eleven o'clock, and assuring himself that the inspector and his men would be able to get a meal, he rang off.

There was no longer any thought of repose in Sir Leonard's mind. His two hours' sleep had done him a world of good, and he felt thoroughly refreshed and fit for whatever the coming hours had in store. At dinner he broke the news to Molly that he would again be away during the best part of the night. She paled a little, and her hands clenched beneath the table, but made no comment, except to express the hope that he was not going into danger. He did his utmost to reassure her, adding that he hoped they would be able to go down to Hampshire the following day, and look forward to the happiest Christmas they had had for years. She brightened a little at that. Molly had not spent the festive season with her husband for some years, and she was almost desperately keen that duty would not call him away from her on this occasion. Invitations to spend Yuletide with them had been sent to her brother and his wife, Major and Mrs Brien and their children, and accepted, but the events that had taken place, since she and Sir Leonard had landed from the *Majestic*, had caused her to fear that, once again, she was about to be disappointed in one of her most cherished desires.

Brien arrived as she was taking coffee in the little drawing room she and her husband always used when alone in the evening – Sir Leonard had gone up to say goodnight to Adrian, and tuck him in his bed, a duty he delighted in performing whenever it was possible for him to do so. Molly made room for Brien on the couch on which she was sitting, and gave him a cup of coffee. He accepted it, regarding her somewhat doubtfully the while. She smiled up at him.

'I am not about to ask you where Leonard is going tonight,' she declared, 'so there's no reason for you to look scared. Are you going also?'

He nodded.

'I've been promised a little outing as a change from hard work,' he grinned. 'I deserve it, Molly, I assure you. Between you and me, I'm actually the hardest-worked man in the Intelligence Service.'

'Of course you are,' she agreed. 'Nobody else does any work really, I suppose?'

'Well, I wouldn't go as far as that,' he confided generously. 'Leonard and his little lot keep up their end, but it's an easy end compared with mine.'

'Oh, yeah!' exclaimed a voice from the door, and Wallace entered the room. 'How do you like my talkie accent?' he asked, helping himself to coffee.

'I think it's awful,' Brien told him candidly. 'Did you collect it in the States?'

'No, from Adrian. He has a great admiration for a gentleman of the name of Jack Oakie, who, he assures me, can say, "Oh, yeah" better than anybody else on the screen. What fairy tale was this fellow telling you, Molly,' he went on, 'when I came in?'

'It was no fairy tale,' asserted Brien stoutly. 'I was assuring your wife that I am the hardest-worked man in the service, which is a self-evident truth.'

'I feel inclined to say "Oh, yeah" again; it really is descriptive.'

He bent down towards Molly. 'Of course that is simply one of his many peculiarities, dear. He really does believe he is one of the world's workers – he doesn't realise that he is only in the office on sufferance.'

'I'll resign tomorrow,' declared the outraged Bill. 'Then,' he added with a sneer, 'we'll see what you can do without me.'

'How can you see, if you've resigned?'

'I have methods of obtaining information,' was the dark retort; 'besides, when the British Secret Service ceases to function, the whole world will know why. "Ah!" will be the comment, "that indefatigable worker, William Brien, no longer controls affairs. They cannot do without him; he is indispensable."'

'The King is dead – long live the King,' retorted Wallace.

Major Brien frowned.

'Leonard,' he observed, 'if I had not known you, and watched over you since you were a grubby little imp in a sailor suit, I would shake the dust of you off my feet, but, remembering our long and, at times, honourable association, and the fact that you cannot get on without me, I will continue to stand by you, in spite of your insults. Virtue is its own reward.'

'What a pity Mr Cousins isn't here,' smiled Molly. 'That is a heaven-sent opportunity for one of his poetical quotations.'

Thus half an hour passed in badinage, but Molly was not deceived. She realised that these two men, whom she had known since they were boys in the same cavalry regiment, who had dared so much and faced so much together, would do anything to prevent her from suffering anxiety or distress, were endeavouring to make it appear that the task they were undertaking that night was nothing out of the ordinary. She knew them both so well, that the more they jested, the more heavy became her heart. But she gave no sign of the apprehension which was beginning to steal over her, except that, when she bade her husband goodnight, there was just a suspicion of fear in her eyes as she smiled up at him. When they had departed, she went up to Adrian's room; stood for a few moments gently stroking the boy's hair. It was always a solace to her to go to her son, when the shadow of uneasiness and suspense regarding her husband was hanging oppressively round her.

Wallace and Brien drove separately to headquarters, as it would be necessary to use both cars. The latter invariably acted as his own chauffeur; Sir Leonard seldom did on account of the handicap of his arm, but Johnson would not be in the way. The Rolls-Royce was a seven-seater, Brien's car a five-seater Vauxhall; there was ample room, therefore, for the men they intended taking with them on their trip into Essex.

It was not until he was in his office that Wallace had an opportunity of imparting to his second-in-command the information he had received over the telephone from Inspector Seymour. Brien listened eagerly, commenting with approval on the action of Willingdon, which had enabled the hiding place of Ictinos and his gang to be discovered, thereby making the raid possible.

'Pretty intelligent fellow, that,' he commended. 'It was jolly quick-witted of him to do what he did. What about it, Leonard?'

Wallace smiled thoughtfully.

'It certainly looks as though he is the sort of man we want,' he nodded, 'especially as we have lost four during the last year.'

'Four!'

'Of course. Cunliffe made the fourth yesterday, poor beggar.'

Brien's teeth came together with a snap.

'I was forgetting him for the moment. Damn that fiend Ictinos! God! If we don't get him tonight—'

'We'll get him sooner or later,' came quickly but resolutely from Wallace. 'But concerning Willingdon do you know anything about him?'

The other shook his head.

'Nothing except that he is looked upon as a smart man.'

'Well, see what you can find out – you know, family record, linguistic ability, and all that sort of thing. If he passes muster, we'll keep an eye on him with a view to stealing him from the Yard.'

Brien grinned.

'Wharton will be pleased. We've had half a dozen from the Special Branch since he's been in charge.'

'How do you make that out? Maddison came to us long before Wharton became assistant-commissioner. Cartright, Henderson, Carter, Reynolds and Cunliffe are the only other fellows who graduated, so to speak, from Scotland Yard.'

'What about Brookfield?'

A look that was seldom seen on Sir Leonard's face darkened it at the mention of that name, rendering it, for the moment, stern, almost forbidding. Brookfield had been the chief actor in the only occurrence that had ever cast a blot on the honour of the British Secret Service during his administration.

'I prefer not to speak of him,' he said in cold, hard tones.

He immediately changed the subject telling his companion of his interview with Sir Peter Nikoleff, and his meeting with the second Stanislaus Ictinos and the latter's daughter Thalia.

'What an extraordinary thing!' exclaimed Brien. 'It's the most remarkable coincidence I've heard of for a long time. There is nothing amazing about meeting a man and his daughter with the same name as the two you're after, but that they should have identical Christian names is—'

'I don't think it's coincidence,' interrupted Wallace.

'What do you mean?'

'I am not quite sure myself yet, but it's quite likely that the Greek we want and his daughter took the names of Sir Peter's friends for some purpose of their own.'

'Or perhaps,' hazarded Brien, 'Nikoleff's friends took the names for some purpose of *their* own.'

Sir Leonard regarded his friend with a look of mock admiration.

'Sometimes, Billy,' he declared, 'your brain gives flashes of real brilliance. Let us go down to the mess room, and see if everyone we want is present.'

CHAPTER SIXTEEN

Down the River

The mess room was the name given to a large apartment in the basement of the building, generally reserved for the use of senior members of the service. It was more a restroom than a mess room, though refreshments could be obtained, and meals were provided, if required, by an ex-sergeant of Artillery. Aided by a retired policeman, both of them with exemplary characters, he presided over the periodic comfort of the men whose duties were usually more abounding in discomfort and danger than in ease and security. Several deep leather armchairs, two or three couches, and other easy chairs were placed in various parts of the room, most of them, on this occasion, being drawn up to one or other of the great roaring fires blazing at either end. Three or four card tables, an equal number of small writing desks, provided with paper, envelopes, and pens, stood in advantageous positions. Maps, bookcases, mostly packed with volumes for reference, one or two pictures, and a few prints adorned the walls. At one end of the chamber was a buffet.

Standing at this, as Sir Leonard and Major Brien entered the room, a sandwich in one hand and a glass in the other, was a man whose powerful physique made it appear as though he were of medium height. As a matter of fact, he was a fraction over six feet tall. His strong, clean-shaven, good-looking face, if anything, added to the impression of strength given by his powerful body. This was Captain Hugh Shannon, generally regarded as the Samson of the Service, thoroughly unassuming, but as capable mentally as he was mighty physically, and extremely popular with his colleagues. He was joking with four of the latter, and Wallace, unobserved, stood watching them for a few moments. His eyes were alight with pride in these men who, under him, served their country without hope of fame or glory, always ready to sacrifice self, home, everything, as members of a silent, efficient service that existed simply and solely for the welfare and security of Great Britain.

There was little Cousins with his slim, boyish figure, and ludicrously wrinkled face, Cartright tall and thin, lantern-jawed, seemingly lugubrious; Hill inclined to corpulency fresh-faced, fair-haired and jolly; Carter, good-looking, athletic, happy-go-lucky, the youngest but by no means the least efficient. The five of them represented all that is best and finest in British manhood. All of them were prepared at any moment to face the most appalling risk, undergo the most perilous ordeal, attempt the most hazardous feat at a word from their leader. In themselves they epitomised the very spirit of heroism, yet they seldom, if ever, spoke of their exploits; then only through necessity. The lives of such men, tragically short as they often are, are lived on a higher, nobler plane than those of ordinary human beings. There is no place or time for the little things of existence, none of the meanness or pettiness that casts such a blot on most of the more selfish and sheltered professions of the world.

To them country is everything and, if in the execution of their duty they lose their lives, they go to their deaths with smiles on their lips, counting it no small honour to lay down their greatest possession for the good of their Motherland.

Cousins was the first to notice the two men standing at the door of the room. His lips twitched, and every wrinkle seemed to proclaim its welcome until a huge smile, in a series of minor smiles, enveloped his face.

'The chief,' he announced.

At once every head was turned in Sir Leonard's direction. He advanced into the room.

'Glad to see you back, Shannon,' he remarked. 'How are you?'

The young giant shook hands warmly.

'As fit as ever, sir,' he replied, 'and tickled to death to be home again.'

'Why? What's wrong with Rome?'

'Rome's all right, sir, but it's tame work acting as a watchdog to an embassy in a placid country like Italy. My only excitement was the discovery of an amazing manservant. He was the complete article in every particular – I've never known such a man. He even seemed to find something to admire in me, and I always understood that no man is a hero to his valet.'

There was a general laugh at that. Cousins with an exaggerated gesture threw an arm in Shannon's direction.

'"In short,"' he quoted, '"he was a perfect cavaliero And to his valet seemed a hero."'

Shannon looked down at the little man; shook his head sorrowfully.

'Still at the same old game, Cousins,' he protested. 'What has Tennyson done to you that you should dare quote from him?'

'Tennyson!' cried Cousins in horror. 'Oh, Hugh, I'm shocked – dismayed. That wasn't Tennyson.'

Shannon turned colour.

'Wasn't it?' he queried. 'I could have sworn—'

'Byron, if I'm not mistaken,' put in Wallace. 'From *Beppo*, wasn't it?'

Cousins beamed with delight.

'Sir,' he declared joyously, 'you are perfectly correct. I am happy to know you.'

'Thanks, Jerry,' smiled Sir Leonard amidst another laugh. 'What was this paragon of a valet, Shannon?'

'A Sicilian, sir; a great lad. I've left him behind with the missus. There's nothing he's not prepared to do for her.'

'You're a courageous man, Hugh,' observed Tommy Carter with a grin. 'Sicilians are great love makers, you know, and—'

A great hand gripped him round the neck, and shook him gently.

'Helen knows how to rule him,' declared Shannon.

'I bet she does,' murmured Cousins. '"She moves a goddess and she looks a queen."'

'What! Again?' remonstrated Brien. 'You're giving us overweight tonight, aren't you?'

'That's because he thinks he's safe when the chief's here,' remarked Cartright drily.

Wallace turned suddenly to Carter, and held out his hand.

'I forgot I hadn't seen you before, Tommy,' he apologised. 'How's Turkey?'

'Fine, sir,' was the reply. 'I've felt like a juvenile lead supported by a bevy of beautiful chorus girls since I've been out there. I almost think now that Turkish girls are the prettiest in the world.'

'Indeed,' commented Wallace with a twinkle in his eye, 'I didn't know you went out to study the females.'

'I didn't, sir,' returned Carter, 'but I couldn't stop their studying me.'

'I suppose they don't get many freaks in Turkey,' murmured Hill, chuckling comfortably. Hill had a habit of indulging in chuckles that can only be described as comfortable.

'Well, gentlemen, we have work before us.' The amused expression left Sir Leonard's face, and he regarded the men before him with grave intensity. Immediately the spirit of facetiousness seemed to depart; every countenance there became eager, purposeful; all eyes were fastened on the face of their leader. 'I am going to ask you to accompany Major Brien and myself on an expedition tonight which is perhaps a trifle out of the ordinary. You are aware of the existence of an organisation – Cousins very much so' – he smiled a trifle grimly – 'the purpose of which is to steal national secrets and sell them to the highest bidder.' He broke off to assure himself that Shannon and Carter had been made acquainted with events; then continued. 'Yesterday Cousins and I might have put an end to the organisation – most of us have, at some time or other, had to face heavier odds than he and I would have been called upon to tackle in the house at Sheppey. But there were reasons then why I was not anxious to have a final settlement with the Greek, Ictinos. One of them is that there is a partner, an influential, wealthy man who, I am convinced, hopes, through the acquired knowledge of the nations' most secret schemes, to proclaim himself dictator of Europe as well as add further to his already vast wealth. He must be unmasked and rendered impotent, and I felt that only through an Ictinos at liberty could that be achieved. Another reason for our abstention was the fact that I had undertaken to recover, if possible, for France, copies of the plans and details of her frontier fortifications which are in the hands of the gang, and which are being used to blackmail her to the tune of two hundred million francs.'

His audience looked intensely interested. One or two of the men gave vent to exclamations, or whistled with amazement.

'Cousins and I,' he went on, 'recovered all documents affecting this country, and also others concerning Germany and Russia, but the very vital French records were not in the house on Sheppey. We discovered that the gang fled to a yacht called the *Electra* which, as you all probably know, belongs to the Greek millionaire, Michael Senostris. The mysterious partner, I feel fairly certain, has the documents we want in his possession. It certainly looks as though he is Senostris. At any rate, I believe that by raiding the *Electra*, we shall not only succeed in unmasking him, but recover the plans, and smash the organisation completely once and for all. We have a lot to settle with Ictinos and his men ourselves,' he added through clenched teeth. 'He foully murdered Cunliffe; he has attempted other things equally foul. None of you will wish Cunliffe to go unavenged.'

There was a murmur of deep abhorrence, forcible enough evidence of the feelings of his six colleagues.

'The *Electra* has been disguised,' he continued, 'and is lying in concealment at the entrance of a creek three miles or so beyond Tilbury. We are going there now, and we are going to raid her. Three men of the Special Branch are keeping watch. As far as possible, I wish to avoid bloodshed, but remember that you will be up against desperate men, four at least of whom are wanted by the police for murder. How many there will be I do not know, for we must naturally include the crew of the yacht, but Ictinos took three from Sheppey with him, Cousins and

I capturing the other two. There is also a girl who may prove as dangerous as the men. I presume you are all armed?' They signified that they were. 'Now, Cousins,' he instructed the little man, 'bring Farrell here.'

A few minutes later the crook was escorted into the room. At sight of him, Shannon exclaimed loudly.

'Do you know him?' asked Brien.

'I used to,' was the reply. 'He acted as one of my sparring partners when I was training for the University heavy-weight championship.'

'More coincidences,' murmured the other.

Farrell stood sheepishly on the fringe of the circle. Except for one quick glance at Shannon he kept his eyes turned on the floor.

'I'm going to give this man a chance to redeem himself,' declared Sir Leonard. 'What with robbery with violence, smash and grab raids, and blackmail, he has pretty well run the whole gamut of crime, but he has not committed murder, and I'm willing to believe that he has an honest desire to make good. Anyhow, I am prepared to give him the opportunity. He is coming with us.'

Nobody demurred. Not only were they too well disciplined for that, but they all knew that Sir Leonard's understanding of human nature was almost faultless; that his judgement of his fellow men was well nigh infallible. They followed him from the mess room at his command, Farrell walking between Cartright and Shannon.

'I'm sorry to find that you have come down to this,' remarked the latter to the crook as he paused in the lobby to put on a heavy overcoat and a soft hat. 'You seemed to be a pretty good sort of fellow in the old days. How did it happen?'

'I guess I always was a wrong 'un,' came the frank reply.

'Fights got scarce, and I began to drink hard. After that I just let myself go.'

'Oh, well, you've a chance in a hundred to wash out the past now. Sir Leonard will stand by you, if you prove you're worth it. Come on!'

Cousins, Shannon, and Carter entered the Rolls-Royce with Wallace; Cartright and Hill sat in the back of Brien's Vauxhall with Farrell between them. Precautions had been taken to ascertain that there were no suspicious characters in the vicinity, and Sir Leonard carefully scrutinised Johnson, laughingly demanding to know if he were in reality the ex-soldier.

Although bitterly cold, the weather offered a striking contrast to that of the previous night. The moon shone down from an almost cloudless sky, rendering headlights practically unnecessary. Once away from London, the two cars made speedy progress, even though the Vauxhall caused a slight delay between Rainham and Wennington with a puncture, but the wheel with the faulty tyre was quickly replaced by Cartwright and Hill, Farrell insisting on lending a hand. Progress became slower as they drew near their destination, and were compelled to travel along a series of narrow by-roads, especially as they were not certain of the way, and signboards were few and far between. However, at five minutes to eleven, the two cars approached the tiny village of Shifton, and were met by a man who had apparently been awaiting their arrival, a couple of hundred yards from the beginning of its one street.

'That you, sir?' asked the voice of Inspector Seymour.

'Yes,' replied Wallace, stepping into the road. 'By Jove!' he added with a shiver, 'it's freezing hard. Anything further to report, Seymour?'

'Nothing, sir. We've taken turns in keeping watch – Willingdon is down there now. From where he is stationed the steamer can be seen quite distinctly, and we're pretty sure nobody has come or gone since we've been watching. The motorboat is still tied up alongside.'

'Good. How far is it to the place where Willingdon is posted?'

'About twenty minutes walk, sir. There are several boats lying thereabouts.'

'We'd better be getting along.'

Wallace collected his force together, Johnson being left in charge of the cars. Led by Seymour, who had been joined by MacAlpine the third detective, the little party made its way along a path running parallel to the creek, Carter carrying a coil of thin, strong rope. It was not easy going. A heterogeneous collection of shrubs and bushes dotted the landscape, at times causing the walkers to step aside on to muddy, marshy ground that gave at every footstep. In places this had frozen, giving off in consequence a loud crackling sound as it was trodden on. Once Farrell, who was following Shannon, slipped and fell, cutting his face on some brambles and slightly twisting his ankle, but, after a slight pause, was able to continue without much discomfort. From what could be seen of it by moonlight, the countryside looked distinctly bleak and uninviting. Here and there tall, gaunt trees were silhouetted against the sky, looking weird and sinister in their naked ugliness. A smell of damp, rotting vegetation offended the nostrils, while a miasmatic vapour rose from the mud left uncovered in the creek by the outgoing tide. Nobody spoke, they were too much occupied in picking their way, apart from which, Wallace had given orders that as little sound as possible was to be made.

At last they reached the mouth of the creek. Here they were no longer offended by the malodorous fumes which had previously caused most of them to hold their handkerchiefs to their noses. A slight breeze brought with it the refreshing tang of sea and seaweed; the lapping of the waves close by, in soft and gentle melody, seemed bent on assuring them that the offensive mud had been left behind. Seymour raised his hand, keeping them back among the bushes. A small figure appeared from close by, could be seen to touch his hat to Sir Leonard.

'Willingdon, sir,' muttered Seymour by way of introduction. He turned to the man. 'Anything doing?' he asked.

'Nothing,' was the reply. 'I've had my eyes glued on the boat ever since I came, but there hasn't been a sign of life.'

Through a pair of night glasses, Wallace studied the dark bulk of the ship lying close to an island a few hundred yards away. From what could be seen of her, she possessed two funnels, an extraordinary amount of superstructure on her decks, and blunt, ugly bows. Obviously intended to pass as a small tramp steamer, Sir Leonard was amused to discover that a vital necessity for a boat professing to carry cargo had been apparently forgotten. There appeared to be no cranes or derricks on board.

'It's the *Electra* all right,' he murmured. 'Wonderful what canvas artistically arranged can do.'

He handed his glasses to Brien, who gazed long and earnestly before returning them to their owner.

'There doesn't seem to be a soul on deck,' he remarked, 'and there's not a light showing anywhere. It looks to me as though there's nobody on the boat.'

'There must be somebody, sir,' put in Willingdon respectfully. 'There were three men aboard the motor-launch on which I came from Tilbury, apart from the fellow we'd been shadowing.'

'Perhaps they went back again,' surmised Brien, 'while you were away in the village.'

'The launch is still there, sir; lying astern, if you notice.'

'Yes; and there is somebody on the deck amidships,' grunted Wallace, as a tiny light could be seen distinctly to flare up and burn for a few seconds before being extinguished.

'Well, that wasn't very brilliant, if they don't want it to be known they're there,' commented Seymour. 'It was obviously somebody lighting a cigarette or pipe.'

'And they've informed us that a watch is being kept,' observed Wallace.

'At that rate,' put in Brien, 'how are we to get out there without being spotted? It's almost as bright as day.'

Sir Leonard turned abruptly to the group of men behind him.

'Where's Farrell?' he demanded.

'Here, sir,' responded Carter, and the crook was pushed forward.

'I brought you here,' Sir Leonard informed him, 'because I thought the moonlight would possibly make it difficult to reach the boat by direct means. Are you still keen on earning that pardon?'

'Yes, sir,' answered Farrell without hesitation.

'Then listen carefully: I want you to row out to the *Electra* by yourself. Go aboard and, if Ictinos is there, tell him that you have escaped from me, and have come to warn him that I have tracked him down here with another man, and am now waiting for assistance in order to make a raid. He'll probably ask you how I found out where he was; but you don't know. If he is puzzled by the fact that I have brought you with me, tell him some yarn about my threatening you with unmentionable tortures, if you don't identify the boat, not believing your story that you've never seen her. You ought to be fairly safe; the very fact that you have escaped and dashed to warn him should give him confidence in you. On the other hand, there is always the chance that he'll shoot you down in any case, but it's a risk you must take.

'Now for the second part of my instructions. Having, I hope, been believed by Ictinos, and thanked for your warning, or whatever he does when any service is performed for him, tell him that there is one way in which he can avoid the raid without putting to sea and, at the same time, get me into his power. I think you will find that any chance of capturing or killing me will appeal to him, and he'll be eager to listen to you. Inform him that I have returned to the village to telephone my headquarters, but that it will be quite an hour before men can reach me there. In the meantime, however, say that I intend to get in touch with Captain Shannon, who returned from Rome today, whose home is in North London, and who will, therefore, be able to reach me sooner. Your idea is this, that Hepburn, if he is aboard, should once again impersonate Shannon, go ashore with two or three men, including yourself to show the way, and, by imposing on me, capture me. If he rises to the bait, well and good. I have an idea that he will, for the man has a perfect obsession to end my career and, I believe, given the chance he'll take it, even if it means running a risk. Is everything clear?'

'Yes, sir,' answered Farrell.

'And you're ready to carry out instructions?'

'Yes, sir.'

At Sir Leonard's suggestion, he repeated them.

'Right. There's your chance; take it. If Hepburn is not aboard, Ictinos will probably make other plans to capture me. There is a chance, of course, that he won't. In that case, manage somehow to drop a lighted match over the side of the boat. I'll understand.

I'm putting a lot of trust in you, Farrell. If you let me down, you're finished. Directly the *Electra* sails a message will be sent to Sheerness asking for destroyers to be dispatched to capture her. It is, therefore, no use your thinking you can play me false, warn Ictinos of the true position, and get away with it.'

'I understand, sir,' returned the man quietly. 'I won't let you down.'

'Put him into a boat, Seymour,' directed Wallace, 'and let him go – Oh, wait a minute! Snap a pair of handcuffs on his wrists. That will make the supposed escape look more realistic. Do you think you'll be able to row with them on, Farrell?'

'I dare say I'll manage, sir.'

There was a click. A few minutes later a small boat left the shore, and the man aboard could be seen laboriously pulling towards the disguised yacht. Ten pairs of eyes anxiously watched him go. The receding tide aided him considerably, and, despite his handicap, and obvious inexperience of rowing, less than ten minutes later he was alongside the yacht. Peering intently through his glasses, Sir Leonard saw the dinghy bump into the hull of the larger vessel with considerable force. Several men appeared on the deck of the latter, and quite a commotion suddenly seemed to be taking place. Someone threw Farrell a rope, and he stood precariously in his little craft talking to the fellow above. Presently the gangway, which had been drawn up out of reach, was lowered, a man ran down, secured the rowing boat, and Farrell climbed aboard the *Electra*.

Wallace sighed.

'The first part of the job seems to have been accomplished,' he observed.

'I hope Farrell doesn't let us down,' murmured Brien.

'He won't,' was the answer, spoken with quiet confidence.

'What's the idea of wanting that fellow Hepburn to impersonate Shannon?'

'I've invented a new game, Billy. You can call it "Replacing a Shannon by a Shannon", if you like. Hepburn, as Shannon, comes ashore, with two or three other men, to capture me. Instead, we capture them. The real Shannon with others, wearing the coats and hats of the prisoners, then take me out to the yacht. We thus get aboard without being suspected.'

A subdued laugh came from the men round him.

'*Mens invicta manet*,' murmured Cousins. 'It's a great idea, sir.'

'Perhaps – if it works!'

CHAPTER SEVENTEEN

Farrell Earns His Pardon

Burdened with the handcuffs, which he regarded every now and then with repugnance, Farrell at first made a hopeless mess of rowing the dinghy. He soon found, however, that the tide was carrying him away from the shore, and all that was really necessary for him to do was to keep her head pointed towards the yacht. It seemed to him to take much longer than ten minutes to reach the latter vessel, but at last she loomed above him. He strove awkwardly to turn the dinghy's bows in order to bring her properly, alongside, but was too late. As she bumped violently into the *Electra*, almost unseating him, he heard the sound of running feet above. His coming had been observed for some time, and the watcher had given the alarm. Voices, chattering excitedly, reached his ears; then a head looked over the railing. He could just discern it.

'Who are you?' came the demand in tones he recognised.

'Is that you, Danson?' he asked. 'Hell! It's good even to hear your blasted voice again. Give me a hand – quick!'

'Farrell!' was Danson's surprised exclamation. 'Where the devil did you come from?'

'Never mind that now. Help me to come aboard, can't you?'

His erstwhile companion threw him a rope which he caught, rising unsteadily to his feet. Farrell heard, with mixed feelings – he hardly knew whether to be glad or apprehensive – the deep tones of Stanislaus Ictinos, as the latter demanded to know what had happened. Danson explained.

'Farrell! Here!' bellowed the Greek. 'How did he come here? How did he know? There is something I do not like about this.'

He looked over the side into the boat below.

'How is it,' he asked curtly, 'that you have found us here? This seems very strange to me, my friend Farrell.'

'Let me come aboard, and I'll soon tell you,' pleaded Farrell. 'Hurry! There's no time to lose.'

'What is that you say? No time to lose! What do you mean?'

The man in the dinghy uttered an exclamation that might have been caused either by fear or by impatience.

'I can't tell you here. What is the matter with you, guv'nor? Why don't you let me come up?'

'Because it looks very suspicious to me that you have found us.'

'It don't make it less suspicious if I'm kept in a boat that's rocking about like a shuttlecock, does it?'

'Tell me where you have come from!'

'London. That swine Wallace brought me here, and I've just escaped. Now you know.'

Exclamations of consternation reached his ears from above. The gangway was lowered, a man ran down and secured the dinghy, and Farrell was told to ascend. He did so, growling to himself the while. He had decided on his way across that, if he adopted an attitude comprising a mixture of resentment, fear, and hatred of Sir Leonard Wallace, he would be most likely to deceive his late comrades. Directly he set foot on the deck, Ictinos on one side and Danson on the other, took him by an arm, and hurried him below into a brilliantly lighted lounge. It took his eyes some moments to get used to the glare. While he stood there blinking, he heard exclamations of astonishment, and presently found himself in an apartment that for luxury could scarcely have been excelled. Before he had time, however, to take in his surroundings, a broadside of questions came from all sides at once. In addition to Ictinos and Danson, there were present Hepburn, Ibsen, Thalia, a dignified-looking old man he had never before set eyes on, and a stout, bearded man in uniform, obviously the captain of the yacht and, just as obviously, a Greek. Thalia seemed to be the only one who was not asking questions; her eyes were fixed on the handcuffs.

'You poor man,' she said, and somehow her voice silenced all others, 'you are in manacles. It was clever of you to escape like that. You have slipped away from the so-clever Monsieur Wallace? Am I not right?'

'You are,' he told her, not without a certain feeling of alarm. Of them all she was the one he most feared. He knew that she would be harder to deceive than her father. 'Can't one of you get these things off?' he asked.

At sight of the handcuffs, the manner of Ictinos had changed towards him considerably. The Greek had obviously become convinced now that, if there was anything suspicious taking place, Farrell was not acting in any manner antagonistic to him. But the slate-blue eyes were troubled and anxious.

'Ibsen,' he ordered, 'get a file, and remove from Farrell those ugly fetters.' He rose, and mixing a strong whisky and soda handed it to the latter. 'Sit down and drink that,' he bade, 'it will do you good.'

Farrell obeyed rather wonderingly. It was unusual for the Greek to show much consideration for those who served him. Setting down his empty glass, the man who was endeavouring to earn his pardon looked at Ictinos, and jerked his head significantly at the old man and the ship's captain. The Greek understood, and smiled.

'It is quite all right, my friend,' he assured the ex-pugilist, 'both these gentlemen can hear what you have to say.'

'OK,' nodded Farrell, leaning forward earnestly. 'Listen, guv'nor; I don't think I owe you much after the way you bolted last night. It was a dirty trick.'

Ictinos shrugged his shoulders.

'How could we help it?' he asked. 'When we heard the shots, we knew the house had been raided, and the underground passage discovered. It would have been foolish to have attempted to save you, and thus been captured or killed ourselves.'

'Oh, well, have it your own way.' Farrell shrugged his shoulders. 'Still I think you might have tried to rescue me – they already had Paul.'

'But tell us how it is you are here. How did you know—'

'I'm coming to that. That swine Wallace, blast him, has had me before him, or some of the others, most of the day trying to get information out of me. I didn't see him personally this afternoon, but this evening he came back, and asked me what I knew about the *Electra*. I told him I knew nothing, but I could see he didn't believe me. Anyhow, I found out that he knew you had gone to a yacht called the *Electra*. Information had reached him that she had left Rochester, and a boat that might be her was lying in a creek about two or three miles from Tilbury.'

He paused to take breath, for he had been speaking rapidly. All eyes were anxiously fixed on his. Ibsen had returned with the file, but stood listening, too interested to use it.

'Continue!' urged Ictinos.

'He got in his car with another fellow, and brought me along. We stopped at a village called – I've forgotten it's name—' which was true – he had. 'Anyway the car was left there, and they came through a lot of bushes and over marshy ground till they could see the yacht. Both of them had a go at asking me if I knew it, if it was the *Electra* and all the rest of it, but I told them I'd never seen the blasted yacht. Hell! If only I had a chance to get back at them. They pulled me about, and shook me until I was fair dizzy. Then they started to return. Wallace told the other fellow that they couldn't investigate by themselves, and that he would ring up for reinforcements – that's the word he used. I also heard him say that the bloke called Shannon was back from Italy at his home in North London, and that they would telephone him as well. He'd be the first to be able to reach them. Well, we'd got about halfway to the village when Wallace slipped and, while the other fellow was helping him, I slung my hook. I think they chased me for a bit, but must have given it up, for when I got to the place where the boats are they were nowhere about. They were in too much of a hurry to telephone I suppose. I didn't know whether to come here or not, in case this wasn't the *Electra*, but I had to get away somewhere, so I risked it.'

He stopped, and looked round him, hoping that his eyes did not show the anxiety he was feeling. But his audience was too concerned to study his facial expressions. Everyone of them looked dismayed, even Thalia showing more consternation than he had ever known her show before. The old man was the first to speak. He addressed Farrell.

'They will know, of course, that you have come here,' he remarked, 'since they suspect this is the *Electra*, and are apparently convinced that you are acquainted with her. Still it is well you came, or we would not know they were so near.' He turned to Ictinos. 'What do you propose to do?' he asked.

'Zere is only vone sing to do,' put in the captain gruffly. 'Ve must sail at vonce.'

'Where to?' demanded Thalia. 'Before we could get far we should have torpedo-boats after us. I think it would be best if we all got in the motor-launch, and went to London.'

'She's right,' agreed Hepburn. 'The sooner we get away the better.'

His face was a sickly white. He was obviously a very scared man. Danson looked in no better case, while Ibsen was nervously playing with the file in his hands. Ictinos sat clenching and unclenching his fists, muttering to himself.

'How has he done this?' he asked presently, addressing no one in particular. 'How could he find out? He is Satan himself, this Wallace. If I could only get my hands on him and that man with him!' Suddenly a gleam came into his eyes. 'Why not?' he demanded and, turning, gripped Farrell by the arm. 'There are only two, you say?'

'Two and the driver,' was the reply.

'Well, that is three. It must be some time before the others can come. On this boat are two officers and ten sailors then there are six of us here, and Villinoff – I am not counting you, Thalia, or you, my friend –' He jerked his head at the old man. 'If we go ashore quickly, and capture these men, we can bring them onboard, and sail away. When the rest come there will be no boat – nobody. They will not know what has happened – perhaps they will think they have come to the wrong place.'

'What about the car?' asked the old man.

'That can be driven away, and left many miles from here. We can arrange to pick up the man who drives it tomorrow, or even later tonight.'

Farrell was delighted that the suggestion had come from Ictinos. It remained only for him to improve on it now. From the expressions on the faces of the others it was easy to see that they regarded favourably the big Greek's scheme, but the old man shook his head.

'I do not think,' he observed, 'that Sir Leonard Wallace is likely to be caught so easily. He may even be expecting an attack, as he will guess Mr Farrell has come to the boat.'

'But we can outnumber him by five to one.'

'That will not matter. Shooting will take place, and the people in the village will perhaps go to his assistance.'

Farrell felt that the time had come for him to make his suggestion. He struck his manacled hands on his knees, as though an idea had suddenly occurred to him.

'Wasn't Shannon the bloke that Hepburn impersonated at Sittingbourne, when he took in that little chap Cousins?' he asked in an eager voice. Ictinos and one or two others nodded. 'Well, what about him making up like that again, going ashore with three or four of us, who could remain in the background, and pretend to Wallace that he had just arrived from London? So long as he got there before the real Shannon it would be a cinch. Once they took Hepburn for the real bloke, he could lead Wallace and his mate into a trap. After that it would be easy enough to down the shover, and drive away the car. Then the three of them could be brought on board, and there needn't be any shooting at all.'

The face of the gorilla-man lighted up. He brought down his hand with a sounding thwack on Farrell's shoulder.

'It is a magnificent idea – this,' he applauded. 'I did not know before you had brains, my friend. We will be saved, and Wallace will be in my power. Ah! What pleasure it will give me to see him die. Hasten, Hepburn, there is no time to lose.'

Farrell's suggestion seemed to meet with general approval, only the principal actor in the suggested drama appearing to dislike the idea. His objections were quickly overruled, however, and he went away to make himself up for the part. While he was thus occupied, Ictinos, his daughter, the captain, and the old man engaged in a conversation in Greek, during which certain documents were taken from a safe, and handed to the latter, who put them away carefully in his pocket. Farrell did not understand a word, which he regretted. It occurred to him that they were discussing something which Sir Leonard Wallace would have found of interest. Now that he had undertaken to betray his late comrades, the ex-pugilist intended doing the job thoroughly. Rather to his own surprise, he felt a glow of enthusiasm, while the thought that he was getting an opportunity to wash out the past caused him to wonder if there was anything else he could do on behalf of the grey-eyed man, for whom he had suddenly conceived a great admiration. Ibsen tried to file through the handcuffs, but he was not an expert and, by the time Hepburn returned, only one had been severed. The one-time actor had been very quick, but had not sacrificed thoroughness for speed. Having seen the real Shannon so recently, Farrell was all the more able to appreciate the make-up, and was astounded at the remarkable resemblance.

Details of the manner in which Wallace was to be trapped were discussed, and it was decided that three members of the crew, and Ibsen, and Danson and Villinoff were to accompany Hepburn. It transpired that the Bulgarian had run his motorboat ashore at Netley, after his escape from Southampton docks, had gone to Rochester, and joined the yacht there. Farrell was also to go with the party to lead the way.

'Now, my friends,' exhorted Ictinos, his eyes gleaming at the thought of, at last, getting Sir Leonard Wallace into his power, 'let there be no mistakes this time. *There must not be.* Wallace is too dangerous to live – look how he has tracked us here; he is a man of devilish cunning. Already he has badly interfered with our schemes. Ah, yes! It will be a great pleasure to have him in my power. There is much I have to settle with him. Go! I await your return impatiently.'

'It is a pity you are so bloodthirsty,' commented the old man, shaking his head regretfully. 'Our plans might have gone better, if you had kept your hands clear of human blood. I will now return to London. Will you come with me, Thalia?'

Farrell heard the girl give an affirmative answer as he followed the others up the companionway. There was not room enough for them all in the dinghy, but one of the yacht's boats had been lowered. The three members of the crew with Hepburn and Farrell, entered this, while Ibsen, Danson, and Villinoff went ashore in the other. Nothing was said until they were close to land; then Hepburn turned to his companion with something that sounded very much like a snarl.

'To hell with your brilliant ideas,' he growled. 'I'm not liking this business at all.'

'Why not?' queried Farrell who, now that he had accomplished his mission satisfactorily, was full of jubilation.

'That fellow Wallace is too damned cute. He must have spotted the deception when I impersonated his chauffeur, and he's bound to know that I took in Cousins by getting myself up as Shannon. I doubt if it will work again. I tell you, I don't like it. What if the real Shannon has arrived when we get there?'

'I don't think you need worry about that,' returned Farrell, smiling to himself.

As the boats ran aground, they heard the staccato beat of a motor engine. The launch was leaving the side of the yacht, and Farrell knew the old man and Thalia were on their way to London. Other ears heard the sound also, and Sir Leonard Wallace, his glasses to his eyes, watched the motorboat swing round the island, and disappear from view. He could see that there were three or four people aboard but, of course, it was impossible to make out their features. There was no time for conjecture, however, Farrell and his companions were stepping ashore. Everything was ready for their reception.

They were allowed to walk for some distance unmolested, until they were out of sight of anyone on the yacht who might be following their progress with night glasses. Farrell, walking ahead, began to wonder where Sir Leonard's party was. Suddenly, however, as he was making his way through a particularly dense section of the underwood, figures rose on all sides. Hepburn and company were completely taken by surprise. Before they could lift a hand to defend themselves, or even raise a cry, they were struck down, the revolvers of the Secret Service men, deftly wielded by the barrels, laying them low. Only one, Ibsen the Swede, retained his senses, Cartright overshooting his mark, and hitting him upon the top of the head, protected by his cap, instead of just above and a little behind the ear. However, he was too dazed to raise an outcry, and sank to the ground holding his head between his hands. Farrell looked round at the dark forms strewn out behind him. The suddenness and celerity of it all rather stupefied him for the moment. Rapidly and quietly the seven men were bound with portions of the rope Carter had brought from the car, and gagged with their own handkerchiefs or scarves. Sir Leonard walked up to Farrell, and patted him on the back.

'Good work!' was all he said, but the ex-pugilist felt immensely gratified.

'What's the idea of giving them the KO, sir?' he asked.

'To keep them quiet,' was the reply. 'If we had merely held them up, and disarmed them, there would probably have been a certain amount of noise which might have been heard on the boat, and cause an alarm. Who are on board?'

'There's Ictinos, the skipper, two ship's officers, and about seven sailors. There was an old man there also, and Miss Thalia, but I heard them say they were going to London. I suppose that was the motorboat taking them away just as we landed.'

'Yes; I saw it. An old man did you say? What was he like?'

Farrell gave a careful description of him, adding that he believed he was the man whom Ictinos had spoken of as his partner. Wallace was deeply interested.

'Do you know if he took anything with him?' he asked with unwonted eagerness for him.

Farrell told him of the documents that had been taken from the safe, which the old man had put in his pocket. Sir Leonard turned with an exclamation of annoyance to Major Brien who had joined them, and was standing by his side listening.

'The French plans for a bet, Bill,' he commented. 'Apparently our work won't be completed tonight after all. It's a pity we couldn't have got aboard before that fellow left.'

'How are you going to find out where he's gone?'

'I think I know,' was the quiet reply.

'Come to think of it, sir,' put in Farrell, 'there can only be about five men on board now besides the three officers and Ictinos. There are three sailors here, and two, at least, must have gone with the launch. I heard the guv'nor mention that there were ten in all.'

'The yacht generally carries a crew of twenty. You're sure of your figures?'

'I'm going on what the guv'nor said. He's not likely to be mistaken.'

'Well, we'll say we have about nine or ten men to deal with. I suppose there is a cook, and probably a steward. Let's have a look at this lot.'

Carefully shielding his tiny torch, Wallace went from one prone man to another, flashing a ray of light on each. The sailors he passed without comment, but stood longer over the four crooks, inspecting them with interest, as Farrell mentioned their names. When they came to Hepburn, Brien gave vent to an exclamation of astonishment.

'Good Lord!' he cried. 'Shannon to the life. Hugh,' he called, 'where are you?'

'Here, sir,' came from some yards away.

'Come, and see yourself.'

Shannon strode up, and gazed silently at the unconscious counterfeit of himself lying at his feet.

'Heavens!' was his only comment, 'am I like that?'

'The Corsican brothers,' observed Cousin, joining the group. 'You note that his shoulders are not quite so hefty as yours,

Hugh.' He bent down, and took hold of one. 'Padded, you see,' he remarked, as he shook it. 'That's how I knew it was not the real blue-eyed boy.'

'Did you know before you were trapped?' asked Farrell with interest.

'I did, battered one.'

'S'truth!'

'Who's this?' asked Sir Leonard, shining the ray of his torch on the face of the fourth crook.

'That's Villinoff, sir, the fellow who was sent to Southampton to croak you.'

'Oh, it is, is it?' The gleam in Sir Leonard's eye passed unnoticed in the darkness, but he was thinking of the action of a curly-headed little boy who had risked his own life to save his father from an assassin's bullet. 'It is a great pity,' he murmured to himself, 'that I cannot settle personally with you.' Abruptly he turned away. 'Seymour,' he called, 'here's a choice collection for the Yard. All wanted for murder as well as other crimes riot perhaps quite so heinous.'

Inspector Seymour sighed a sigh of contentment and satisfaction. He regarded the prostrate quartet almost with eyes of affection, after which he transferred his attention to Farrell.

'What about the bracelets?' he demanded. 'Want to keep them on?'

Farrell held up the wrist to which the handcuffs still hung, nodding to the one that had been filed through.

'They tried to get them off,' he explained.

'One perfectly good pair of handcuffs gone west,' groaned the inspector. 'Oh, well, I suppose it was in a good cause.'

He unlocked and removed it, much to Farrell's relief. Handcuffs were not the sort of ornaments the latter would wear from choice. Sir Leonard stood a little apart talking in low tones to Brien. Presently he called the other Secret Service men round him.

'Major Brien will come on the yacht with me,' he announced, 'as the other man supposedly captured by Hepburn and his gang of cut-throats, Shannon will, of course, go as Hepburn, and I think Farrell had better come too, so that he can answer any questions that may be asked before we ascend the gangway. Cousins, and Cartright, make yourselves resemble Ranson and Ibsen sufficiently to pass muster in an open boat in the moonlight – their caps should do. Once aboard it doesn't matter what you look like. Seymour, Carter, and Hill, put on those seamen's berets, and try to look as much like them as you can. Willingdon, and MacFarlane will stay and guard the prisoners. Hurry, all of you, it's about time we started.'

The men were quickly ready. Shannon merely took Hepburn's hat, the one he had been wearing being of a different colour. Their coats were identical in cut, material and length; there was no necessity, therefore, to change them. Sir Leonard, Brien, Farrell, and Shannon, rowed by Carter, and Hill, the latter with the borrowed berets pulled well down on their heads, left in the first boat. They were followed closely by Seymour, Cousins, and Cartright in the dinghy. It was only when they were halfway across that Farrell remembered what had been said concerning Johnson and the car. He told Sir Leonard, who promptly assured him that it did not matter. Their progress was undoubtedly being closely observed, for they were hailed as soon as they ran under the lee of the yacht. Shannon answered gruffly. Sir Leonard, and Brien, as prearranged, had their hands tied lightly behind their backs, a jerk being all that would be required to free them. The boat glided alongside the gangway, and Farrell roughly ordered the two supposed prisoners to ascend.

'So you have them,' came the exultant voice of Ictinos.

'Yes; we have them all right,' called back Farrell, putting as much triumph as he could into his tones.

Sir Leonard, and Brien stepped on the deck of the disguised yacht, and found themselves face-to-face with Ictinos, and the bearded captain.

'At last,' boomed the former, 'you are in my power, Sir Leonard. We have much to settle, is it not so? You will discover that it is dangerous to oppose Stanislaus Ictinos. Tonight you and I will conclude our little feud.'

Wallace bowed mockingly.

'As you say,' he agreed, 'tonight we will conclude our little feud.'

CHAPTER EIGHTEEN

The Elusive Greek

Ictinos gave orders to Farrell, and the pretended Hepburn to bring the prisoners down to the saloon, and led the way, accompanied by the captain. Carter, and Hill, keeping well out of the moonlight, awaited the coming of their companions in the other boat. As soon as they were joined by Seymour, Cousins, and Cartright, the quintet proceeded quietly and methodically to seize the ship. They found an officer in his cabin writing a letter and, almost before the astonished man gathered that they were not friends, he was tied up, gagged, and deposited on his bunk. Another deck cabin contained a man busily engaged in restringing a mandolin. From various indications it was obvious that he was the engineer. He was quickly rendered helpless in the same manner as the navigating officer. Both cabin doors were locked, and they were left to their own, not very happy, reflections. Three seamen were discovered in their quarters in the fo'c'sle, and quickly overpowered; another in the lamp room suffered the same fate; a fourth was found in the galley with a cook. There they met with a certain amount of resistance, due to the fact that Seymour, before entering, had bumped against a stanchion, and expressed his feelings with a typically British oath. Both men showed fight, but a full-blooded uppercut from Carter quickly laid the sailor low; the cook, however, a saucepan in one hand, a carving knife in the other, strove desperately to keep them off. Eventually he was pummelled into unconsciousness, though not before a considerable amount of noise had been created. Nobody appeared from the saloon to find out the cause of the disturbance, and thereafter the five men distributed themselves about the deck, keeping watch until Sir Leonard came up, or they were summoned below. They had satisfied themselves that everybody in the ship was accounted for apart from the men in the saloon.

Wallace and Brien gazed round them with an air of approval as Farrell and Shannon pushed them into the beautifully furnished apartment, that looked more like a lady's boudoir than the saloon of a ship, even though that ship was a privately owned pleasure yacht. Costly tapestries and exquisite little etchings adorned the walls of fumed oak; silken curtains of a delicate tint of blue hung before the doors and portholes, a wonderful carpet of the same colour, into which their feet sank ankle deep, covered the floor; the chairs and settees were upholstered in silk brocade of a slightly deeper shade of blue; the small, exquisitely carved tables, of which there were four, were covered by brocaded cloths of the same colour as the curtains.

'Very nice,' observed Sir Leonard.

Ictinos frowned a little. It would have pleased him better, if this man, whom he believed to be in his power, had shown alarm, or at least a measure of consternation. He made a mental promise that, in a few minutes, he would give himself the satisfaction of witnessing the Englishman writhe in agony.

'I am glad you like it,' he replied mockingly.

He and the captain of the yacht sat down behind one of the tables. Without being invited, Wallace sank into another chair, his example being followed, a moment later, by Brien. Over them stood Farrell, and Shannon. Again Ictinos frowned.

'You take things very coolly,' he growled, 'but I have no objection to your seeking comfort for the moment. Soon there will be no comfort, I promise you, Sir Leonard Wallace.'

'What do you propose to do with us?' asked Sir Leonard with an air of polite interest.

The Greek's eyes flashed.

'I am going to exact recompense from you,' he declared emphatically, 'for all you have caused me to lose; make you pay to the uttermost for the indignities you have put on me and the misfortunes you have caused me.'

'Oh! And how are you going to do that?'

'You will see.' He turned to Brien. 'I was not anticipating a triumph, which would bring into my power the redoubtable Major Brien' – he pronounced it 'Brion' – 'as well as the so great Sir Leonard. So great!' he repeated with a deep laugh of contempt. 'My friends, your fame is, after all, made like the egg-shell – it is not solid. You think you are so wonderful, yet you are deceived by a clever actor, who can make himself exactly like one of your own men. Look at him! Is his impersonation of your Shannon not perfect in every respect?' He pointed to the powerful man standing behind Brien's chair. 'Even I, who have seen it before, marvel. To me it looks more complete than ever.'

'It certainly is excellent,' commented Sir Leonard, turning, and winking slightly at his assistant, who bit his underlip as though to suppress a smile. 'In fact,' went on Wallace, 'he looks more like Shannon than anybody but Shannon could look.'

'What do you mean?' demanded Ictinos. 'Levity will not help you to escape from the fate in store for you.'

'Well, what is that fate?' queried Sir Leonard.

'Presently you will be taken on deck; you will be gagged so that you cannot make any outcry. The ship will sail. Then you will be hanged from a mast by your ankles. If, when dawn breaks, you are not dead, you will be hanged by your neck, so that you will then quickly expire.'

'You brute! You inhuman brute!' burst from between Brien's clenched teeth.

'As for you, Major, I will not be quite so severe – you will be stabbed, yes! A little pain, a little blood, and it is all over.'

As he spoke he was looking at his captives; he did not notice the expression on Shannon's face, but the captain did, and it troubled him. He spoke rapidly to Ictinos in Greek. A threatening frown overshadowed the latter's countenance, as he darted a look at his supposed underling.

'Why is it you glare like that?' he demanded. 'Do you object to my programme?'

With an effort Shannon controlled himself.

'I object to cruelty,' he remarked quietly.

'Ah, bah! Who are you to talk of cruelty? And why do you speak in that voice now? The play is over. You are no longer Shannon.'

'He *is* Shannon,' came in quiet tones from Sir Leonard. 'It is you who have been deceived, Stanislaus Ictinos.'

He rose and, at the same time, slipped his hands from the cord that had apparently bound them. Brien immediately stood by his

side, his own hands freed. For a few seconds Ictinos was too amazed
to make a movement. Those slate-blue eyes of his, registering
incredulity and horror, almost bulged from his head. The captain
uttered a gasp, and shrank back in his chair, his face as pale as
death. Then, with a mighty roar, Ictinos was on his feet, glaring
murder at the men standing opposite him. But he dare make no
move; he was outnumbered, and they now held revolvers in their
hands; all, that is, except Farrell, who had shrunk back a little,
watching the scene with fascinated eyes. A pregnant silence, almost
overpowering in its deadliness, reigned in the saloon for several
moments. Glancing at the skipper, Wallace decided that he would
be no trouble. The man was a mere catspaw; was overwhelmed by
the manner in which the tables had been turned. Ictinos looked
Shannon up and down, and presently he spoke, the words coming
from him as though they were being drawn out.

'It is true?' he asked. 'You are not Hepburn?'

'No,' replied Shannon; 'I am certainly not Hepburn. He and
the other cut-throats you employed are ashore in the hands of the
police.'

'Then who was it came on board – with you?'

'They were my men,' Wallace told him. 'The ship is, by this
time, in their hands. It is no use thinking of resisting, Ictinos. You
are my prisoner.'

Abruptly, with terrible ferocity, the Greek turned on Farrell.

'You betrayed me!' he roared. 'It was all lies the story you told.
Fool that I was to believe you. May you rot in the deepest hell,
you – you—' He used a word that would not be countenanced by
the Patriarch or the Holy Synod of the Orthodox Greek Church.

'Enough of this!' snapped Sir Leonard. 'Call Seymour down,
Shannon, and let this fellow be handcuffed. It'll be a police job.

Hardly worth pulling him in under the Official Secrets Act, when there are at least two charges of murder, and several of incitement to murder, against him.'

Suddenly, with a despairing sort of effort, the yacht's captain made a dash for the door near which he stood. Sir Leonard's revolver spoke once and, with a groan, the sailor crashed to the floor.

'Smashed knee cap,' commented Wallace; 'damn silly to try and get away like that.'

But abruptly the saloon was plunged into darkness. Ictinos had taken advantage of the diversion caused by the skipper's action, the switches of the lights being close behind him. There was a choking cry, a heavy form collided with Wallace, sending him staggering across the saloon, and the pounding of racing feet could be heard receding in the distance. Sir Leonard groped his way across to the switches, and once again the room was brilliantly lit. He cast a hurried glance round. Close by lay the captain groaning with pain; on the other side Farrell was lying on his face, his legs drawn up as though in the throes of agony. The haft of a knife showed in the middle of his back. Apparently bent on vengeance, Ictinos had flung himself on Farrell as soon as the lights were out, stabbed him, and bolted along an alleyway to the left of the saloon. Shannon and Brien had gone after him.

Wallace bent down, and examined the ex-pugilist. The man was still breathing and, from the position of the wound, he judged there was just a chance that his life might be saved. Hurrying out of the saloon, he ran up the companion-way, and called. His men came to him immediately. They had heard the shot, and had been standing by in expectation of being required. Sir Leonard sent Hill down to attend to Farrell, with Cousins to assist him. Hill had qualified as a doctor, before patriotism, first class detective instincts, and a spirit of adventure had taken him into the Secret Service. Directly they had gone below, Wallace dispatched the other three to help search for Ictinos, he himself running along the alleyway that the Greek had taken.

He passed several cabins, glancing perfunctorily in each as he went by, but knowing full well that the gorilla-man would not have attempted to take refuge in any of them. Almost subconsciously he was aware that all the cabins and the alleyway were brilliantly illumined, and the reason why no light had been discernible from the shore dawned on him. The whole of the yacht's hull had been covered by canvas or, more probably, wooden casing. He resolved to investigate later on. At the end of the passage he came to a small smoking room on the far side of which was a companion-way. He ascended this, emerging on deck close to the stern. There he paused a moment, wondering which way to turn. As he stood hesitant Seymour dashed up.

'He's on the bridge, sir,' he cried. 'Captain Shannon and Major Brien have got him.'

His statement turned out to be somewhat premature. They ran towards the bridge, and quickly caught sight of three forms struggling desperately on the starboard side. Suddenly one tore himself loose, and sprang into the sea. Wallace hurried to the rail, and glanced down. At first he could see nothing, but, after a few moments, caught sight of a head. Ictinos was swimming strongly for the little island. Shannon, too, had glimpsed him from the bridge and, throwing off his overcoat and shoes, dived in without hesitation after him. Sir Leonard fingered his revolver. To him Ictinos was an easy mark, even in the deceptive light of the moon, but he could not bring himself to shoot a defenceless man, though the latter had lost all right to considerations of humanity and mercy. Shannon was a powerful swimmer, and it was quickly evident that he was rapidly gaining on the Greek. Wallace ran to the gangway on the port side.

'Brien, Seymour, Carter,' he called, 'come with me. Cartright stay on watch here.'

He tore down the gangway, followed by the three men. Tumbling into one of the boats, they cast off, Seymour and Carter taking the oars. Once round the yacht's bows they headed for the island, making rapid progress. Nothing could be seen of the Greek and his pursuer for some minutes; then Brien caught sight of them close inshore, pointing them out to his companions. As they looked, the Greek was seen to scramble up the shelving bank, but Shannon was close behind him. They disappeared out of the moonlight into the darkness caused by the shadow of a group of trees. Three minutes later the boat touched bottom, and Wallace and his party sprang ashore. Seymour remained behind, while the others hastened towards the spot where Ictinos and Shannon had disappeared.

When they drew near, the laboured breathing of men locked together in mortal combat could be heard, and presently, from the shadows, rolled the two, wrestling desperately. The onlookers stood spellbound, watching fascinated, hardly daring to breathe. The combatants, each struggling frantically to get the upper hand, were never in the same position for more than a second or two at a time. There was something terrifying about the contest, one felt that both men had resolved to fight until one of them was dead. With the pale rays of the moon throwing a ghostly light upon the scene, a more uncanny spectacle could hardly be imagined. The great arms of the Greek, thrown round his opponent, were being exerted to the full in an effort to crush him. Shannon had one hand under his antagonist's massive jaw, pushing his head back, the other was locked round his neck. Their legs were entwined in a hold that no ordinary means could have broken. Minutes went by without either one or the other gaining the slightest advantage, but the mighty Greek had found his match. Never before had he met any man who could stand up to him, but in Shannon he was opposed to an individual whose strength was a by-word in the circles in which he moved. Inch by inch the Greek's head began to go back before that terrific pressure, until, at last, with a deep bellow of agony, he was forced to release his grip on his antagonist's body. For a fraction of a second they lay as though taking a rest, but suddenly Ictinos managed to bend his knee, and drive it with sickening force into Shannon's abdomen. With a suppressed groan the latter rolled over, momentarily winded. The Greek staggered to his feet, gathered himself together, and threw himself at the disabled man. Shannon, however, saw what was coming; succeeded, barely in time, in twisting aside, causing Ictinos to miss his grip. Then the Englishman rose slowly; braced himself. He was rapidly recovering from the blow in his stomach, and was doing his utmost to avoid the other until his strength returned. But Ictinos was up again now. For a moment or two they stood eyeing each other, the perspiration, despite the bitter cold of the night, pouring in streams down their faces.

Abruptly they were at it again, swaying in the moonlight like two great monsters of some other world, grotesque, terrifying, altogether barbarian, symbolic of man's primeval passions in the raw. Ictinos had the longer reach, but on their feet Shannon had the advantage of height. Legs again entwined, their arms locked together like bands of steel, each strove for the mastery. But the Englishman had obtained a grip with his right arm on his antagonist's left that was slowly but surely breaking it. Suddenly with a snap that startled the stillness of the night it went, and a howl that was more animal than human broke from the lips of the Greek. He tore himself away and, in that moment, Shannon caught him on the point of the jaw with a left hook that sent him staggering back several yards. Following up his advantage the Englishman drove in a straight right that would have felled an ox. Ictinos spun round, dropped in a crumpled heap, and lay still. Shannon sank slowly to the ground and sat, his head between his hands, drinking in the air in great gulps.

The spectators of that herculean combat ran forward to his assistance. He refused their aid, assuring them that he would be quite all right when he had regained his breath. They turned their attention to Ictinos, therefore, and found him quite unconscious. In addition to his left arm, Sir Leonard found that his jaw was fractured.

'Hill will have quite a lot of doctoring to do tonight,' he commented grimly, adding with a smile: 'I'm glad you and I are on the same side, Shannon. Billy, do you think you and Carter can carry this fellow to the boat?'

They found it a pretty difficult task, but managed it, Wallace lending what assistance he could. By the time Ictinos had been deposited in the bottom of the boat, Shannon, apparently fully recovered, joined them. They clambered aboard, and rowed back to the yacht.

'Whatever you say or do in the future, Hugh Shannon,' remarked Carter, as they sped across the water, 'even if it's the most ridiculous statement or action possible to be imagined, I'll agree with it. I'm taking no risks after what I've seen tonight.'

Shannon laughed.

'At all events,' he observed, 'I think I've taught this Greek Johnny not to go playing about with my identity. I don't like people impersonating me. I hope there's somewhere on that boat where I can get dry – I'm wet and beastly cold.'

'Didn't you enjoy your dip?' asked Carter with an air of innocence.

'Didn't notice it,' was the retort.

Before going aboard they stopped for a little while to inspect the side of the yacht. As Sir Leonard had half guessed the hull was covered from stem to stern, from the deck to the waterline, with a casing of wood which had been clamped on in sections, each part fitting into the other, giving a totally different effect and shape to the whole boat. It was very ingenious, but whether it would be convincing in a close-up by daylight remained to be seen. The name, now showing on each side of the bows, was *Canopus*. He afterwards discovered that the top-hamper which had been noticeable from the shore and one of the funnels were constructed of canvas stiffened out with wood, and painted the same colour as the rest of the ship.

Cousins met them at the head of the gangway with the news that Farrell was in a precarious condition, but Hill thought he would recover, if he could be got to hospital reasonably quickly. Ictinos was carried below, where his jaw and arm were at once attended to by the Secret Service man who had once been a doctor. The saloon had been turned into an emergency dressing station, and with Farrell, the captain, and now Ictinos, Hill had his hands full. Seymour stayed to help him. Shannon found a dressing gown, which he donned, while his clothes were drying in the engine room. He also discovered a cabinet packed with wines and spirits of all kinds, and helped himself to a stiff whisky. Wallace blessed the fact that under the bridge was a well-equipped wireless cabin. A message was sent to Tilbury asking for a strong force of river police, and giving instructions that the local hospital should be asked to prepare for the reception of a dangerously wounded man. That done Wallace, assisted by Brien, Cartright, Cousins, and Carter, commenced a systematic search of the yacht.

The saloon was the first to come in for examination, and not a square inch of space escaped the intensive scrutiny of those keen-eyed experts. They even took care to assure themselves that there were no secret hiding places under the deck or behind the bulkhead. But nothing of interest came to light, unless a considerable sum of money in banknotes of large denomination found in the safe, could be said to have impressed Sir Leonard, because he made a note of their numbers. Satisfied that they had overlooked nothing in the saloon, they went from cabin to cabin, spending a considerable time in one that had obviously been used by Ictinos. Even there they made no discovery of note, a file of documents in a locked attaché case only giving them information which was already known, at least, to Sir Leonard. In another cabin was found a large box full of grease paints, crêpe hair, nose paste, and all the other materials necessary for an actor's make-up. There was also an extensive wardrobe suggesting that the owner had played many parts. In the bottom of the make-up box was a significant document in which the story of Hepburn's crime was set down unblushingly in black and white, almost as though its author were intensely proud of the vile deed that had caused him to become a fugitive from justice. Wallace glanced it through, and handed it to Cousins with a grim smile.

'Take charge of that,' he directed. 'Scotland Yard will find it very interesting. It is extraordinary how a warped sense of vanity will often cause criminals to write incriminating records of that nature, or keep papers or articles that, if found, can be used in evidence against them.'

'Although he writes as though he gloried in the murder he committed,' commented Cousins, 'the ending rather suggests that his conscience has been pricking him. Look!'

The others followed his pointing finger, and read: '"Which way I turn is hell, Myself am hell."'

'You would take particular notice of that,' grinned Carter. 'It's a quotation, isn't it, Jerry?'

Cousins regarded him sorrowfully.

'It is obvious,' he observed, 'that you do not know your Milton. It is interesting,' he added reflectively, 'how many of the old poets and dramatists liked to write about hell and Satan. '"Hell hath no limits, nor is circumscribed In one self place; for where we are is hell, And where hell is there must we ever be."'

'That's a beastly morbid idea anyhow,' remarked Carter. 'Is that some more of your friend Milton?'

'No, it isn't,' snapped Cousins; 'it's Marlowe.'

'Marlowe and Milton mean the same to me,' grinned the other, adding in a burst of generosity: 'They both wrote pretty good stuff.'

'Ah, bah!' growled Cousins irritably. 'You're the sort of ignoramus who thinks Milton is a disinfectant and Marlowe—'

'A seaport in northern France,' put in Cartright.

Cousins subdued him with a look of deep contempt not unmixed with commiseration.

From the cabins they went to the bridge. In the chartroom was found the log-book, which Sir Leonard studied carefully with the assistance of Cousins, making certain notes of entries that interested him. At length they descended to the engine room, where they found Shannon collecting his partially dry clothing. He showed no effects at all now of the terrific struggle he had had with Ictinos, and smiled cheerfully at the humorous comments of Carter and Cousins on the brevity of the dressing gown he was wearing. It certainly had never been intended for a man of his size. Suddenly realising that, now Shannon was with them, there was nobody on deck, Sir Leonard sent Cousins up to keep watch; then led his party through the small, compact engine room and stokehold. By this time he was convinced that the documents he was so anxious to procure were not on the yacht; that, in fact, they were those, which the old man, described by Farrell, had put away in his pocket, and taken ashore. But he had no intention of leaving any likely nook or cranny unexamined, the engine room of a boat containing many possible hiding places. The furnaces showed signs of having been attended to fairly recently, while there was a pressure of steam sufficiently high to enable the yacht to sail at a moment's notice.

'Hasn't it occurred to you as curious,' asked Brien, as they stood together in the stokehold, 'that nowhere have we found any proof that Senostris is in partnership with Ictinos, except in the knowledge that he owns this boat, and also, of course, from what Farrell told us of the old man he met on board?'

'You think that was Senostris then?'

'Yes; don't you? The description certainly seemed to fit the Greek as I remember him.'

Sir Leonard smiled. He was about to reply, when Carter came running to him. The latter wore a look of deep perturbation.

'Cousins heard the sound of shots coming from the direction of the saloon, sir,' he reported, speaking in rapid tones. 'He went to investigate, and found the door locked; then came and shouted down to us. Cartright and Shannon have gone up.'

Without a word Sir Leonard made a dash for the ladder leading to the fiddley; clambered up, followed by the other two. A minute later they were on deck, had passed through the door at the top of the saloon companion-way, and were racing down the stairs. They reached the bottom just as Shannon, throwing himself like a battering-ram at the door for the third time, burst it in. He fell full length, but they jumped over him and entered, standing aghast at the scene that met their eyes. Lolling over the body of Farrell, that lay stretched out on a couch, was Hill, blood pouring copiously from a wound in his neck; sitting on the floor, his head resting against a table, was Seymour, shot through the chest. The captain of the yacht was half-sitting, half-reclining on a settee, in his eyes a look of horror. Of Ictinos there was no sign. After one comprehensive, horror-stricken glance, Wallace acted promptly.

'Quick!' he ordered, pointing to Hill: 'Staunch the flow of blood, or he'll bleed to death; then attend to Seymour.' At once Cousins and Cartright were on their knees by the side of their colleague. 'Where did he go?' snapped Wallace, turning on the captain.

The latter pointed to the door on the opposite side of the saloon. It was found to be locked and, in preference to waiting while it was being battered down, Sir Leonard led the way on deck followed by Brien, Shannon, and Carter. As they ran along in search of Ictinos they heard the rapid beat of a motor engine coming momentarily nearer.

'The police boat,' exclaimed Brien.

He was wrong. It was the launch, belonging to the yacht, returning. The Greek, from a hiding place in the bows, either recognised it, or took a chance. He stood up, shouted something in a loud voice, which must have caused his fractured jaw intense pain, and plunged over the side. The men seeking for him amidships, heard the shout, saw him jump. Quick as lightning Wallace fired; then the four of them tore to the bows. They were just in time to see him being hauled aboard the launch, which turned, and rapidly made back the way it had come. The Englishmen fired, but the men on the motorboat lay sheltered from the bullets, even the steersman, crouching amidships, being protected by the little cabin behind him. Before long they were out of range.

'By Jove!' commented Brien, 'that fellow is as slippery as four eels rolled into one. He must have had a nerve to jump overboard with his jaw and an arm broken.'

'Nerve of that sort is easy to conjure up,' observed Wallace grimly, 'when the alternative is execution by hanging.'

'Can't think how it happened,' put in Carter in puzzled tones. 'He was searched when we brought him aboard, and everything taken from him. Where did he get the revolver?'

'We'll soon find out,' returned Sir Leonard. They walked back along the deck; descended to the saloon. 'I'll get him yet,' he added vehemently, 'and before many hours are past. Next time he won't have a chance of getting away.'

CHAPTER NINETEEN

Sir Peter Nikoleff Stays in Bed

They entered the saloon to find that Cousins and Cartright had succeeded in stopping the flow of blood from Hill's neck. He now lay on the floor, the wound tightly bandaged by hands skilled through experience in the grim school of necessity. Wallace and Brien knelt. down and examined Seymour. Their relief was great when they were able to satisfy themselves that, though nasty, his wound was not dangerous. Apparently the bullet had been deflected by a rib, and was now lodged below the right lung. The inspector opened his eyes as they were binding him with bandages taken from the yacht's surgical stores. He smiled a little.

'Did you get him, sir?' he whispered to Wallace.

The latter warned him not to speak and, leaving him in the hands of his companions, walked across to the captain.

'Now,' he addressed the bearded man sternly, 'perhaps you will tell me what happened. How did Ictinos escape?'

The Greek hesitated for a moment; then spoke sullenly.

Sir Leonard could make little sense from the disconnected and badly phrased narrative of the other, and called Cousins to his assistance. The little man soon had the skipper talking volubly in his own language and, after putting a few questions to him, turned and translated for the benefit of his chief.

'It appears, sir,' he said, 'that after Ictinos had been attended to, Hill went back to Farrell, leaving Seymour to keep an eye on the Greek. Occasionally the inspector's attention was taken away by Hill's requirements and, when that happened, Ictinos opened his eyes and looked round, proving that he had already regained consciousness, although they did not know it. Eventually, when Seymour went to help Hill raise Farrell to a more comfortable position, and required the use of both hands, he laid his revolver on a table. Ictinos saw his opportunity, and took it. While their backs were turned, he slipped off the couch, grabbed the gun, and crept to the door. Before he got there, Seymour saw what had happened, and made a spring for him, but was stopped by the bullet in his chest. Then, as Hill was getting up to tackle him, he was shot also. The Greek quickly locked this door, went across the saloon and out the other, locking that.'

'All through a little carelessness on Seymour's part,' commented Wallace. 'It was criminally foolish to put down his revolver like that, even if he did think Ictinos was still unconscious. The other fellow wasn't, anyway. Is there hope of Hill's recovery?'

'I think so, sir, if that bandage can be kept undisturbed until we get him to hospital. I'm rather afraid, though, that carrying him into the police boat, and then ashore at Tilbury, not to mention the vibration, when he's on his way there, may prove fatal.'

Wallace stood in deep thought. He looked worried; rather an unusual state for him to be in, but he was thinking of the two dangerously wounded men. To move them at all was a risk; to transfer them from the yacht to the police boat, allow them to undergo the jolting to they would certainly be subject on the launch, and carried ashore at Tilbury might easily, as Cousins remarked, prove fatal. Suddenly he made up his mind. He gave orders for the captain to be carried to the bridge – he was unable to walk on account of his shattered knee – and the assistant officer to be released under guard. That done, the engineer and the three men from the fo'c'sle were sent down into the engine room under the watchful eyes of Shannon and Carter, and ordered to stoke-up. Sir Leonard was about to send Cousins ashore with instructions to Willingdon and MacAlpine to bring the other prisoners aboard, when the police boat from Tilbury arrived.

'You've taken a long time,' commented Wallace to the inspector in charge.

'We had some difficulty in finding this creek, sir,' was the explanation. 'There are about a dozen of these inlets within half a mile, and most of the entrances look alike.'

Sir Leonard rapidly described the events of the past hour or so, and told him what he wanted done. The inspector had brought a dozen men with him. Half of them were immediately sent to collect the captives ashore, while the rest were distributed on the yacht, two replacing Brien and Cartright on the bridge, three relieving Shannon and Carter, while the other stood by within call. Twenty minutes later the three sailors with Danson, Hepburn, Villinoff, and Ibsen were aboard. The four criminals were handcuffed together in a circle, and locked in a small but strong baggage-room astern. Now in full possession of their senses, they were white-faced and terror-stricken. No doubt each was thinking of what the near future held in store for him. The three seamen were taken forward, and directed to haul up the anchor. MacAlpine and Willingdon were sent ashore with orders to drive their taxi back to London. Cousins and Cartright stayed aboard to look after the wounded men; to see that they were conveyed to hospital at the earliest possible moment; afterwards to return to headquarters with a report concerning their condition. Having assured himself that the inspector in charge fully understood his instructions, Wallace descended into the dinghy with Brien, Carter, and Shannon. They pushed off from the disguised yacht, as she began to glide from the anchorage which Ictinos had apparently considered safe from prying Secret Service eyes.

Sir Leonard and his companions made their way back to Shifton with a great deal of difficulty. The moon had set and, although they now used electric torches, they found it laborious going. Every now and again they lost the path, where it had become obscured by the tangled undergrowth, and wandered aside, sinking into yielding, evil-smelling marshland, sometimes nearly up to their knees. It took even longer to return than it had to come, and they were heartily glad when, at last, they struck solid ground, and walked into the sleeping hamlet. Not a sound disturbed the stillness, even the dogs were asleep and, with not a glimmer of light showing from any direction, they felt almost as though they had entered a village deserted by all its inhabitants, whether human or animal.

'Fancy living in a spot like this,' commented Brien, as they strode through the place, their footsteps, on the frozen surface of the road, making enough sound, they felt, to disturb any sleepers. 'Can't think what dwellers hereabouts can possibly find to do.'

'They're mostly agricultural labourers, I suppose,' observed Shannon. 'Hardy toilers of the soil who rise at four and bed down at nine.'

'That sounds almost poetical,' laughed Carter. 'It's a lucky thing

Cousins isn't here or he'd be spouting something about "winding herds lowing slowly o'er the leas".'

'Aren't you getting a bit mixed?' queried Brien. 'What are winding herds anyway?'

'The municipal authorities of Folkestone,' laughed Shannon, 'would be a bit perturbed to see them lowing slowly o'er the leas.'

Sir Leonard trudged on, taking no part in the light conversation of his companions. He seemed to be in deep, almost gloomy thought. They came to the cars; found Johnson very much on the alert.

'I'm afraid you've had a long and chilly wait,' remarked Wallace, speaking for the first time since leaving the yacht.

'I managed to keep fairly warm with the rugs inside, sir,' replied the chauffeur.

He held open the door for his employer, who stepped in; then turned, and smiled at Carter and Shannon.

'You two had better go in Major Brien's car,' he suggested. 'I'm going to think, and I'm afraid you would find me a very dull companion. Stop at the hospital in Tilbury on the way, Johnson,' he added.

'Am I to drive back to headquarters?' asked Brien.

'Yes; we'll go there first.'

'Then the night's work is not yet done?' returned the deputy chief lightly.

'It certainly is *not* done,' was the emphatic reply. 'Before we can think of relaxing, we're going to get those documents which France so badly needs and, with them, Ictinos and his partner. If we leave it till daylight we may be too late.' He looked at his watch. 'Ten past two,' he muttered. 'We've very little time.'

Brien walked to his car followed by Shannon and Carter. All

three had caught something of Sir Leonard's gravity now. No time was lost in returning to London, the pause at Tilbury being as brief as possible. Sir Leonard himself interviewed the house surgeon on duty at the hospital, explaining the condition in which the wounded men, particularly Farrell and Hill, were, and insisting that they were to receive the very best of attention, even if it meant calling in the finest surgeons in London. He was assured that everything possible would be done for them.

If the truth were told, the young medical man was greatly impressed by the coming of such an important visitor. Sir Leonard's card had been brought to him when he had been reclining at his case in the surgeons' room, bemoaning the fact that there was not more work of an interesting nature, requiring a higher degree of skill than was usually the case in Tilbury hospital, for he was exceedingly keen on his profession. He had been notified by the police that a badly injured man would be brought in, but as no details had been given, had thought little of it, putting it down as an accident in the docks or perhaps a stabbing affray. The sight of Sir Leonard's card caused him to open his eyes, not because he had ever heard of the Chief of the Secret Service, or that on the little piece of pasteboard was engraved the latter's designation – which of course it was not – but because the words *Sir Leonard Wallace, Foreign Office, London* looked very intriguing in themselves. When he heard that he was to receive four wounded men, one of whom would be under police guard, and that the Foreign Office itself took all responsibility for them, he became very curious indeed, while all his professional instincts were aroused at the thought that before him was the kind of specialist work he yearned for. Sir Leonard, watching him closely, was satisfied. He knew that the casualties would be in good hands.

The two cars tore rapidly through the night, once Tilbury was left behind and, with little traffic to delay them, arrived in quick time in Whitehall. All the way Sir Leonard sat, his chin sunk on his breast, staring into vacancy. His were not particularly pleasant thoughts, for he realised that, by bringing to a successful termination the work he intended to accomplish before daylight, he would probably cause a great deal of suffering to many thousands of innocent human beings, perhaps bring more distress on a world already in the throes of trouble and tribulation. It was not the eventual capture of Ictinos, the final disrupture of his organisation, that was causing the two deep lines to appear between his eyes; it was not even the necessity of obtaining possession of the plans and details concerning the French frontier fortifications. There were greater issues even than that at stake, but no thought of shirking his duty, as he saw it, occurred to his mind. As always, he faced what was ahead, without endeavouring to find a means of side-tracking it, calmly, judicially, logically. His course lay clear before him – he would take it without hesitation. Nevertheless, he regretted the necessity that might cause a catastrophe.

He only remained at his headquarters long enough to study once again the papers he had brought from the *Electra*, and the notes he had made from her logbook. He then rang up the hospital at Tilbury, was told that the reception of the wounded men was at that moment taking place, and was assured that the two, whose lives were in danger, had survived the transportation from the yacht to the hospital, were, in fact, doing better than expected. Greatly relieved, he turned away from the telephone. Sir Leonard's anxiety had not been centred merely in the condition of Hill, he had been as worried over Farrell. The man may have been a crook, but he had nobly carried out the task assigned to him as the price of his pardon, and Sir Leonard intended to see that he obtained the chance of redemption he had earned. A few minutes' conversation with his assistants, who were awaiting him in Major Brien's room, and the four once again left the building, all, on this occasion, entering Wallace's car. Johnson had received his instructions, and the Rolls-Royce was quickly on its way, running swiftly and noiselessly through the slumbering streets. They came to one of London's most famous residential quarters, and Johnson slowed down. Brien turned to Sir Leonard with a look of astonishment in his eyes.

'What are we going to do here?' he asked.

'Raid a certain house,' was the quiet reply. 'It's going to be a devilish awkward job too.' Suddenly he picked up the speaking tube. 'Drive round the square, Johnson,' he ordered sharply, 'and let that car pull up before you stop.'

The driver promptly turned to the left, and began to encircle the garden in the centre of the square, thus avoiding a taxicab which had appeared on the northern side.

'Ictinos is in that taxi for a bet,' murmured Sir Leonard. 'If so, the problem of obtaining an entrance into the house is solved. Stand-by, everybody, to jump out, and make a dash for it.'

The cab drew up before a residence, like all others in complete darkness. It was a house well known to Brien.

'Why,' he cried, 'that belongs to—'

'Of course it does,' snapped Wallace. 'He's the mysterious partner of Ictinos. Come along!'

'Well, I'm—' began the astonished Major Brien.

There was no time for more. The Rolls-Royce was drawing up some yards behind the other car, and Sir Leonard, revolver in hand, had already sprung on to the pavement. A great, hulking figure of a man tottered out of the taxi, supported by another, smaller fellow. Even in the gloom it was possible to see that his face was bandaged, and his left arm in something that resembled a sling. He appeared to be in the last stages of exhaustion to judge from the manner in which he lolled over the shoulder of his companion, but he turned his head sharply enough as he caught the sound of running feet. A deep cry that was something between a groan and a shout of alarm broke from him, as he recognised the four men then passing under the rays thrown from a street lamp. His hand went to the pocket of the seaman's coat he wore, but Wallace had reached him, was holding his revolver close to the bandaged face of the adversary who had given him so much trouble.

'You won't get away this time, Stanislaus Ictinos,' he ground out in low, tense tones.

The Greek was either too ill or too dejected by the unexpected appearance of the Secret Service men to make any resistance. The fellow with him, whose whole appearance, apart from the beret he wore, denoted that he was a sailor, started back, leaving Ictinos staggering drunkenly on the side-walk. Shannon and Carter, however, quickly took hold of him, supporting him between them. Descending from his perch, the taxi-driver peered curiously from one to the other.

'Nah! then,' he began aggressively, 'what's all this 'ere—' He caught the sound of feet approaching slowly but with determined tread. 'That's a copper,' he asserted. 'I reckon 'e'd better 'ave a look at you fellers. 'Ere, officer—'

Sir Leonard gave a slight nod to Brien, who took the Cockney gently by the arm, and led him protesting towards the approaching constable. He whispered a few words in the latter's ear. To the driver's surprise, the policeman drew himself up, and saluted smartly.

'You'd better hop it quick,' he suggested to the taxi man. 'You're not wanted here.'

'But – but what abaht my fare?' protested the surprised man.

'How much is it?' asked Brien.

'Eight an' a tanner, guv'nor,' replied the other hopefully.

'The gentleman wasn't asking how much you would sell your car for,' interposed the policeman scornfully.

'Blimy! I've driven those two blokes all the way from Woolwich.'

'Here you are.' Brien handed him a ten shilling note.

He took it with a word of thanks. A few moments later the taxi was out of the square, not before Sir Leonard had taken a sharp look into its interior, however. He eyed the policeman reflectively as he approached with Brien, acknowledging his salute with a nod.

'I may want help,' he decided. 'Ring up the Yard, and ask them to send along a van with half a dozen men inside. It is to wait here.'

'Outside this house, sir?'

'Outside this house.'

'But – perhaps you don't know whose residence this is, sir?'

'I certainly do,' Wallace informed him. 'Now hurry off!'

Without another word the man obeyed. Sir Leonard looked anxiously from window to window.

'We don't seem to have aroused anyone,' he commented. 'Still one never knows. Run up the steps, Bill, and ring the night bell. Bring these two along,' he added to Carter and Shannon.

They waited outside the door for some minutes before there was any sign of life from within. Brien had rung again, was about to ring a third time, when a light flared up in the hall showing through the stained glass of the door. Immediately Wallace pushed the sailor forward with Ictinos close behind him.

'When they open,' he ordered in a tense whisper, 'tell them you have brought Stanislaus Ictinos from the *Electra*.'

The feel of a revolver muzzle in his back persuaded the man that it would be distinctly foolish to disregard this stern Englishman's commands, had he felt inclined to do so. He swallowed a trifle convulsively. The door was unlocked and unbarred then drawn open a little way, the chain not having been removed. The pale oval of a face looked out.

'Who is there?' asked a voice somewhat tremulously.

Sir Leonard smiled to himself. There was little resistance to be feared from that quarter. He poked the barrel of his revolver into the seaman's back. The latter swallowed once more.

'I am from the *Electra*,' he told the man inside. 'I have brought Stanislaus Ictinos.'

With an exclamation the servant quickly unfastened the chain; pulled the door wide open. Immediately the four Englishmen, pushing Ictinos and the sailor unceremoniously before them, entered the house. The footman uttered a cry of fear as he beheld the uncompromising countenances of the uninvited guests; cowered back fearfully as Brien's weapon was pointed at him.

'Shut the door, but don't lock it!' ordered the latter.

The trembling man obeyed. At Sir Leonard's command, he afterwards led them across the great hall into a small reception room, where the lights were switched on. The injured Ictinos, who was too dazed apparently to take any interest in the proceedings, and the sailor were both searched, each being found to possess an automatic which was confiscated. Both men were then pushed into chairs, and told that, if they moved, they did so at their own peril.

'Don't take your eyes off them,' warned Wallace, addressing Shannon and Carter. 'You know what a slippery customer Ictinos is, even though he's somewhat the worse for wear. Shoot if he makes an attempt to escape. Now then,' he turned to the quaking servant; 'take this gentleman and me to your master.'

'But, sir,' protested the man, 'he is not here. He has gone away.'

'Lead on!' ordered Wallace sternly. 'And don't make a noise. He may be making preparations to go, but I'm sure he hasn't gone yet.'

Without further objection the footman preceded them across the hall, and up the broad, beautifully carpeted staircase; then along a wide corridor. He stopped a few yards beyond the gallery overlooking the stairs, dumbly indicating a closed door.

'Take him back, Billy, and leave him in the care of Shannon and Carter,' whispered Wallace. 'After you have handed him over, rejoin me.'

Brien nodded, and brusquely drove the servant before him down the stairs. Sir Leonard contemplated the massive door before which he stood for some moments; then, shrugging his shoulders, softly turned the handle. As he had anticipated, it was not locked, and he quietly stepped into the room. The sound of regular breathing reached his ears, and a gentle sigh of satisfaction escaped him. Feeling round cautiously in the dark it was some moments before his fingers encountered the electric light switches, but he refrained from turning on the illumination, waiting for Brien to rejoin him. It was not long before he heard the latter.

'Are you there, Leonard?' came in a whisper that was hardly a whisper at all, so faint was it.

For answer Sir Leonard reached out, found his friend's arm, and pressed it. A moment later he pulled down a switch. A single light, high up in the ornamental ceiling, blazed into life. The intruders gazed round them curiously. They found themselves in a great, lofty bedchamber decorated expensively but somewhat sombrely. The furniture was of Chinese blackwood, wondrously carved, but giving a distinctly funereal tone to the apartment, the deep carpet was elephant grey in colour, the hangings round the great four-poster bed being also of that hue. Toilet articles of gold on the dressing table, silver-grey wallpaper, and a cheerful blaze in the great open fireplace were all that relieved the depressing atmosphere of a truly remarkable chamber. A door on the opposite side of the apartment, over which hung a silk curtain also elephant grey in colour, obviously led to a dressing room. The electric lights were cunningly concealed in the ornamental work of the ceiling.

Neither their entrance nor the sudden radiance had disturbed the sleeper in the bed. They walked across the room, and looked down at him as he lay, his head cushioned in a pillow of the softest silk, one arm, uncovered, thrown over the satin coverlet. Whether their intense gaze disturbed his slumbers, or he roused in the natural order of things, it would be difficult to say, but suddenly his eyes opened. He looked earnestly at one, transferred his gaze to the other, but not the slightest sign of fear or even of curiosity showed in his face and, in that moment, Sir Leonard felt a great admiration for the man. His ruddy complexion looked ruddier than ever, his bushy white hair and beard more unkempt than usual, but his eyes, opened so recently from probably untroubled sleep, were sharp and bright and, in them, was actually an expression of friendliness. He was the first to speak.

'Sir Leonard,' he remarked in conversational tones, 'I am not quite sure whether I should be sincere if I said this is a pleasure, but, at least, I assure you that I am always more pleased to see you than most people, even though, on the present occasion, the hour is somewhat unusual, and my position distinctly informal.'

'I think you know why I have come, Sir Peter,' returned Wallace. 'I have discovered, without doubt, that you are the mysterious partner, in fact the actual head of the organisation of which Stanislaus Ictinos is the supposed leader.'

Sir Peter Nikoleff raised himself on one elbow.

'You surely have not come to me thus unceremoniously at this hour' – he looked at a small gold clock standing on the bedside table. The hands showed that the time was twenty minutes to four – 'in order to relate fairy tales to me.'

'Need we fence?' returned Wallace a trifle wearily. 'You probably know me well enough to realise that I do not take stupid chances, or act on a sudden suspicion. I am perfectly well aware that you are the real seller of secrets, the man who thought that by stealing the confidential schemes of nations, and holding them up for auction or ransom not only to enrich himself, but to gain a power that would be unique.'

Sir Peter looked at his accuser steadfastly.

'How did you arrive at this extraordinary conviction?' he asked. 'I thought that you were of the opinion that my friend Senostris was the villain of the piece.'

'I never quite believed in Senostris' guilt. I know him too well as a man of quiet, unassuming character, uninterested in anything apart from his own very mild hobbies. If you want the truth, Nikoleff, I began to suspect you when you introduced a man and a girl to me in this house yesterday as Stanislaus and Thalia Ictinos who had just come to you from Greece. Your vanity made you think that I would never associate you with such an organisation, and, having met your friends with that name, would necessarily conclude that my information was wrong. Thus the real Ictinos could be shielded, and carry on his nefarious work under your orders as before. For a man as astute as you it was a positively feeble attempt to put me off the track. You made the mistake of taking it for granted that I was going on hearsay, and did not realise, until I admitted as much, that I had not only heard of the real Mr and Miss Ictinos, but had actually seen them, and been present when they were discussing their plans.

'Once my suspicions were roused against you it was not difficult to substantiate them. I put out searching enquiries; discovered, among other things, that the man and his daughter you had calculated to astonish me by producing as Stanislaus and Thalia Ictinos were, in truth, retainers of your family called Nikki, who had been sent from Athens to you in the hope that you would obtain for them employment in England. Various other items of information, into which I need not enter, came quickly into my hands to strengthen my belief that you were the man I wanted. Proof positive came with the intelligence that three weeks ago Michael Senostris, at your request, lent you the *Electra* for two months, or until such time as your own yacht, which had been damaged in a collision, had been repaired. Tonight on the *Electra* I studied the logbook. I cannot speak Greek, but I had the assistance of a man who can, and I know enough about the language to be able to read it without a great deal of effort. The captain of the yacht is conscientious, but very unwise. I copied this entry, or rather translated it from the logbook under today's date –' he took a notebook from his pocket, opened it, and read: "Orders received from Sir Peter Nikoleff, temporary owner, to disguise yacht with the prepared planks of wood and canvas superstructure in readiness on board. Alterations duly carried out. Sir Peter came aboard and expressed approval". Sir Leonard closed the book, and returned it to his pocket. 'I am afraid you can hardly find an argument sound enough to disprove that,' he observed drily.

For the first time Sir Peter showed perturbation. He sat bolt upright in bed.

'This is a ridiculous position in which to hold an interview with you,' he protested. 'I feel I am rather at a disadvantage. If you permit, I will rise, and don a dressing gown.'

'I'd rather you stayed where you are at present,' was the reply.

The ex-Greek was about to ignore the suggestion; made as though to get out of bed, but a revolver flashed in Sir Leonard's hand. Sir Peter sank back on his pillows.

'So you threaten me?'

'I want you to realise,' came the retort, 'that you are my prisoner.'

'Prisoner! On what charge?'

'Certain charges under the Official Secrets Act, and also the criminal charge of being accessory to murders and other misdemeanours committed by your partner Stanislaus Ictinos.'

'That is ridiculous,' spluttered Nikoleff. 'You cannot do it. Whatever I may have done, and I admit nothing, I have certainly not been a party to murder.'

'Your mistake was in associating yourself with a bloodthirsty brute like Ictinos. In protecting your joint secrets he committed murder; you can hardly expect, therefore, to avoid being charged as accessory. Altogether, Sir Peter, for a man who has certain control on the money markets of the world, and has more than one nation in his pocket so to speak, you haven't shone in this business. The manner in which you prepared your poor catspaws for their new names yesterday for instance was not brilliant. I'm afraid the unnecessary use of, and the emphasis you laid on, the Stanislaus and Thalia rather suggested to my mind that you were priming them. They certainly fell in with the hidden command with credit to themselves.'

'And you are really convinced of my guilt?'

'Absolutely. I must admit that I do not think that you, probably the richest man in the world today, were very interested in the financial gain expected to accrue from your projects. Your supreme idea was to get nations at your feet in order that you could blackmail them into agreeing to anything you demanded. Ultimately you hoped to become dictator of Europe. The idea, Sir Peter, was colossal, but the preliminary execution has been puerile, simply because you chose Ictinos as the man to carry out your schemes. I have talked enough. Before going any further, I want the copies of the documents and plans relative to the French frontier fortifications which you brought away from the *Electra* tonight.'

Nikoleff started. He was too big a man to endeavour to fence with the astute Englishman confronting him. He knew he had been unmasked, and was sensible enough to see that a futile attempt at bluff would not pay. But he was naturally very much surprised at the revelation of Sir Leonard's knowledge.

'How did you know I was on the *Electra* tonight?' he demanded.

Wallace laughed.

'Does that matter? You left Ictinos in the belief that he was about to trap me – as it happened I trapped him. At the moment he is downstairs under guard. His band of cut-throats is locked up to await trial, the *Electra* is in the hands of the police at Tilbury. You left her in the company of Thalia Ictinos, and in your pocket were the documents I want. Where are they?'

'Sir Leonard,' observed Nikoleff quietly, 'you are a wonderful man.'

'Where are those papers?'

'What does that matter to you? Suppose I have them, how can documents of such a nature possibly interest you?'

'I have pledged myself to recover them for France. You will save time and trouble by handing them over.'

'Ah! So there is now an *entente cordiale* between the secret services of France and Britain. That is most interesting. My friend, if you suspect that those papers are in this house, I am afraid you will have to search for them. Shall I sit by, and tell you whether you are hot or cold?'

Wallace turned to Brien.

'Put on all the lights, Bill,' he directed, 'and search this bedroom and the adjoining apartment. I don't think the documents will be far away.'

He was watching Sir Peter narrowly as he spoke without appearing to do so. Out of the corner of his eye he noticed the old man subconsciously touch a certain portion of his anatomy. At once Wallace was on him, had called his colleague to his assistance. For a few moments there was a violent tumult in the bed; then Wallace and Brien rose. In the former's hand was a thin silken belt, which, with its double folds, really consisted of a long, strongly made pocket. Wallace had torn it from its position round Sir Peter's waist under his pyjama jacket, having guessed from the latter's involuntary movement where the precious papers were. He extracted them now, and examined them with a quiet air of triumph. Sir Peter, his torn jacket hanging in silken ribbons from his body, lay back on his pillows as though exhausted.

CHAPTER TWENTY

'The Affair is Finished'

Sir Leonard quickly satisfied himself that the documents he was holding were in truth those so badly wanted by the French government. He put them away into an inside pocket of his coat, and contemplated the recumbent financier.

'It is a pity you resisted,' he commented. 'After all the result was the same, and, if there is one thing I hate, it is having to use force on people against whom I have no personal animosity.'

Sir Peter opened his eyes, and looked at the speaker.

'So you have no personal animosity against me?' he remarked.

'None. Why should I have?'

'I am glad of that, because, strangely enough, though you are the first man who has ever frustrated a scheme of mine, I feel no ill-will towards you. In the past, if anyone dared to attempt to thwart me, he was made to regret it – oh, yes; regret it very much! In the present case, for the first time in my life, I feel inclined to admit that I am beaten. I have little desire to ruin you, Sir Leonard.

Perhaps it is because I am growing old, and am beginning to realise the futility of vengeance.'

The Chief of the Secret Service smiled.

'Do you think you could ruin me if you wished?' he asked.

'But of course. You must know yourself that I could. Are you forgetting the political strings I can pull? Why, my friend, I could bring down your government if I desired. Ruining an individual, even though he possesses the power of Sir Leonard Wallace, would hardly be a more difficult operation.'

'Why this sudden boastfulness? Allow me to remind you, Sir Peter, that you are my prisoner.'

'Do you mean to say' – the old man sat up in bed – 'that you still persist in believing that you can make me a common captive, and hand me over to be dealt with by the law like any malefactor?'

'Why not? If you offend, you are subject to punishment as well as any other man. Why should you be exempt?'

'Because of my power; because of my money! My dear sir, the government would not dare to prosecute me. Inform the country that I am to be tried, and what would happen?' He laughed softly. 'Take my advice, Sir Leonard, and do not attempt impossibilities. You have won; you have broken up the organisation I formed, recovered the secrets I schemed for, in one case which I obtained myself – I refer to those documents in your pocket, which cost me a lot of money and all my persuasive powers. What more can you want? What good can it do you to place me in the very humiliating position of a man on trial for felony?'

'It will do me no good,' returned Wallace doggedly, 'but I have my duty to do.'

'Bah! Is it your duty to throw the world into a state of chaos? Listen, my friend! If you dared apprehend me, tomorrow, or rather today, there would come a state of confusion such as Europe and America have seldom seen. It is not boasting to remind you that I wield tremendous influence in the affairs of the world both financial and political. I am all-powerful, and you know it well. Arrest me, and markets will crash, securities will come tumbling down, governments will fall. Sir Leonard, I must not be touched. Surely you yourself realise all this?'

Wallace nodded. His face was grim and stern.

'Yes; I realise it,' he returned. 'Nevertheless I repeat once more: you are my prisoner. What is done with you after I hand you over to Scotland Yard is not my affair. My duty concludes when I place before the government the proofs that will convict you.'

Sir Peter stared at him a trifle wildly. There was a tense pause of a few moments' duration; then:

'Do you think the government would put me on trial?' came almost in a sneer.

'There would be no alternative. But why argue about it? Will you be kind enough to rise now, and dress? I will send for your valet, if you wish.'

Again the financier's eyes showed perturbation. Little beads of perspiration appeared on his forehead.

'Never have I met a man so obdurate,' he confessed. 'Listen,' he leant forward: 'I do not care so much that my arrest would throw the world into disorder. It would be impossible, however, for me to stand in the dock to be tried by a judge and a jury, the cynosure of curious, sensation-seeking eyes – I who up to now have been the greatest, most powerful force in Europe and America. A position of such humiliation is not possible for me. There must be a way to avoid that, even for a man of your intractable sense of what you call duty.'

Sir Leonard's face hardened.

'You are merely thinking of yourself,' he accused.

'Have you no thought for the thousands who might be ruined by your fate?'

'Have you?' countered the other sharply. 'You would be the guilty one, not I. During the years that have passed there have been two or three cases of world-known financiers coming to grief. You remember well what the result was; the misery, the suffering, the distress that afflicted so many people. And what power had those men when compared with mine? Where their ruin affected thousands, mine would affect millions. Think of that, Sir Leonard, and ponder on it.'

'I have thought about it, and I have sought for a way out, not for your sake, for the sake of others, but my duty has remained perfectly clear. The government, as I have already said, will have to decide, when I put all the facts before it. There is another thing,' he added, 'of which you appear to have lost sight. Ictinos will be placed on his trial. Do you imagine, for one moment, that he will keep silent about your part in his activities?'

Sir Peter actually smiled.

'He will never mention my name,' he declared with confidence.

'A man on trial for his life, apart from the other things, and such a man as Ictinos, would not hesitate.'

'You are wrong,' persisted the other. 'He will never speak.'

Wallace shrugged his shoulders.

'There are other considerations as well,' he remarked. 'If, by some chance, the British government declined to prosecute, there are other nations who would; France, for instance.'

'France would never dare; too many French affairs are in my hands. Besides, my friend, the man from whom I obtained those documents, which you have taken from me, holds a position in the French government which is almost unassailable.'

'Who is he?'

The financier laughed softly.

'Do you think I would tell? You would like to hand on the information to Monsieur Damien no doubt.'

'I certainly should.'

Sir Peter sat slowly nodding his head.

'I understand now,' he commented, without troubling to state what it was he understood. 'It must be a curse to be so outrageously honest as you, Sir Leonard.'

'We are wasting time,' retorted the other brusquely. 'Come on; get up!'

'I decline to do so. It is not my hour for rising.'

'Then we shall have to make you—'

'Be reasonable, my friend! Let me make one more appeal to you. Providing you leave my name out of this affair, take what you have got, and go, I will pay to you and your friend there one million pounds. Do you agree?'

'You are now becoming senile,' retorted Wallace curtly. 'Get up!'

He took hold of the financier's arm. The latter sighed, and stepped to the floor.

'I was afraid bribery would not work,' he confessed. 'Nothing, not even a million pounds, can shake that probity of yours apparently. I will dress myself. It would be degrading to have a valet present under such circumstances.'

He walked towards the dressing room followed by Brien, who was obeying a significant nod from Sir Leonard. For a moment the latter felt like sinking into a chair. He was weary, not so much physically as mentally, the realisation of the responsibility he was taking, in unmasking Sir Peter, having contributed mostly to that condition. But squaring his shoulders he shook off the lethargy, and commenced a search of the room. In ten minutes Sir Peter returned, accompanied by the watchful Brien. He was clothed in a lounge suit, but had not troubled to brush his hair or comb his beard, which looked more unkempt than ever. Walking to the bed, he sat down.

'I am dressed, as you see,' he remarked. 'What a pity you came here when you did. By ten o'clock I should have been on my way to the continent by air. I was foolish in thinking myself safe, when a man like you was on the track. Ah, well! It is over. I have had a good innings, and my life has been full and triumphant.'

A spasm of pain crossed his face. Wallace frowned a little. The man looked ill; his complexion was no longer ruddy, there was a greyness about it that held almost the suggestion of death.

'Are you ill?' he demanded, stepping forward.

'I am dying,' was the quiet reply. 'When dressing I swallowed a capsule of an obscure and very deadly poison which has no known antidote. Its name I prefer to keep to myself. Do not blame your friend, Sir Leonard. The box I took it from looked very much as though it might contain studs, and I acted in a manner to give the impression that I was indeed selecting and using one. I think I will lie down, if you have no objection.'

He sank back. Wallace lifted his legs on to the bed, and remained watching him. Brien, close by, stood with a face of tragedy. Both sensed instinctively that it was hopeless to endeavour to save Sir Peter's life. It required no very great acumen to see that he was sinking rapidly; long before a doctor could be summoned, the deadly work would have been accomplished. The dying man opened his eyes, which had closed when he sank back on to the pillows, and smiled painfully.

'I have gained a partial victory,' he whispered. 'There will be no humiliation for me in arrest and imprisonment now and, at the same time, you will still have to face the fact that you will have been the cause of throwing Europe and the United States into financial chaos.' He paused for breath, a little foam appeared on his ashen lips. 'Still I bear no ill-will,' he went on. 'I have – chosen this way – it is best.'

A groan broke from him, his body writhed convulsively for some minutes; then lay still. Sir Leonard turned away, and dabbed his forehead with a pocket handkerchief. Both he and Brien were nearly as pale as the man lying dead on the bed.

'I am sorry, Leonard,' murmured the latter.

Wallace forced a smile.

'You weren't to know,' he replied. 'It never occurred to me that he would do a thing like that. A force all his life, he meant to be a force at the end. Perhaps, after all, it's the best thing that could have happened in the circumstances. We may be able to keep his name out of this affair, and save too big a crash in financial circles.'

'But won't his death cause that in any case?'

'I think I see a way out.' He turned, and looked once more at the still form on the bed. 'To think,' he murmured, 'that a man of his power and wealth should devise and organise an enterprise of such a nature. It is inconceivable.' He shrugged his shoulders. 'Forget he's dead, Bill.'

Brien stared at him in astonishment.

'What – what do you mean?' he asked.

'Forget he's dead – at least for the present. I wonder if that instrument is connected up,' he added, eyeing the bedside telephone. He lifted the receiver, and listened. 'It is,' he remarked in a tone of satisfaction.

First he rang up the Foreign Secretary's house demanding that that gentleman be awakened, a proceeding that took some time. When the sleepy but interested voice of the statesman came over the wire, asking to know why he had been disturbed, Wallace refused to give any explanation, but insisted almost bluntly on his coming to Grosvenor Square at once, ringing off in the midst of the minister's astonished questions. It took even longer to get through to the Home Secretary, who was distinctly brusque at being awakened at what he described as an ungodly hour of the morning. His presence was also demanded as soon as possible in Sir Peter Nikoleff's residence, Wallace assuring him that there was vital reason for his attendance there.

'Like a lot of old women with their questions,' he commented somewhat unreasonably, as he replaced the receiver. 'Come along, Bill; we'll go downstairs.'

They left the room, taking care to lock all doors giving access to it, and pocketing the keys. They found Ictinos sitting practically as they had left him, his head sunk forward on his breast; the sailor looked up at their entrance and scowled; the footman eyed them fearfully. Shannon and Carter sat at their ease smoking, but very much on the alert. They rose as Wallace entered, and reported that the prisoners had been perfectly tractable. He nodded shortly, went up to the servant, and regarded him sternly.

'Why didn't you tell me your master was ill?' he demanded to Brien's astonishment.

'Ill, sir!' faltered the man. 'He was not ill when I saw him last.'

'Well, he is now. My friend and I went to interview him concerning this man,' he indicated Ictinos, 'and found him seriously – in fact critically ill. He will have to be moved to a nursing home.'

'Shall I call his secretaries and valet, sir?'

'Presently. At the moment you must stay where you are.'

'But what have I done? I—'

'Be quiet!' came the curt order. Wallace turned to Carter. 'Go and let the police officers in,' he directed. 'Bring them here.'

Suddenly he found the eyes of Ictinos fixed on him. The Greek had raised his head and, despite his unkempt and haggard appearance, looked very much on the alert. He had been very interested in Wallace's conversation with the servant, the look on his face denoting that he was puzzled. A few minutes went by, and Carter entered the room followed by an inspector of police, a sergeant, and two constables. They all wore expressions of intense curiosity. Sir Leonard pointed to the Greek.

'This man,' he stated, 'is Stanislaus Ictinos of Greek nationality. He was leader of a gang engaged in stealing and offering for sale official secrets. He escaped from me a few hours ago, and, I suppose, sought sanctuary here in the hope that Sir Peter Nikoleff, being of Greek birth, might help him. Apart from his offences under the Official Secrets Act, he has committed two murders, at least, and various other crimes. Take him away, inspector, and watch him carefully. He's a slippery customer. I will communicate with the Commissioner later this morning. I am making no charge against this fellow at present,' he indicated the seaman, 'but keep him locked up until you hear from me.'

The inspector smiled with deep satisfaction.

'Come along!' he bade the two prisoners.

They rose to their feet, Ictinos with a scowl, the other sullenly. The sergeant and constables took possession of them, and walked them away. At the door Ictinos turned, and shook the fist of his uninjured arm at Wallace.

'Curse you!' he mumbled from amidst the bandages round his jaw. 'Somebody will get you yet, and I hope it is soon, you devil.'

'So you've recovered your voice,' commented Wallace. 'I was beginning to think Captain Shannon had knocked it out of you.'

Ictinos uttered an expletive which was pointed if ungentlemanly.

'Come along,' ordered the sergeant, giving him a shove. 'Don't be so playful!'

Wallace turned to speak to Brien, taking no further notice of the gorilla-man. The lights were now on in the hall, but the policemen did not stop to admire the palace-like splendour of that vast space. They had a job on hand, which they were bent on performing, and marched with their prisoners to the front door without glancing either to right or left. There, however, they halted with surprise, as a scream rang out behind them. From the gallery above a beautiful girl, whose face was strikingly pale, had observed their progress.

'My father!' she cried, tore down the stairs, ran lightly across the hall, and flung herself into the arms of Ictinos. 'What have they done to you?' she sobbed.

Sir Leonard and his companions heard the commotion, and hurried out of the room. They were just in time to witness the meeting of father and daughter. The embrace terminated abruptly. Thalia stepped back, and Ictinos, planting himself against the wall, an expression of triumph on his face, raised the revolver she had pushed into his hand.

'If any man makes a movement,' he boomed, 'I will shoot to kill.' The policemen stood astounded. Wallace smiled. 'Ah!' snarled the Greek, noticing the smile, 'the so-great Wallace thinks I do not mean what I say. Thanks to my daughter Thalia, I will prove it.'

'Oh! How are you going to do that?' asked Sir Leonard in a tone of interest.

He actually began to advance across the hall. Ictinos watched his progress, at first a look almost of fascination in his wicked, slate-blue eyes, quickly changing to one of mingled delight and ferocity.

'The nearer you come the surer the mark,' he sneered. 'You are unarmed, my friend Wallace. What can you do?'

'Be careful, Father!' cried Thalia. 'Remember—'

She never finished the warning. Like lightning Sir Leonard's hand went to his pocket, at the same time he threw himself on the floor and, as he rolled over, fired in reply to the shot which Ictinos had sent viciously, a fraction of a second too late, where his adversary had been. The Greek howled with pain and rage as the gun dropped from his shattered hand. At once the police were on him; ran him and the sailor out of the house. Thalia, screaming maledictions, made as though to follow, but the inspector barred the way.

'Shall I take the woman too, sir?' he asked, as Sir Leonard rose languidly from the floor.

The latter shook his head, and advanced towards the girl. Her lips curled with scorn as she stood looking at him, her great eyes glaring hatred. He reflected that he had seldom seen a more beautiful creature. Her slim body was wrapped in a peignoir of pale blue silk which seemed to enhance her loveliness. Full of charm, altogether glamorous, it was difficult to realise that she was anything but a sweet, captivating girl.

'No,' he decided. 'I have no desire to make any charge against her. Please remember,' he added to Thalia, 'that you are lucky to be allowed your freedom.'

'Send me to prison if you wish,' she retorted. 'I have no desire to be under any obligation to you.'

'Perhaps not; nevertheless it might be to your future advantage, if you reflected on the truism that crime does not pay. Go into that room,' he pointed to the apartment he had recently vacated, 'and stay there until you are told you can go. Carter, Shannon, go with her, and keep that servant there too for the time being. Perhaps you'd better accompany them, Bill,' he added.

She walked across the hall with studied insolence, every step she took the very acme of grace, and disappeared from view followed by her temporary guards. The sergeant of police re-entered the house.

'He struggled like hell, sir,' he reported descriptively, 'even though he has all them wounds. Still we've got him in the van now with four men holding him down.'

'Good,' returned Wallace. 'Take him away, and lock him up in the strongest cell you have.'

He saw the inspector and sergeant out, and closed the door upon them. Turning he found that the household had been aroused by the noise. Startled men and women in various stages of *déshabillé* stood on the stairs or peering down from the gallery. An elderly, keen-eyed man, clothed in a dark blue dressing gown, approached him. Sir Leonard knew him well. He was Sir Peter's principal secretary.

'What has happened, sir? Has there been—'

'Send all those people back to bed,' ordered Wallace; 'You can tell them the police have arrested a dangerous criminal who sought refuge here if you like. But get them back to their quarters; then return to me.'

After a barely perceptible show of hesitation the secretary did as he was ordered. Wallace waited by the front door, intending to open it himself when the two statesmen arrived. Three or four minutes went by; then the man who had been in Sir Peter Nikoleff's service for many years came back.

'They have all gone to their rooms, Sir Leonard,' he announced quietly.

At that moment they heard the sound of a car drawing up outside the house.

'Open the door, Anstruther,' directed Wallace.

The elderly man obeyed, his look of perplexity increasing. When he observed the thin, ascetic face of the Foreign Secretary, as the latter ascended the steps, his astonishment knew no bounds. He stood aside to allow the statesman to enter, was about to close the door, when another car drew up. Out of it sprang a figure muffled up to the chin in a thick overcoat, who hurried into the house as though not in the very best of tempers. Anstruther started back with an exclamation of sheer wonderment. He had recognised the Home Secretary. The latter caught sight of Wallace greeting his colleague of the Cabinet, and strode across to him.

'What's all this ,Wallace?' he demanded. 'Why have you called us up at this unearthly hour, and brought us here?'

'You'll know all about it in a minute,' was the reply. 'Anstruther,' he called, as the secretary approached, 'take us to a room where we can talk.'

The elderly man led them into an apartment towards the back of the hall, fitted up as an office, apparently his own sanctum. He offered them chairs; then took a decanter of whisky, soda siphon, and glasses from a cellaret, and placed them on a table within easy reach. Wallace accepted a drink gratefully; he felt he needed it.

'Would you like me to call Sir Peter?' asked Anstruther, surprise still showing in his expression.

Sir Leonard took a deep drink.

'It wouldn't be any use I'm afraid,' he remarked with a sigh.

The secretary saw something in his face that caused him to gasp. His own paled.

'What do you mean, sir?' he asked in a hoarse voice.

The others also had sensed that something was wrong. They leant forward staring into Sir Leonard's eyes.

'You must be prepared for a shock,' observed the latter quietly. 'I am very sorry to have to tell you—' he paused deliberately, giving them time to prepare for what was coming.

'What? In God's name, what?' cried Anstruther, now thoroughly alarmed.

'Sir Peter is dead!'

His announcement was received in complete silence. The three men who had heard it sat as though carved out of stone, pale-faced, horror-stricken, incapable for some minutes of movement of any kind. Anstruther was the first to speak.

'Sir Peter – dead!' he whispered incredulously. 'Why, he was perfectly fit when I saw him last.'

Sir Leonard rose, set down his glass on an adjacent table, and placed his hand on the secretary's shoulder.

'I have known you, Anstruther, for some time,' he said. 'You are, to the best of my knowledge, a man of absolute integrity and honour. It is because of that that I am admitting you to my confidence in this tragic affair, as well as the necessity I feel in having somebody connected with Sir Peter's household to aid me in the scheme I have in mind. I can rely absolutely on you?'

'Of course, Sir Leonard,' replied the white-faced man, 'but what—'

'Sir Peter committed suicide in the presence of Major Brien and myself about twenty minutes ago.'

This dramatic announcement had them all on their feet. Again horror held them in shocked immobility; their faces were ghastly.

'But – but why should he have done that?' gasped the Home Secretary at last.

'Because I had discovered that he was the real head of the organisation that has lately caused so much anxiety by its procuration of national secrets for sale to interested powers.'

'Impossible!' came from the two statesmen in one voice.

'I cannot believe that—' began Anstruther.

'Sit down, gentlemen, and listen to me.'

They obeyed, the horror on their faces having given way, at least in two cases, to utter incredulity. Then, still standing where he was, Sir Leonard quietly but graphically related everything that had happened from the time he had stepped ashore from the *Majestic* until the arrival of the two cabinet ministers in the house, including the conversation he had had with Sir Peter Nikoleff, and the latter's efforts to persuade him to keep silent about his part in the conspiracy. When he had finished he sat down, and drained the contents of his glass. For some seconds there was a profound silence then the Foreign Secretary spoke.

'We could never have brought him to trial,' he dared in a hoarse voice. 'He was right – we would not have dared to do it.'

'We should have had to,' interposed the other statesman brusquely. 'It would have been our duty.'

'Think of what would have happened.'

'Think of what will happen in any case,' was the retort. 'But, gentlemen,' murmured Anstruther – he looked like a man on the verge of death – 'this is appalling. I had no idea—'

'Of course you hadn't,' Wallace interrupted. 'I know that. Tell me: is the effect of his sudden death likely to be very disastrous, even if we hush up the reason for it?'

'It will be catastrophic,' replied the secretary in a hushed voice. 'He practically had control of the money markets of the world. Almost every nation will suffer; there will be chaos in some; very few will escape without being shaken to their foundations.'

The four men sought each other's eyes, in their own the fear of terrible things.

'But,' protested Wallace, 'if he had become seriously ill, and died, say after a few days spent in unconsciousness, utterly unable to deal with his affairs, surely there would not be such a world-shaking repercussion?'

'No,' replied Anstruther; 'for there would then be time for me and the other secretaries, managers, and agents to adjust things in expectation of his death. Even then there would be a certain reaction in the world's markets, nothing very serious of course. But what is the use of discussing what—'

Sir Leonard leant forward; held the eyes of the others.

'Sir Peter is going to become seriously ill,' he declared; 'so seriously ill that he can only be seen by Anstruther here. He will be placed in a nursing home under the care of a well-known doctor. In three or four days he will die.'

His listeners looked at him in bewilderment, but gradually a gleam of understanding came into their eyes.

'You mean—' began the Foreign Secretary.

'I mean that only we four and Major Brien know that he is dead now, how he died, and why he died. You, Anstruther, must have him removed to the nursing home tonight. I will select the home, and guarantee the silence of the matron, the special nurses employed, and the doctors. The sooner everything is done the better.'

'Is it possible?' murmured the Home Secretary.

'Leave that part to me,' was the confident reply. 'All the rest is in Anstruther's hands. I am sure we can rely on him.'

The secretary appeared to be a broken man. He seemed to have aged years since he had met Sir Leonard in the hall less than half an hour previously, but he nodded his head emphatically enough.

'You can rely on me,' he declared.

'There is no reason why you gentlemen should remain here, unless you wish to,' remarked Wallace to the two statesmen. 'Anstruther and I will deal with everything.'

They declared their intention of stopping. They had both been very friendly with Sir Peter, and thought it might give point to the reported story of his serious illness, if they were seen about. Wallace agreed with them. Announcing his intention of making the necessary arrangements at once, he handed the keys of Sir Peter's bedroom over to Anstruther; then left the three men. Turning into the room wherein Thalia sat with her custodians he told her to go to bed. She rose from her chair, eyeing him with intense hatred.

'You will be sorry – oh, so sorry for tonight's work,' she threatened. 'If my father dies, you die also – nothing will save you.'

'Take my advice,' he returned calmly, 'and try and remove the kinks from your mind. You'll only end by landing yourself in serious trouble. It would be as well if you went back to your own country at the earliest possible moment.'

'Remember my words,' was her only reply to that.

She turned on her heel, and walked away. Wallace beckoned to the footman.

'You are not a prisoner,' he told him, 'so you need not look frightened. You can go to the domestic quarters, but remain awake and within call. Your master's illness may necessitate your being wanted at any moment.'

Greatly relieved that he was apparently no longer an object of suspicion the man departed. Sir Leonard told his assistants to make themselves comfortable until his return, and left the house. Giving Johnson certain explicit directions, he entered the car, and was driven away.

The British Secret Service includes among its members all sorts and conditions of people cloaking their activities under the guise of almost every profession it is possible to mention. The greater number of these live abroad, but there are also individuals in Great Britain, holding more or less important civil posts, whose connection with the government department controlled by Sir Leonard Wallace would never be suspected. Among these are two of London's most famous physicians. One of them is the nominal head of a nursing home in Mayfair of which the matron and the principal nurses on her staff are also trusted members of Sir Leonard's organisation. The advantages of such an arrangement in connection with a department of the nature of the Secret Service will be too obvious to need explanation. Not infrequently the existence of a nursing home staffed by nurses, and visited by doctors in Sir Leonard's confidence, has been found of the utmost value. To the house of one of these medical men Wallace was driven on this occasion. Although the hour was so early he found that the man he had gone to visit had already risen. For ten minutes they were closeted together, after which they both left in Sir Leonard's car for the nursing home. The matron and two nurses were called, and a short conference took place.

Half an hour after leaving Grosvenor Square, Wallace re-entered Sir Peter Nikoleff's house accompanied by the doctor and one of the nurses. Anstruther was called, and the four of them went up to the room where the great financier lay dead. The secretary was dispatched to rouse the household, and quickly the news spread that Sir Peter was desperately ill. Servants, with anxious faces, were soon rushing hither and thither, conveying to the bedroom various articles demanded by the doctor, which the nurse always took in at the door. Sir Leonard rejoined the two statesmen; gratefully accepted a cup of coffee handed to him by a footman.

'Double pneumonia,' he declared succinctly.

The Cabinet ministers made no reply, except to nod their heads. In the eyes of each, as they regarded the Chief of the Secret Service, was an expression of frank admiration, not unmixed with a look of profound relief. Shortly afterwards they took their leave, warmly shaking Anstruther by the hand, as he stood holding the door open for them. Soon after their departure an ambulance arrived. With the doctor on one side, the nurse on the other, the body of Sir Peter was carried down the stairs and out of the house. Sir Leonard and the secretary followed behind. Pale-faced, wide-eyed servants, and other members of the household, strove to catch a glimpse of their employer as he passed by, but they could see little of his face, blankets being drawn almost up to the closed eyes. Anstruther and Sir Leonard stood on the steps watching until the ambulance glided out of the square on its way to the nursing home; the former, despite the fact that he was clad only in pyjamas and a dressing gown, apparently impervious to the bitter cold; then they re-entered the house. In the centre of the hall, frowning as though in perplexity, stood Thalia Ictinos. Wallace walked up to her. The same look of hatred as before was in her eyes as she watched his approach.

'When you came back on the launch with Sir Peter,' he asked, 'did he seem ill?'

She started a little.

'So you know that we came here together,' she murmured.

'Of course. That is why I came to ask Sir Peter what connection there was between him and your father. Unfortunately I found him too – er – ill to give me any information.' She gave an almost imperceptible sigh of relief, which he was quick to notice. 'Perhaps you will tell me,' he added.

'I have nothing to tell you,' she returned sharply.

'At least,' he urged, 'you will answer my first question.'

'He did not seem ill. Several times he shivered with the cold that was all.'

Turning she walked away from him. Sir Leonard watched her ascend the stairs; then joined Anstruther in his sanctum. The latter was engaged in telephoning a carefully framed report of Sir Peter Nikoleff's supposed illness to the press. Waiting until he had finished, Wallace had a few words with him, shook hands, and went to rejoin his assistants. They had been supplied with refreshments, and had made themselves very comfortable.

'The affair is finished,' he remarked simply. 'Let us go.'

As they crossed the hall, Anstruther the secretary walked heavily up the stairs. He was on his way to the room so recently and tragically visited by the Angel of Death. The four Secret Service men took their seats in Sir Leonard's car. Brien whistled softly.

'Do you realise,' he remarked, 'that it is only forty-eight hours since you landed from the *Majestic*?'

'Forty-eight hours!' repeated Wallace. 'It seems like forty-eight years.'

CHAPTER TWENTY-ONE

Yuletide Peace

Christmas is essentially a festival for the children, and on this occasion particularly there was great jubilation among the younger members of the Wallace and Brien families, the reason being that, for the first time for years, the house party held annually in Sir Leonard's beautiful residence in New Forest, was complete. There were present, besides Sir Leonard and Lady Wallace and Adrian, Major and Mrs Brien and their children, and Wing-Commander and Mrs Kendal. As Cecil Kendal is Molly's brother, and Mrs Kendal the sister of Mrs Brien, it was indeed a family party. But, despite the general happiness of everybody, the blissful elation of the children, it is certain that the greatest joy was felt by Molly. To have her husband with her at any time is always her greatest pleasure, to have him at home in that season, which is the very epitome of happiness, was the acme of bliss to her, especially as four years had passed since they had spent the Yuletide together. Her heart was full of thankfulness and, for the time being at least, the shadow of anxiety and suspense, which overhung such a large part of her life, had departed, leaving her without a care in the world. The two days of intense strain, which Sir Leonard had spent immediately on his return from the United States, had left him careworn; there were little wrinkles at the corners of his eyes that she had never seen before. She asked no questions, for she was careful never to interfere or intrude in any way in his official life; nevertheless she knew he had undergone a great deal, had suffered severely. But rapidly, under her devoted care, he recovered all the heartiness and *joie de vivre* which was so typically part of his character.

Wallace himself entered into the spirit of the season thoroughly. Of the three men he was the most boisterous. Always planning games and expeditions for the children, he took part in them with thorough abandon, appearing to enjoy himself every bit as much as they, which probably he was. Christmas Day itself was an enormous success, and neither he, Brien, nor Kendal spared themselves in their efforts to make it noteworthy, a real red-letter day in the lives of their children and their wives. The *pièce de resistance* was an enormous Christmas tree at which three Santa Clauses appeared carrying sacks of presents, and staged a friendly dispute concerning their right to the title of Father Christmas. The fun waxed fast and furious, reaching a perfect climax, when they agreed that the old man of Yuletide was in reality triplets, and proceeded to distribute gifts to the ladies and the youngsters amidst screams of delight and uproarious merriment. The servants were not forgotten, and were included in the general merry-making round the Christmas tree, receiving their presents and joining in the hilarity with great good will. Altogether it was a memorable occasion.

The only serious note during the whole of that day was struck at the end of dinner, when the ladies had left their men to port and cigars, and betaken themselves to the cosy seats round the huge fire in the smaller of the two drawing rooms. Sir Leonard, feeling pleasantly tired after his exertions, allowed himself to relax, and sat, eyes half closed, listening to the conversation of his companions. Suddenly Kendal leant across the table, and addressed him.

'Bad luck on old Nikoleff being struck down with double pneumonia, isn't it?' he observed. 'They say there's no hope of his recovery.'

'He died this morning,' returned Sir Leonard calmly.

Brien glanced at him sharply; Cecil Kendal whistled long and thoughtfully.

'That will mean a pretty hectic upset, won't it?' he asked.

'Not now. You see his death was more or less expected, and by this time everything has been adjusted in anticipation of it. Of course, countries for which he had floated huge loans will feel the draught a bit, but nothing to the extent they would have done if, for instance, he had died without warning.'

'I see. I never could make head or tail of finance. It has me beaten every time. There was a bit of a crisis in financial circles on the day he was taken ill, wasn't there?'

Sir Leonard nodded.

'Yes; quite an exciting and anxious time, I believe, but things began to quieten down twenty-four hours afterwards, and yesterday they were almost normal. I take off my hat to Anstruther,' he added, glancing at Brien, 'he has engineered things admirably – proved himself a wizard in fact.'

His words carried a deeper meaning than Kendal suspected, but Brien understood, and the latter's lips curved in a slight smile.

'Who is Anstruther?' asked Cecil.

'Sir Peter's chief secretary. The man behind the scenes, who has spent about twenty-five years in carrying out Nikoleff's orders and studying his methods. A very fine fellow. He was deeply attached to Sir Peter, but even he wasn't acquainted with all the financier's undertakings.'

Kendal gazed at his brother-in-law with a new admiration in his eyes.

'Is there anything you don't know?' he asked.

Wallace nodded his head solemnly.

'So much,' he stated, 'that sometimes I am appalled at my ignorance.'

Kendal grinned; then became serious once more.

'Poor Nikoleff,' he murmured. 'I knew him a bit – he seemed a decent old boy.'

'He was,' agreed Sir Leonard, 'but, like a great many men of his extraordinary mental brilliance, he had a kink. Still he's gone now, and the kink has gone with him.' He raised his glass. 'May he rest in peace,' he added.

The others followed his example, and drained their glasses to the memory of the man who had been the greatest force in the world.

'By the way, Leonard,' pursued Cecil, putting down his glass as though its position on the table were a most important matter, 'from hints, signs, and portents I rather suspect that you've had a pretty hectic time lately. What have you been up to?'

'Cecil, your use of the word hectic is becoming monotonous,' admonished his brother-in-law. 'Try something else.'

'Come on, out with it,' persisted the other in persuasive tones, 'or is it one of those frightful secrets you keep shut up in your reticent breast? I'm always keen on hearing about your adventures, you know; flatter myself that I have once or twice proved useful. Do you remember Luis de Correa?'

Wallace smiled reminiscently.

'I do,' he admitted. 'A crook, but a sportsman. As I have not heard of his committing any transgressions lately, I am almost inclined to believe that he has decided to be honest.'

'What about this yarn. Mustn't I hear it?'

'I don't suppose it will do any harm, if you really want to know. Billy let me in for the business. He thought I'd enjoyed myself too much in the States, I suppose.'

Brien made a grimace. Sir Leonard then told his brother-in-law of his encounter with Stanislaus and Thalia Ictinos, leaving out all mention of Sir Peter Nikoleff's connection with the conspiracy, and making it appear that he had found the documents, so important to France, when a boat called the *Canopus*, which Ictinos had hired, had been raided. Kendal listened entranced, not uttering a word until the narrative was concluded; then he gave vent to his feelings.

'Great Scott!' he exclaimed. 'What a perfectly bloodthirsty brute that fellow Ictinos must be. Hanging's too good for a fellow like that. How are the invalids?'

'All out of danger, I'm thankful to say. It was touch and go with Hill and Farrell, but they're progressing well now. Maddison, too, has had a streaky time, but he's well on the road to recovery. Of course you knew it was young Cunliffe's funeral Billy and I went up to attend yesterday.'

Cecil nodded.

'You fellows do take risks,' he murmured. 'I almost wish I could get into the game.'

'My dear Cecil,' protested Wallace in mock alarm, 'don't talk like that. What on earth would the RAF do without you?'

Kendal grinned.

'Lots,' he returned nonchalantly. 'Will Farrell receive the King's pardon?'

'It has already been arranged,' put in Brien. 'Furthermore Leonard is going to set him up in a little business.'

Cecil nodded understandingly.

'You've a soft heart, brother-in-law,' he declared, 'even though you are a stern, grim ogre of a Secret Service man. Have you handed over those French plans to Monsieur what's-his-name yet?'

Wallace and Brien laughed.

'Handed them over!' exclaimed the latter. 'Why, as soon as Leonard got Damien on the phone, and told him he had them, the dear old chap jumped into an aeroplane and descended on us amidst a torrent of te deums and benedictions.'

'He certainly was delighted,' agreed Sir Leonard, 'and I don't mind admitting a peculiar pleasure in being of use to him. I like him, and I like France.'

'Have you men deserted us entirely, and on Christmas night too?' enquired the plaintive voice of Lady Molly from the doorway.

'We haven't moved, dear,' protested her husband. 'It was you who deserted us.'

'When are you coming?'

'At once!' cried the three men together.

As they crossed the hall, Brien took Sir Leonard's arm. Kendal was ahead of them.

'Where was Senostris all the time?' he asked.

'In the south of France,' was the reply. 'When he returns to England, I'll have to take him into my confidence to a certain extent before handing him back his yacht and its crew.'

'Anstruther told me that Thalia Ictinos was nosing about Sir

Peter's rooms a lot before he turned her out of the house. I suppose she was after the French plans.'

'Of course she was,' nodded Sir Leonard, 'and I daresay she is mighty puzzled to know what has become of them. She tried twice to get into the nursing home to see Nikoleff. Now she seems to have disappeared.'

'I wonder if we'll ever hear of her again!'

They did.

But that is another story.

ALSO IN THE SERIES

To discover more great books and to
place an order visit our website at
allisonandbusby.com

Don't forget to sign up to our free newsletter at
allisonandbusby.com/newsletter
for latest releases, events and exclusive offers

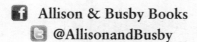 **Allison & Busby Books**
   @AllisonandBusby

You can also call us on
020 7580 1080
for orders, queries
and reading recommendations